Something Shady

Pamela Morsi

JOVE BOOKS, NEW YORK

SOMETHING SHADY

A Jove Book / published by arrangement with
the author

PRINTING HISTORY
Jove edition / July 1995

ISBN: 0-515-11628-9

A JOVE BOOK®
Jove Books are published by The Berkley Publishing Group,
200 Madison Avenue, New York, New York 10016.
JOVE and the "J" design are trademarks
belonging to Jove Publications, Inc.

PRINTED IN THE UNITED STATES OF AMERICA

10 9 8 7 6 5 4 3 2 1

Jove titles by Pamela Morsi

MARRYING STONE
RUNABOUT
GARTERS
WILD OATS

For my husband
who gave up all that was dear and familiar
to become an all-American boy.

And for my late father-in-law
who wisely counseled his son to marry
a simple country girl.

It worked out so well for me.

Chapter One

CLAIRE BARKLEY GLANCED nervously around the deserted hallway of Venice High School. The only sound discernible in the warm stillness of the afternoon was the distant thud of hammers and screech of saws as the workmen in the still-unfinished part of the building continued their toil. The new school building, a marvel of the latest in fireproof architecture, was two levels of locally produced brick, winged with grand staircases on each end. A real, permanent public high school had been the dream of the parents of the Venice, Missouri, community. Claire, like most of her classmates, accepted the new school and all that it represented with indifference, it being the prerogative of youth to disregard what their elders value.

The click of heels at the far end of the hall caused Claire to flatten herself against the threshold of the nearest door frame. Holding her breath, she watched Miss Dudley, the high school girls' Commerce teacher, walk toward the south doorway without even raising her head from the papers she was riffling through. When she was safely out of the building, Claire let out a great sigh of relief. She was so nervous her palms were sweating. And so excited her heart was pounding like a drum. The last thing in the world that she wanted was to have to explain her presence to some starch-hearted adult.

Adults never listened anyway, Claire thought to herself. And anytime that they did, they always managed to hear something she had never said. Except for Aunt Gertrude, of course. Aunt

1

Gertrude was not at all like the others. The truth of that statement washed over Claire with a pale shock of embarrassment followed by cheeks flushed with mortification. *Aunt Gertrude was more different than she'd ever imagined.*

Quickly she checked up and down the length of the building again to assure herself that she was alone. She had to find Teddy and talk to him. She had to talk to someone or she would simply burst with the news. Once more she began to tiptoe down the shadowed side of the hallway.

Claire Barkley was a plain-looking young woman of sixteen years. Her straight brown hair was tied severely at the nape of her neck and then twisted in three long sausage curls that hung halfway down her back. Her features were slightly sharp, but softened by wide doelike brown eyes made larger by round gold-rimmed spectacles. Her clothes, while well cut and of fine quality cloth, were as brown and dowdy as she was herself. She had no sense of her own style and the fashion popular with the other high school girls, the middy dress with its loose sloppy blouse and circular skirt, was not at all attractive on her chubby, wide-hipped frame.

Claire Barkley was exactly what she appeared to be, a bookish banker's daughter. But, she was more. And today that extra aspect of her nature was heightened. Heightened by the secret that she carried. A secret of scandal.

With continued surreptitious caution and light careful steps, she made her way to the library room. He would be there as he was every afternoon between the end of classes and the beginning of football practice. She knew his schedule and his habits as well as she did her own, though she'd never deliberately taken note of them. There had simply always been a bond between the two of them. It had been there in her earliest memories and it was still as strong today. For all these years she'd marveled at it, but now she finally understood it. She now knew exactly why.

Soundlessly, glancing up and down the hallway to assure herself that she had not been seen, Claire slipped through the doorway. The room was nearly empty. Not just deserted, empty. It still smelled of fresh lead paint, and the hint of sawdust in the air itched her nose.

The plan for the high school library room was a grand one. The entire outside wall was a row of tall graceful windows that poured light in from the afternoon sun. Long study desks, sturdy enough to last several generations, gleamed with unscarred newness. Rows and rows of fine oak bookshelves stood in precise lines three feet apart. Map tables stood conveniently at the end of the shelf ranges. But there were no maps upon them. They were as empty as the bookshelves. In fact, the only books in this library were the ones sitting open in front of Teodor Stefanski, whose brow was furrowed in concentration as he studied.

"Teddy." Claire whispered his name in deference to the quiet of the room.

The young man looked up, surprised that his lonely study place had been invaded.

"Claire?" His puzzled expression showed a hint of concern. "What are you doing here? Is something wrong?"

She walked toward him, willing herself not to fidget. "Teddy," she said, "we have to talk."

Immediately he rose from his seat with as much gentlemanly grace as any slightly overgrown, awkward young man could manage and pulled out the chair on the opposite side of the table.

As she sat down, he gazed at her questioningly. The two had been friends since childhood. At one time their talks had been an hourly occasion. Teddy never had a thought or a scrape that he hadn't shared with Claire, and she hadn't believed that things were real until she'd told them to Teddy. But high school had changed that a bit. Their exchange of confidences had dwindled down. They both had other friends. He played sports. She was in the Lady Lits, the school's reading club. They moved in different circles. Still, it was not as if some event had broken their friendship or as if they had ceased to be interested in each other's lives. The direction of their paths simply no longer ran parallel, but this afternoon they were about to converge once more.

Teddy gave her a warm and familiar grin. "If you're worried about your place at the head of the class," he said with gentle teasing, "I can tell you with some certainty that me and John Milton are not getting on so well."

Claire smiled back at him, nostalgic at his banter. Academic competitors as well as playmates, their early years had been indelibly woven together. When they had discovered that due to the two-year difference in their ages Teddy would be going off to attend Miss Duberry's Day School, while Claire would be staying home alone, the two had created such a row with their parents that ultimately the adults had been forced to take action. Little Claire, not yet five, had been led before Miss Duberry to demonstrate that she could read and write as well as any of the teacher's current students. And Teddy's father, at turns strict and indulgent, tempted the head mistress with a new roof for her building. Finally, the old lady agreed that certainly Claire Barkley should be allowed to attend school along with Teddy Stefanski. They had been in the same classes together ever since.

Now Teddy was the star fullback of the Venice High School football team. A big, strong, good-looking Polish immigrant's son, his father owned the most prosperous business in town, Stefanski Brickyards.

As Claire gazed across the table at his so-familiar face, sandy hair, and pale blue eyes, she sought something concrete, something definite. She sought something she'd had no cause to look for in the past.

"Well, Claire?" he asked curiously. "What is it?"

She took a deep breath, gathering her courage. "I've discovered a rather startling bit of information."

Teddy raised his brows in unspoken question.

Claire trembled slightly and found herself too embarrassed to look him in the eye. "I don't know quite how to begin," she admitted.

Teddy heard the anxiety in her voice. "Begin with one precise thesis statement defining the nature of your discussion," he said.

When she glanced over at him sharply, his smile was warm and reassuring. "You're the one who helped me with English, remember?"

She nodded. She did remember. But somehow what she had to say could not be summed up as easily as an essay on progress or a diatribe on politics. Claire bit her lip nervously. Her cheeks were pale with concern. "Some things in this world cannot be confined to a precise thesis statement."

"Then be as imprecise and rambling as you need to be," he told her. "You know that whenever you talk to me, Claire, I'm listening."

She turned her eyes from him to gaze out the new twelve-light windows that let the sunshine in to warm them and kept the crisp autumn afternoon breeze outside. Protected. They had always been protected. She turned to face him once more.

"Two days ago," she began, "Mama sent me up to the attic to find my old skates. Lester the Pester had been whining for a week about wanting skates; the little brat can't even wait for winter to get here. Mama said that he could have my old ones, and nothing would do but that he have them immediately."

Claire heard herself rambling nervously and hesitated.

Teddy gave her an understanding grin. Lester Barkley, age eleven, was the bane of his older sister's existence. Teddy easily concurred that the pesky rascal should be placed behind bars at the earliest possibility.

"My offer's still open to drown him in Mueller's fish pond," he said.

Claire smiled slightly and shook her head. "Once I got into the attic," she continued, "I began looking around. You know how it is up there."

Teddy nodded. He had spent more than a couple of rainy afternoons with Claire rummaging through the worldly possessions of the city's first family.

"I was looking through some old dresses, the funny ones with the bustles in the back. I thought that they must be Mama's because they were very dazzling and brightly colored."

She hesitated once more, nervously biting her lip. "Underneath them there was a book."

"A book?"

"A . . . a journal, a diary I guess." Claire covered her cheeks guiltily. "Honestly, I thought that it was Mama's, probably some of her recipes."

"But it wasn't," Teddy said.

She shook her head. "It was written by Aunt Gertrude. It was . . . I suppose it was Aunt Gertrude's journal."

"Really?" Teddy sounded more delighted than horrified. Like Claire, Teddy had long been an admirer of Miss Gertrude Barkley, Claire's eccentric aunt and Venice, Missouri's, major literary figure. Aunt Gertrude lived a solitary, but rather unconventional life in the Barkley house, tending only to her immense flower garden at the side of the house and to her writing. And periodically she scandalized the entire town with her startling ideas and outlandish behavior. Her two published novels were considered reprehensible and highly improper, though most of the townsfolk who said so had read them both from cover to cover.

But to Teddy and Claire, the sprightly, bright-eyed spinster could always be counted upon to be a sanctuary in times of trouble. And Teddy and Claire had run into it upon several occasions. Despite being a spinster lady and a bit of a scandal, when Gertrude Barkley spoke, both her brother, George Barkley, and Teddy's father, Mikolai Stefanski, listened.

"So did you read it?" Teddy asked eagerly.

No amount of begging, pleading, or cajoling had ever succeeded in the young people being allowed to peruse even one paragraph of Aunt Gertrude's infamous fiction.

"I didn't mean to," Claire began plaintively. "I was just going to look at it for a second and then, well, I just got interested and the more I read, well, I couldn't stop."

"You don't have to make your confession to me. I'd love to read it, too!" Teddy said immediately. "Is it from her childhood or after she started writing?"

Claire swallowed nervously. "I suppose she was only a little older than us. It's dated 1898."

"That's the year my father brought us to town," Teddy said.

"Yes, I know."

"Did she mention us?"

Claire nodded. "Your father was building your house next door to ours. Aunt Gertrude watched you to keep you out of the way of the builders."

"Really?" Teddy was surprised. "I thought Mrs. Thomas had always kept me. Miss Gertrude, too? Father never mentioned that."

Claire sighed heavily and rubbed her temples. "There were a lot of things nobody ever mentioned."

Teddy saw the pain in Claire's expression and his own brow furrowed with concern.

"What is it, Claire?"

"It's something . . . something rather shady."

"What?"

"Your father and Aunt Gertrude . . ." She hesitated, her face flaming with humiliation. "Your father and Aunt Gertrude had a *love affair*." She spoke the last words only a little above a whisper.

"A love affair?" Teddy repeated the words as if he didn't understand them. His eyes widened and he sat back in his chair, stunned. "Father? And Miss Gertrude?"

Claire nodded.

Teddy sat, stunned, shaking his head. "I can't believe it."

"I wouldn't have," Claire said. "But it's all in the journal. Their secret meetings, their vows of undying love, their . . . their—" Claire dropped her gaze unable to look at him. "Their lust of the flesh."

The euphemistic term heard most often from the reverend sounded scandalous on her lips.

Teddy choked.

Claire covered her face.

The silence in the huge, empty library was oppressive. The very predictable, understandable, familiar world of their childhood suddenly was turned topsy-turvy. The two young people stared out on a bleak adult horizon upon which they hesitated to embark.

"Father and Miss Gertrude." Teddy's voice was still full of disbelief. "I can't even imagine it."

"They've always been unusually friendly," Claire pointed out.

Teddy nodded. "Father has never really seen any purpose in having friends, but he's always made an exception for Miss Gertrude."

"Think of those long talks they have in the garden. That hazel tree they always talk about having planted together."

"They talk about shrubbery and fertilizers," Teddy protested. "Don't they?"

Claire shrugged. "According to Aunt Gertrude's diary, they've talked about more than that."

Once more the silence of disbelieving contemplation settled upon them. The rustle of autumn leaves could be heard outside the window.

"If they were in love," Teddy asked, "why didn't they marry?"

"My grandfather was opposed to the match," Claire whispered, melancholy in her voice. "Your father being an immigrant and a Catholic, too, Grandpapa didn't want him in the family."

Teddy nodded. He was not unfamiliar with prejudice. But as a star football player for the team, his Polish heritage and religious background paled in the minds of the townsfolk before his ability to move a small inflated pigskin forward for yards at a time. Teddy had no unusual accent and grew up in Protestant churches. He saw no limits or disadvantages in his own life, but he knew they had been there for his father.

Strangely, Mikolai Stefanski never spoke of the difficulties of life in his adopted country, he only spoke of his pride in being American.

Teddy's father had been barely out of his teens when he'd come to America. He'd had a sick wife and then a young baby to support and only a strong back and a willingness to work to recommend him. A peasant's son, he could barely read and write in Polish. English had been a complete mystery to him. But he'd persevered, alone. Teddy had often wondered how.

"Actually, it explains a lot," he said.

Claire looked up surprised, then thoughtful. "Yes, it does," she agreed. "I always knew that I was nothing like Lester the Pester. I've always been more like you."

Teddy couldn't follow her logic. His thoughts continued in their own direction. "I've wondered for years why Father never remarried. No wonder he wants me to stay and run the business. When I go off to college he'll have no one. A man like Father, a man with no friends, needs a wife."

"And Aunt Gertrude should have had a husband, too," Claire said sadly. "She deserves one. She should have had one!"

"Yes," Teddy agreed. "And a family of her own. She always liked children, us at least."

Claire made a tiny pained sound and Teddy realized that she was crying.

"Claire? What is it?"

She was biting her lip, trying to hold the tears that were welling in her eyes.

"Is there more?"

She nodded as the tears burst through and trickled down her cheeks. She rummaged through her pocketbook until she found a hankie with which to dab her eyes.

Teddy reached across the table to pat her hand. He had always dried her tears when they were children, but they were children no more. Ineffectually he offered what little comfort he could.

Claire bravely looked up at him. She raised her chin with dramatic solemnity and spoke as if her words came straight from a morality play.

"You can't play fast and loose with the rules of society without ultimately having to pay," she said, and then returned to the contemplation of her handkerchief, choking with sorrow on the stark sadness of her own words.

Teddy looked at her, puzzled. Her brown eyes were red-rimmed and swimming with tears. Her slightly untidy brown hair was coming loose from the ribbon that tied it at the nape. And her expression was one of anguish.

"What are you talking about?" he asked.

She looked up at him. Bravely she reached across and grasped his wrist. It was an attempt to comfort him as he tried to comfort her.

"They had a child, Teddy," she whispered. "Aunt Gertrude and Mr. Stefanski had a child that next year."

Teddy's jaw dropped open and he stared in patent disbelief. "A child? That's impossible."

"It's not impossible, Teddy. It's true. I read it in her diary," Claire said.

"But how . . . where—"

Teddy realized the course of the questions that he was asking and blushed. "I mean . . . how can this be true?"

Claire shook her head.

"I don't know. I don't know anymore, Teddy. That's where the journal stopped. She just stopped. She said she wasn't writing anymore. But it is there. It is there in her own handwriting. In 1899 she and Mikolai Stefanski had a child, a healthy little girl."

Claire waited a long moment before she continued. "1899, Teddy," she said, letting the number of the year sink in. "It must be me. I must be their child."

"What?"

"Oh, Teddy, I think I'm your *sister*."

Chapter Two

⁓⁓

GERTRUDE BARKLEY STEPPED out of the Dooley Shaving Parlor and Tonsorial Surgery at the corner of Main Street and B Avenue. The several wide-eyed males loitering in the doorway gave the locally infamous spinster a wide berth. She smiled at the fellows, almost ruefully.

"Good morning, gentlemen."

Her greeting met with mumbled response from the few who had not been struck mute by the sight before them. The rest continued to stare with as much astonishment and awe as when the circus elephant had been paraded down Main Street last spring.

Gertrude knew, without their shocked expressions, that she had done it again. The quiet town of Venice, Missouri, was fated for another uproar. And once again she was the cause.

With a determined smile, she hastened her step. Her head felt light. Not as if she were about to faint, something Gertrude Barkley was not prone to, but as if a weight had been lifted from her. And indeed it had. Thirty-seven years' growth of her dark brown hair now lay on the barber's pine-plank floor. What was left curved about her jawline with only the barest indication of a need to curl upward.

Her chin was held high, a common occurrence, but now easier to manage as she made her way through the busy downtown boulevard that was the center of the small Missouri community. People were looking at her. That was not unusual.

Being a nationally recognized author and unquestionably the most famous citizen in town, notoriety was to be expected. Today's attention, however, was more direct. On the streets of Venice this morning, the townspeople busy upon errands stopped and stared at the sight, a woman with her hair cut.

"Lovely day," Gertrude pointed out politely as she passed Naomi Pruitt frozen in her tracks.

The woman stammered haughtily and her head shook until the load of flowers and fruit decorating her broad-brimmed hat trembled dangerously.

Gertrude was tempted to laugh out loud, but she concealed her humor as best she could and continued onward.

Old Mr. Wentworth, whose eyesight was reportedly badly failing, apparently managed a glimpse of her. His near-toothless mouth opened in shock, causing his cigar to fall to the sidewalk.

"You've dropped something, sir," Gertrude whispered lightly as she passed beside him.

As she made her way down the broad, clean brick sidewalks of Main Street, people stepped back, giving her a clear path. Gertrude was much used to being the center of speculation and attention. And she had been aware of the reaction her haircut was likely to generate. It wasn't that she enjoyed oversetting the neighbors. In truth, it bothered her that she could disconcert them so easily. Still, it was worth it. She shook her head lightly, marveling in the feeling. It was freedom. More than that, it was new, so new that newness was an total sensory singularity.

Gertrude laughed lightly at her own foolishness. An action that startled the awestruck Main Street onlookers as further evidence of a woman gone mad.

She ignored them. This was what she had needed, Gertrude thought. She had suffered the doldrums most of the summer. She'd spent endless hours with Principal Shue planning the accoutrements for the new high school. She had dutifully aided her sister-in-law in making curtains for the meeting hall of the Crusading Knights of the Mystic Circle. And she'd worked long hours on the new novel, the final book of the DuPree trilogy. Not any of these activities had served to make her feel younger, stronger, or even alive. But upon this pleasant fall morning in 1915, her new haircut did.

Her next destination was the Barkley Bank. Her midyear royalties money had been wired to her yesterday. It would have been simple to have her brother, George, who was the town banker, deposit it for her. She was not, however, willing to do that. This was *her* money. Money that she had made herself. It was not an allotment, a legacy, or a stipend. Her success had been hard-won and a subject of great disbelief among the locals. She would deposit the money herself so that all the gossips would immediately know. And if she must do it with a brand-new haircut, so much the better.

The bank was at the center of town, the oldest building on Main Street, a fact that was obvious to the most casual onlooker. Up and down both sides of the street were buildings of all sizes and styles, but they had one thing in common. Each and every building, like the sidewalks, the curbs, and the street, was bright red brick, Stefanski Brick. Formed and fired at the Stefanski Brickyards on the west side of town. The bank, however, built by her father and now run by her brother, predated the brickyards and was constructed of smooth brown river rock. It stood in sharp contrast to the other buildings and as a monument to the Barkley tradition of going their own way. Gertrude Barkley understood that perfectly. She often wondered why her brother did not.

She opened the wide front door of the building. It was free of the traditional bank bars and in itself was a work of art, composed of delicate beveled window-glass hand-painted with the words "Barkley Bank." It was a testament to the mentality of the community. If preeminent criminals like Jesse James, the

Youngers, and the Daltons had not seen fit to rob the bank, the community was not about to be fearful of the current crop of no-account lowlifes.

Gertrude stepped inside smiling broadly, her head high. The bank was not full of people; two or three, however, were present. Ethel Duberry, a former teacher, and a well-known stickler for good form, glanced momentarily at Gertrude's shorn locks and then hastily looked away as if she had chanced to see her underwear. With a quick nod, she hurried out the door as if suddenly aware of a quite urgent appointment.

Chester Fallon, a farmer from the nearby valley, was standing at the counter, cheerfully paying off his seed debt. When he turned to leave he caught sight of Gertrude. He looked her up and down with disapproval and then pushed past her with mumbled words about the "wildness of town women."

Grantham Mitts, perhaps the town's most elderly citizen and known to every member of the community as simply "Old Grandpa," sat contentedly upon the small waiting bench at the far side of the room. He rocked back and forth contentedly and quietly sang to himself the words of "Taney County Bad Companions."

Gertrude nodded pleasantly to him. At least he was not shocked by her new bobbed hair. In some ways it was unfortunate that everyone wasn't as unconcerned with this world as was Old Grandpa.

Determined to remain in good humor, she stepped up to the counter and greeted the bank teller.

"Good day to you, Mr. Harris," she said brightly. The pinched-looking young man with thick glasses glanced up from the stack of paper money he was counting and opened his mouth as if to speak. The words apparently stuck in his throat as he gazed at Gertrude in stupefaction.

She politely ignored the bug-eyed stare.

George Barkley, who was deep in concentration at his desk,

must have sensed something amiss, and he glanced up from his account books. He did a quick up-and-down perusal of his sister, then his eyes came up again, this time staring in horror.

"What have you done!" His whisper came out almost as a hiss.

With increased purpose, Mr. Harris turned his full attention back to the money he counted.

"Good morning, George," she answered her brother evenly. "I've merely come to present my deposit."

It took only a second for George Barkley to make his way through the small half-door at the far end of the counter. Gertrude had clearly done it this time. Her brother descended upon her like the wrath of God. Red-faced and teeth clenched, she would have almost been able to swear that steam was coming out his ears. He was standing before her, puffed up, at full height, and ready to blow, when the tinkle of the bell sounded at the doorway.

As one, the brother and sister turned toward the intrusion. Mikolai Stefanski stepped into the near-empty bank building.

"Good morning," he said, greeting them. To George he offered a polite nod. Gertrude received a slight bow, a gesture lingering from his European manners.

"Stefanski," George ground out in minimal response.

"It's a beautiful day," Gertrude said brightly.

"So it is," Stefanski agreed. "And the trolley, it runs on time."

Most people would have no idea how the one thing concerned the other, but Gertrude Barkley knew Mikolai Stefanski better than most people in town. She smiled at him.

"You've come with your payroll, I suppose," George said.

"Every Thursday," Stefanski replied. He glanced once more at Gertrude and her brother. "Mr. Harris can help me."

George gave his sister an assessing look and almost sighed in frustration. Stefanski Brickyards was the biggest payroll in town. He never left it for his assistant, and certainly not for Mr. Harris.

"Let me get your books," he said. He gestured to Harris to assist Gertrude.

"I want to deposit my royalties," she told him.

The young man took the telegraph receipt from her and nodded. He stepped away from the counter and Gertrude and Mikolai Stefanski stood quietly together, alone.

Gertrude turned her head to smile at him lightly. She was very aware of him. How could she not be? Somehow the big near-empty bank building was dwarfed by his presence. He was not a tall man, nor was he excessively large. He was of medium height and muscular build. But he was a giant, somehow. He had been that way since the first day she had seen him over seventeen years ago. He had been poor then, and ragged. His wagon weathered and rusty. His English then was broken and accented to the point of being indecipherable. His young son perched upon his knee, the two were grimy with road dust and near indigent as they rode into town. Even then he had seemed larger than life to Gertrude. His shoulders were as broad as an ox and he was as muscled as if, like Atlas, he carried the weight of the world. He was a man to be gazed upon with wonder and mystery. A man to give flesh and blood to her romantic fantasies.

Gooseflesh fluttered up her arms and skittered across the tender flesh upon the back of her exposed neck. She cleared her throat. She was momentarily at a loss as to what to say. Stefanski's eyes were a pale hazel color that was neither quite green nor brown. His brow was well defined and heavily garlanded with bushy eyebrows that almost grew together over the bridge of his nose. His face was wide and strong-featured, but somehow it retained a handsomeness in that strength.

"It's a lovely day," she chattered nervously, and then remembered that she'd mentioned that to him already.

He nodded politely in agreement.

Perhaps it was his ambition that made the man seem so large, Gertrude thought. Seventeen years ago he'd arrived in town in a decrepit wagon. Today he was the city's foremost citizen and had her brother, the banker, rushing to do his bidding.

"You have cut your hair," he said.

Gertrude turned to face him, her eyes wide.

"Yes, I . . . this morning, I had it cut."

He nodded. "I noticed right away," he said.

"Do you like it?" she asked. Immediately she wished she could cut her tongue out. Of course he wouldn't like it. Only fast city women cut their hair. Doing it was a craziness, a bid for freedom that Gertrude needed. It was not something for which she could expect approval.

To her surprise, Stefanski nodded slightly. "It suits you, Miss Gertrude," he said. "I believe that it suits you."

It was past midmorning when Mikolai Stefanski caught the Interurban trolley back to the brickyards. The trolley master nodded at him respectfully as he settled himself in the broad, shiny open coach with polished pine seats. He had not chosen the deep green color of the cars. When he'd ordered them he had assumed they would be black or brown. But he liked them. Green went well with red, especially Stefanski red. And Venice, Missouri, was almost completely that color. The transit company was just another business venture that Mikolai had begun for the good of his workers. It had turned out better than expected. And for the good of the town.

The trolley slowed as it passed the crosstrack at Wentworth Street. There were only two lines. One ran down Main Street from the brickyards in the west to the Barkley house on the city's far east side. The other track ran from the shanties of the south river side to the new high school building just north of town. Transfers were made for free so that anyone in Venice could go all the way across town in only a few minutes for the cost of five cents. Stefanski was understandably proud of that accomplishment.

"Main Station!" the trolley master called out.

As the car hesitated at the stop, Mikolai looked about him. A lot had changed about Venice, Missouri, since he had arrived here in the summer of 1898. And Stefanski was proud to think that many of the changes could be directly credited to him.

Venice was a town that galena had built. Mining for the bluish gray ore that was mostly lead had begun in the lean years just after the Civil War. Merchants and businessmen, like the Barkleys, had hurried in to feed, clothe, house, and ultimately relieve the get-rich-quick miners of their gains. By the time Stefanski had arrived, the mines were almost all played out and the town was dying. There was no industry, no work for the common man. Stefanski had changed that.

He glanced toward the rows of fine brick buildings running on either side of the street. The day he'd first come to Venice, the buildings along Main Street had all been rotting clapboard.

Now, the cleanly swept streets were slick paving brick, fired from Stefanski kilns. Finer thoroughfares couldn't be found in St. Louis or Kansas City. They were a far cry from the muddy trail he'd ventured upon the day he'd arrived. He'd driven his worn-out wagon into town with baby Teodor upon his knee. The thick Missouri mud that made up the city's roadways was as bogging as driving a mule team through half-baked taffy. Mikolai Stefanski had changed all that, too. Venice, Missouri, continued to exist, it could be argued, because Mikolai Stefanski had chosen to settle there. Certainly, the clay was rich and good for brick. Perhaps another brickyard might have opened. But no other businessman could have been as driven to succeed as was Stefanski. And the entire town had benefited from his ambition. Mikolai was pleased, but did not think himself a better man for his accomplishments. Ambition and success were all that he had. Neither warmed a man's heart, or his bed, on a cold winter night.

He urged his thoughts back to matters of real importance. The week's payroll was completed and his accounts in balance. The dedication tea for the new high school was this week. He should remind Mrs. Thomas, his housekeeper, to brush his best coat. He had the new issue of *Architectural Digest* at his office. He should bring it home for Teddy. That wouldn't seem as if he were pushing. The boy was interested. Pastor Wilkerson claimed that some of the Negroes declared that they were tired of being relegated to standing room at the back of the church pews and were hoping to recruit their own preacher and build their own house of worship. He should find out if they would accept money or materials from him. Josh Patrick was still not back to work after nearly a month. The man claimed he was sick unto death. Stefanski suspected he was merely sick of working. But something would have to be done about the man's wife and two children.

Ultimately the concerns and cares of the day settled in his mind and he allowed his thoughts to linger upon the memory of a face. It was the face of Gertrude Barkley. It was a face he'd seen and admired for years. There was a time . . . well, it was a time long ago. Today that face had looked different. It looked different with her new shorter hair and he thought he liked it. The short dark brown curls bounced around her head, one falling down across her brow. She'd looked her very best, dressed for town. There had been a tautness about her as she had absently pushed the stray lock back with a gloved hand, revealing those sparkling bright brown eyes.

His eyes softened at the memory and the right side of his lip curled slightly into an almost dreamy smile.

Yes, he liked Miss Gertrude's short hair. For Miss Gertrude, that is, he amended to himself quickly. Normally women should look like what they are, normal women. But Miss Gertrude was an unusual woman. It suited her to appear unusual.

Stefanski knew that his thoughts didn't quite make sense, but he wasn't exactly sure where his reasoning went astray. Bobbed hair was generally the province of young women, young, fast women. And if he had had a daughter, Stefanski was sure that he would not at all approve. But Miss Gertrude was neither young nor fast. On her, the bouncy curls at her jawline and nape were more appealing than dangerous. Miss Gertrude was attractive in her own way; he'd always thought so. And the boyishly short haircut somehow accented the unexpected femininity of her features.

Yes, Stefanski decided, he liked Gertrude Barkley's new haircut. But then, it could not be denied that he liked Gertrude Barkley.

She'd been out on Sunday afternoon wrapping pinestraw around the trunk of the hazel tree. Their hazel tree. He always thought of it that way. They had planted it together.

"Do you think that will encourage our tree to produce something we can eat this year?" he'd asked her from the edge of his porch.

She glanced up, already grinning. She had a wide, big smile that came to her lips easily.

"I remain optimistic, Mr. Stefanski," she said.

Optimistic. That was a good word to describe Gertrude Barkley. He had been drawn to that sunny purpose right from the beginning. She had talked him into that tree. Maneuvered him into it, he supposed. Still, he didn't regret its existence. The hazel tree had been planted the year that they had met. The year that he had come to town. It was a tall, straight, shady haven they had planted together.

It was seventeen years ago, yet he remembered that day as vividly as if it were painted upon his memory. He was tired, he was hot and sweaty, not at all a fine condition in which to receive a young lady. But Gertrude Barkley didn't wait for invitation, she merely appeared in his yard. Or rather in her own yard, at the border of his own.

He was running a string along dig stakes that marked the border of his property. His house was nearly finished and he proposed to built a wall.

"Good afternoon, Mr. Stefanski," Gertrude greeted him with the cheerful politeness that he had come to expect.

Immediately he came to his feet and doffed his worn glove hat respectfully. He bowed slightly before he remembered that people didn't do that in America. He was raised as a peasant. Trained to show deference to his betters. Of course, in America a man had no betters. But with someone like Gertrude Barkley, it was hard to remember that.

"Miss Gwere-tood," he said in acknowledgment. He heard the sound of her name coming from his lips and knew that it wasn't quite right. English was still very difficult for him, the strange names especially. But for this young woman, his neighbor, he would practice until he got it right.

She was tall for a woman, standing just a couple of inches shorter than himself. She held her head high and her posture always seemed excessively straight. Somehow that rigidness seemed to enhance the soft feminine curves of her body. At least for Mikolai it did.

"It's a lovely day, is it not?" she began. She continued to talk, but Mikolai lost the thread of the conversation. It was very hard to concentrate on translating her words when all he could think about was how coarse and dirty he must appear.

He was dressed in his heavy workingman's duckings and hobnail boots; his hair and brow were drenched with sweat from the warmth of the afternoon. He had not bothered to shave that morning.

Gertrude smiled a little uneasily at him.

He realized that she must have asked him a question. He had no idea what it might be.

"Excuses?" he said, and then remembered that it was supposed to be "Excuse me." He didn't go back and correct himself. Perhaps she hadn't noticed.

He knew how he must appear to her. Uncouth, unlearned, unapproachable. Still, she did not seem to be at all afraid of him. Maybe she should be. There was something about her nearness that was distinctly unsettling. He hadn't been with a woman in a very long time.

He was still a young man then, only twenty-one. But he had none of the lightness or carefree air of youth. He was stark and solemn and determined. But Miss Gertrude . . . Miss Gertrude was laughter and life and . . . her warmth of spirit lured him like a lighted window on a shivery winter's night.

With a gentle smile she gestured to something behind him. He turned to see what had captured her attention. In the sand, some distance away, his son was playing in the dirt. The boy's bright blond hair gleamed in the sunshine and he was galloping tiny wooden horses up and down the hills and valleys he had dug in the loose dirt.

"Hello, Teddy!" she called out to the little boy.

He had told her that the boy's name was Teodor. She had shortened it to Teddy. It sounded very American. Mikolai liked the way that it sounded.

Teddy raised his little pudgy chin and smiled at the adults watching him, his face grimy from the afternoon's adventure.

"He is such a nice baby, Mr. Stefanski," she said.

She was speaking more slowly now, carefully. Mikolai glanced back at his son with pride. Haltingly, he sorted through his meager vocabulary to come up with the right words.

"He is good boy," he said carefully. "Today new . . ." The noun eluded him. In frustration Stefanski pointed to his own mouth. "New . . . *zab*, how do you say?"

"He has a new tooth?"

He sighed gratefully and nodded. "Yes, new tooth. My son, Teodor, has new tooth."

Gertrude smiled at him. Willingly she joined him in a quiet moment of unconcealed pride. It was one of the things that he longed for most, someone to share the joys of his life, the small successes, the private jokes.

He caught himself. Miss Gertrude didn't come out of her house to share anything with her neighbor but the afternoon sunshine. He cleared his throat, deliberately pretending to be anxious to get back to work. Still the woman lingered.

"Are you enjoying the weather?" she asked him.

Stefanski looked around startled. For a moment he had been unaware if it was spring or fall.

"Hot," he managed to comment.

"Yes, it is quite warm for such hard work," she agreed. "Whatever are you building, Mr. Stefanski?"

He looked at her in puzzlement for a long moment and then pointed to the huge red brick edifice behind him. "House," he said.

"No, not the house." Gertrude laughed lightly. "I know that you are building a house. What are you building here?" She pointed to the stakes and string and the partially leveled ground. "Are you building a wall here?"

"Yes! A wall," he said, feeling foolish. Of course she knew he was building a house. Everyone in Venice knew. It was nearly completed and he and Teodor were already living there. He hoped to complete the inside finish work during winter's bad weather. There was still much to do, but the brickyards were more important right now. Business was booming and he must not allow himself to be distracted. Competitors were everywhere, eager and anxious to relieve him of his customers if possible. "I build wall," he told her.

"That's not a good idea, Mr. Stefanski," she answered.

His brow furrowed "No?"

"No," Gertrude stated emphatically.

He hesitated thoughtfully, giving her words ample consideration. He couldn't lay claim to understanding American ways. Sometimes they made perfect sense. At other times they were unfathomable. Like Mr. Barkley, Miss Gertrude's father, being angry at him for building the house. Mikolai knew that the old man was furious about it, but for the life of him he couldn't figure out why. The woman before him probably understood perfectly. Still, he thought the wall a necessity.

"Yes, wall is good idea," he told her. "Stefanski is here. Line here. Your papa there." He pointed to the stakes for the east side of the wall. "This is mine," he stated firmly, indicating the stakes on the west side. "Clear line, no trouble."

He looked up at Gertrude searchingly. He knew his explanation was poor; he willed her to understand.

"Of course you are right, Mr. Stefanski," she said finally.

It took a moment for her words to sink in. Her words didn't, however, match her expression. She hadn't really agreed with him. There was more to be said, he was certain. He waited, leaning against his shovel, to hear what she had to say.

"It's such a shame about your porch."

He raised a curious eyebrow. "Porch?"

"Such a lovely porch on your house," she said, gesturing toward it.

Stefanski looked behind him at the wide expanse of covered porchway on the huge brick house. She liked his porch. He felt a moment of pleasure. It was the latest design. He'd seen it in a new American magazine. He'd hardly been able to read the words, but he'd carefully studied the drawings.

"Both the front and the side," Miss Gertrude continued with a sigh of approval.

He nodded. He wanted to talk to her about airflow, bearing walls, living traffic patterns, and ascetics versus function. He wanted to explain to her about the designer's ideas and how he felt he had improved upon them. He wanted to tell her the whys as well as the what of it. But it was too much explanation for his meager vocabulary.

"It's good porch," he admitted modestly.

"Yes," Miss Gertrude agreed effusively. "And it is such a shame that all you'll be able to see is a brick wall. Not a very pretty view."

Stefanski eyed her speculatively. Even in an unfamiliar language he knew when he was being maneuvered. He didn't resist it.

"My bricks . . . very pretty," he said.

Gertrude nodded. "Oh yes, of course, they are lovely bricks. They are the most attractive I have ever seen."

"Strong brick," he said. "Very pretty and very strong."

"They certainly seem so," she concurred. "But don't you see bricks all day?"

"What?"

"Don't you see bricks all day?"

"Yes, I work all day, every day," he said, more than a bit of pride in his tone.

"So don't you think that perhaps when you are not working that you'd like to see something else?"

He looked thoughtful then and shrugged. "See your house?" he asked, not particularly pleased with the prospect.

"Not just our house, Mr. Stefanski. The woods and the lane and . . . Why, I'm sure that from your porch in winter one could see Buffalo Mountain. Have you ever seen Buffalo Mountain?"

"Buffalo Mountain?"

Mikolai had not even heard of the place.

"It's a lovely view on clear winter days," Gertrude assured him. She turned to point in the direction of the far-off hill that could barely be glimpsed that afternoon as a gray haze on the horizon. He heard the near-breathless enthusiasm in her voice and was drawn to it. He moved up to stand directly behind her, leaning forward slightly to follow the direction of her hand with his eyes. He caught the scent of her. Closing his eyes, he took in a deep breath. Rose water. She must rinse her hair in rose water.

"Do you see it?"

She turned her head then and she was close. Very close. Close enough that in a movement, a small and very natural movement, his lips could touch her.

Mikolai abruptly stood to his full height. His blood was pounding through his veins and he could still smell the soft, feminine fragrance that tempted him.

"Can't see," he said truthfully, though his words were more brusque than he'd intended.

"No, it's not truly very visible this time of year," Miss Gertrude admitted. "Winter is when we can most usually see it, when you will be able to see it from your porch."

Mikolai was having difficulty concentrating on what she was saying. The unexpected reaction to her nearness disconcerted him. "Sit on the porch in winter?" he asked.

Miss Gertrude was momentarily speechless. She stuttered momentarily. "Wh-wh-wh-why no. Of course no one would sit on a porch in bad weather. But frequently it will still be quite pleasant here in the winter and we can see snow on top of the mountain in the distance."

"Snow?" He repeated the word slowly. It sounded familiar, but he couldn't remember its meaning.

"Snow . . . white . . . like rain, it comes from the sky."

Miss Gertrude made curious little wavy motions with her

fingers that at first he didn't understand, then suddenly he nodded as if he could see what was in her thoughts.

"*Snieg,*" he said.

"*Snieg?*"

"*Snieg* is 'snow'."

"Yes," Miss Gertrude said, laughing. "*Snieg* on the mountain, very pretty."

"Pretty," Stefanski agreed. He laughed with her companionably.

"You have snow in your country?" she asked.

His eyes narrowed. He felt stung. "Amerika is my country," he said.

She flushed. He had embarrassed her. He was sorry, but she'd pricked his pride.

"Yes, yes, of course America is your country now," she said. "I was simply thinking of the country where you grew up."

He nodded at her and then gazed off into the distance toward the mountain that couldn't be seen. He should apologize for snapping at her. She couldn't understand what it meant for him to be an American, all that he had given up, all that he longed for that was yet to be realized. He wanted to explain, to confide, but there were too many words, or no words at all.

"Much snow in Poland," he said simply. "Much snow, much cold."

For a moment he was there once more. The soft rolling hills of Galicia, green and fertile-looking so much like this Missouri that he now called home. He imagined himself once more working the fields with his father and brothers. Laughing with them, talking with them. He was not a strange, silent foreigner, but a clever hardworking son who hated baths, teased his sister, played tricks upon his brothers, and made his father chuckle.

He could see those fields again, hear those voices in his native tongue. And in his mind, once more he scaled that tallest peak, near Lida's house, where he stole his first kiss and gazed southward into the distance at the mountains of Carpathia.

"There was hill," he said finally.

He turned to regard Gertrude directly. His gaze was somber, but not without warmth. "For children very pretty."

Gertrude's eyes widened. They simply looked at each other for a long moment.

"Then you were very lucky that your father didn't build a high brick wall around your house so that you couldn't see it."

"What?" He was momentarily puzzled. He'd forgotten the purpose of their conversation. His expression turned wry. He bent his knee and propped his foot upon one of the marking stakes in the ground.

"Clear line, no trouble," he stated firmly once more.

Miss Gertrude nodded. "But does it have to be a wall?" she asked. "Couldn't we mark the line another way? With a shrub perhaps, or a tree."

Stefanski's expression turned thoughtful and he rubbed his chin. A wall would be better, still he wanted to please her. He wanted to have her smile at him again.

"A fruit tree would be nice," she said. "You could plant a fruit tree here, it wouldn't block your view and we would have no question about the property line."

Mikolai took time to consider that, his brow furrowed thoughtfully. Miss Gertrude continued to look at him hopefully.

"Is there some kind of tree that you like? Something that perhaps will remind you of your home in Poland? Or maybe a good-luck tree? My Aunt Hilly used to say magnolias are good luck."

Stefanski was thoughtful for a long moment.

"Hazel tree," he said.

"Hazel?" Gertrude nodded slowly. "I don't know if they will

grow very well this far south," she said. "I suppose we could try."

Suddenly Mikolai wanted very much to try. He also wanted to talk. He wanted to tell her the story of the hazel tree. He searched his mind for the words, the phrases necessary to tell the tale.

"Children's story," he said simply.

"There is a children's story about the hazel tree?" she asked, smiling. "You must tell me."

He hesitated only a moment before nodding. He sorted the story out in his head. When the Virgin Mary was fleeing King Herod she had sought shelter in the forest.

"Mother of God in trees," he said.

Gertrude's eyebrows raised in surprise. Mikolai continued, inexpertly explaining how the Virgin had asked the aspen trees to hide her and the Christ child so that the king would not find them and slay them.

"She talk to aspens."

He knew that was not quite what he meant. The aspens had been afraid of the king and they had begun to tremble in fear and pleaded with Mary to go away, for the king might find her there and would cut them down.

"Aspens say, 'Go away,'" he explained haltingly as he leaned back on his shovel and rested his elbow on the handle, relaxed in his pose.

The hazel tree heard what was happening in the aspens and bid the Madonna to come its way. It enfolded the Madonna and Child safely in its wide leaves and the king's men didn't see them and rode right by.

"Mary hid in hazel tree."

Miss Gertrude listened politely, nodding.

The hazel tree was blessed for its good deed and since that day, aspens shake even in the absence of the slightest breeze, trembling and fearful to the end of time. But the hazel grows strong and tall, shading any who pass by, and perpetually safe from storms and lightning.

"Hazel tree good for house, good for us."

Miss Gertrude smiled. Clearly she did not understand.

Mikolai sighed heavily. "We plant hazel for line," he said finally. "Same like wall and no trouble."

"Oh yes, let us plant a tree," Gertrude agreed. "It will serve just as well to mark the property and be something shady for the yard, too."

They smiled together for a long minute.

"Someday I tell story of hazel tree again," he promised.

She laughed then, delightedly. "Now all we'll have to fight about is who owns the hazelnuts?"

"Brickyards!" the trolley master called out, startling Mikolai from his reverie. A man shouldn't be dreaming of a woman when the workday was still upon him.

Chapter Three

GERTRUDE BARKLEY SAT writing at her desk near the window of her second-floor apartment in the Barkley house. It wasn't really an apartment, merely two connecting rooms that were set aside for her personal use. But she liked to call it her apartment, the use of the term gave her a feeling of independence.

Of course, she *was* independent. She had always been quick to remind anyone who suggested otherwise that she had her own rather successful career as a novelist and therefore her own money. Hadn't she made a deposit at the bank just that morning? Simply because she chose to continue to live in the house in which she was born—her father's house, now her brother's house—did not in any way diminish the fact that she was a modern, self-sufficient, self-reliant woman. If some unlettered, ignorant people in the town thought her to be an aging, dependent spinster, it was merely their mistake.

Her concern this afternoon, however, was not her own position in the community of Venice, Missouri, but rather the fictional position of Weston Carlisle, the illegitimate son of Tye DuPree, patriarch of the DuPree family of Carlisle, Virginia, that concerned her.

After her interesting and almost infamous outing of the morning, Gertrude had decided that what she needed was to concentrate all her thoughts and energies upon the new book. There were problems aplenty in her fiction, without having to deal with those in her real life.

With Tyler DuPree, the family patriarch, dead, his second wife Alexandria was nearly insane with grief. His handsome twin sons, Granville and Lafayette, were in dire straits due to their war records with the Confederacy. And his daughter, young Blessida, was mindlessly in love with the no-good Yankee colonel. It would have to be Weston Carlisle, the scorned interloper, who would save the DuPree fortune from the evil carpetbaggers.

Gertrude had created the DuPrees more than ten years earlier. Lying alone and sleepless in the polished cherrywood bed that had been her sixteenth birthday present, and staring through the darkness at the chubby cherubs in flight upon her bedposts, she had fancied a different family and a different world. It was a world of heroism and honor. One of passion and romance. In all ways, a world very different from the one in which she lived her life.

At first she had just walked around making up the story in her head. Inattention in the Barkley house did not go unnoticed. And distraction was not thought a minor annoyance. Her brother had called her scatterbrained. Her sister-in-law more kindly had said distracted. Her father had put his foot down.

"Spinsterhood is making your brain go soft!" he'd declared adamantly. "For the sake of your good sense, Gerty, accept the next man who walks across this threshold!"

She might have followed her father's advice, but the old fellow died shortly thereafter. He simply fell asleep in church one Sunday morning and never woke up.

After the appropriate year of mourning, Gertrude found herself to be on the wrong side of twenty and considered completely and irrevocably on-the-shelf. Gertrude Barkley, spinster.

But strangely, no longer having to worry about finding a proper husband was not heartbreaking. In fact, Gertrude found it to be a liberating experience. She no longer need concern herself about her behavior or her future. Spinsters were supposed to be eccentric and unconventional. It was this sense of being unshackled by social custom that had led her to begin writing.

She had been making up stories for her own entertainment since childhood and had tried her hand at putting them on paper when she was still in her teens. With the story of the DuPrees in the back of her mind, continuing to steal into her everyday thoughts, Gertrude decided that writing it down might be challenging and diverting. When she had put pen to paper she found, to her surprise, that she had a real knack for it. Although her first attempt at a novel was doomed for obscurity, among other things she had outgrown, she tried again. Her thousand-page multigenerational saga she entitled *The DuPrees of Carlisle Place* had happily found a home with a New York publisher. And her new poignant and passionate vision of the Old South had only whetted the appetite of the reading public. They had clamored for more and she had given them that in *The DuPrees in Gray*.

Now three years after the success of that novel, Gertrude was trying valiantly to properly end the family's troubles in the final volume of their story, *Triumph of the DuPrees*. It wasn't easy.

Gertrude leaned back in her chair and lightly tapped the top of her fountain pen against her teeth. The short locks that had shocked the good people of Venice were now unattractively tied up in curling rags. The style, or rather lack of it, gave her rather straight, pointed features even more severity than usual and only the absence of a wart on her nose kept it from being absolutely witchy. But she was writing, and in the privacy of her apartment she saw no reason to stand on ceremony. If a woman looked good all of the time, Gertrude postulated, she could never see any improvement.

Glancing down at what she had just written, she shook her

head. Weston had been a villain practically since his birth in the tiny little backstreet house where Tye had kept his mistress. Mistress. It was such an intriguing, exciting term.

Son of the mistress, however, was not quite so. And turning him into the man of the hour would require a bit of doing, even for Gertrude. She was not sure what could possibly bring about such a transformation.

Staring thoughtfully at nothingness outside her window, Gertrude's attention was captured by the rowdy old mockingbird that lived in the hazel tree. Their hazel tree. He was loudly chasing away a bright red cardinal foolish enough to encroach upon his territory. As she watched, the stranger hurried off into the distance, beaten, and the mockingbird lit on his favorite spot near the topmost limb almost eye to eye with Gertrude.

She smiled at him. The two had a lot in common, she thought. Neither was exceptionally attractive or particularly talented. Both of them did a good deal of what they did best and fought like the very devil to be allowed to do it.

"I suppose you have a brother and sister-in-law somewhere yourself," she said to the bird.

The gray-and-white-feathered creature looked in her direction and raised its beak as if in disdain, then lowered it as if giving a cut direct. Gertrude laughed out loud and shook her head.

"Oh dear," she said to herself. "The situation in this town is getting pretty desperate when even the birds look down their noses at me."

In actuality, she was proud of the controversy she stirred up.

"You are an interesting woman," Mikolai Stefanski had said to her once. She smiled to herself and she thought of him that morning. He liked her hair. He thought she was interesting. It was little enough. Still, she wanted to hug herself.

The mockingbird flew away on some unknown errand, but Gertrude continued to stare at the hazel tree outside her window. It was almost impossible to believe that she had planted that tree and now it was nearly as tall as the house. Wryly she thought that it probably grew so tall because it never bothered to produce any hazelnuts. Still, time certainly did pass quickly. Seventeen years. She sighed heavily in disbelief. Seventeen years.

A smile came to her face as she thought back on that long-ago day, a spring day in her youth. That was the first day that she knew. She had suspected before, but that day she knew, for then and all time. Hastily she pushed the thought away. It was a childish fancy and it was high time she put all thoughts of it away for good.

It had started with Prudence and George. In those days everything started with Prudence and George, the two of them just recently wed and in a constant stir over something.

"Oh, I cannot bear it. I just cannot bear it." Gertrude had heard her sister-in-law's whining travail before she'd even come down the stairs. "It will block our view completely and be tantamount to an eyesore on our very own property."

Standing upon the imported Brussels carpet in the narrow foyer, Prudence Barkley, the new bride of Gertrude's younger brother George, was leaning heavily against her husband as she wrung her hands and cried plaintively. The mass of blond curls on the back of her head shook with the vibrations of her sobs.

"I can't bear it, George. I tell you, I can't bear it."

"For heaven's sake, whatever is she sniveling about now?" Gertrude asked.

They both looked up toward her on the stair landing. Gertrude folded her arms across her chest in disgust. At the sight, Prudence burst into full-blown tears and hurried from the room.

"Pru!" George called after her, but she was already gone.

He glared up at his sister. "Gerty, could you please be nice to her? You know how tender her feelings are."

Gertrude rolled her eyes. "I know that she's a watering pot, if that's what you mean. But *I* don't have to cater to her, George Barkley. She's your wife, you'll have to deal with her."

George's surprise marriage to Prudence Margrove was an event completely beyond Gertrude's understanding. Her brother at eighteen was far too young to take on the responsibilities of being a husband. And rather than the young blushing bride being joyous and fulfilled, Pru seemed childish, silly, and completely unhappy.

"I deal with Prudence just fine," her brother answered through clenched teeth. "All I'm asking of you is that you try to get along with her."

"I thought new brides were supposed to be blushing and happy. From all the sobbing and misery I've seen from yours, I swear it's turning me off marriage completely."

"I don't exactly see fellows beating down the door to ask for your hand," her brother pointed out unkindly.

"It's a good thing," Gertrude shot back. "Because I don't know of any in this town that I would have."

"Have you ever heard that beggars can't be choosers?" he asked.

Gertrude stuck her tongue out at him in an infantile gesture of revenge.

George huffed pompously.

The two had never been the best of friends, but as a little brother, Gertrude thought George was not too bad. She actually didn't even mind Pru, except lately she seemed to be whining or crying nearly all the time. It was the change in the house that made things so difficult.

"So what's all the fuss about today?" Gertrude asked as she descended the stairs.

George made a gesture of frustration toward the west window. "Oh, the crazy German is building a wall around his castle."

"What? Mr. Stefanski?"

"Who else?"

"He's not German, he's Polish," she corrected.

"I don't care if he's the King of Spain. It's not enough that he builds a house as big as a church out of bright red brick, but now he's planning to surround it with an eight-foot wall. We won't even be able to see down the street except from the second floor."

Gertrude's brow furrowed. "Have you talked to him about it?"

George snorted unkindly. "Who can talk to him? The man doesn't even speak English."

"He understands if you speak slowly."

George's tone was haughty. "I suppose I just can't talk slowly enough."

"Oh, George, you're getting as bad as Papa. The lot was for sale and the man bought it. You certainly can't continue to hold that against him."

"I can if he turns the neighborhood into a brickyard."

"He just has one small kiln in the backyard that he's using to make the brick for his house. I'm sure he is not planning to expand his business on this street, it's simply not practical."

"And they do say that these Polish folks are practical," George acknowledged. "Of course, that's far from all they say about them."

Gertrude eyed her brother disdainfully. "I think, George, that you would do well to consider less what people say about the Polish and more about what Mr. Stefanski says about himself."

"If you think he's such a talker, you talk to him," George challenged.

"I certainly will."

Gertrude had traipsed outside, her nose in the air, leaving her brother standing in the foyer. She was not afraid of any man or woman living. And having grown up with the stubbornness of both her father and brother to contend with, she knew a great deal about negotiating with the masculine sex.

The wide plank front porch was swept neatly clean and the railing around it was pristine white. The Barkleys believed that houses should be white. The Barkleys held a lot of beliefs like that. Preferences indulged with such consistency that they had become convictions.

Gertrude made her way to the west side of the house. It was barren of trees or shrubs. For all twenty years of Gertrude's life this side of the house was a wide-open meadow that separated the Barkley home from the rest of the town of Venice. Although the Barkleys had never owned the land, they had always thought of the meadow as their buffer from the rest of the community, the moat around their castle that no foreign knight could ever assail.

Mikolai Stefanski couldn't have known that. He'd settled in Venice because he liked the composition of the clay. Gertrude assumed that he'd bought the meadow for a similar reason. He'd bought the land because it was for sale. Her father and her brother would never forgive him that transgression.

Gertrude, of course, had forgiven him. But then, she'd fallen in love with him. That day, that hour, that place, she had fallen in love with him. And there was just no help for it.

Determinedly she shook her head and stared down once more at the page of paper before her. She would not think about Mikolai Stefanski. She wouldn't think about him. It might show on her face, or someone might hear it in her voice. If she was not very careful, one of these days he might realize how she felt and she would lose him completely. It was painful to love from afar. But more so not to love at all.

"Love," she said aloud. "He has to fall in love."

She tapped the pen against her teeth once more as she thought it. If Weston Carlisle was to be a changed man, it would take love to change him. Yes, love could change Weston. Falling in love could change any man.

Mikolai stepped out of the neat little square brick building near the gate of the Stefanski Brickyards. Dressed in his shirtsleeves, gleaming white, he was creased and wilted from a hard day's work. His broad shoulders and muscled physique gave the impression of a big and powerful man. His brow was thick and severe in a perpetual frown and his tawny blond hair was parted down the middle and slicked away from his face with J. B. Bristol's Healthy Hair Tonic. His aspect spoke neither of wealth nor prominence, but rather of distance, isolation, as if invisible boundaries yawned all around him.

He glanced down at his watch, noting that it was almost a full minute before six o'clock. Believing without question in the adage "A full day's work for a day's pay," he waited. He allowed his gaze to roam with pride along the dusty bustling distances of the yard. Everywhere he looked men and machines were busy and productive. This was his place of business. He had built it himself with nothing but the sweat of his brow and the desperation to prove that he could succeed. And it was exactly what he had always wanted it to be. Stacks of perfect, finished brick, trademark bright red, lay waiting for distribution near the fancy arched gateway to the property. So far, 1915 had been a very good year for brick, despite the increased popularity of concrete and steel building materials. And Stefanski Brick was the most popular brick in the state of Missouri.

With pride he turned his attention toward the tempering shed. The rhythmic grind of the soft-mud pug mill was like music to his ears. Tons of the raw materials of Stefanski Brick, clay and slate and sand, were being blended and stirred in the large, mechanically operated vat.

A vacuum-operated plunger then pushed the mixed clay

product into oiled brick molds that were struck, tapped, and dumped onto drying pallets.

As Stefanski watched, a pallet was filled and Jimmy Terrell, a young off-bearer, hoisted it up on a two-wheel cart and headed toward the drying house. After a week or so in that building, which utilized both the drying agent of the ancients, sunshine, and the preferred method of the moderns, a coal-fired furnace, the *green* bricks would be ready for the kiln.

The brickyards were a maze of modern industrial activity. These were workingmen at work. A thing, Stefanski believed, that was as much to be reverenced as anything seen in a church. A man's worth, his nature, even his soul, was irrevocably tied to his purpose. And excepting those few intended for life in prayer or contemplating philosophy, a man's purpose was his work.

In the distance Stefanski gazed at the four beehive-style downdraft kilns smoldering like redbrick igloos. They turned the best clay in Missouri into the finest brick west of the Mississippi.

Once more he pulled his watch from his pocket and glanced down at it. Six o'clock exactly. He reached up to clang the bell beside the door. It was quitting time at the brickyards.

Work did not stop immediately, but rather speeded up perceptibly as the men hurried to finish their current tasks before heading home. Stefanski was no wrathful industrial overlord, but brickyard jobs were hard to come by and well compensated. The workers believed that despite the hard, backbreaking work, hundreds of other men coveted their livelihood.

Within a couple of minutes the men were gathering up their lunch buckets for the trip home. Making their way through the gates, they were tired and hungry and eager to go to comfortable homes with happy well-fed children and the woman of their choice. Some of them may have envied the brickyard's owner. But some days, he envied them.

Retrieving his coat from the office, Stefanski walked out of the yard. Only a small night crew was left to stoke the furnaces. He securely locked the tall, wrought-iron gate that bore his name in fancy script of twisted metal and hurried to catch the cable car.

Truthfully, he was entirely willing to wait fifteen minutes for another car. But he knew his men, and they would hold the trolley until he got there. The riders at this first stop being all his brickyard employees, and as the owner of the trolley service itself, it was unlikely that anyone would dare to leave Mikolai Stefanski stranded. It was therefore almost a favor to the workers and the trolley master that he quickened his step.

Just as he had expected, the Venice Interurban sat patiently at the end of the line waiting for him to board.

He nodded his thanks to the trolley master as he stepped on and dropped his nickel in the slot. An empty seat was waiting for him, but, as always, he did not take it. The deference paid to him by his employees was an embarrassment. And truly he preferred to stand. In America all men were equal. He knew what it felt to be less than other men. He would never allow himself the vanity to feel better than them.

The cable car chugged off at a breezy twenty miles per hour pace. All around him the men he knew, the men whose livelihoods depended upon him, laughed and talked together in casual camaraderie. Stefanski listened, but did not join in. He rode the trolley to be part of them. It would have been quicker and easier for him to drive his new Packard to the brickyards. But he needed these men, their talk, their lives. Even if he was, of necessity, upon the edges of the world around him, he needed the human connection no matter how tenuous.

With some exceptions the men around him were near his own age, thirty-eight. Pete Wilson was probably closer to fifty than he cared to admit and Jimmy Terrell was barely in his twenties though he was a father of four. They were the sons of miners and tenant farmers and hired hands who sought a better life for themselves and their children in town. Stefanski understood that better than they knew. He too had come to this place to create something better for his son, something better than he had ever had for himself.

Ultimately, as always these cool fall days, the talk turned to football. It was a subject dear to the heart of Mikolai Stefanski. Not simply for the excitement it afforded or the challenge of the team, but for the door that it offered. Stefanski was aware of that door and was grateful for it.

"Did you see that score on the Harvard–Cornell game?" Tom Acres asked the men around him rhetorically. "Who'd of thought the Crimson could ever be beaten ten–aught?"

"Harvard's not the power no more," Avery Parks stated emphatically. "It's Notre Dame that knows how to play the game these days."

"Forward pass is all they know," Tom snorted. "Throwing the football is for cowards and Catholics. I don't want a thing to do with it."

Pete Wilson's eyes widened and with a somewhat frantic expression he kicked Tom under the seat and made a slight nod toward Stefanski.

Tom's ears and neck brightened with the flush of embarrassment. "Not that I'm saying Catholics is cowards," he corrected. "They just has their own ways that's different from Americans."

Although hearing exactly what had been said, Stefanski's face revealed nothing as he turned it to the breeze, watching Main Street pass by.

"Well, I'd say, we've got the best mix of both kinds of football," Tate Bounty piped in with welcome tact. "Avery's boy can sure toss that pigskin toward the post and with Teddy

Stefanski at the crux of our wedge we're going to run right over every team in the state."

Stefanski's face continued to be void of expression, but pride surged through him.

"See, Teddy ain't coward enough to play Catholic football," Tom said proudly. "It's almost as if he was one of us. Ouch!"

Pete kicked him once more beneath the seat.

Stefanski continued to gaze out at the passing street, his face giving no indication that he was amused and even somewhat pleased. In some way Tom was right. Teodor, his only son, was no coward. America was no place for cowards. And the boy *was* almost one of them. He was more than almost. He was an American.

"Mikolai, we are strangers here!" Lida had raved at him in Polish one long-ago night in the cold, drafty Chicago apartment they had shared. "We will always be strangers."

"But that child you carry," he said to her. "Our *dziecko* will not be a stranger here, my wife. He will be an American."

Still she cried as if her heart would break. It had made him feel helpless and angry.

"Can you be so selfish?" he asked with tight-lipped fury. "To return to Poland, to Galicia, is to gift our child with the slavery of the Austrian yoke. Here, in America, he can be whatever he can be. This is a land of freedom. We can offer it as a gift to our generations."

Lida hadn't understood freedom or the Austrian yoke. She had only grasped the cold of the dirty, cramped apartment and the drudgery of Chicago immigrant life. She hadn't been able to even exchange a greeting with the loud boisterous Italians who shared their building or the dour Germans who sold them bread and meat. She had missed her mother and her sisters, friends and celebrations, and dancing the polka in a freshly shorn field. In the America that Lida had seen, there had been no friends, no fields, no dancing; only hard work and bad food as Mikolai worked his apprenticeship at the brickyards in Chicago and saved his money.

"Have patience, Lida," he told her so many times. "Trust your husband and have patience. I can make a good life for us in this new country."

Stefanski hadn't lied to her. He had made a very good life. He was the wealthiest man in town and the city's chief benefactor. But Lida hadn't been able to wait. That spring, only days after Teodor was born, she'd taken sick and died. He'd paid cash money from his stash of hoarded pennies to bring the physician. But she'd died anyway.

He pushed the sad thought from him. It did no good to blame himself and guilt was wasted effort. Still, he felt guilty. He had been right to come to America. Perhaps he had been wrong to bring a wife like Lida to a country where she had no friends. But he couldn't regret his son, Lida's son and his pride, his American legacy.

As the Interurban chugged down the line, Stefanski turned slightly to pick up the thread of the conversation. Football was still the topic.

"Cochem's was first to visualize passing as a worthy offense," Parks was saying. "So it's Missouri-made and a good thing, too, if you ask me. A lot less hurt and injury to the players than the way it's been played in past years."

"Well, if we can just wallop the devil out of Rogers next weekend," Tate Bounty said, "I don't care if they do it old-fashioned or newfangled—just so they do it."

There were laughs of good-humored agreement all around.

The trolley slowed for a stop at Pickens Street and the trolley master announced it in his usual boisterous voice. Three stalwart matrons returning from the Algonquin Society meeting boarded. The men, feeling a sudden need to mind their manners, fell silent. The ladies, however, felt no such compunction.

"Well, I definitely think that Pastor Wilkerson must speak with her," Naomi Pruitt stated firmly. "It's perfectly clear to me that the woman has lost whatever good sense she might have at one time possessed."

"Oh, I don't know," Claudy Mitts said shyly, wringing her hands, her big eyes wide and confused. "Oh dear, oh dear."

"It certainly must be lowering for the Barkleys," her companion, Oleander Wentworth, said.

Oleander was smaller than her hat and the forceful shaking of her head posed frightful danger to Miss Mitts at her side as well as the miscellaneous birds and fruit residing upon its rim.

"Poor Prudence, my heart goes out to her," Naomi was saying in a manner that belied her words. "Gertrude is just more than a woman should have to bear. Acting the fool, writing those unseemly stories, and now getting that *fast* haircut."

"Oh, I don't know," Claudy declared again. "Oh dear."

"They say she walked right into the barbershop, bold as brass, and asked poor Hank Dooley to bob it for her," Oleander said.

"I'll bet Hank's wife will never hear the end of it," Naomi replied.

Oleander giggled like a young girl. Something she hadn't been for at least forty years.

Claudy looked uncomfortable. "Oh, I don't know," she said. "Oh dear, oh dear."

None of the men on the Interuruban, including Mikolai Stefanski, could have avoided hearing the ladies' discussion. Stefanski, however, might well have been the only man on the trolley that was interested in it.

As the Interurban made its way farther and farther east on Main Street, more and more riders were let off until at the end of the line, directly in front of the Barkley house, it was only himself and Oleander Wentworth.

Mikolai hurriedly took the steps ahead of the older woman, turning to doff his hat politely before offering his hand in assistance. The matron looked down her long, narrow, almost avianic nose at him for a half minute before allowing him to help her.

"A good evening to you, Mrs. Wentworth," he said when she was safely on solid ground.

"Mr. Stefanski." Her answer was politely civil and nothing more. Exactly what Mikolai had expected.

Dinner at the Barkley house was barely finished at eight o'clock. Prudence insisted on having it served fashionably late and upon it being called dinner.

For that reason, George Barkley, who rarely saw fit to comment on anything his wife managed to accomplish, did speak up about the meal. "It was a wonderful supper, Pru," he said joylessly. "Even if we did nearly faint from hunger waiting on it."

Prudence, who only a few short years ago would have burst into tears at such criticism, merely gave her husband a predictably miffed expression and stepped away to turn up the lights. All up and down the main streets of Venice electric lights blazed. But in the Barkley house the bright yellow glow of gas lamps still provided illumination.

"Little Lester," Prudence said to her son as she seated herself in the dark mohair overstuffed armchair that was officially *Mother's.* "It's time for you to brush your teeth and get ready for bed."

Her tone was childish, almost descending into baby talk.

The young boy, sprawled out leisurely upon the hundred-year-old carpeting brought from Virginia, ignored his mother completely. Pulling a rather dingy-looking bean bag from his trouser pocket, he undid the tie string and poured out the well-used collection of tweeties, agates, cat-eyes, and taws.

With complete unconcern he began to count out his marbles on the parlor rug.

"Don't put those dirty things on the carpeting, Little Lester," she said to him.

George began riffling through the paper, speaking to the family group assembled as if they were there merely to hear his thoughts.

"It would be a pretty foolish thing if the Knights were to elect any other man as Sublime Kalifa this year," he stated.

His family made no comment, except for his wife who once again spoke to Lester. "Darling, I said the marbles are not for the rug."

"Last year they chose old Wentworth over me, but it won't happen again," George assured them. "No one has done more for the Mystic Circle than I have. I deserve to be Sublime Kalifa and everybody knows it."

No one argued. Lester continued to stir his marbles on the rug and his mother spoke to him once more.

"Now, now, Little Lester, put those marbles back in the bag. They make such a mess for Mommy to clean up."

The youngster seemed not to hear.

"Why in charitable donations alone I'm already the most benevolent man in town," George continued. "Except for that grubby, redbrick Polack, and thank God not even a fool would vote some foreigner to head the Mystic Circle."

"Darling? Darling? Are you listening to Mommy?" Prudence asked.

Lester wasn't.

"Claire, do you want to play a game of Parcheesi with me?" Gertrude questioned her niece as the young woman walked into the room.

Claire seemed nervous and flustered. Her face had been flushed all through dinner. Her mother had asked her more than once if she was feverish, even suggesting a dose of bitters.

"I can't tonight, Aunt Gertrude," she answered with a fluttery little giggle that was quite unlike her. "Although you know that I'd love to. I truly enjoy every minute that I spend with you. I hope that you know that. I think you are terrific."

"Claire!" Prudence scolded. "I do wish you wouldn't use that word. 'Terrific' comes from the word 'terrifying,' surely you do not think of your aunt as frightening in any way."

"Mama, everyone in school says 'terrific.' It means great, wonderful. Aunt Gertrude knows what it means."

"Still, it is slang," her mother complained. "And I don't like it."

"You don't mind it, do you, Aunt Gertrude?"

Gertrude laughed lightly. "Well, no. I guess I did know that you weren't in terror of me. I always assumed that if you weren't enjoying yourself in my presence, you were then quite the little actress."

"I never act with you, Aunt Gertrude." Claire's answer was solemn in the extreme. "I am truly, sincerely, honestly happy for every moment that we have together."

Her declaration was quite puzzling to Gertrude and she might have suggested a dose of bitters herself.

"Lester," Pru said, breaking the flow of the conversation. "Precious, please put up those marbles and go upstairs now."

George Barkley's paper rattled. "Lester Barkley, mind your mother! For heaven's sake, Prudence. You always complain that I never talk to you and then when I'm speaking about something important you pay more attention to the boy than you do to me."

He went back to reading without waiting for a response. It was a good thing. Pru's eyes welled up, but she set her chin in anger, holding back all other emotions.

Lester shot a quick look in his father's direction and then another at his mother. Reassured, he immediately returned to doing exactly what he wanted to.

The knocker on the front door sounded at that moment and Claire jumped nervously as if a gun had been fired.

"Who in the world could that be?" George Barkley barked, annoyance clear in his voice.

"It's Teddy," Claire answered quickly. "We have a history test tomorrow and we are going to study together."

"Teddy?" the three adults questioned in unison.

Barkley raised an eyebrow. "We haven't seen him around in a while." He sniffed disapprovingly. "I suppose his marks are falling drastically without your help."

"Oh no, Papa," Claire answered proudly. "Teddy is still at the top of the class."

"Little Lester, would you please put those marbles in the bag and take yourself on up to bed." Pru's voice was as whining as a child's.

Claire hurried to the foyer and opened the door for Teddy.

"Hello," he said. "Am I late or early?"

Claire giggled. It was one of their private jokes that as far as George Barkley was concerned, Teddy Stefanski could never do anything right.

"Late, very late," Claire whispered. "It's Little Lester's bedtime and the fight is on."

Teddy grinned. "What round is it and who's highest in the score?"

"About the fifth, I'd say. And so far Lester has landed all the punches."

"Terrific," Teddy commented.

A moment later the young man was standing in the parlor looking very red-faced and very large, but smiling nonetheless, with Claire at his side.

"Good evening, Mr. Barkley, Mrs. Barkley."

Lester looked up at him challengingly.

"Hi, *brat*."

Prudence huffed in shock at the word.

"I meant no insult, Mrs. Barkley," Teddy added hastily. "Remember *brat* is the Polish word for 'brother.'"

"Oh yes," she said, sighing gratefully. "It's been so long since we've seen you, I'd forgotten that."

Lester's eyes had narrowed angrily. He had not forgotten. It was the only Polish word that Teddy ever used and he only used it for Lester.

"Well, doesn't old Aunt Gertrude get a hello and a kiss?" she asked.

Teddy hesitated a moment and his voice cracked nervously. "Miss Gertrude." Dutifully he leaned down and placed a peck on the woman's cheek.

She grasped his hands in her own. "We've missed seeing you around here," Gertrude told him, smiling.

"Yes, we have indeed, Teddy," Prudence chimed in. "Haven't we, George?"

Barkley rattled his paper once more to look over the edge of it at the young man in the doorway. "Hello, Stefanski," he said before going back to his reading.

"So, Teddy?" Gertrude asked. "What are our chances against Rogers?"

Teddy was looking at her stupidly. He had spent much of the afternoon trying to imagine her and his father together. It had to be some kind of mistake, he was sure. Claire had misread something in the diary. It just never could have happened.

"Rogers?"

"The football game."

"Oh, the game, oh . . . it's going to be a good game," he said as if the speech were rehearsed. "We'll be playing our hardest and I'm sure Rogers will be, too. May the best team win."

Gertrude laughed delightedly at his little speech. She had always openly adored the young man, almost as much as her own niece and nephew. But tonight Teddy Stefanski, ill at ease, saw more in that affection than he'd ever considered before.

"Well, I'll be there on the sidelines cheering you on." Gertrude shook her fist in the air in a gesture reminiscent of the high school yell-leader. "Go Venice!" she cried with a youthful chuckle.

"Gertrude, really." Prudence tutted in disapproval. Her attention was only momentary, however, as Lester pulled back the rug that was slowing his practice shots. "Now, Little Lester," his mother attempted scolding once more. "Don't disturb the rug, darling. It's time for you to put your toys away and go to bed."

The boy did not appear to be so inclined.

"So," Gertrude said. "You and Claire are going to be studying homework together again."

"What? Oh yes, ma'am," Teddy stammered uneasily. "Studying. I'm just here to be studying."

The young man turned uncomfortably to glance at Claire. Gertrude gave her niece a speculative glance. The young woman only lowered her eyes.

"Why don't you two go on into the library, then," Gertrude said. "The sooner you get started on your homework, the sooner you'll be finished."

"Yes, yes," Claire said. "We'll be in the library. We can study there without disturbing anyone."

She glanced meaningfully at Teddy, who made gracious apologies as they nearly fled to the privacy of the library in the far west corner of the back of the house.

They heard the newspaper rattle once more. "Leave the door open!" her father called out.

"George, please, we do not shout," Prudence scolded with annoyance.

"I do," her husband answered gruffly.

"Lester, dear," Pru continued. "Didn't I tell you to pick up your things and go up to bed?"

Safe inside the relative sanctuary of the musty old library, Claire and Teddy shared a long look and sighed gratefully.

"I could hardly look her in the eye," the young man confessed.

Claire nodded. "It's been like that for me all evening."

"Where is it?" Teddy asked, glancing around.

The heavily draped room had been the preserve of Claire's grandfather, Grover Barkley. He had been dead since Claire was a baby, but the room still smelled slightly of his aromatic cigars. Claire hurried over to the bookshelf and climbed the narrow fruitwood ladder kept there. Secreted behind two volumes of a rarely used Latin dictionary was the infamous journal, its cloth cover dusty and faded with time.

Claire held it out before her as if it were an explosive ready to detonate.

"Here it is," she said.

Teddy hesitated momentarily to take it. It was bad enough for Claire to read her aunt's private words. For him, only an interested stranger, it seemed a crime.

"I don't know if . . ."

"Teddy, you are the only one in the world I can trust with this," she told him. Shaking her head dramatically, Claire put her hands together prayerfully as if beseeching him. "And I just can't bear the weight of this knowledge alone."

Her pleading, as always, won him over. Teddy accepted the book from her hand and together they sat, side by side, at the library table.

He opened the book up before him and Claire began to leaf through it.

"The first part was very unorganized," she explained. "It is just sort of a calendar of some very boring day-to-day activities. Start reading here."

She pointed to a place almost midway through the journal. No date was written at the top of the page, but from the entry before it, several pages earlier, it was the early summer of 1898.

With Claire leaning over his shoulder, the two began silently to read the words that were written.

I saw him today. Him, you ask? Him who? (Or whom.) The man of my dreams. The man of my destiny. And no, I have not run from home. I am not now sitting in a garret above a street café in Paris. I am within the comfort and warmth of my very own home. Fate has seen fit to send the man to me.

My first sight of his face, his form, was in the meadow west of the house. Standing amid the early wildflowers, the breeze tousled his hair. The sun gleaming through its burnished color turning it to gold. I saw him there and he turned to look at me. He had a shovel in his hands. He was building a wall. It was a wall between us. It was between us then. Right there at the beginning. It was there immediately.

The flash of passion, the lure of romance, the temptation of love. And as I gazed upon his visage for the very first time, I knew in my heart that this man, this exquisite masculine creature, this strange foreigner who had traversed the stormy seas and crossed the gaunt and empty plains, had done so because heaven and fortune intended him for me.

His name is Mikolai. Nicholas, from the Greek. Meaning "victorious people." The patron saint of children. A generous and giving name. Is my Mikolai generous and giving? Only if he gives his love. Only if he gives his love to me.

He is not a suave and tender man. He is forceful and primordial. There is no elegance about him. Except the natural elegance of manhood in the prime of life.

"Papa!" I heard a child's call.

A toddler came running toward him, giggling and grinning, holding a captured dragonfly before him in his chubby hands. He pulled the child up into his arms and accepted the offering with grace and pride.

"Where is the boy's mother?" I thought the words, not spake them.

He looked at me, directly at me, and I could see the emptiness in his eyes, like an abyss where a soul should be.

"She is dead," his heart answered.

And I knew I was placed on this earth to bring joy back to this man's sad world. To bring love back into his life. And to bring life back into mine. He owns me, this man, this hero of mine. He owns my heart, my soul. He owns my body. It is his now, today, just for the asking.

Teddy leaned back in the library chair and stared at the book before him as if it were a snake.

"Oh, my gosh," he said, amazed. "It's worse than you even said."

"So you believe me now?" Claire asked.

He nodded. "Golly, Claire, what are we going to do?"

"What else can we do? We must bring them back together."

Chapter Four

MIKOLAI STEFANSKI SAT casually glancing through the evening paper in the sparsely furnished masculine office in the far east corner of his big brick house. He loved his house. It was a symbol of his affluence, his achievement, his Americanization.

In Galicia, the partitioned part of Poland held by Austria where he was born, Mikolai had lived in a thatched-roof serf's cottage that was cold enough to freeze the water in his washbowl from October to March. When his father had died, they hadn't even had that. Living as unwelcome additions in the cottages of relatives and friends, his mother had not lasted the first winter.

After that his Uncle Leos had stared resentfully across his crowded supper table at the five extra mouths he had inherited. It was no wonder that his brothers, Bartos and Dawid, left to look for work and never returned. And then his sweet sister Edda married a grizzly old friend of Uncle Leos's. The lecherous old man had wanted the pretty fifteen-year-old body in his bed so badly, he'd agreed to take their youngest brother, Rhysio, to raise. Edda's sacrifice was for naught. Rhysio had been stricken with typhoid the next year. He was buried in the churchyard with *Matka* and *Tatus,* his mother and father, before his sixth birthday.

With a deep sigh of regret and sadness, Mikolai folded the paper and lay it upon his lap as he gazed once more around the lush, marvelously paneled room that was his own. With his family dead and scattered, his victory seemed a hollow one.

Still, there was Teodor. It was all for Teodor, he reminded himself. His Teodor would have a life in America. He would never be caught between old ways and new. He was an American. That was all that mattered.

In the front hallway the huge German ten-day clock rang out the quarter hour. It was after nine and Teodor was still not home. Frequently, Mikolai was honest enough to admit, he worried about his son when he was out. A young handsome man with more money than good sense could get into a lot of trouble. Mikolai had always dreamed of his son taking over the brickyards. Stefanski and Son. He had almost had the very first sign painted that way. Fortunately, his good sense had held.

In his son's future plans, which the young man shared across the dinner table with his father, there were big and exciting things, faraway places and unusual happenings. The Stefanski Brickyards was not often mentioned in Teodor's dreams.

His son had plans for college. Notre Dame. He would play football for the great coach. And earn a fine education in the process. Then he would go back East, New York, Boston, Philadelphia, and he would conquer those places.

Mikolai's heart ached to think of his son, his only son, the only person in his life, so far away. But children were like delicate wildflowers. A man who tried to press them close to his body and keep them safe would only crush them.

Nothing could foul the young man's plans for college, Mikolai decided. He would see to it that nothing did.

Steps and the rattle of the front door indicated that the subject of Mikolai's thoughts had just returned to the house.

"Teodor!" Stefanski called out. "Come here, please."

A moment later the handsome young man stuck his head through the doorway.

"Evening, Father," he said. "Sorry I'm late."

"No matter," Mikolai answered with a shake of his head. "Sit," he said. "Sit here, Teodor. I want to talk with you."

Teddy looked uncharacteristically a bit ill at ease, but joined his father in the study. The two big leather tufted armchairs sat opposite each other. And although the younger man knew one of the chairs was considered to belong to him, he sat in it rather hesitantly.

"What did you want to talk about, Father?"

Mikolai shook his head, smiling. "Nothing of importance. Nothing really. I just want to talk to my son. When you were small you delighted to tell me everything. Now I hear about you from strangers on the trolley."

"Who was talking about me on the trolley?"

"They talk of football," he answered. "And when the men talk of football, they talk of Teodor Stefanski."

There was more than a modicum of pride in the older man's tone.

Teddy nodded, but Mikolai noted that his son did not appear as cocky and confident as usual. His concentration seemed to be on the Aubusson carpeting rather than on the heartfelt compliment he was being given.

Mikolai's bushy blond eyebrows furrowed. "Is something not good, Teodor?" he asked.

Teddy looked up quickly. "No," he assured his father quickly. "Everything is fine, Father, just fine."

Mikolai wasn't easily convinced. "Fine, yes," he said convincingly. He stared at his son a long minute. "Yes, I'm sure all is fine or you would tell me otherwise."

Teddy's cheeks flushed with guilt. The young man and his father were closer than might be expected. Mikolai Stefanski had not simply tried to be mother and father to the boy. He had tried to be the doting grandparent, the stern uncle, the cautious older brother, and the carefree friend. Teddy had been the centerpiece of his ambition, his goal, his life. And the young man was very much aware of the fact.

"I . . . ah . . . nothing's wrong at school if that's what you're thinking."

Mikolai's expression never changed. "That's good," he said, obviously still waiting.

Running a nervous hand through his hair, Teddy looked up at his father in frustration. "It's not really something I can discuss with you, Father," he said. "It's . . . well, it's personal."

"Ahhhhhh," Mikolai said with exaggerated comprehension. "I understand personal." He continued to nod thoughtfully. "When I was young, I too had things that were too personal to speak of with my father."

The two looked at each other for a long moment. Slowly Mikolai's expression lightened. "Just do not allow anything personal to keep you from schoolwork. A man must know more than play football if he is to go to college."

"Don't worry, Father," Teddy said.

Mikolai raised his bushy eyebrows in exaggerated surprise. "Teodor! To worry is the duty of a father."

Teddy grinned at his attempt at humor. "And I know you always do your duty." As the young man's smile faded, he hurried to begin a new subject for conversation. "What's happening at the brickyard?"

Mikolai shrugged. "We are making bricks."

Teddy grinned. "As hard as I sweat there during the summers, I still miss the place when I start back to school."

"Hard work is good for the soul," his father replied. "But the soul of a young man shines with goodness anyway."

Momentarily Teddy looked uneasy again. Hastily he continued talking. "How are the sales going? Are you having another record year?" he asked.

"Sales are fair, but not like the past," Mikolai answered.

"The steel-and-concrete builders are really taking a cut into the business," Teddy said, nodding knowledgeably.

"Yes," his father admitted. "But we continue to do well enough. This is to be expected. Fashions change even in buildings. We must be at peace with the variations, even if we've no wish to conform to them."

Teddy nodded. "And the new stylized bricking is a great start. Beauty is our advantage, we must use it to compete."

Mikolai acknowledged his son's words with pride and respect for the younger man's discernment. "Yes we must, Teodor, and we will," he said. "But we compete with the civility of gentlemen. Stefanski's is no longer a new, struggling brickyard, youthful and full of energy, growing by leaps. We are an old established business now. Like a man in middle years we do not run as fast or risk the dangerous trails, but we continue to journey down the road nonetheless."

"You talk like you're getting old, Father," Teddy said.

Mikolai shrugged. "Yes, perhaps I am getting old. The brickyard gets established, the man gets old."

"You're not even forty," his son reminded him.

"No, I am still healthy and strong. But in my heart I am no longer the young boy fresh from Poland, eager as a bridegroom and foolish as a pup.

"I can't imagine you as ever foolish."

Mikolai's expression darkened slightly. "A man can be very foolish when he is young."

Teddy's brow furrowed as he stared at his father. His next question came out half stuttered and ill-conceived.

"Have you ever been foolish about women, Father?"

Momentarily surprised, Mikolai stared at his son for an instant before laughing out loud.

"All men are *eternally* foolish about women, Teodor. It is simply the way of nature."

Stefanski's chuckle was a warm, strong, masculine sound,

most welcomed by his son. Teddy joined in his father's humor, but his own laughter held a strained quality that Mikolai fortunately did not notice.

When the noisy humor faded, Teddy felt compelled to ask his next question.

"What was my mother like?"

"Your mother? Ah, Teodor, you know this story only too well," he said. "Lida was very beautiful, my son. She was kind and gentle and very much a woman to be admired. I had known her since she was a babe in her mother's arms. I desired her from the time she became a woman."

Mikolai paused. He really had no desire to say more, but his son continued to stare at him hopefully.

"She was a curvy little woman, little tiny hands and feet, but such legs." Mikolai smiled fondly. "Lida had legs to inspire the poets. Oh, how they inspired me. There was no other girl in the village that I yearned for so. And I was not alone. All the lads in the village sighed after her as if she were a goddess come to bless our fields."

Teddy gave his father a long, thoughtful look. "You must have loved her very much."

Mikolai glanced up, his expression sobering somewhat. Momentarily thoughtful, he gave his son a long measuring look as he considered the best course. The complete truth vied against a more acceptable tale. Stefanski saw the young man before him, a strong, honest young man. The kind of young man that he should deal with openly and with frankness. He shook his head.

"No, Teodor," he said quietly. "I failed your mother. Failed her because I never loved her at all."

Teddy's eyes widened in surprise; he was clearly shaken by his answer. "You never loved my mother?"

Mikolai felt the disillusionment that swept his son and worried that he should have kept the truth to himself. But

Teddy was no longer a child. If he was old enough to ask about love, he was old enough to know the truth about it.

He glanced around the room at the symbols of those things he had achieved as if the presence of them might offer him strength. "I didn't love her. I needed her. I needed her, Teodor, because I was afraid."

"Afraid?"

"Yes," Mikolai admitted frankly. "I was afraid. I had decided to come to America. It was what I wanted, what I felt that I must do. The old world was so crowded. There was no room for a man with ambitions. I knew I must strike out, but I was afraid to leave all that I knew. With a woman beside me, a beautiful woman, a woman other men would envy, to depend upon me, I thought I would become fearless."

Mikolai looked deep into his son's eyes, willing him to understand. "Your mother never wanted America, Teodor. She wanted me, but not this place. It was my dream and I swept her into it."

"I'm sure she was never sorry," Teddy told him quietly.

"I do not know if she was ever sorry. But I am," he answered. "Had I not brought her here, she'd still be in Poland, maybe be a jolly, fat granny sitting in the morning mass with a bright-colored babushka covering her hair."

Silence lingered in the chestnut-paneled study as Mikolai sat, his vulnerability unshielded from the young man who shared his name.

"Maybe not, Father," Teddy said quietly. "Maybe if she'd married someone else she would still have died too young."

Mikolai turned to regard his son. He smiled.

"You are a good son, Teodor," he said. "I cannot so much regret marrying your mother, because I am so proud to have you for my son."

Teddy blushed, embarrassed at the approbation in his father's words. The young man cleared his throat and deftly shifted the direction of the conversation.

"Have you ever been in love with someone else, Father? Have you ever felt with another woman that you were in love?"

Mikolai shook his head and laughed humorlessly. "Love is a thing for young men, Teodor, like yourself. Young men with light hearts and few worries." Mikolai sighed. "I have never been such a man."

"You have never been in love?" Teddy's tone was rife with disbelief.

Mikolai raised a curious eyebrow. He leaned forward in his chair slightly, making his words seem more confidential. "No, I have not been in love," he answered his son quietly. "If we are talking about *being in love*. If you are asking me if I have made love to women other than your mother, of course I have."

Teddy cleared his throat nervously. His father's steady gaze was unnerving. "I didn't mean to pry."

Mikolai sat back into the comfort of the heavily tufted leather armchair and eyed his son thoughtfully. "I do not suppose that it is prying to ask such questions of a father," he said finally. "Who else should a young man ask?"

Teddy's face was blazing red from the flesh around his collar to the bright pink tips of his ears. "You don't need to tell me anything," Teddy assured him.

"No, perhaps I should. My father was in his grave before I was the age you are now. I don't truly know what is right or wrong to say to my son. But the truth is what I would give to another man who asked it of me. Surely I should offer no less to my own flesh."

"Father, really you needn't—"

Mikolai held up a hand to halt Teddy's protest. "From time to time," he said with matter-of-fact clarity, "I have sought the company of accessible women. It is not a thing of which I speak with any pride."

"I should not have made you speak of it at all," Teddy said.

"No, you are wrong about that, Teodor," he said. "I'm sure you have questions about such things. What I have told you in the past about men and women could just as easily have been said about dogs or horses. But with humans there is more involved and it is not unseemly that we speak of that."

"I never meant—" Teddy began.

"What are your questions, Teodor?" his father asked. "I will be as honest as I am able."

Teddy's brow was furrowed with concern. Clearly his thoughts were in a whirl. It took him several minutes to formulate his question.

"Who were these 'accessible women'?" he asked.

Mikolai seemed almost as uncomfortable with the question as Teddy was. But he'd decided to be frank and open with his son and he was not going to back down.

He cleared his throat, willing his words to honesty. "There was an older woman when you were a baby," he said. "She was a widow and greatly admired my strong back. I left her when I left Chicago."

He hesitated, letting that memory spill out and be gone before dredging up another. "Several years ago I assisted a wronged wife in a commensurate revenge upon her husband. It was mutually satisfying for a couple of months." Mikolai scanned his son's face for signs of shock or disgust.

"There have been others from time to time. A few quite memorable, some I can hardly recall. In a few instances I admit to having lowered myself to consort with a more unsavory type of female. This is not the kind of thing I would wish for you, Teodor. Not merely to avoid the danger of disease, but also for the sordidness of it. I clearly understand the urge to seek release in the female body. But I would encourage you to wait for a woman that you can honor and respect and openly call your own. The pleasure of these unsanctioned pairings is fleeting. And a certain distaste at one's actions lingers."

"Was there never anyone that you wanted to marry?" Teddy asked.

"Marry?" Mikolai paused. For him this was an abrupt change of subject. Marrying a woman or bedding her were distinctly different propositions in Mikolai's mind.

"There was one woman that I'd thought would make a good wife," he said. "But her father would never hear of it."

The dedication ceremony for the new high school was held at five-thirty in the afternoon. The hour was personally affirmed by Prudence Barkley as appropriate for the occasion of high tea.

It was to be attended by all the important people of the town. At least that's what George Barkley told Gertrude when he insisted that she be there.

Gertrude hadn't argued overmuch. She had a very chic-looking new waistcoat and skirt that it would shortly be too cool to wear. She took the opportunity offered to show off her new finery. She wanted all of George's "important people" to see her in her new clothes and fast haircut. It gave them something to talk about. It was, in fact, sort of her own brand of public service.

The site of the tea was the main hallway entrance to the school. The polished oak floors gleamed with brightness and the elaborate scrollwork done by the finish carpenters was more suited, Gertrude thought, to the confines of a church than a place of learning. But then Gertrude liked the smoother, sleeker, more modern style just coming into fashion.

The ladies of the Algonquin Society were furnishing refreshments. Without bothering to check the table, Gertrude knew that there would be heaping plates of Mrs. Ponder's honey-cured ham, Oleander Wentworth's fancy okra pickles, and her sister-in-law Pru's delicate ladyfingers. Gertrude had seen it all before and tasted it many times. For tonight she was content to drink her cup of elderberry punch and stand quietly content upon the sidelines.

Of course, she was not allowed this luxury for very long.

Hank Dooley sidled up to her, grinning. "How's the haircut?" he asked with a snorty giggle. "My woman is fit to be tied about it."

"I rather like it, Mr. Dooley," she answered with confident politeness.

"Yer do?"

"Yes," Gertrude insisted. "It's so cool off my neck and so light. I cannot imagine why a woman would want to carry around a bushel-load of hair upon the top of her head."

Hank guffawed as if she had told a very good tale. He seemed ready to say more when he apparently caught sight of his wife from the corner of his eye.

"Well, jest let me say this, Miss Gertrude," he whispered. "That when you're a-needing a trim, you could get it done in Mansfield or Conners. My woman don't like you in the barbershop a bit."

"I'll be happy to take my business elsewhere, Mr. Dooley," she said, smiling. She glanced around the room to catch Mrs. Dooley watching her and she gave the woman a cheery little wave.

"Oh, Lord," Hank complained and hurriedly moved away.

Her respite lasted only a couple of minutes before Doc Ponder made his way in her direction.

"How are you doing, Gertrude?" he asked. "I trust no visits to my office to mean that you are in good health."

"I am indeed feeling very well, Doc," she said. She wanted to simply leave it at that, but the doctor didn't move on. His hesitation became so long it proved to be embarrassing and

Gertrude finally was forced to spout the inquiry that politeness demanded. "How are you, Doc?"

"Well, I've been busy," he said. "Of course you understand that. Doctoring is not all that I do. Like yourself I have a book to write."

"Yes," Gertrude said evenly and gazed off into the crowd, hoping her inattention would discourage this discussion.

It didn't.

"I've told you about *my* book, haven't I? Well, of course I have," he continued without waiting for a reply. "It is the culmination of all my observations about the nature of people and their fate. The genetic predisposition of caste and class. I'm thinking now of calling it *What's in a Name*. Do you like that?"

"Catchy title," Gertrude answered vaguely.

"Of course, when you understand where it comes from. You know that our surnames, when we first got them, were dependent upon our role in the communities. The miller was called Miller and the smith called Smith. That was the way it worked. And I think, Miss Gertrude, that if you look closely that is still the way that it works."

Gertrude was not at all interested in looking closely.

"If you begin to look at people and the places that they hold in society, you'll find that the Millers and Smiths of this world are still tradesmen. And the great families that once held land in medieval Europe still rule the world."

"I am aware of your theory, Doctor," Gertrude said.

"It's more than a theory. If you look at Darwin, Engels, any of those thinkers could tell you, genetic determinism is as much a reality of human existence as living and dying."

The doctor sighed proudly and patted himself upon his ample stomach. "That's why people who declare that some classes are oppressed and that we should stop that oppression are just barking up the wrong tree. Why, even the Bible says that the poor will always be with us. Huge groups of people are born on this earth merely to serve those whose genetic superiority will naturally allow them to rise to the top."

"And we can kind of know exactly whether we were meant to serve or to be served based upon our surnames?" Gertrude asked skeptically.

"Well, not totally. Some people have changed their names or taken names they never deserved. Some people's names don't mean anything. But it's a clue. And it's important. We must teach the lower classes not to resist their genetic fate and to be grateful for the life that they have, lowly though it may be."

"I'm sure that's a course I wouldn't want to teach," Gertrude said.

"And you certainly should not," the doctor hastened to assure her. "You are not genetically disposed in that direction."

"But I suppose that you are," Gertrude said.

"Teach? Me? Heavens no. Think of my name. Think of my name, Gertrude. Ponder. I'm a philosopher. I am here on this earth to contemplate the truths, not to teach them."

The doctor gave a self-satisfied sigh.

"Ah, but the writing," he said. "It's really difficult. That taking the time to put everything down in pen and ink. It's a truly thankless job. But then you should know that."

"Yes."

"Although fiction is of course very different from what I write," he said.

"Oh no," Gertrude corrected him. "It is the same, exactly."

Doc Ponder nodded, then his expression grew puzzled. "What did you m—"

"Excuse me, Doc," Gertrude interrupted. "I have to get another cup of this wonderful punch."

She eased into the crowd as quickly and adroitly as she could. Her route toward the punch bowl was a circuitous one, taking her on the edge of one polite conversation after another.

"And we have six business-quality typewriting machines," Miss Dudley was telling her eager listeners. She was absolutely glowing from the attention.

"I've always felt that a school for our own children would be the best investment we could make in our future," her brother George said to a group of posturing older men. More than likely, Gertrude thought, they were potential voters of the Crusading Knights of the Mystic Circle.

"I add just a little bit of lemon juice to it and it brings the stains out every time," Mrs. Pugh said to Mrs. Wilkerson.

"Every time!" The minister's wife seemed awed by the prospect.

Finally, Gertrude found herself at the punch table. Her heart thudded dramatically as she caught sight of the man in a handsome gray broadcloth vest who was already there.

"Mr. Stefanski," she said, stepping up to stand beside him. "How nice to see you here."

Turning with surprise, Stefanski bowed over her hand in that formal, rather continental way he had, and smiled at her.

"Miss Gertrude," he said. "As always, it is a distinct pleasure to see you."

She grinned broadly. She loved his accent. It was much improved from when she first met him, but he was, and forever would be, foreign-sounding, despite his now having a very, very good grasp of the English language.

"May I pour you a cup of punch?" he asked.

"Let me pour for you," she suggested. "After all, if not for you, sir, we might not be here tonight."

He cleared his throat uncomfortably and as Gertrude dipped punch for both him and herself, she let the subject drop.

Mikolai Stefanski's contribution to the community of Venice was unmatched. And his contribution to the new high school was a tremendous one, and also the worst-kept secret in town.

He had, it was said, begun with the proposal of furnishing all the brick. Ultimately it was his deep pockets that had paid almost exclusively for the building. Despite the contributions of the city fathers and the generous charity of the Knights of the Mystic Circle, without Stefanski there would have been no school.

His modesty on the subject allowed the community as a whole to take bows for what they had accomplished. But Gertrude felt that she, at the very least, should acknowledge what he had done.

"It's a beautiful school," she said. "I wish I could have gone here."

He nodded solemnly. "I wish I could have gone to school anywhere," he said. "But I am glad for Teodor. And your Claire, of course."

"Of course.

"I heard Miss Dudley say that they have typewriter machines here in the school for the young people to learn to typewrite upon."

"That is a good thing," he said. "I have one in my office, but I haven't learned to do much with it."

"Many novelists are now using them," Gertrude said. "It is the latest thing to now send your manuscripts to the publisher already neatly printed upon pages."

"Perhaps you will take up typewriting then," he said.

"Perhaps," she insisted with a shake of her head. "But maybe not. They are much too fast for me. I like to think about what I am saying. A pen and paper give me sufficient time to do just that."

"For me it is the same, but for a different reason," he said. "I have to think up the words in Polish and then translate them to English before I write them down."

They smiled at each other momentarily and the conversation waned. Gertrude felt somewhat nervous. She had so recently allowed herself the luxury of daydreaming about Mr. Stefanski.

It was a reckless thing to do. They were friends. Beyond that, the only thing they shared was a shady tree. Reveling in the pleasure of standing close to him in a public place was foolishness in the extreme.

"I was talking to Doc Ponder about his book," Gertrude said quickly. She was almost chattering with the need to converse, to distract her thoughts from the smooth wide expanse of his suit coat and the fragrance of his hair tonic.

"Ah . . ." Mikolai nodded sagely. "I have heard the good doctor's peculiar interpretations of the makeup of the human race."

"He's such a fool," Gertrude stated harshly. "Believing that people's lives are predetermined at birth by who their parents and grandparents were."

Mikolai nodded. "Yes, I think I have been a great disappointment to him. He keeps hoping, I think, that my business will fail and that I will take up the scythe and sharecropping."

Gertrude laughed lightly at his words. "I suppose he would have me give up writing for forestry," she suggested. "Barkley does mean birch woods, you know."

"Does it?" he asked, grinning. "Perhaps we should have planted a birch together instead of a hazel."

"We would have certainly gathered just as many hazelnuts," she answered. "I truly am at a loss as to why that tree doesn't produce."

"Perhaps it just isn't time," Mikolai said. "Nature has its own calendar for things and it is often a mystery to us."

"That's true," she agreed. "But still I wish something would happen to give nature a little push before we're both too old to appreciate its bounty."

It was pitch-black in Claire Barkley's bedroom as she stuffed the hem of her pink princess petticoat all around the doorframe cracks. It was the only way she could ensure that no telltale light shining through might be noticed by her mother. When she was certain that all was secure, she brought out the coal-oil lantern that she had secreted in her armoire. The hiss of the gas lamps might be detected by her mother's sharp ears, but burning coal oil was as quiet as the night itself.

She struck a match on the bottom of her dressing table and removed the globe to light the wick. The immediate brightness of the room was a little frightening. She stood silently, stiff as a stone waiting for the sound of Prudence Barkley's feet padding down the hallway toward her room. As the long minute passed without any evidence of movement in the house, Claire let out a deep sigh, set the globe on the lamp, and seated herself at the dressing table.

From the middle drawer, beneath a rainbow of hair ribbons and hat flounces, Claire brought out the diary. She held it to her chest as if making a wish and then let go a long heartfelt sigh.

She had already read it all, of course. Every word was seared upon her memory for all time. Still, she could not resist the beauty of it, the wonder of it, the incredible truth of it.

Knowing exactly the passage that she was looking for, Claire leafed through the book eagerly. Easily she found the page of part of the story she called simply "The Kiss."

Her eyes dreamy, she held the worn yellowed pages beneath the flickering glow of the coal oil and read once more the first sweet, touching moment of love between the two wonderful people that she now knew to be her parents.

It was sugary sweet, often purple prose that captured her heart as the diary told the tale of a determined young woman, misunderstood and often mistreated, flying in the face of her father's wrath to seek the man who loved her. And that man, strong, heroic, noble, unable to control the force of passions that the innocent young woman drew from him.

"Liebchen," Claire whispered aloud. It was Mikolai's pet name for Gertrude. She sighed heavily and closed the journal.

She brought it up against her chest to touch her physically as it had already touched her heart. She gave her own graceful sigh of true love.

"It's so beautiful," she whispered to herself as joyous tears gathered in the corners of her eyes. She sat up straighter and fumbled for the handkerchief in the pocket of her flannel gown. She wiped her eyes and stared once more with wonder at the fading ink and the yellowed pages before her.

"Oh, Aunt Gertrude, Mr. Stefanski, my . . . my parents."

Somehow, she thought she had always known it. How could her grouchy father and her boring mother ever have conjured enough intensity to create such a child as herself?

Of course, she, a young woman of such inexplicably fervent feelings, would have to have been the fruit of a passionate, ill-fated union.

"Oh, I vow, I vow, Gertrude and Mikolai, that with every breath in my body I will see that you have not loved in vain. You will be together again. Together for all time and no man will again put you asunder. I am the child of your love. And I will see to it."

She sighed dramatically.

"And Teddy will help me."

Chapter Five

"AND HE CALLED her *liebchen*," Claire whispered to Teddy as the two made their way through the noisy, crowded hallway of the Venice High School building. The fall morning was crisp and bright and the leaves outside the windows were a splash of dazzling color, but the two young people were too preoccupied to notice.

"Father doesn't speak German. Why would he call her a German name?" Teddy asked.

Claire shrugged with unconcern. "Maybe it's the same in Polish."

Teddy's brow furrowed and he shook his head. "I don't think so."

"Anyway, don't you see that we have to do something and we've got to do it now," Claire told him. "We can't turn back time, but as their closest relatives and the people who love them most in the world we've got to get them together."

The young man nodded. "Yeah, I guess that we do."

"They've loved each other so long," Claire's voice was wistful. "Gosh, they're both nearly forty. They just have to be together for what time they have left. Together for their twilight years."

Teddy nodded in solemn agreement. "Father told me last night that he'd never been in love."

"What?" Claire looked at her friend askance. "Of course he was in love. The journal says so. He must be lying to you."

Teddy shrugged. "But he did say that there was a woman he wanted to marry but that her father was against it."

Claire's eyes widened with joyous delight. "See, I told you!"

"It must have been Miss Gertrude," he said. "I just can't imagine anyone else in town he might have wanted to marry."

"Of course it wasn't anybody else. Oh, Teddy," she sighed dramatically. "It's all so romantic. We've just got to get them together and this time we will all live happily ever after."

"I don't know how we are going to do that," he said. "Both of them definitely have minds of their own. And they've lived next door to each other for years. I'd think if they wanted to get back together, they would have after your grandfather died."

"But then Aunt Gertrude was in mourning," Claire explained. "I'm sure she couldn't go against her father's wishes while she was still in mourning for him. And after giving me up, do you think they could just be together like nothing happened while another couple raised me as their own?"

Teddy considered that. "No, I guess not."

"So now it's up to us. We have to find a way to remind them of the love that they shared. To let them know that there are no longer any barriers to it. To make them see that their children *want* them to be together."

"It would be good for Father to have someone when I've gone to college. I hate to think of him alone in that big old house."

"And poor Aunt Gertrude," Claire said. "Don't you know how trapped she must feel living her whole life hemmed in by George and Prudence?"

"George and Prudence?"

Claire flushed slightly and gave an arrogant toss to her head. "I refuse to call those people 'mother' and 'father.' They may be Lester's parents, but they are not mine. I can't yet call Aunt Gertrude and Mr. Stefanski 'mom' and 'dad,' but I can quit speaking the lie I've been forced to live."

Claire's tone was overly dramatic, but Teddy didn't really notice. He was pensive, trying to imagine Mikolai Stefanski—who, his son was sure, could do anything—being thwarted in love.

"Father seemed pretty certain last night that he'd never been in love," he said.

"Don't be ridiculous. Nobody lives as long as Mr. Stefanski and Aunt Gertrude without having been in love," Claire declared with the certainty of youth. "It was just such a heartbreak for him. That's it, Teddy. He lost not only the woman of his heart, but his own daughter, too. He's probably put it out of his mind completely."

"I don't know, Claire, that doesn't sound much like my father."

Teddy was just about to point out how unlike Mikolai Stefanski it would be to shirk responsibility for a child and to allow his own flesh and blood to be raised by George Barkley. It was a puzzling concept and he meant to bring it up for discussion, but he was momentarily distracted.

"Hi, Teddy! Hi, Claire." The voice that called out was that of Olive Widmeyer, the most popular girl in the senior class.

"Hello, Olive." Teddy's voice cracked slightly and he flushed in annoyance at the sound.

The pretty young woman, nearly bouncing with enthusiasm, reached out to grab Claire's wrist, giggling with excitement and delight. "I just spoke with Miss Dudley and Principal Shue and you will honestly never guess."

Claire probably couldn't guess and Teddy was far beyond even trying.

Oliver Widmeyer was Venice High School's version of the femme fatale. Since the differences between the girls and boys first became apparent, Olive had become to the young men of the town the true symbol of all that was good and fine and wonderful about the great state of Missouri. The boys on the football team spoke of Olive often, and with near reverence. The young gentlemen of more literary bent composed sonnets that used her name in rhyme. Even the staid old professors were known to avert their eyes and clear their throats nervously in her presence.

Certainly her cornsilk-blond curls hung prettily down the middle of her back. Her big blue eyes were wide-spaced and expressive. And her bright, winning smile seemed to light up her face with a magic glow of friendliness. But it was none of these qualities that captured the attention of the male population. To the boys of the varsity, Olive was known simply as "The Bosom." And like the others, Teddy Stefanski was mindlessly enchanted by the way those robustly feminine mounds of flesh filled up the front of her middy blouse.

"They are going to let us have a dance." Olive was squealing with delight. "A real dance after the football game in celebration of our victory over Rogers. Isn't it terrific?"

"Terrific," Teddy agreed.

Claire looked puzzled. "What if we don't beat Rogers?"

Olive's eyes widened in distress. "Oh, but we will beat them." She turned her pretty face up to the silent young man beside her. "We will beat them, won't we, Teddy?"

"Of course," he squeaked and then cleared his throat with a deep bass sound. "Of course, we'll beat them, Olive."

"And then we can dance and dance," she said wistfully, adding a delighted giggle. "It's all arranged. All we have to do is come up with some chaperones."

"Ah." Claire nodded understanding.

"I'll take care of all the plans and the decorations, but I know you'll be much better than me at getting parents to come as chaperones."

It was true, of course. When Olive talked to adults about fun or parties, they always seemed worried, as if unleashing all her youthful vitality and beauty upon the world might be dangerous. When Claire brought up the same ideas, people were generally more indulgent.

"All right, I'll round up the chaperones. What about your parents?" Claire asked.

Olive wrinkled her nose slightly. "Only as the last resort," she said. "My father is such an old fuddy-duddy. He gets mad at every boy who wants to dance with me. I was thinking about your folks, Claire. Could you ask them?"

"I suppose so. I'm sure Mama would love to come. It's just if she can talk my father into it."

"Well, tell her we're counting on them," Olive said. "See you. Bye, Teddy."

"Bye," he managed to get out.

As the young woman hurried off, Teddy turned his head to follow her figure. Olive flittered out of range, her smile ceaselessly beaming, her breasts perpetually bouncing.

Teddy stopped stone-still in the hallway, his gaze lingering after her. His expression part lovelorn lothario, part pouting puppy dog.

Claire couldn't help but notice. A flair of unexpected jealousy welled up inside her. Immediately she pushed it away. By all consensus, Olive Widmeyer was the prettiest girl in school. And she was nice to everybody, that couldn't be argued. Teddy certainly deserved the prettiest girl and a nice one, too. As his sister, Claire decided suddenly, she shouldn't wish him anything less.

"She's lovely," Claire commented with honesty.

"Huh? Oh, Olive, yeah, she's something all right," Teddy agreed.

"I think you should ask her to the dance."

Teddy's eyes widened and he stared at Claire as if she'd lost her mind. "*Me* ask *her*, I— What dance?"

"The one she was just talking about. Didn't you hear what she was saying?"

"Guess not," he admitted.

In truth, he wasn't sure that he'd even be able to breathe, let alone listen, when he was in her presence.

"We're going to have a dance after the game with Rogers. A victory dance, I suppose."

"What if we don't win?"

"Teddy, you just told Olive that we would."

"I did?"

Claire shook her head and laughed in amused disbelief. "You did, and I do think that you should ask her to the dance."

Teddy looked somewhat daunted at the prospect. "Oh, Claire, I don't think she'd go out with me."

"Of course she would," she assured him. "She'd be a fool not to. You're terrific."

Teddy looked at her, askance at the unexpected recommendation. "You just think that 'cause I've finally learned to read John Milton."

Claire laughed. "I think it because it's quite true. I think she's terrific, too."

"She's terrific all right," he said. "In the old-fashioned sense of that word. She scares me to death."

"Don't be silly. Fullbacks don't get scared," she assured him. "And I do think that you should take Olive to the dance. But first things first. We won't have a dance unless we get some chaperones."

"Chaperones? Yeah, good idea."

"I suppose we could start with my parents," she said somewhat less than enthusiastically.

Stopping in midstride, she grinned broadly. "That's it!"

"What?"

"My parents."

Teddy raised a questioning eyebrow.

"I'll get Aunt Gertrude and your father to chaperone. They will have to spend the whole evening together and they'll probably dance together and, oh, Teddy, this is going to be wonderful."

Alexandria DuPree was such a tragic figure, Gertrude acknowledged to herself as she gazed at the words she had just written so neatly on white vellum. She sighed heavily. It was hard to believe that the beautiful and courageous young heroine that she had created to be Tyler DuPree's second, much younger wife had turned into such a sad and almost pitiful war widow. It was shame, Gertrude thought, but it had to be so.

Tyler had married her when she was only the very ambitious and attractive young daughter of a drunken white-trash overseer. DuPree had not loved her, not the way he had loved his first wife, but he had wanted her. He had wanted her more than any woman since Mona, Weston's mother, had seduced him into betraying his marriage vows. His inconstancy had hastened his dear wife's death and to his dying day Tyler DuPree had never forgiven himself.

But still, he was a man. And as a man, his greatest weakness was his own passion. When Alexandria's drunken pa had been killed for cheating in a game of cards, DuPree had saved her and her mother from an uncertain fate. His cold embrace had never warmed the beautiful young woman in his arms, but she was very grateful. And it was that gratitude that ensured Alexandria would be loyal to her husband's memory.

Yes, she would have to keep Carlisle Place together for the perpetuity of the DuPree family. It was a sacrifice for a woman still young, a woman who would never know the stir of hot passions or be blessed with the gift of a child of her own. It was a sacrifice that was as expected and unheralded as the sunrise. Alexandria DuPree could rightfully anticipate to live forty more years. Alone.

Inexplicably, tears came to Gertrude's eyes, blurring the words before her. She fumbled with her skirt pocket, retrieving her handkerchief. Weeping was not something that she was prone to, but lately during this book, this last book of the DuPree saga, she'd found herself overwrought more than once. In all honesty she couldn't quite understand it.

She leaned back in her chair and stared thoughtfully into oblivion. This book was meant to bring the DuPree family full circle. It was supposed to show the triumph of the human heart over the devastation of war. But somehow when she looked at her characters, she didn't see courageous people starting over. She saw sad, wounded people. People whose shattered lives left them only dreams unfulfilled.

Gertrude sniffed loudly as once more the tears threatened. With disgust she wiped her eyes and rose to her feet. This was foolishness. Plain foolishness. She was intolerant of that in others; she hated it in herself. A good cup of tea would get her back on track, she decided. It would slice through the web of sentimentality that was obscuring her vision.

Wearing her knitted house slippers, her steps were silent in the hall as she made her way through the familiar passages of the house where she'd been born, the house where she had lived her life, the house where she would probably always be until the day she was dressed in a shroud and laid out in the front parlor.

It was not, however, her house.

When she reached the bottom of the stairs, she heard Prudence humming. In a flash she recalled that it was Wednesday. Wednesday was the maid's day off and baking day for the Barkley family. Gertrude knew that her sister-in-law would be up to her earlobes in bread dough. She hesitated and almost turned back to her apartment. Pru enjoyed the baking, it was one of the few activities that she truly seemed to relish and without ever being told, Gertrude understood that her interruption would be more of an intrusion. Prudence seemed to have so few truly joyous moments in her life, Gertrude hated to intrude upon the ones that she had. But this morning the need to escape her work was stronger than her wish to be kind to her sister-in-law.

Gertrude made her way down the long hallway parallel to the stairs and into the kitchen.

Prudence was there, as Gertrude knew she would be, looking flushed and pink and domestic in a snowy white apron and a starched cap.

"Oh, Gertrude," she said lightly, without the slightest hint of disappointment at the encroachment upon her private time. "I didn't expect you to pop in. Have you finished for the day?"

She answered with a negative shake of her head. "I'm just in for a cup of tea," Gertrude told her by way of apology. "I promise not to get in your way."

"Don't be silly," she replied. "Having tea is certainly no trouble in comparison to the mess I'm making." She indicated the giant mixing bowl where the dough was left to rise and the floury remains of her kneading that still dusted the huge breadboard.

"Help yourself," she told Gertrude. "The water may still be warm."

Gertrude thanked her sister-in-law politely and picked up the water kettle from the cool part of the back of the stove. She tested the metal with a quick pat of the flat of her hand and determined that it wasn't hot enough to suit. She placed it upon the hot metal lid of the cookstove. Leaning indolently against the cupboard, she waited with some impatience.

Prudence was humming again. She turned and kneaded and pounded the dough against the board and sounded as delighted with her task as if she were walking out at a cotillion. Gertrude eyes her sister-in-law with some curiosity. Prudence was a good mother, a devoted wife, and an unfailingly dependable friend to the community. She made bread each week, not just to feed her own family, but to send to the widows and orphans and to the unmentionable folks who lived in shanties on the far south side. Prudence was quiet, dutiful, and boring. Not at all saintly material, but Gertrude knew her to be closer to that rank than many more well-known philantropists would ever come.

"Claire has asked me to chaperone a school dance," Gertrude said, breaking the silence of the warm, sunny kitchen.

Prudence nodded as her thickly buttered hands formed the broad loaves of white dough and laid them carefully in the oblong tin pans.

"That will be nice for you," she said. "You need to get out more."

Gertrude chuckled lightly. "I think it is you that should get out more, Prudence. According to my brother and your husband I am getting out far too often," she told her.

"Oh, whatever do you mean?"

"My brother George thinks his sister causes a scene every time she goes out in public."

Prudence's brow furrowed with concern. "I hope he hasn't hurt your feelings, Gertrude," she said. "George is simply not himself lately." She turned from her labors long enough to sigh heavily. "He wants so badly to be chosen Sublime Kalifa."

"I can't imagine why," Gertrude answered with a shake of her head. "It's just a social club, for heaven's sake. George acts as if he's trying to be elected King of England."

Prudence nodded with agreement, but her expression was troubled. "It's such a gesture of respect from the community to be chosen," she said. "George needs that."

"George *is* respected in the community," Gertrude declared truthfully. "He's the banker, after all."

"That's it, Gertrude," she said. "George feels like he's inherited that respect from Mr. Barkley, just like he did his money, his position, even his home." Her expression was serious as she turned to face Gertrude. "Being elected Sublime Kalifa is something that neither his father nor grandfather ever did. It will prove that George has earned his place in this community for the things that *he* has done."

Prudence became very quiet for a long moment and stared soberly at the long row of pans brimming with gleaming white bread dough. "It will prove that he's earned his place in this community in spite of the things that he has done."

The silence in the room was large, enormous, unfathomable.

Gertrude took two steps across the room and embraced her sister-in-law, her own concerns and the hot water on the stove completely forgotten.

"Oh, Pru, that was such a long time ago," Gertrude whispered against the younger woman's cap-covered hair.

Her expression somber, Prudence answered her honestly. "The smaller the town," she said, "the longer the memory."

A knock on the door and the sound of her aunt's voice requesting entrance startled Claire and she dropped the diary to the floor. She spent most of her spare time now reading it and rereading it. The words written there had taken on a life of their own in her young mind.

Hurriedly she pushed those most secret scribblings under her bed and piled her shoes on top of it. Her heart was pounding like a tom-tom, just the way she was sure Aunt Gertrude's heart had pounded on that day so long ago when she had secretly met the man she loved, the man her father refused to allow her to marry, the man with whom she had conceived a child of love.

Claire's face was flaming red at the thought, but she could do little about it and quickly she sat down on her bed and smoothed her nightgown once before checking again to ensure that the diary was well hidden.

"Come in, Aunt Gertrude," she called out.

"Are you all right?" her aunt asked as she came through the doorway. "You look a little flushed."

"Oh, I'm fine, fine," she answered nervously. "Perhaps I got too much sun today. Why do you ask?"

"Well, it's very late for you to be up," Gertrude said. "You're going to be yawning through your classes tomorrow, I suspect. What have you been reading?"

Claire felt the color staining her cheeks, "Oh, nothing," she insisted quickly. "I've just been sitting here thinking about things."

Gertrude raised a questioning eyebrow and came over to sit on the edge of the bed beside her. She was dressed in her nightwear, a white muslin gown trimmed in soft pink silk ribbon and her hair was covered with a shadow lace cap. Claire had seen her aunt hundreds of times looking this same way, but tonight somehow she saw her differently. She was no longer simply dear eccentric Aunt Gertrude, but rather a woman who had thrown caution and decency to the winds. And who, for that crime, had become her mother.

"What sort of things are you thinking about?" Gertrude asked her. "You certainly have a strange expression on your face."

"Oh, just things," Claire answered guiltily.

Gertrude smiled and hugged her tightly. "I understand, dear," she said. "I remember that when I was your age, my mind was simply awhirl with the possibilities. I wanted to do so many things. There were so many places I wanted to go."

She sighed as she contemplated the memory.

Claire eyed her aunt thoughtfully a moment before she spoke. "I'm sure you dreamed about places and things," she said evenly. "Did you ever dream about falling in love, Aunt Gertrude?"

Her aunt's eyes widened in surprise. Fluttering a bit nervously, she seemed hesitant to answer. "I'm sure that all young girls dream about that," she admitted before adding, "they'd simply be old women in young faces if they didn't." She chuckled as if she'd made a fine joke, but somehow her laughter did not quite ring true.

Claire did not even smile and she wasn't about to be put off by her aunt's feeble attempt at humor.

"I don't want to know about all young girls, Aunt Gertrude. I want to know about you. Didn't you dream about falling in love?"

Gertrude cleared her throat. She was obviously very uncomfortable with the subject. "Well, of course I thought about it upon occasion," she admitted. "But nothing really ever—" She glanced up nervously and gave Claire a long, rather pained look. "Don't you think that this sort of thing would be better discussed with your mother?"

"What on earth could Mama know about love?" Claire asked, her eyes wide with sincere surprise. "She married George Barkley!"

Gertrude appeared slightly aghast at her niece's words, then her expression softened. "What a strange thing for you to say, Claire," her aunt scolded. "I can only count it as the foolish words of youth. Your parents are very much in love and have been since they were your age."

Claire gave her a doubtful expression. "Mama has nothing on her mind but Lester the Pester. And Papa—" She rolled her eyes. "He certainly doesn't strike me as having ever been an ardent swain."

Gertrude laughed good-naturedly. "Oh, but you don't know him as well as I do," she said. "Your father was quite the lovelorn romantic in his youth."

Claire shook her head, disbelieving. "I suppose that's why he's so grouchy now."

Gertrude's good mood vanished almost immediately and she looked uncomfortable once more. She answered slowly as if carefully choosing her words. "I'm sure it's upsetting to you the way your father flies off the handle at everything. But it's just his way."

"His way is certainly what he gets around here," she answered. "I hate how he tries to tell you what to do all the time. Mama apparently doesn't mind, but he's got no right to treat you like . . . like . . ."

"Like a sister?" Gertrude asked softly. She wrapped a loving arm around Claire's shoulder. "Your father is just very worried about this election of the Crusading Knights of the Mystic Circle. He's wanted to be Sublime Kalifa for years now. It really means a lot to him." Gertrude patted her comfortingly. "And, honestly, I think he might have been elected last year if I hadn't decided to wear that split skirt and ride astride at the Founder's Day Parade."

"It was a beautiful skirt, Aunt Gertrude," Claire told her, quickly rising to her defense.

Her aunt smiled broadly at her. "Oh yes, I thought so, too, and you know I don't mind at all tweaking the noses of the gossips. But I should have remembered that ultimately everything I do comes to rest on George's shoulders," she said. "That's what happens when you are the head of the family. And that's why the rest of us must try to be as very understanding as we possibly can. Your poor father has had all of it to contend with since your grandfather died."

"I still don't like him telling you what to do," Claire said.

Gertrude leaned closely and spoke conspiratorially. "Well, darling," she whispered, "if it will make you feel better to know it, I hardly listen."

Claire laughed with her aunt, delightedly for a moment before realizing that she had been very cleverly led away from the subject she wished to discuss.

"Oh, Aunt Gertrude, you've made me forget what I am about," she said. "I want to hear it from you. I want you to tell me about falling in love."

Gertrude smoothed the hair from the young girl's face and looked into her eyes for a long moment. "Truly," she told her. "I'm sure I know nothing at all about it."

"Of course you do," Claire insisted.

Gertrude shook her head determinedly. "Falling in love is a bit like catching the chicken pox. Most everyone does, but it's not something that you can make happen." She hesitated just an instant too long before adding, "And when it is going to happen, there is really nothing you can do to avoid it."

Chapter Six

❧❧

"HURRY, AUNT GERTRUDE, the game is almost ready to start," Claire declared as the two women made their way through the crowd gathered at the side of the open field near the high school.

The day was chilly and gray and threatening rain. The people present looked almost as dreary as the sky overhead.

In her navy blue middy sweater and shepherd-check skirt, Claire looked very much like every other young female in attendance. Gertrude, on the other hand, was sporting a new three-piece-style afternoon costume that was more chic and fashionable than anything heretofore seen in the town of Venice. The bright rose-colored linen jacket and skirt with the candy-striped collar and cuffs stood out among the more primly dressed matrons in their gray silks and serges. And the trim little boyish cap with the bright pink aigrette only drew more attention to her short-cropped curls. It was a little extraordinary for football game attire, but Claire had begged her to chaperone the victory dance afterward, and Gertrude couldn't really attend such a function without a little bit of style.

The young woman continued to weave through the crowd.

"For heaven's sake, Claire," Gertrude called out. "Where are you going? We can see perfectly well from here."

Claire stopped only to glance around once more, then,

apparently sighting a spot she liked better, hurried on. "Over here, Aunt Gertrude, this is terrific," she said.

Gertrude somewhat unwillingly followed her niece to the very front row of the crowd, standing only just to the right of the circle of congregating players. The area was mostly men with their smelly cigars and for the life of her, Gertrude couldn't see what made this place better than one a little farther to the edge. She was about to say that very thing to Claire when she spotted Mikolai Stefanski beside her.

"Well, hello," she said, a bit surprised. It wasn't that she hadn't known that he would attend his son's football game. But the two rarely saw each other away from their own gardens. Now they found themselves thrown into conversation several times within the same week.

Sedately dressed as any businessman present, he bowed slightly. "Good afternoon, Miss Gertrude."

With the warmth his presence was known to bring stealing over her, Gertrude deliberately sought an expression of nonchalance as she glanced around at the crowd.

She found that many of the gentlemen and most of the ladies dressed soberly in clothing to match the darkening skies were staring at her.

She smoothed her skirt. "It seems I am a bit overdressed for this occasion," she said to Stefanski. "Even when I don't mean to draw attention, it seems that I do."

He too glanced around the crowd before returning his gaze to her. His expression was warm, but the lines of his face were straight and sober. "Not overdressed, Miss Gertrude, merely a ray of sunshine on this cloudy day."

Gertrude laughed at his rather poetic compliment.

"Why thank you, sir," she answered with playful exaggeration. "As always, you are more than a friendly neighbor, you are my knight gallant."

He smiled then, broadly. "I am a man who can appreciate a lady in a pretty dress," he answered.

Gertrude was pleased. The "pretty dress" was the latest couture creation and she had paid dearly for it. It had come all the way on the train from a New York mail-order house. She had thought herself quite the fashion rebel when she'd put it on this morning, and looked forward to being the most dazzling chaperone at the high school dance. The dress had earned her Mikolai Stefanski's smile. If she never wore it again, it was worth the price.

"I look rather like the goldfinch among the sparrows," she admitted, blushing as she glanced once more at the row after row of ladies and gentlemen dressed in gray and brown.

Mikolai answered her words with frank solemnity. "You look the goldfinch, Miss Gertrude, because you *are* a goldfinch. And a goldfinch is always a welcome sight, Miss Gertrude. I would not wish such a bird to hide itself in feathers meant for sparrows."

His compliment was made without the least bit of smile or gesture to indicate it as flattery. Gertrude felt a flutter in her heart. How could a woman not be in love with this man? The thought was as natural as it was startling. Her heart pounded. She shouldn't be thinking such things. Not in public, not standing next to him.

"Thank you very much, Mr. Stefanski," she said, her tone overly proper and her expression sober. "As always, I value your opinion."

Mikolai glanced at her, obviously puzzled at her abrupt change in behavior. He cleared his throat unnecessarily and gave her the very slightest of nods before turning his attention back to the empty field before them.

Gertrude did the same. She straightened her striped collar and brushed her striped cuffs, her cheeks glowing. For some inexplicable reason, Claire scooted over, forcing Gertrude to stand even closer to Stefanski. She could hardly move without brushing against his coat. In her current state of mental agitation, that should be avoided at all costs.

With a blow of the whistle, the referee set the large oblique-shaped pigskin ball at the center of the field and the players on both teams hurried to their assigned positions. The young men from Rogers, who had arrived on the morning train, had only their coach and a few parents to applaud them.

The hometown boys, however, were loudly cheered. Gertrude was close enough to hear the coach give them their words of encouragement.

"Remember, boys, no push and pull," he cautioned. "Don't flinch, don't foul, and hit the line hard."

With a clap of dismissal, the Venice varsity hurried out to take their stance and defend their goal.

Gertrude clapped with excited encouragement, though the sound of her cheering was muffled by her white afternoon gloves. She knew most of the boys on the team. Their parents had been her childhood friends and she had watched the progress of their little lives at a writer's respectable distance, keenly observing. If she had had a son of her own, he too might be playing on this team.

The thought was a melancholy one and she pushed it away. And a woman didn't need a son of her own to appreciate the strength and grace of an athlete in his youthful prime.

"For heaven's sake, Gertrude, why did you have to stand this near the sidelines!" The words were spoken in a gruff scold by her brother, arriving late.

Gertrude startled, moving guiltily as far away from Stefanski as possible. "Claire picked this place," she answered quickly. "It seems as good to me as any other."

Barkley huffed, disgruntled. He glanced over Gertrude's head. "Afternoon, Stefanski."

"Barkley," was the reply.

George turned his attention back to his sister. "It's just foolish of you to let Claire make such a decision. You might as easily let Prudence make a choice, neither one of them has any sense at all."

"I like where we are standing just fine," Gertrude lied to her brother. At that moment she wished herself far away from the man at her side. "I think it's, as the children say, terrific. If you don't like it, you can stand elsewhere."

George's cheeks puffed up. "The family should stand together. How else will the head of the family be able to give directions to its lesser members? If you and Claire had waited for us as you should have, this problem would have never come up."

Gertrude's eyes narrowed and she looked downright belligerent. "No *problem* has come up. Claire and I will stand where we want, and you may stand wherever it pleases you to do so."

George flushed slightly and lowered his voice to a near whisper. "Good Lord, Gerty, don't defy me in public. You know I'm up for Sublime Kalifa. Half of the Knights of the Mystic Circle are probably watching us right now."

Gertrude answered him just as quietly. "Don't tell me what to do, George Barkley, and I won't defy you."

Her brother nodded as if accepting the truth and then he looked at her more closely. "What is this outfit you're wearing?" he asked.

Gertrude was saved answering when Prudence sidled up to her husband, full panic in her voice.

"Little Lester got away from me in the crowd!" she exclaimed. "I can't find him anywhere."

"Mrs. Barkley." George's voice was loud and stern. It was clear that his words were meant as much for the crowd around him as the woman he addressed. "As a wife you are almost totally worthless." The men in that group smiled and nodded to each other in approval of a good and well-done setdown by a man who definitely wore the trousers in his own household.

Prudence was too well bred to give a reply and the two dove off into the crowd to find their missing offspring, leaving Claire and Gertrude to their own devices.

Gertrude stifled the sigh of relief that escaped from her lips. Glancing up, she saw that it had not gone unnoticed by the man at her side.

"George is a little nervous these days," she said by way of explanation.

Stefanski nodded. "Were I voting for Sublime Kalifa, he would get my vote," he said. "The man must have fine qualities for such ladies as yourself and Mrs. Barkley to put up with him all these years."

The foibles of George Barkley had been a shared topic of humor between the two of them for years. Her brother, although being very near their own age, had always acted as if he were from their parents' generation instead of their own.

The teasing quality of his words evoked that friendly, safe feeling. And Gertrude smiled as she turned her attention to the field. She was not about to make a fool of herself.

The young men had taken their positions. Scanning the group, her eyes alighted upon young Teddy Stefanski. Nearing six feet in height and weighing about one hundred sixty pounds, he was one of the larger boys on the team. His knitted team shirt in a lustrous royal blue fit closely along his back and shoulders, accurately portraying his stalwart physique. The same could not be said, however, of his baggy front-laced football knickers that were cut to oversize proportion to accommodate the thick knee pads that were worn for safety.

The huge gray pants did, however, emphasize the narrowness of the young man's waist and the attractive curve of his well-muscled calves.

In a flash of nostalgic memory, Gertrude was reminded of the young man's father, who had looked similar so very few years earlier. She turned to Stefanski beside her.

"Teddy favors you so much," she said.

Stefanski seemed surprised at her words and glanced with curiosity at his son on the field.

"Does he?"

"He looks exactly as I remember you on the day you came to town."

"I wasn't aware that you even noticed me way back then," Mikolai answered.

As they watched, Teddy took his place in the line of defense. He reached into the lone back pocket of his knickers and retrieved his leather helmet. He slipped the protective cap on his head and half squatted, hands on knees, ready for the kickoff.

"He looks like me, you think?"

"Yes, very much so."

Stefanski shook his head. "I see only Teodor," he told her.

She nodded. "Yes, I'm sure that's the kind of man you are," she said.

He looked at her questioningly, but Gertrude was saved explanation by the sound of the whistle. The center, Roy Bert Pugh, leaned down into his three-point stance, reaching one arm out into the neutral zone to clasp the football. The opposing team jockeyed for position at the line hoping to lure an overeager Venice man into an early, illegal motion. Their temptation was not heeded by the single-minded linemen.

"Hike!" Paul Parks, the young quarterback, called.

With a flash of movement, the center shot the ball back through his legs at a thirty-five-degree angle, directly into the hands of the quarterback.

Parks, with a casualness that belied the gang of determined

young men headed his way, dropped the pigskin to the ground in front of him. The instant that it landed with a plopping sound in the short-cut grass, he kicked it with a powerful whoosh that sent it hurtling over the rush of men coming toward him.

The game was on. As the young men ran and blocked and hit, the friends and family on the sidelines clapped and cheered and hollered encouragement. Gertrude was enjoying the game. It lifted her spirits and made her seem, at least for a short while, a part of something, an accepted member of a kind of community.

When the team managed to hold the line, forcing Rogers into a turnover, Claire turned to ask her aunt in giddy delight, "Aren't they terrific?"

Gertrude smiled at the flushed and glowing young woman at her side. "Yes, I think they rather are," she answered.

The varsity almost scored on their first possession, but was held tight by Rogers's goal-line defense. When the ball was turned over, the coach called for suspension of the time clock and the young men all ran to the sidelines to huddle.

The cheering crowd hardly had time to draw a breath when Delfane Ponder, the yell-leader, wearing a team sweater with his navy worsted knickers, raced onto the field. He held his black tin megaphone up to his lips and hollered.

"Who's straight as a shot and sure as a stream?"

The crowd answered, "Our team! Our team!"

"Who's tough as they come and square on the beam?"

"Our team! Our team!"

"Hurrah! Hurrah! Hurrah rah rah! Venice High School! Rah! Rah! Rah!"

Much shouting and clapping followed this exchange, as much for young Mr. Ponder's way with words as for the young fellows playing football.

When the referee's whistle sounded once more, the young

men were back on the field. Within minutes Roy Bert forced a fumble and Clifford Bounty gratefully lay down upon it, recovering the ball.

Without conscious intent, Gertrude's attention was drawn to the silent man at her side. Mikolai Stefanski watched the game with the solemnity of a judge.

"They are really playing well," she said.

Mikolai nodded. "That is good," he said. "I can't always tell if we are winning since the people yell just as loudly when we lose."

Gertrude's eyes widened. "You don't understand the game?"

He shook his head. "I keep thinking I will have Teodor to explain it to me. But when we talk there are always more important things."

Momentarily Gertrude accepted his words with solemnity, then a little grin twitched into the corner of her mouth and her eyes lit up with amusement.

"Something more important than football, Mr. Stefanski? Why, in this town that could only be baseball and we can't play that game in this crisp fall weather."

Stefanski furrowed his brow, but Gertrude looked close enough to detect an appreciable sparkle in his murky hazel eyes.

"I listen to what is said," Mikolai admitted. "I know that my boy hits the line." He paused thoughtfully. "I just don't know why."

Gertrude laughed then and shook her head, tossing those curls that weren't sufficiently secured by her hat.

"I'm not sure I know *why* either," she admitted. "But I think I can explain the rules of the game."

She stepped closer to him and he lowered his head slightly to listen to her words.

"The field is one hundred yards long," she said as she indicated the distance between the two goalposts.

Stefanski dutifully looked at them both and nodded.

"Each team," Gertrude continued, "has a goal to defend, although they switch goals at the middle of the game."

"Ah," Mikolai said, nodding. "That explains why they run one way for so long and then suddenly they run the other way."

Gertrude laughed. "I guess it would be hard not to notice that," she admitted.

"When a team gets the ball," she continued, "they get four chances to make ten yards toward the other team's goal. The chances are called 'downs.' Because they start with the ball down on the grass."

Mikolai was listening intently.

"Do you understand me so far?" she asked.

"The team gets four downs to make ten yards," he said.

Gertrude smiled proudly at him. "If they don't make the ten yards they have to give up the ball to the other team. If they do make the ten yards they get four more chances to make ten more yards."

"Why four chances?" he asked. "Why not three or a half dozen?"

Gertrude shrugged. "Actually it used to be just three chances, but they changed the rule a few years ago. I suppose it was just too hard for the high school athletes to move the ball that far. Usually on the last down, they kick it so that the other team will have to start way back next to their own goal."

"That's a good idea," Mikolai commented. "So now I understand how they get the ball, but how do they make the points," he asked.

"When they cross the line under the goalpost they score points," she said, pointing to the H-shaped structures at each end of the field.

"How many points?" Mikolai asked her.

"Different ways across the goal line mean different points," she answered. "A touchdown, that's when you deliberately carry or pass the ball across the goal line, is the best. It's worth six points."

Mikolai nodded thoughtfully. "Touchdown is best," he said.

"If you drop-kick it from anywhere in the field and get it through the uprights on the goalpost it's worth three points."

"Through the uprights?"

"Between the top part of the H," she said.

"But," she added, "if you drop-kick it for the extra point after the touchdown, it's only worth one point. You get a chance for extra points after the touchdown."

"The touchdown is the best," he agreed.

"Now, if you cross your own goal with the ball it's called a touchback and you don't get any points, unless the other team tackles you back there. When that happens it's called a safety and they get two points for that."

"Who gets two points?"

"The other team."

"That doesn't sound very safe to me."

Gertrude gave him a quick look and recognized from the glitter in his eyes that he was joking.

"You're teasing me!"

"I assure you, Miss Gertrude, that Polish gentlemen never tease," he said.

"And you are a Polish gentleman?"

"Certainly not!" he replied. "I'm an American workingman, caring only about football and given to teasing interesting women."

Gertrude grinned at him broadly. He was amused and amusing. She felt suddenly young and happy and alive.

From the corner of her eye she caught sight of her niece and turned to glance at her. The expression on Claire's face was dreamy and strange. Gertrude could not recall ever seeing the young girl look quite so fanciful and she stared back at her, puzzled.

Mikolai must have seen it, too. Gertrude felt the soft, warm brush of breath against her cheek. Mr. Stefanski was leaning in closely to whisper.

"Young Miss Claire looks wistful," he said. "I suspect it is time for her also to fall in love."

"Fall in love?" Gertrude asked in a startled whisper. "What do you mean, 'her also'?"

His tone was confidential. "My Teodor has been asking about love. I suspect it's just their time of life. Youth is so enamored of love," he said.

"Yes, I suppose so," Gertrude answered. Suddenly, quite uncomfortably, she realized that she was once more standing altogether too close to Mr. Stefanski.

With deliberate nonchalance she moved slightly away and determinedly turned her attention once more to the football game. It was a good thing. Only a minute later Teddy took a handoff from the quarterback and went through the line, just to the left of the center. Like magic, he ran right through the huge string of young men and thirty-five more exciting yards for a touchdown.

The Venice crowd went wild. The personages of the city, famous for modesty and decorum, jumped up and down for joy. Claire was alternately cheering and crying. George Barkley was roaring in a very unbankerlike manner. Little Lester, who had managed once more to get free of his mother, was swaggering as if he personally had made the touchdown and telling anyone who would listen that Teddy Stefanski was his neighbor.

To her horror, Gertrude found herself clutching Mikolai Stefanski's hand in her own. They were close, so very close. She looked down at their intertwined fingers. Palms melded together in joy and pride and . . . and something more. Slowly, oh so slowly, as if moved by a force against both their wills the clasped hands rose up between them. Her eyes were wide as she gazed into his. And then for an instance, only an instance, his lips touched the curved knuckles in her snowy white glove.

Chapter Seven

⊱ ⊰

IT WAS, THANKFULLY, a victory dance. The varsity had nosed out Rogers in the last ten minutes of the game. Teddy Stefanski was the hero of the day and the young man had been unable to maintain a dignified and modest decorum and had actually jumped for joy. He hadn't been the only person excited. On the sidelines the people of Venice had been screaming madly. It was as if a football victory over the nearby town were as important as a cure for consumption or peace in Eastern Europe.

Gertrude might have been as excited as the rest had she not been embarrassed. Mikolai Stefanski had kissed her hand, in public, and she was certain that somehow she was to blame. Had she encouraged him? Had he somehow seen her unrequited love staring out at him from her eyes? Whatever the truth, Gertrude was horrified at what had happened. She could only be grateful that the crowd was too roused to notice such a tasty gossip morsel occurring in their midst.

This evening, she vowed quietly to herself as she took an observing position under the shelter of the dance pavilion, she would be the model of propriety. Not because she had such great respect for propriety, but merely for the tremendous opportunity it presented to practice self-discipline. She was, after all, no longer a young girl. Being unusual and eccentric was all well and good, but she was neither frivolous nor youth-crazed. And she certainly didn't want to appear so, especially not to Mikolai Stefanski. There was no sight more pitiful than a woman past her prime pretending to be young once more.

Gertrude glanced down at her new dress and privately reassured herself that looking fashionable did not mean looking young. She was not like an aging coquette grasping for the last bit of excitement in a narrowing life, but rather a modern, free-thinking woman of independent means.

She smiled slightly at her own private joke. Miss Gertrude Barkley, authoress, was as much a character of her creation as Alexandria DuPree or Weston Carlisle.

Deliberately pushing the thought from her, Gertrude took note of her surroundings. The dance pavilion at Monument Park was decorated in Japanese lanterns, to be lit as the darkness of evening came upon them, and boughs of brightly colored leaves and shrubbery. The girls who had done the decorations were to be commended, she thought. It was one thing to spruce up a spring dance with bright new blossoms. It was quite another to try the same course in the chill of October. But the young ladies had done admirably. The bright red leaves of burning bush and the blazing yellow of maple were interspersed along the pavilion railing among orange oak boughs and fragrant dark green cedar. In its own way October could be more beautiful than May.

Monument Park no longer had the sparse newness that she remembered from her own days as a young woman. The former cattle pasture had been turned into a park by the far-thinking and civic-minded of her own youth. Her father had had a good deal to do with that. Mostly he had wanted to end the pasturing of cattle in the city limits, but he also was intelligent enough to believe that a park in the center of town was a good idea.

The idea of dedicating it to Civil War heroes had been a bit trickier. Even today, feeling ran high in the area that had been for the Confederacy, but later occupied by Union forces. It was her father, a true Virginian, who had suggested that a monument with no war or army specified could be whatever the people wanted it to be. Confederates could remember their war dead. Union sympathizers could eulogize theirs. And people with no interest in long-ago wars could simply enjoy the beauty of a lovely park. Truly a monument that was all things to all people.

Gertrude smiled to herself. Her father could be blamed for many things. But inevitably he had to be thanked for many, also.

The gentlemen of the band were turning up. They were local men whose hardworking days were enlivened by the bright blue-and-white uniforms they donned upon every possible occasion and the boisterous, booming music that they presented. Gertrude listened as they sought perfect harmony among the men themselves and the instruments they played.

The plucking of strings and the tooting of horns was random and unmelodic, but it was a fit background accompaniment for the arriving young people. Gaggles of young girls arrived, chattering with the vibrancy of violin strings. The sturdy young men, their expressions serious, were like the trombones and tubas making very few notes, but striking them with great impression. The couples looked sheepish, knowing they were on display. Like the clarinets and trumpets they knew they were meant to take the lead and not sure if the breadth of their scale was sufficient for the job. Gertrude listened as their excited young voices blended together with more noise and exuberance than was strictly necessary.

Teddy Stefanski arrived, with the pretty young Widmeyer girl on his arm, looking very much the conquering hero. He was cheered by all, clapped upon the back by those closest to him, and roundly venerated as the champion of the day's competition.

Gertrude put aside her personal pride of the young man she had known so well and so long, and watched him with a writer's eye. He was handsome, sincere, chivalrous. In the short, swift years that she had honed her writing skills, he had grown from chubby toddler with a stinking diaper and a penchant for eating dirt to a stalwart warrior with grace and honor.

Maybe she should write him into her story, she thought. Immediately she discarded the idea. No, he was far too young. There were no characters in her story that would be his age. If he were older, she mused thoughtfully. No, if he were older he would be like Mr. Stefanski and she had certainly used him for an heroic model too frequently as it was.

Gertrude continued to watch the scene unfolding before her. Pretty young Olive fairly glowed with excitement and cheerfulness. Paul Parks appeared near mesmerized by her every word. Roy Bert Pugh kept his eyes on his shoes, only occasionally glancing up to look at one of the young ladies surrounding him. Delfane Ponder was acting as victorious and debonair as his yell-leader status would allow him. And Tappy Smith was not too grown-up that he didn't try to steal Edith Rittman's new hair ribbon. They were happy young people, innocent and unconcerned, eager and anxious to begin their lives, to begin the dance.

Gertrude, herself, had not attended a dance in years. Not since she was young enough to be one of these gaily dressed ladies giggling so attractively as they were led across the floor. And that was more years ago than she cared to think about.

Of course there were all those balls and soirees at Carlisle House. Crystal chandeliers with a hundred candles and dozens of French dancing slippers gliding across gleaming marble floors. All those exciting, dramatic people in frock coats and hoop-skirts. Gertrude shook her head, smiling. She wondered what people would think if they knew that the dances she'd created with paper and pen were more real to her than any she'd attended here in Monument Park.

Her rumination was abruptly interrupted by a sprightly trumpet blast and the striking up of the band. She clapped politely, as did all in the crowd, her gloved hands effectively rendering her applause inaudible. It was the gentlemen who truly were allowed to show their appreciation, loudly and with shouts and whistles. Perhaps that was why the world always seemed to cater to their choices.

Certainly it was the gentlemen who decided who would dance. The first number was such a dazzling ragtime tune that toes began tapping all over the pavilion and in only a moment the single-sex huddles that had formed on either side of the floor dissipated as the young men hurried to get the choicest partners onto the dance floor.

Up on heels and down on toes, various types of Turkey Trot, Grizzly Bear, and Bunny Hug broke out all along the broad circle of sawdust-strewn polished oak.

Unlike many women of her generation who were shocked by the wild, cavorting rhythms of ragtime, Gertrude watched in awe of their movements, so happy, so full of life. She understood their need for movement and envied them their opportunity to do so. Dancing was an exuberant mystical union of body and music. It could dull grief, enhance love, and refill the empty soul. Gertrude knew that because her soul had been empty more than once. It had been a long time since she'd danced. Oh, the Christmas that Prudence had gotten the new Victrola, George had danced with her. But he'd done so reluctantly and the parlor of the Barkley house could in no way be compared with dancing at the pavilion at Monument Park. Her father had danced with her at Prudence and George's wedding, but that was a lifetime ago. A woman should dance more often, she thought to herself. And a woman needed more dancing as she got older than she did when she was young.

Her thoughts continued in that direction. Perhaps a dance was what was needed in the new book. Her brow furrowed as she considered the notion. Since the end of the war the gaiety had certainly gone out of the DuPree family saga. Even as the writer, she found the story line too often beset with overcast skies and concerned expressions. She imagined Grandville and Lafayette dressed in tattered reconstructions of their once-proud gray uniforms, twirling ladies upon their arms once more. Gertrude sighed aloud at the hopeful expectation. It would be lovely. It would be symbolic. It would be poignant. She considered seriously.

She needed a big new scene utilizing the near ruin of the Carlisle House. And a dance would be fun to write. It would lift her own spirits as well as poor Blessida's, and hers certainly needed lifting. The poor pale beauty had just recently discovered her scallywag lover to be untrue and had begun to waste away with the sorrow of his faithlessness.

Yes, a dance in the new book might be just the thing. She let her imagination run free with the prospect. What kind of dance? A holiday would be nice, May Day or Christmas. She shook her head. Dancing around the maypole was much too wrought with symbolism. And although a Christmas dance would be colorful and bright, Christmas was truly a holiday for children and she had no interesting child characters in the story.

She chewed her lip and stared sightlessly at the gathering crowd. It would be foolish to pretend that Alexandria might suddenly just want to have a gala. Gertrude had worked too hard to make Tyler's widow hard-edged, determined, and unfrivolous. It would have to be something truly important to move her to enter society once more. It would have to be a charity ball.

Gertrude's eyes widened and her heart beat faster. She could have a charity ball to raise money to save Carlisle House from the tax assessors. Gertrude laid a hand upon her heart that was pounding joyously in anticipation. It was such a good idea she wondered why she hadn't thought of it before. A charity ball would certainly be the only thing that would draw the old guard out in their made-over gowns and dilapidated carriages.

Of course, the old guard had no money now. Her thoughts slowed as she considered. The carpetbaggers were the only ones with money.

"A Carpetbaggers' Ball," she whispered.

That was it! She almost laughed aloud. Weston would organize a ball at Carlisle House. He knew all the uppity Yankees with money. Those people would pay dearly to be a part of an authentic genteel Southern ball with the old guard in attendance. And for Carlisle House even Miss Evica DuPree Humbrington would make an appearance. It was perfect. It was wonderful. She could hardly wait.

"Aunt Gertrude? Are you all right?"

Startled, Gertrude found her niece standing at her side. "Claire, I didn't hear you come up."

"What were you doing, Aunt Gertrude? You had such a peculiar expression on your face."

Gertrude shrugged and smiled, only slightly embarrassed. "I was just thinking about my book. Sometimes I just get rather caught up in my plotting."

Claire nodded, clearly understanding.

"Why aren't you dancing?" Gertrude asked her.

The young woman waved away the question with unconcern. "I'm not really much of a dancer," she admitted. "Besides, I wanted to talk to you."

"To me? That's probably a good idea. I really know nothing about being a chaperone," Gertrude told her with a light, self-derisive laugh. "I still think it would have been better to ask your parents. Prudence could have used a night out and your father would have loved to be seen here doing his civic duty. He's running for Sublime Kalifa, you know."

"I know," Claire answered with a long-suffering sigh. "But I wanted *you* here."

"I can't imagine why."

Claire was momentarily speechless, then with a strange flash of expression she answered quickly, "Father is such an old fuddy-duddy. He gets mad at every boy who wants to dance with me."

"Really?" Gertrude was surprised. She had no idea what a "fuddy-duddy" might be, but she wouldn't be surprised if her brother was one. However, George rarely seemed to even notice Claire or her adolescent angst. Gertrude had always thought him to be much like their father, as unconcerned about Claire's personal life as Grover Barkley had been about her own.

"Claire, if you'd like for me to talk to him," she suggested.

"Oh no!" Claire answered hurriedly. "Really, it's nothing. I . . . I . . . I just wanted to talk to you, actually."

"About what?"

"I think you are just terrific for speaking with Mr. Stefanski at the game," she said.

Gertrude looked embarrassed and slightly shocked. "Whatever do you mean?" She asked, thinking guiltily about the warm, glowing feeling that a tête-à-tête with Mr. Stefanski always brought her and, even more regrettable, about the fretful moment when she found herself holding his hand.

"Just that you are always very nice to him," Claire said. "And a lot of people aren't. I mean they are, 'cause he is, I guess, the richest man in town. But they don't speak to him because they like him. I could see that you actually like him."

Gertrude felt her face glow guiltily. Had Claire turned to see them? Had the clasped hands not escaped her notice? Had she witnessed the touch of his lips upon her aunt's glove?

"Being polite to a neighbor is no more than my duty,"

Gertrude answered. Inwardly she winced at her own words. She sounded as pompous as her brother George.

Claire picked at her nail nervously and glanced about as if looking for someone. "Teddy says his father is so lonely," she told Gertrude. "I'm just glad that you seem to enjoy talking to him."

Her brow furrowing, Gertrude eyed her niece questioningly. "Mr. Stefanski, lonely? I don't think so."

To Gertrude's mind the idea of such a man as Mikolai Stefanski feeling loneliness was absurd. Of course, she realized, Claire was far too young to understand that men, with their social clubs, their saloons and beer gardens, their billiard parlors and their houses of ill fame, hardly had to time to even *be* alone. It was the long-suffering women in their lives who begged heaven for children to alleviate the emptiness of their days.

"Mr. Stefanski is a very busy man. I doubt seriously if he has time to be lonely."

"Everyone has time to be lonely, Aunt Gertrude," Claire said. "Why, with your writing and gardening and helping out in the house, you must be one of the busiest women in town."

She stared at her niece, puzzled. "But surely, Claire, you don't think I'm lonely."

The young girl blushed sheepishly. Apparently she did.

Gertrude was affronted. "Why, I have you and Lester and your parents," she said. "I'm sure that I could never be lonely."

"No, of course . . ." Claire began, but it was too late to backtrack. She had suggested that her aunt was a lonely woman. And quite suddenly Gertrude felt exactly that.

"Good evening Miss Dudley, Principal Shue." Mikolai Stefanski greeted the two politely as he made his way to the gaily decorated dance pavilion. He was still dressed in the gray suit he'd worn to the game, but he'd straightened his tie and combed his hair in deference to the higher degree of formality the occasion demanded.

He had never chaperoned a dance in his life and he wouldn't be doing it now if he could have thought of any way out of it.

"All the other parents have already done their part," Teddy had assured him. "It's really your turn, Father. Just think of it as another civic duty."

Mikolai had civic duties aplenty and would have gratefully been willing to forgo this one. He was a single man from a foreign culture. He was to chaperone here, to watch these young people for social misstep. He was not entirely sure if he would recognize a misstep if he saw one. And he was certain he wouldn't know how to correct it even if he did.

Wandering over to the far side of the pavilion, he found an out-of-the-way place where he hoped that he could go unnoticed. He stared at the cavorting dancers out on the floor. He knew little of ragtime but its name and its sound. He was not much of a dancer himself. And he was certain as he watched the young people that while he might manage a polka or a waltz, he would never be able to sweep the floor with this exciting new American dance.

His Lida had been such a dancer. She would have loved this music, this evening. In his mind's eye he could see her, young and full of life once more, dancing in a shorn field in the cool, crisp Polish autumn. She was strong and lithe and sensual. When she moved, the gentle sway of her body enticed the watcher. An occasional spin or gust of breeze would gently stir the hem of her skirt giving a tantalizing glimpse of her long, shapely, yes, wonderful legs. He himself had first felt the stirrings of lust for her as she moved so gracefully upon another man's arm.

Ah, lust. He almost smiled. Lust and youth, two things little valued when you have them, much treasured when long gone. His infrequent couplings were no longer inspired by lust. When the stirrings of the flesh plagued him, he sought release where he could. If a suitable female could not be found, he merely waited for the desire to pass. The mind-numbing, heart-pounding, blood-rushing craving of lust was a thing of memory to Mikolai Stefanski. Lida had inspired his lust. Other women had honed it and celebrated it. Time and age had dulled the edge and replaced its grinding ecstasy with pleasant satisfaction. He might not miss youth, but he did miss lust. Inexplicably the image of Gertrude Barkley, dressed smartly in pink and staring up into his eyes, assailed him.

Mikolai cleared his throat unnecessarily and adjusted his tie. He was here to do his civic duty, he reminded himself. To rekindle old feelings for women long gone or relive private memories too intimate to come to light was a foolish pastime.

At that moment Teddy and young Miss Widmeyer passed immediately in front of him. Teddy didn't even notice his father, his attention held completely by the dance and his partner.

Mikolai eyed the two young people warily. Their bodies were very close together. Her arms were around his neck and his hands rested firm but unmoving upon her hipbones. Olive shimmied very discreetly in step, still her bosom bounced lively against Teddy's chest and the sashay of her skirt revealed more than just a little of her stocking-covered calf.

His brow furrowing, Mikolai watched his son with the attractive young woman in his arms. He was a father. And he worried. Remembering his own youthful lust for Lida, Mikolai could well imagine what his son, still glowing from the thrill of his proud football victory, must be experiencing so close to the soft, yielding flesh of an innocent young girl.

It was Teodor's time for lust and love. Mikolai would not try to deny him that. Still, a father worried. A father couldn't help that. Mikolai wanted so much for his son. He had created a business for him. He wanted to hand it to him like a gift. But it was a gift that Teodor did not appear to yearn for. He yearned, it seemed, for other things. Excitement. College. Travel. If that was what Teodor wanted, he would try to see that his dreams came true.

Sometimes Mikolai wondered why the offspring should seek such different things than the sire. He shook his head. That was just the way of things. And a good father didn't try to hinder his son's nature. Mikolai wanted for Teddy everything that he himself had not had. Plus more—things he did not even know. He wanted that for him, also.

As the young couple twirled upon the dance floor, Mikolai saw his son's body pressed so closely to the warm, young flesh of Miss Olive Widmeyer. Love. Lust. Mikolai wanted those things for his son also.

The dance ended and the young people clapped politely. Mikolai joined in the applause. He made a point to nod respectfully to the bandleader, Abe Hulbert. Abe worked as a brick mason at the Stefanski yards. Acknowledging his talent was the same as voicing personal approval. Hulbert accepted the unspoken praise offered by his boss with proud good grace and began bouncing off another jaunty tune.

Mikolai turned his attention once more to the dance floor. To his surprise he saw young Miss Widmeyer being led into the next two-step by quarterback Parks. His own son, Teddy, was partnerless and headed toward him.

"What on earth could cause a healthy young man to leave the beautiful Miss Widmeyer in the arms of Mr. Parks?" he asked his son as Teddy stepped up beside him.

His son shrugged and smiled. "Thought I'd better check on my balding gray-haired father, make sure that you are on the job and know what you are doing," he said.

Mikolai gave a huff that would have sounded disgruntled to the ears of anyone other than his son. "My hair may be getting gray, Teodor Stefanski, but it is not falling out. And I am on the job as you've requested. As for knowing what I am to do," he said, "I thought that fathers were not meant to understand the youth of these days."

Teddy nodded with a teasing grin. "That's exactly right. What *you* don't know won't hurt *us*."

Another couple passed directly in front of them. The young man was hunched down and holding his partner way too close for acceptable propriety. The woman in his arms, seemingly unaware of the risqué positioning, continued to wiggle and trot in perfect time with the loud music blaring across the dance floor.

"They are dancing very close," Mikolai pointed out.

"That's the way it's done," Teddy answered. "It's all the rage, snuggle up and spoon."

"I do suppose it is pretty safe to get close to a girl when everyone is watching," Mikolai said.

"It's the music that makes it all right," Teddy said. "Trying moves like that without the ragtime ringing is a good way for a fellow to get his face slapped."

"I would imagine so," his father replied.

"Guess that's why we thank God for the music."

The two men, father and son, laughed together in a private understanding.

"How on earth do they learn to dance like that?" Mikolai asked him.

"It's syncopated motion, Father," Teddy answered. "You just let yourself go with the music."

"In my day if we had 'let ourselves go with the music' in such a way, the fathers of these young women would have been after us with a sharpened scythe."

Teddy chuckled. "Then it's really not so different than in our day," he said. "All the fellows joke about outraged papas with shotguns."

Mikolai nodded, but his tone was serious. "Then it is best to keep your wits about you, Teodor. An unexpected bride could mean big changes in your future."

Blushing, Teddy shook his head. "It's only dancing, Father," he said. "Olive and I—I mean, gee, she's so pretty she scares me to death."

Mikolai heard the honesty in his son's voice and deftly maneuvered a change of subject. "Tell me more about this syncopated motion. I know that it is dancing, but of such a variety I have never seen. Truthfully, even as a young fellow I had trouble mastering the simple steps of country dances," he admitted. "I don't believe I could ever have managed to learn such a complicated series of motions."

Teddy turned to observe his fellow dancers more assessingly. "The motions just come rather natural," he said. "When the rhythm gets onto the floor, the dance just takes over the dancers."

"It does seem somewhat a dance to come natural to the young," Mikolai said, observing without envy the athletic grace of youth. "But an old fellow like me, no I don't think anything is so natural anymore."

"With a woman in your arms," Teddy said. "I wouldn't be surprised if you feel young again."

Mikolai shot Teddy a quick look. His son was gazing at him with round-eyed speculation.

"A woman?" His gaze shifted back to the dancers once more. He was horrified at what he thought his son had suggested. Camaraderie with one's offspring was all well and good, but a decent man would never seek female companionship among the lady friends of his son.

"These are merely young girls, Teodor," he said in a whisper meant to convey his shock. "If I were to ask one to dance, I would *expect* her father to come for me with the shotgun you mentioned."

"I didn't mean . . . I didn't mean one of those girls, Father. I meant a woman, a woman your own age."

"A woman my own age?"

"Sure, there are older women here, too. Why don't you find one of them to take a turn upon the floor with?"

Mikolai shook his head conclusively. "Dancing, like love, Teodor, is for the young."

Chapter Eight

THE LATE-AFTERNOON sun was riding low on the horizon when Mikolai helped Principal Shue light the Japanese lanterns. The young people had hardly taken a break from the dancing and it was only when the band declared a hiatus that they gathered in large noisy groups around the refreshment tables.

It was from behind one of those tables that Mikolai spotted Gertrude Barkley. She was still wearing her bright pink dress with the silly little hat. The costume made her look fashionable and lively. The strange faraway look in her eyes made her interesting. It was *interesting* more than *fashionable* or *lively* that attracted Mikolai's attention.

"You are enjoying yourself, Miss Gertrude?" he asked as the music began once more and the young people rushed away from the platters of ladyfingers and shortbreads.

She startled at the words spoken beside her.

"Oh, Mr. Stefanski," she said. "I'm afraid you caught me napping. Well, not napping. I was thinking about my book," she told him.

"Ah—" He drew the syllable out to great length giving it infinite meaning. "Then please do continue, as I, as well as your other readers, anxiously await the final chapter of the DuPree saga."

Gertrude's eyes widened. "You read my books, Mr. Stefanski?"

"I'm afraid no," he answered with a wistful shake of his

117

head. "I have taught myself to read some English, but not enough for a book."

She was looking at him so closely. She always seemed to look at him that way. It was puzzling.

"Then why are you anxious for my new book?" she asked with a surprising intentness.

His expression was serious, but he kept his voice light. "There is very little excitement in this town, Miss Gertrude. It is only the discussion of your books that gets the community to talk about something other than sports."

She smiled at him then. The big, broad, genuine smile that he would always associate with Miss Gertrude Barkley. "But you are a great fan of sports, Mr. Stefanski."

"Yes, but a prince who eats pheasant every day soon becomes unmoved by its flavor."

She laughed out loud at that and it pleased him.

"So what brings you to the dance tonight?" she asked him in that charming manner she had that made his most inconsequential conversation seem important. "Do you often attend these high school soirees?"

"Me?" He looked surprised. "Why no, Miss Gertrude, I do not. This is my very first. And I am here because your niece and my son would not take *no* for an answer."

Gertrude chuckled. "I found that to be true, also. I really felt that Claire should invite her parents to chaperone instead of her aunt, but she claims her father is a fuddy-duddy and she didn't want him here."

"What on earth is a fuddy-duddy?"

"I have no idea." She shook her head, causing her soft shorn curls to flutter about her face attractively.

"I assume that it is not something *terrific*," Mikolai said solemnly.

She giggled. "I think not."

"Well, whatever it is," he noted wryly, hoping to make her

laugh again, "if George Barkley is one, I find myself assured that it is not something I would want to be."

She did laugh then, wholeheartedly. So much so that heads turned. He saw her sheepishly cover her smile as she cleared her throat.

"Is that why you haven't joined the Mystic Circle? Because George is praying fervently to be chosen Sublime Kalifa."

Mikolai said nothing for a moment and watched Gertrude's cheeks color up as realization dawned upon her. He answered lightly. "I have little time for boys' clubs, and the Crusading Knights of the Mystic Circle have little tolerance for immigrants."

Gertrude's smile had disappeared completely, replaced by an expression of hapless guilt. It was well known that many of the men's lodges and societies had secret rules that were designed to keep out other races and religions. In her banter, Gertrude had forgotten that Mikolai, though very much a part of the town of Venice, Missouri, would in some ways forever be an outsider.

It was something that did not cause Mikolai Stefanski any grave concern. The unspoken rules that shut him out from the upper levels of the small-town society would always be there for him. But Teddy would not be shut out. His Teodor was as American as any of them. And that was really the only thing that mattered.

Gertrude was obviously horrified at what she had said. He saw her discomfort and quickly sought to alleviate it. In her own way, choosing to be a spinster and a writer, she was as much an outcast as he was himself. He refused to allow her to suffer one moment's anguish over the rigidity of a community that suffered her presence only with great complaint.

"Would you care to dance, Miss Gertrude?"

He was surprised to hear his own words. He had never intended to dance that evening. He'd certainly never intended to partner Miss Gertrude. But the band was playing a schottische, a dance from Scotland that was a slower version of the polkas of his youth. They certainly could dance it, although he didn't want to.

"Oh no, I couldn't, Mr. Stefanski," she said, her cheeks bright pink and glowing. "We are, we are chaperones."

He had wanted her to refuse. He had hoped that she would. But he was disappointed that she did. Suddenly he wanted to dance with her very much.

"Oh, please, Miss Gertrude," he said. "Just once around the floor to show these youths how it is really done. We can consider it merely another service to our community."

He held out his hand to her, his big, ugly workingman's hand. "Do let us try it," he said.

And with only the slightest hesitation, she placed her small gloved fingers within his grasp. As respectful and genteel as any Southern gentleman who ever danced with a society belle, Mikolai led Gertrude onto the dance floor.

The bouncing rhythm of the schottische was rapid and enthusiastic. His fine boots tapped loudly against the wooden floor and her bright pink dress swirled around her limbs in exuberant fashion. Together they pranced around the floor until both were nearly out of breath. It was more from exhaustion than design that Mikolai halted their progress in front of the bandstand.

"Don't give up the floor, Mr. Stefanski," Abe Hulbert admonished him from the bandstand.

"This is not the music I danced to as a boy," Mikolai told him with good-natured gravity.

"Oh, well how about this?" Hulbert said.

To their total surprise, Abe tapped his wand on the music stand and the schottische dance tune faltered and faded. As murmurs began among the dancers, Hulbert directed the musicians once more and suddenly they were playing a waltz.

The beautiful strains of "After the Ball," a tune popular in the dancing days of the high school parents, were as familiar to Mikolai and Gertrude as anyone. To the young people present it was, as they phrased it, "old hat." To Mikolai it was music that recalled his past. Like the sweet strains of Strauss, he loved it and yet an ache of sorts formed in his chest.

A flash of memory ripped through his consciousness. He could see *Matka* and *Tatus,* his mother and father, dancing the waltz together once more, the clear blue sky of Polish autumn above their heads, an itinerant fiddler playing their tune. He was there watching and clapping with his brothers and sisters. He was young and happy and had his whole life in front of him. He had no idea what sorrow and loneliness that life would bring.

The tune the band played was as familiar as his memory. And it was as if the past had suddenly confronted him, unbidden. His family, his people, his youth, they were all very far away. The past could never be retrieved again. The leaden weight that settled in his heart was grief for its loss.

"Mr. Stefanski? Is something wrong?" Gertrude asked.

Mikolai looked down at the familiar face beside him. He must look the idiot, he thought. Standing on the dance floor lost in the past like a doddering old fool. Determinedly he pushed away the feelings that plagued him and turned to Gertrude, bowing regally over her hand.

"I am stunned by my good fortune, Miss Barkley," he said. "I believe this dance is especially for us."

She blushed as prettily as a young girl. "Should we waltz, do you think? We are chaperones."

"I can only think that this particular dance was meant for chaperones," he said. "And you, Miss Barkley, are never one to allow such a gift to pass you by."

"You are undoubtedly right," she admitted, laughing almost

gaily. "A chance like this is so rare, we mustn't waste it," she said. "We may not get another."

With exceptional care he took her gloved hand in his own, and placed his other at her surprisingly narrow waist. She was the perfect size, he realized. She was neither so small that he must stoop over nor so statuesque that he need remember to stand his full height. Her form, while not one to garner appreciative remarks from casual male observers, was feminine and shapely. The inevitable changes of age made her sufficient curves softer, more soothing, infinitely approachable. Mikolai felt a sudden desire to approach.

They were close, it seemed, very close, as they began an impressive glide across the floor. The steps of the waltz were the same anywhere, but the way Mikolai had learned it in Poland had more glissade than Missourians were accustomed to.

Gertrude adjusted to the extended float easily. Leading her in the dance was as effortless as breathing. It felt strangely familiar to have her in his arms, as if they had practiced moving in harmony together all their lives. It felt so easy, so without care.

Mikolai looked down into her face. Her shorn curls, thick and dark, fluttered at her jawline. The rosewater fragrance of that hair was familiar and yet still quite alluring. She was prettily flushed and smiling at him with delight. He had pleased her with this dance. He was glad. He'd been afraid that having kissed her hand, strictly a gesture of friendship on his part, might cause her to distance herself from him. She had not. It seemed in fact that even as they danced a respectable arm's length apart, there was nothing separating them and no one in the world apart from themselves. He forgot the prying eyes of the town matrons who gazed at them speculatively. And the exuberant young people all around who tolerantly accepted the old-fashioned waltz as they waited for more ragtime to begin.

He forgot about the sad, choking memories the song had provoked in his heart. He forgot that he was almost forty years old. And that romance and passion were for the young. He was strong and graceful and was floating across the floor with a lovely woman in his arms. Her pretty pink dress swirling with the grace of a fancy ball gown. So sweet, so familiar, so caring, and he just couldn't help himself. He fell in love.

It had merely been a friendly dance at the Monument Park dancing pavilion, Gertrude reminded herself. There had been no great ballroom and no underlying intrigue. Nothing of the romance or drama of her novels. But it had been glorious. Gertrude had enjoyed it. It was far from the grandeur of Carlisle Place. And Mr. Stefanski was perhaps no elegant cavalier, although he was certainly more than merely attractive. And he danced quite well and in the continental fashion that was so romantic. That was a surprise. It was all a surprise, and a surprising pleasure. Gertrude wanted just to hug herself. She had been in his arms, really in his arms. And it was more wonderful than any fantasy she had ever imagined.

She was humming the tune as she allowed herself the luxury of reliving every moment of the dance. She had excused herself from the gentleman's company and was making her way back to the refreshment table.

She knew that, without a doubt, she had caused a bit of a scene. The schottische was bad enough, but a waltz! She was glad that George had not been there to see it. He would have scolded her. Of course, he scolded her all the time and she never let it worry her much. But she didn't want him to ruin it. She didn't want to remember it as just another inappropriate action that upset her brother. It was her moment in Mikolai Stefanski's arms. She wanted to cherish it always.

George was, of course, sure to hear about it. It was best, she decided, to mend up the fences as quickly as possible. With that

in mind she hurried back to the relative obscurity of the ladies'
culinary offering of punch and cookies. Her presence would
make her seem unconcerned about what had happened. It
would also force the gossips to wait to talk about her until she
was out of sight.

The fast-paced modern rhythm now being played by the band
was extremely popular with the young people and the dance
floor was crowded with hopping, trotting ragtime revelers. Not
wishing to walk through the group, Gertrude took the steps
down from the pavilion and walked around the building to the
other side.

The evening was delightfully cool and now full darkness had
settled upon them. She gazed off into the maze of pathways
that wove their way through the interior of the park. By day
they were attractive promenades for children and their parents.
Tonight they looked very forbidden and very private.

She smiled to herself. In her novels those paths would be
secret trysting places for star-crossed lovers. But here in
Venice, Missouri, they were only the empty, unilluminated
trails of Monument Park.

Gertrude was still thinking joyfully, happily, of Mikolai and
the dance as she approached the refreshment table from the
back. The profuse growth of English ivy that cooled this west
side of the pavilion on hot summer days hid her arrival from
view.

When she heard her name mentioned, she stopped still. The
sound of voices was quite clear.

"It's like something I've never seen in my life," Oleander
Wentworth declared sotto voce. "Gallivanting across the floor
with that immigrant Stefanski, as if she had just cause to be
there."

"Oh dear, oh dear." Claudy Mitts sounded near overwrought
with anxiety.

"You would think that the woman would have the common

decency to know her place," Naomi Pruitt agreed. "But Gertrude Barkley simply has no boundaries when it comes to bad taste and scandalous ways."

"Oh dear, oh dear dear," Claudy whined.

Behind the anonymous screen of ivy, Gertrude merely stopped and shook her head. The tittle-tattle had already commenced. And she'd only stopped dancing less than five minutes earlier. She stiffened her lip, determined to be philosophical about it. She was quite accustomed to being the pot likker in the gossip boil of Venice, Missouri, and truly she didn't mind. Giving these ladies a cause to fuss and fret about was almost a duty, she told herself. Still, she couldn't like it.

"And the way that man was grinning at her," Oleander continued. "It was without dignity and positively bordered upon crass."

"You are being too kind to the woman," Naomi told her. "The gentleman, although he is a foreigner and undoubtedly quite lowborn, is just as aware as we ourselves of what is proper behavior. He must have been as ill at ease with her untoward behavior as the rest of us. Have you ever seen such an expression upon his face in your life?"

"No, I haven't," Oleander answered.

"No, never," Claudy Mitts agreed.

"My point exactly," Naomi said. "The poor unfortunate fellow was trying to smooth over her outrageous behavior as best he could."

Gertrude raised an eyebrow at that. Defending Mikolai Stefanski from *her*, that certainly was serious, she thought.

"Now, ladies, ladies," interrupted Amanda Ponder, the doctor's wife. "I think you are misconstruing the situation."

The other women quieted immediately. As the doctor's wife and the mother of four rather delicate boys and a woman of impeccable reputation, Mrs. Ponder's words and opinions could not easily be discarded. "I think you are being far too harsh on Miss Barkley," she said.

Behind the wall of ivy, Gertrude grinned. She had not imagined Amanda Ponder to be a champion of hers. In fact, the woman had always seemed not to like her. Probably because the doctor spent innumerable time boring Gertrude with the horrible book on genetic predisposition that he was writing. His wife clearly didn't appreciate that he thought Gertrude Barkley to be his colleague. Amanda Ponder had even once suggested to her that writing books was a man's business and that it was unhealthy for a woman's delicate constitution.

But apparently she had changed her mind and it pleased Gertrude to hear the woman take up her defense.

"It was a simple schottische they intended," Mrs. Ponder told the ladies. "It certainly was not Gertrude's fault that the band chose to change the dance in the middle of the tune."

The woman's tone was even and sincere. "And even with the waltz, she behaved herself with perfect decorum."

"Thank heavens for that," Oleander declared with a huff of disapproval. "I wouldn't put it past the woman to begin gyrating to that horrible loudness that is coming from the bandstand. I will not flatter the sound by calling it music."

"And no doubt that is what she has in mind next," Naomi said. "Wearing colors infinitely more suited for a woman half her age and consorting upon the dance floor as if *she* were still one of our young persons."

"Oh dear, oh dear," Claudy added in.

"I'd swear the woman must think she is one of those romantic heroines in those disreputable books that she writes."

"That certainly makes perfect sense to me," Oleander agreed. "I have always thought that she must long for a disgraceful life in order to write about it so habitually."

"You've read her books?" Mrs. Ponder asked in a startled whisper.

"Oh dear, oh dear."

"Certainly not," Oleander answered. "But everyone knows what is in them."

"Yes," Naomi put in, as if the idea had just dawned upon her. "It must be that she writes about the things that she wants to do, but has never had any opportunity for, being closely guarded by her family, and a spinster."

"Exactly," Mrs. Ponder agreed.

Oleander huffed disagreeably. "She is simply a scandal and George Barkley ought to put a stop to it," she declared.

"Oh, but can't you see," Mrs. Ponder continued, "that she's more to be pitied than censured."

"Pitied?" the three asked with surprise.

Listening, the hair on the back of Gertrude's neck stood on end.

"Certainly," Amanda said. "Going to the barber for that bob, wearing those bright clothes, dancing, it's all part of it, you know."

"Part of what?" Claudy Mitts asked.

"Why, *the change*."

Mrs. Ponder whispered the words, but they were perfectly audible to the women around her, and to Gertrude Barkley behind the curtain of English ivy.

"Ohhhhh." All these women made sounds of agreement and sudden understanding.

"Is she old enough for that?" Oleander asked.

"Oh, certainly," Amanda Ponder assured them. "It's a well-known fact that with woman who've never, well, you know—produced fruit—it comes upon them early."

"I've heard that," Naomi said.

"And it's absolutely true," Amanda said. "A doctor's wife knows these things, believe me."

"Did the doctor tell you that she was going through *it*?" Oleander asked in an excited whisper.

"Not in so many words," Amanda responded, hedging. "A doctor must maintain the privacy of his patients, of course."

"Of course."

"But after twenty-seven years, I can read him pretty well, you know."

"You know virtually everything that he does," Naomi agreed.

"And it explains a lot," Amanda said.

"Oh yes, it does indeed." They all concurred.

"Oh dear, oh dear," Claudy Mitts chirped in.

"Poor old thing," Oleander said sadly. "I suppose it is our Christian duty to forgive a moment of her silly foolishness. *The change* can be so distressing. I myself had to take to bed for six months. Of course, I've always been a woman of delicate constitution."

"Oh dear, yes, Sister has always been delicate," Claudy Mitts verified.

"And for a woman who has never married," Amanda added, "it can be even more so. Knowing finally for certain that youth has passed you by and that you have 'wasted your substance.'"

"Oh dear, oh dear."

"Poor Gertrude," Amanda Ponder stated with high drama. "Youth is only a faint glimmer in her memory now and she has no children, no grandchildren. Her batter is spoilt and her seed is soured. She stares off into a empty horizon."

"Oh dear, oh dear."

"We should be more understanding," Mrs. Ponder concluded.

"I suppose we should," Oleander agreed. "Such a vision would unhinge any woman."

"And Gertrude Barkley never was that snug to the gate," Naomi Pruitt added snidely.

Behind the ivy Gertrude stood still as a stone, her face as pale as alabaster. Her heart was pounding. The truth was no refuge. She had been to Doc Ponder over a year ago with questions about her *female* trouble. Her menses were changed and irregular. She had hoped for another answer than the one she suspected, but the doctor gave her no other. It was early signs of the change, he'd told her. His expression had been pitying, but she hadn't needed pity. She accepted his verdict and the finality of nature with calm good grace. But she had not expected to find her most personal realities discussed by the Algonquin Society.

Had it been another day, another time, Gertrude might have shrugged off the unkind words and hurtful gossip. But her anger, raw and righteous, quickly touched on the vulnerable spots in her heart. Those places she had carelessly left exposed by need to be held in the arms of the man that she loved. These women pitied her. She shuddered although there was no chill in the night air. They pitied her. Once more she heard their spiteful words. And she pitied herself.

Her books *were* her life. She *did* live through them. They were the only interruptions in the ponderous monotony that was her existence. She had *wasted her substance* by being in love with a man for seventeen years who had never given her even the slightest glimmer of hope or acknowledgment.

She turned from the pavilion and began to walk. How right they were. If they only knew. She escaped her life in bits and pieces of the stories she told. She escaped because there was nothing here to keep her, nothing real. People loved her stories. They brought excitement and pleasure to her readers. But that wasn't why she wrote them. She wrote them to fill the giant void that yawned in her own existence. An existence typical of an old-maid aunt in a small Missouri town. An existence typically without life or love or passion. She had none, so she created her own.

She swallowed hard as she felt the tears welling in her eyes.

Daily, she fooled herself into believing that the path she'd chosen was the one that she had wanted. Only in the darkest hours of her night could she admit that it was not choice that kept her unmarried and bereft of motherhood, but rather lack of choice. The only man she had ever wanted had never asked her. But it was worse than that. Had she held on to spinsterhood only because her love was unrequited, she could see herself as a heroine. The truth was infinitely more lowering.

The man that she wanted had never asked her. Moreover, no man at all had ever asked. No earnest gentleman had soberly bid for her hand, no courtly squire, not even a clumsy farmer. There had never been, would never be, any romance in her life, not ever. No kiss, no touch, no trembling embrace. There would be no physical union with another human being. There would never be children.

A choking sound escaped from her throat. She'd thought that she was content with that. She'd had Claire and Lester, it was enough, she had told herself. It was more than many women were lucky enough to have. To watch two healthy youngsters grow and live was a great and precious gift. Even if the two would never call her mother. And she had Mr. Stefanski, dear Mikolai. He was just next door and she could watch him go and come every day. She could talk to him in the yard. They could laugh together about her brother, George.

And there were her books. Her sweet creations where life and love were inseparable commodities and all things worked out for the best for everyone. The honorable were honored and the unworthy received just punishment. Those who craved love found it and it remained unwavering ever after.

The real world had not seen fit to grant her passion, companionship, or offspring. She had promised herself not to weep or grieve for that loss again. But the facts were cruel, simple, and certain. She would not be a man's wife. She would be no one's lover. She would never hold a small little body next to her breast and look up into eyes that adored her to whisper,

"I have borne you a child, a gift of my body, a symbol of our love, an infinite perpetuity of our union." She would never say it. Her womb was vacant and withered. But worse, much worse than an empty womb was an empty heart. And her own was, for now and forever more, a interminable void.

The tears did fall then, in wrenching sobs of desolation. She was not old yet, she was merely having *the change*, but old age would come. And she would meet it with no more to show for her life than she had today. She was an aging spinster, hopelessly in love with a man she could only call her friend.

She began to run. Clutching her hands to her face, she ran into the darkness, the emptiness of unlighted pathways of the park. She ran from her thoughts. She ran from her tears. But she could not escape from her reality.

Chapter Nine

HE WAS BOTHERED by his thoughts. It was not something that he let happen to himself often. Mikolai wandered out of the bright and lively dance pavilion to the more quiet solitude of the shadowed grounds. He'd enjoyed the dance. He'd enjoyed it very much. Miss Gertrude was as light on her feet as she was lively in conversation. But that raw, vulnerable moment when he knew that he loved her lingered with him. He didn't try to puzzle out his feelings, merely to rid himself of them.

He supposed it was not that unusual for a man at his stage in life to begin to look back, to try to find those pleasures that he'd missed in youth, but he fought against it. He could not allow himself to love now. If he was to have fallen in love, it should have been with Lida.

It was only seeing his son reaching adulthood that made him so fanciful. When a man has taken upon himself the duty and ambition to raise his child well, it was understandable that he might feel unsettled to see that task coming to an end. The future for a man nearing forty who has made his mark and had a secure business might not be as exciting as when he was twenty. But it was certainly not something to bring on melancholia. And imagining himself *in love* was certainly that.

He checked his pocket for his pipe and found it missing. The foolishness of the gesture surprised him. He'd given up tobacco years ago. The smoke tended to irritate young Teodor's eyes. He had done away with the pipe as easily as he had done away with so many other things that he had enjoyed. He'd given them up for his child. Maybe he would take it up again when his son went off to the faraway college back East. Maybe he wouldn't.

From the corner of his eye he spotted movement in the distant shadows and turned his glance in that direction. His bushy brow furrowed. At first he didn't quite believe what he saw, or understand what he did believe. Miss Gertrude Barkley, who always moved across the earth with such unconscious purpose and grace, was rushing away from the pavilion. She had her arms clasped tightly against her chest, an aspect suggesting a need to comfort an aching heart. As he watched, her hasty steps quickened into a run. She was fleeing.

A strange knot of concern formed in his chest. He raised his hand to hail her and thought to call out, but knew without undue consideration that attracting attention to her departure would be unthinkable. Immediately, knowing not his purpose or his errand, Mikolai hurried after her. Somehow he had to.

Leaving behind the brightly colored light of the lanterns, the grounds were shrouded in night and shadow. The moon was a mere sliver in the autumn sky, turned like the edge of a teacup pouring out the last dregs of luster on the night. He hurried through that darkness.

She was a good distance ahead of him when he reached the maze of trails. Empty and deserted, the shaded pathways were illuminated only by the occasional beams of moonlight that stole through the trees. Mikolai was very much aware of the roots, rocks, and loose gravel at his feet, all very capable of bringing him head over heels at any moment, but he didn't slow his step. Something was wrong, very wrong, with Gertrude Barkley. And somehow it was his purpose to set it right again.

It was at a small moonlit clearing, within a ring of cottonwood trees, that he spotted her. She was racing ahead blindly, unheeding, as if real demons chased her. He feared for her safety.

"Miss Gertrude! Miss Gertrude!" he called as he ran. "Miss Gertrude, it's me, Stefanski."

At first his cries went unanswered. But he knew the minute she heard his voice. She stopped still in the path and turned to look in his direction. Her little hat was askew and her shorn curls were wild with disorder. He was close enough to see her expression. It was one of horror.

"Miss Gertrude, it's me, Stefanski," he repeated again.

Immediately, with pride more innate than acquired, she raised her chin and straightened her hat.

He wondered suddenly if he should have followed her. Wasn't a person, especially a person like Gertrude Barkley, to be allowed moments of solitary grief? He had no idea as to the cause of her distress. His intrusion could be unwanted to the point of rude. But somehow he had had to follow and now he was here. He was not going away without doing something to help.

He continued toward her, but he slowed his pace as he approached. He gave her time to dab ineffectually at the tears that had reddened her eyes and attempt to stiffen the lovely lower lip that trembled so tenaciously.

"Miss Gertrude, I saw you running," he explained. He spoke his words slowly and quietly as if he were afraid to frighten her. "I was worried."

"Oh, Mr. Stefanski, you shouldn't trouble yourself," she declared with only a slight catch in her voice. She tossed her head in the grand manner that she had and smiled at him in dazzling pretense. "I am perfectly fine."

She was flushed and her eyes were swollen, but she held herself straight with rigid self-control. "I was only . . . only . . ."

He stood in front of her now. He was looking down into her

eyes. He was in love with her, but he pushed that thought away. They were friends, friends of long-standing. If a man was not there to comfort a friend, he was not much of a friend.

"Miss Gertrude," he whispered. "I cannot bear to see you crying."

"It's just a silly female foolishness," she assured him.

Her face was all starkness and shadows; he stepped closer to see her more clearly.

"If it is something I have said or done, Miss Gertrude—" he began.

"You?" Her voice sounded horrified. "No, of course it doesn't concern you. Why would you think—?"

The nonchalance in her tone broke apart. She covered her mouth with her clasped hands and turned away from him. She was silent, ominously silent, in her suffering. He was helpless. It was the shaking of her shoulders that finally moved him to action. It was those mourning tremors that drew him closer.

"Miss Gertrude, please, no," he said, raking a hand through his hair uncomfortably, before laying his palms gently upon her shoulders.

Mikolai stood behind her, in a quandary as to what to say or do. He felt the ill-suited sensation of being powerless. Defenseless against the intensity of her feelings and the unfamiliarity of his own.

In his well-ordered life he dealt with problems in the same direct, effective style he used for forging brick from earth. Emotions were as unwanted and unwelcome as topsoil in clay. And women, women seemed to Mikolai to be all emotion. Beautiful and delicate forms, too full of feeling to ever fire into anything strong and sturdy. He was not used to the emotions of women. He had no idea how to handle them. The women he had some skill in handling charged extra for any display of feelings. And certainly misery was not an emotion usually requested for purchase. His experience with the finer ladies of the community was a distant one at best. And his memory of his impatience with his late wife's tears was not one he wished to conjure up.

His sister, Edda, had shed many tears over her unhappy life. More than once she had turned to him in sorrow. And he had comforted her with a strong shoulder and a willing ear.

But Miss Gertrude was not his sister. Neither was she his wife. To offer comfort to her was something totally new and a thing for which he was in no way prepared. His intellect offered him no counsel, so he allowed his heart to lead him.

"Sweet Gertrude," he whispered softly into her hair. Without giving himself time to worry about his actions, he turned her to face him. He wrapped his arms around her and pulled her tightly against his chest. "Shhhhhhh, don't cry," he murmured. "It will all be fine."

Somehow the inappropriate embrace seemed perfectly right and reasonable. Holding her in his arms felt perfect, just as it had upon the dance floor. It seemed so right and reasonable to fit her cheek against his throat, to stroke the smooth soft curls away from her face.

"Hush, my sweet, my so very sweet."

His tenderness did not immediately ease her grief, rather it appeared to encourage it.

Sobs broke from her in great rushing torrents. Her body quaked as if his comfort had unleashed a flood of feelings inside her. A dam of propriety that had held her in check broke through with great calamity.

"Oh, Mikolai, I am so miserable," she whimpered.

The sound of his given name upon her lips caused his heart to beat faster. "Oh, Miss Gertrude, dear Miss Gertrude," he consoled her. "It can't be as bad as all that." He pulled her more protectively against his chest. "I'm here. You are safe. Everything will be fine."

He felt the dampness of her tears soak through the smooth satin stripe worsted of his lapel.

"There, there," he said. "Just let it out, I'm here and you are safe."

Gertrude cried as though her heart were breaking. And he held her. Firmly, securely, as if somehow his strength would transmit through his embrace and give her the fortitude to bear the pain that tortured her.

Mikolai closed his eyes. For one tender moment he allowed himself the sheer rapture of her body against his own. He had never held her before. Not like this. Never even in his dreams. Her soft feminine bosom was pressed close against his muscled, unyielding chest. It was nothing like the embrace of a dance. There was no formality, no illusion of propriety. He held her to him as if she were a dear possession of his heart, which she was.

"My dear Gertrude, my dear, dear Gertrude," he said softly. "If I could take the sadness from your heart, please know that I would. Yes, know that I would."

Her tears were like mortar binding them together. He held her against him, tightly. But it was not close enough. Could it ever be close enough? Close enough to meld her heart with his own.

"My Gertrude, my own dear Gertrude," he whispered against her.

The sweet scent of her hair filled his nostrils. Rose water. He loved her hair. Those short, bouncy locks that flabbergasted his neighbors were a delight to him.

He pushed one shorn curl away from her face. She was regaining her self-control, but he was loath to release her from his arms.

His hands began to move up and down her back, stroking, caressing. The straightness of her back from the expanse between her shoulder blades to the gentle curve at her waist felt alarmingly pleasing to his touch. His reaction was as powerful as it was male. She was soft and feminine and oh, so very welcome in his arms. The tension in the front of his trousers quickened. The strong sweet yearning that he'd relegated to youth assailed him. Lust, sweet lust. Desire. And need. The blood pounded in his veins. It deafened him. For one wonderful instant he allowed his hand to rest upon the smooth round curve of her derriere. Heaven.

He jumped back from her as if he'd touched a hot stove. He realized, almost too late, the inappropriateness of his action. She was still crying and he could only be grateful that she hadn't noticed the impropriety.

"Miss Gertrude, you must tell me what is wrong," he said, grasping only her hand now and keeping her body at a good and proper distance from his own. "Whatever has made you cry this way? Tell me, Miss Gertrude, perhaps I can fix it."

Gertrude quietly harnessed the most extreme of her emotions. He watched as she made a valiant effort to return to her more normal behavior.

"You must forgive me, Mr. Stefanski," she told him through tearful hiccups. "I am not myself."

"You most certainly are yourself, Miss Gertrude," Mikolai corrected gently. "You are merely yourself, distressed. Now you must tell me what has happened."

"It is nothing, really."

"It is something definitely. And you must tell me. I may be able to fix it," he said with the certainty of a man who has often bent his world to his resolve. "And I certainly will if it is within my power."

Bravely she attempted to smile. She wiped her eyes and straightened her hair. "It can't be fixed, I'm afraid," she said, feigning lightness. "Not now, not ever."

He continued to hold her hand, somehow unwilling to break the connection between them completely.

"Let me try," he pleaded. "You will never know that I cannot remedy the trouble if you fail to ask for my help."

She looked up at him then. In the moonlight her tear-brightened eyes shone like stars. He could have gotten lost in them.

"My life has passed me by, Mr. Stefanski," she said quietly. Her eyes welled up again with sorrow and she turned from him. "It has passed me by and I can never get it back."

Her words startled him. "It's my fault," he said quickly, before he realized that he had hidden his new, strange feelings for her in his heart.

She ignored his acknowledgment of culpability. "I'm a spoiled, silly spinster, Mr. Stefanski. As you see, that cannot be fixed," she said. "I have chosen my life and lived it as I wished. But I have chosen badly and have no one to blame but myself."

"Miss Gertrude, please let me—"

"Don't trouble yourself over me, Mr. Stefanski. I am sure Doc Ponder would call it a mere attack of the vapors. I'm just an aging spinster who has suddenly discovered that she is disappointed."

She turned from him then and hurried away. Mikolai stood in the clearing watching her go. Hurting. Understanding. Wondering.

"Dear, dear Gertrude," he whispered to the night sky.

In the concealing darkness of the shrubbery at the far side of the moonlit clearing, Teddy Stefanski and Claire Barkley hid, crouching in silence. They stared in shock at the lovers' silhouette before them. They could not hear the words spoken, but they could hear Aunt Gertrude's crying and could see the tenderness in which she was held by Teddy's father. After she left, they watched as he stood bereft, still gazing thoughtfully for several minutes at the path she had taken. Finally he had raked his hair with consternation and began walking back toward the pavilion.

When he was out of sight, Claire gave a long, confounded sigh and dropped to the ground, sitting Indian-style in the grassy undergrowth.

"Oh, Teddy!" she exclaimed with disbelief. "It's all true, every bit of it."

He nodded slowly. "Truly, Claire, I didn't believe—well, I did believe—but I just couldn't—I mean—really it was just so—"

"I know," Claire agreed. "Did you see them dancing? What perfection. They must have danced together a million times."

"Father always said he didn't care for dancing."

Claire was almost beside herself with excitement. "Even knowing it—seeing it—I thought it almost like a fairy tale, but it's real, Teddy. It's really real."

The two sat thoughtfully side by side, trying to make sense of an adult world that they weren't completely prepared to understand.

When Claire had caught sight of Mikolai Stefanski running off into the darkness of the trees her curiosity had been piqued. It had taken only a couple of minutes to find Teddy and decide to follow him.

"Who would have thought old people could still feel that . . . that passionate about each other," Teddy said.

Claire nodded. "They are obviously still in love," she told him.

"Can't be anything else," he agreed. "And we've brought them back together."

"Yes, we've done that."

Teddy sighed wistfully. "Now, I guess all we have to do is wait for them to make an announcement."

"An announcement of what?" Claire asked him. "For heaven's sake, Teddy, didn't you see the way that she ran away from him?"

"Well, sure."

"That's not the way people end up happily ever after, is it?" Her tone was superior and facetious.

"Of course not, but—"

"They still don't believe that they can be together," she said. "They are still trying to keep the whole thing a big secret."

"Why would they do that?"

"Because of the scandal."

"What scandal?"

"The scandal of having me!" Claire answered with annoyance. "I am the child of their unsanctioned love. They must keep that secret, especially from me."

"There's no need for that. You already know," Teddy said.

"But they don't know that I know."

"Then we should tell them."

"Teddy Stefanski, football is rotting your brain," she declared. "Do you expect that I can just walk up to them and say I know that I am their illegitimate daughter?"

Teddy blanched. "Well, no."

"They have to tell us, you and me. To be together again, they have to be honest and confess everything. But they can't tell us because it would hurt us, maybe ruin our lives. It's like a penance, don't you see. They can't be together because of us. Their love for you and their guilt over me keeps them apart forever."

The young man's brow furrowed in concern. "So we're back to where we started from."

"Not exactly," Claire said. "We know that the journal is all true. And we know that they still love each other."

Teddy nodded. "But if they can't be together because of you, how are we going to change that?"

"I don't know," she admitted. "But I'll think of something. Come on, we'd better get back. Olive is going to be wondering what happened to you."

Teddy helped her to her feet and they brushed their grass-stained clothing halfheartedly as they made their way down the path.

"If we could just come up with some compelling reason for them to admit what happened," she said.

"After keeping a secret this long," Teddy said, shaking his head, "nothing would make my father tell."

"There is always something, Teddy. Some way to bring the truth to light. We'll just have to figure out what it is."

"You've got a plan, I can tell," Teddy said.

Claire grinned up at him. "You know me too well," she said. "Actually I don't have a plan yet, but I'm working on it."

"And you can bet I'm going to be heavily involved." Teddy's tone was complaining, but Claire didn't take his lack of enthusiasm as anything for concern.

"You want them to be happy as much as I do," she said.

He could do nothing else but nod in agreement. "But how are we going to do that?"

"I don't know, but I'll think of something."

Claire was still thinking when they came around one darkened corner of the path to be confronted with the large and very excitable form of Principal Shue.

"What on earth is going on here?"

The two stopped stone-still, staring at him in surprise.

"When I heard that two young people had been seen stealing away among the trees, I was shocked. I could never have imagined it would have been you two."

Chapter Ten

❦

MIKOLAI WAS ANGRY. That was clear. He had spoken very little since their encounter with Principal Shue, but his face was set in a stern, forbidding mask.

That must, Gertrude thought, have the children trembling in their boots.

What Gertrude herself felt was more guilt than rage. Teddy and Claire had been caught coming out of the darkness of the park. But they had had to get in there to get out. Gertrude should have been watching when they headed that direction in the first place. But she hadn't been.

She had left them alone, so concerned with her own silly, hopeless feelings that she'd forgotten that her purpose for being at the dance was to safeguard her niece and the other young ladies and gentlemen present. Now Claire and Teddy had only barely escaped a scandal.

They *had* escaped. Thanks to Mr. Stefanski, who now sat, so sturdy and dependable, beside her. The front seat of the expensive automobile was heavily padded and luxurious. In Gertrude's current state, she wanted to lean back into the soft cushions and let her mind go blank with relief. That was not, however, possible.

Emotions were definitely fueling the driving as Mikolai turned the Stefanski Packard onto Main Street and continued traveling eastward at a very good clip, the engine firing powerfully on all twelve cylinders. He barely hesitated at the yellow caution lantern meant to remind drivers, if the bumpy tracks did not, that the Interurban passed this way every twenty minutes.

The dance at Monument Park was still continuing, hopefully with none, or at least few, the wiser. Principal Shue would be the one to escort Olive Widmeyer home. The story given out was that Claire had become suddenly ill and that Teddy and his father were hurrying her and her aunt home. It wasn't a perfect alibi, but it seemed likely to work.

Getting Teddy and Claire away from the dance and into the care of their chaperones as quickly as possible was the principal's main concern.

Gertrude could hear the young people in the backseat whispering to each other. There seemed to be an argument of some sort going on. So far their stories had been the same. They were simply admiring the night sky and accidentally wandered off into the darkness of the trees. It didn't seem too plausible a story, but the adults had all pretended to accept it.

Mostly Principal Shue accepted it because Mikolai had encouraged him to do so. He was the most powerful man in Venice, Missouri. No one could doubt that. Until tonight, Gertrude had not, to her knowledge, ever seen him use that power. It was indicative of the seriousness of the situation that he had been forced to do so tonight.

Glancing over at his somber visage behind the steering wheel, Gertrude felt somewhat like the rescued damsel in distress. This evening Mikolai Stefanski had been her brave and chivalrous Southern gentleman who had held her while she cried, dried her lonely tears, and then eagerly defended the sacred honor of her beloved niece. He was much like a character from one of her novels. But that should be of great surprise only to people other than herself.

He didn't look much like the gentlemen in her novels. Those men were made of words, words like honor and glory and greatness. The man beside her was flesh and blood; warm, living flesh and blood. The reality of that made gooseflesh tingle across her skin.

She could smell the alluring masculine scent that was his alone, only the faintest hint of the fragrant hair tonic obscured it. She could feel the warmth of his body so close to her own. His shoulders were wide and strong and seemed able to bear burdens, both tangible and evanescent. His hands were smooth and sure as he guided them homeward. She could trust this man. He could soothe her in times of trouble. She had known that instinctively for years. Now she knew it from experience.

The whispers in the backseat stopped abruptly and a long, anticipatory silence followed. Teddy cleared his throat.

"Father, Miss Gertrude," he said in a deep resonant voice that belied his tender years, "Claire and I have decided to get married."

"What!"

Gertrude gasped the word in shock, but the sound of it was lost as Mikolai slammed his foot down full-force on the brake pedal. The shiny new yellow-and-brown four-door Packard skidded slightly on the brick pavement before coming to a complete stop next to the curb directly in front of the Barkley National Bank.

Gertrude was thrown forward and then rocked back into the plush navy seat cushions, her curls bouncing and her hat knocked askew.

Before she could gather her wits about her, Mikolai Stefanski had his door open and was stepping out onto the brick paved street.

He barked curtly over his shoulder. "Teodor, may I speak with you privately for a moment."

His request sounded very much like an order and young Teddy scampered to comply.

Gertrude's eyes widened and her complexion paled. A

heavy, frightened knot formed in her stomach as she watched the two step out of hearing distance of the ladies. In vivid detail her mind conjured the memory of her father raging at her brother George. Words had been said, angry words, hurtful words, words that would never be forgotten. She had wanted to stop those words from being said, but she had not been brave enough to do it.

Today she was no longer the hesitant, uncertain young woman she had been in those days. And for a moment she thought to follow them, to get between the father and son and this time prevent the schism that last time she had not understood. But the sight of the two talking calmly as they strolled down the clean brick sidewalk allayed her fears.

She sighed deeply with relief. Mikolai Stefanski was not Grover Barkley. And apparently he did not feel the need to bully Teddy as her father had bullied George.

More relaxed, she turned to Claire who was sitting silently, expectantly, in the backseat. She appeared totally unconcerned with the Stefanski family drama playing out upon the Main Street sidewalk. All of her attention was focused upon her aunt. She seemed to be waiting. Waiting to hear what her aunt might say.

Gertrude was in a quandary. She didn't really want to say anything. Should she speak with Claire? Should she ask questions? It wasn't really her place. She had no experience in raising children. And even less in youthful affairs of the heart. Counseling her niece was not at all what she wanted to be doing.

What Gertrude wanted right now was simply to go home to the solitude of her apartment, to drink a nice warm cup of tea and snuggle deeply beneath her bedcovers. She wanted to let her emotions run rampant until they were spilled and her heartache was spent. She wanted to recall once more, with anguish, the unkind words that hurt her. And be soothed again within the warm comforting feel of Mr. Stefanski's arms around her.

But her niece still sat staring at her expectantly. She had been selfish once tonight, she would allow herself no second indulgence. She had been a buffer between Claire and her parents for years now. It was a job she'd taken on willingly, lovingly. It didn't seem that that would change.

"Claire, darling," she said with quiet calmness. "This is all very sudden."

"Yes," she admitted very quietly. "I suppose that it is."

She was looking at her aunt so expectantly that Gertrude became somewhat uncomfortable. She adored Teddy. She considered him a wonderful young man, but he surely wasn't old enough to be anyone's husband. And he certainly was not yet man enough to be a husband to Claire.

"I suppose this has something to do with our conversation about love the other evening," Gertrude said, attempting to mask her discomfort by a show of sophistication.

"Yes, I guess it does," Claire answered.

Gertrude was thoughtful for a moment. "Mr. Stefanski was saying that Teddy had spoken about that subject to him also."

A sudden unexpected excitement sparkled in the young woman's eyes. "So you *have* been talking about it," she said delightedly.

Puzzled by her words, Gertrude frowned. "Well, yes, I suppose we have, still we never expected—"

As her words trailed off she looked hopefully at her niece, thinking the young woman would speak up, shed some light upon this abrupt revelation. Claire continued to look at Gertrude as if it were she who should be doing the explaining. She was clearly excited, eager. Gertrude could imagine no cause for such behavior, but as the silence lingered once more, she became certain that her niece would be volunteering no information.

"Well," Gertrude began bravely as she shot a quick glance out the window to assure herself that the Stefanskis were still speaking civilly, "I suppose I can assume that you two are in love."

"What? Oh yes, Teddy and I. We're very much in love," Claire answered in a matter-of-fact fashion that was completely devoid of any passion or deep feeling.

"You, ah . . . you have thought this over carefully, haven't you?"

"Sure, sure," Claire replied. "That's what we were doing tonight. Talking it over. We want to get married. It seems like a pretty good idea, don't you think? It's really terrific."

"Well, I don't know, Claire," Gertrude answered cautiously. "Marriage is a very big step and you are both so very young."

"Age has nothing to do with it," Claire answered quickly. "I'm the same age as Mother was when she got married."

Her words sent a shaft of surprise and fear through her aunt's heart. It was, to Gertrude, as if her words were reverberating against the inside of the fancy, well-apportioned Packard. "*I'm the same age as Mother*" was a frightening statement to hear.

Gertrude leaned sideways in the seat so that she could look into Claire's eyes, and reached for the young woman's hand.

Her niece seemed calm and collected. It was Gertrude who trembled. She held the young, slim hand in her own for a long, frightful moment before asking the question that hesitated upon her lips.

"Claire, you must tell me the truth right now," she said. Gertrude bit her lip nervously as she chose her words. "Have you and Teddy . . . have you done anything . . . anything for which you should be ashamed?"

"Ashamed?" Claire's expression was puzzled. "What do you mean?"

The young girl had barely got the question out of her mouth when it became obvious by the widening of her eyes and the startled gasp that came out of her mouth that she knew exactly what her aunt meant.

"Of course we haven't!" Claire was clearly shocked by the question. "Aunt Gertrude, we wouldn't . . . we couldn't . . . certainly not!"

"Thank heavens," Gertrude sighed.

"How could you even think that?" Claire asked.

"I apologize, truly, dear Claire, I am very sorry to have even suggested such a thing," Gertrude answered. "Please forgive me. My only excuse is that this has just been such a complete surprise to me. Why, Teddy has not even called upon you. What on earth is your father going to say?"

Claire, still reeling from her aunt's appalling suggestion, was flippant. "I don't care at all what he has to say. I want to hear what you have to say, Aunt Gertrude. I've been waiting to hear it for a very long time."

Standing very much alone on the Main Street sidewalk, young Teddy watched a little nervously as Mikolai reined in his temper with iron control. He knew that his father would never strike him or scold him beyond what he deserved. But the elder Stefanski looked as if he were far from being pleased with his only son.

"I know that this is America," he said quietly as he began to pace the clean-swept brick walk in front of the bank. "But even here there are rules to obey, conventions to be honored!"

Teddy swallowed tensely and nodded.

"In my heart," his father continued more quietly, "I do not believe that you have compromised this young woman who has been your friend since childhood. Please reassure me, Teodor, that this is correct."

Teddy stared into the face of his father's fury, not with fear but with anguish. He was humiliated beyond belief. He had not, to his knowledge, ever directly lied to his father. Tonight he had compounded deceit upon deceit and he no longer had any clue as to how to stop.

"Of course I haven't compromised her, Father," he said. "You know I would never do anything to hurt Claire."

The words he spoke were perfectly true, although at the moment he was thinking that it might be extremely pleasurable to wring Claire Barkley's neck.

"It'll be terrific," she had whispered to him in the quiet darkness of the backseat of the Packard. "I was trying to think of a plan and here one has just been dropped into our laps."

"This is not a plan, Claire, it's lunacy."

"It's not lunacy, it's brilliant!" she'd insisted. "We tell them that we want to get married. People get married all the time; there is no reason in the world why they shouldn't believe it."

"We can't tell them that, Claire," Teddy protested. "What will they think about tonight? What on earth will they say?"

"They'll think that it's high time to confess the truth. They can't allow a half brother and sister to marry. They will simply have to tell us everything."

"It won't work, Claire. It will just get us in more trouble."

"It will work. And I'm not at all afraid of trouble. Especially when I know that it is for a good cause."

Teddy had argued as long as he dared. But, as with every crazy idea that Claire Barkley had ever come up with, ultimately he had gone along. Now he had to face his father.

"Why is it, Teodor, that you would escort one young lady to a dance and then claim to want to marry another?" Mikolai asked, bringing Teddy's thoughts abruptly back to the present.

"Oh . . . ah . . ." Teddy vainly searched his brain for a reasonable answer. It would make no sense to do what he had just done. He knew that. But Claire was always leading into things that didn't make much sense.

"I didn't realize it at the time?" Teddy answered.

"Didn't realize what?" Mikolai asked.

"That . . . that I wanted to marry Claire," he said. "Yes, that's it." He nodded enthusiastically, approving of his own reasoning. "I didn't realize it until tonight."

His father was looking at him thoughtfully. The light from the big round bulb that hung from the light pole in front of the bank was not brilliant enough to reveal details, but still Mikolai searched his son's face.

"You want to marry this young woman, but you just thought of it tonight?"

Teddy's smile faded. Maybe his reasoning was not as good as he had thought.

"No, I had wanted to before," he assured his father. He continued lamely. "But then I thought that maybe I might rather have a wife like Olive, so I asked Olive to the dance, but now I know that she is not the one for me."

Mikolai raised one heavy brow skeptically as he eyed his son. "What brought you to this conclusion?"

Teddy swallowed. "Well," he began. "I . . . I just wasn't comfortable with Olive. I want to be comfortable with the woman that I marry."

Mikolai continued to look at his son as if he couldn't quite understand him, but he finally nodded in tacit agreement. "Yes, I suppose that is a reasonable expectation."

"And Claire and I have been friends for years," Teddy pointed out hurriedly.

His father nodded. "Friendship could be a fine basis for a marriage, I imagine. Although I think that there should perhaps be more."

"Oh, there is more," Teddy assured him quickly.

But when his father gave him a questioning look, clearly waiting for Teddy to elaborate, he could think of nothing further to say. So he kept his silence.

"You simply want to get married?" his father finally continued.

"Ah . . . yes, that's what we want."

"The idea just came to you tonight?"

"Well, not totally," Teddy hedged. "But I was able to sort of make my mind up, so to speak, about it tonight."

Mikolai stopped his pacing and faced his son. His expression was stern. "I believe you to be a very bright young man, Teodor," he said. "I don't say that because you are my son, but because I believe it to be true."

"Thank you, Father." Teddy was almost cringing from the sting of his own guilt.

"When I was your age I was a married man on my way to America," he continued. "So I know that a man can make his own decisions without the wisdom of advanced years."

Teddy nodded.

"But this does not seem to be a plan that you have thought out too carefully," his father said. "You plan to marry in the middle of your last year at the high school?"

Teddy's eyes widened.

"I didn't mean to marry now," he said.

"You don't mean to marry now?"

"Ah . . . no, not now, I guess. Later, yes, we mean to marry later." Teddy stumbled nervously over the words.

"You plan to marry and not go to college?" his father said.

"After college," Teddy answered. "We'll marry after college."

"After college?" Mikolai asked.

"Yeah, sure," Teddy said agreeably. "After college is fine with us. That'd be terrific."

Teddy heard his father's sigh of relief as the older man slung a loving arm around his shoulder.

"Then there is time." He patted his son on the back affectionately. "You had me frightened there for a moment."

"I didn't mean to scare you," Teddy said.

Mikolai shook his head. "No, don't apologize. I should thank you. I haven't felt my heart pumping so frantically in a good long time."

Teddy sighed with relief. His father's anger had completely dissipated. It was over. He began to relax at his father's side.

"So you think to marry the Barkley girl," Mikolai said.

Immediately Teddy's stomach tightened once more.

"Ah . . . well, yes, I think so."

"I like her," Mikolai said. "I've always liked her. She's a smart girl."

"Yeah, yeah, she is," Teddy agreed.

"She reminds me of her Aunt Gertrude."

Teddy eyed his father a little more shrewdly. "Yes, well, everyone says that she's like Miss Gertrude. More like Miss Gertrude than either her mother or father."

Mikolai nodded. "That's good. But marriage, Teddy"—his father made a small sound of disapproval—"marriage is a thing that will need to be handled properly."

"You don't think I should marry her?" Teddy asked.

"I think you should do what you think best, but a man doesn't just announce his intention to wed."

"No, I guess not," he admitted.

"You must speak with George Barkley, of course. It shows a great lack of respect, I think, not to."

"I have to speak with Mr. Barkley?" Teddy was daunted at the prospect. He hated the lie that he was perpetrating. He certainly didn't want to draw anyone else in on it.

"Or I can speak on your behalf, of course," Mikolai assured him. "That's how we did it in Poland."

"You let someone else speak for you?"

"Yes." His father was thoughtful for a long moment as the memories assailed him. "I'll be your *swat*."

"My *swat*?"

"The negotiator for your wedding," his father explained.

"I need a negotiator?"

"Perhaps not here, but in Poland, yes, always," Mikolai told him.

"Why?" Teddy looked at his father curiously. "Seems like it would look better if a fellow just spoke up for himself."

"In Poland the groom never speaks to the bride's family," he said. "Never. Not until all the details are settled."

"Why not?"

"It's the tradition," Mikolai answered. "And to protect his reputation, I suppose."

Teddy's expression was curious. "Why would a man need to protect his reputation?"

"Well, if a suitor were to be rejected by a woman or her family, it would just be very embarrassing for everyone."

"Yes, I guess so."

"So he never talks to them directly," Mikolai explained. "That way if the match doesn't work out, everyone can simply pretend that he was never even interested in her."

Teddy shook his head in wonder. "Still, it does seem strange that a man wouldn't even do his own proposing for a bride."

"It is not the Polish way. In fact, talking about the wedding at all is considered bad luck for the marriage," he said. "So even the *swat* never mentions it."

They had returned to the Packard, but Teddy made no move to join the ladies inside. He was intrigued with these stories of Poland that he had never heard.

"How do they propose if they never talk about it?"

"Well," Mikolai said, propping his foot up on the front tire and leaning forward to rest his hand on his chin. "When I went to ask for your mother, my Uncle Leos went with me. He said to your grandfather, 'I hear that you have a fine goose to sell and we were hoping that we could get you to part with it.'"

Teddy laughed out loud. "You pretended you were buying a goose."

"No, not really," Mikolai assured him. "It was just a way of speaking. It was the way that things were done. The old man knew what we wanted and why we were there."

"So what did he say, 'Yes, you can buy my goose'?"

Mikolai shook his head. "No, not that. It is never that easy. I presented the old man with a bottle of vodka. That was how he answered me."

"Oh?"

"If he had just said thank you and taken it, it would have meant that he didn't favor me for a son-in-law. That would have been the end of it. I would have gone away and nothing would have ever been said about it again."

"But he didn't just thank you and take it?" Teddy said.

"No, he opened the vodka and poured some for himself and for the *swat*," Mikolai answered. "That meant that he was agreeable to the match."

"And then that was all there was to it?" Teddy asked.

"No, of course not. Even in Poland the bride gets to have her say."

"So what did my mother do? Offer to be a goose?"

Mikolai shook his head. "The old man called for her to bring me a glass for the vodka. If your mother had left the room or asked someone else to fetch it, it would have meant that she didn't want to marry me."

"But she did."

"Yes, she did," Mikolai said. "She brought me the glass and poured the vodka. Then she tasted it before she handed it to me. That way we all knew that she was as eager for the match as I."

Teddy shook his head in disbelief. "It's a strange way to ask a girl to marry you."

"Yes, it is strange," Mikolai admitted. He was quiet, thoughtful for a moment. "I like America better. You just ask Claire and she says yes and we talk to her father."

Teddy glanced hopefully inside the car. He had explained

himself to his father, but he hadn't made any progress on getting him to talk about Miss Gertrude. He hoped futilely that Claire was having more luck getting the truth.

"Ah, yeah," he said vaguely. "I just have to ask her and talk to her father. But I don't think that there is any hurry. I don't want to talk to her father yet."

"No," Mikolai agreed. "There is no hurry. Unless you are worried that some other fellow may come and steal her away."

"Some other fellow?" Teddy was incredulous. "Oh, she wouldn't marry anyone else," he assured his father hurriedly. "I . . . I mean we are not going to get married until after college, so there is no need to rush into anything."

Mikolai nodded agreement and then added in a low, even tone that was deceptively mild. "No need to rush into anything, especially not into the darkness of Monument Park."

Chapter Eleven

≈≈

THE MORNING AIR was crisp and cold. Perfect, Mikolai thought, for September. He had two kilns firing and three more on the cool. The brick business was going very well. The brick business was his life and his livelihood. Which in no way explained why he had left his foreman in charge and was headed home early in the middle of the day.

"I'm going home early today, Toppett," he said. "I'm sure you can handle everything here."

"Yessir," the foreman answered, looking momentarily surprised. Although the boss frequently ran errands, he rarely left work before the other men. "All we're a-needin' is to see that railcar loaded."

Stefanski nodded crisply. "Once we free up some space in the drying shed, put all the off-bearers to work getting the yard bricks inside. The weather may change on us any day and I don't want that stock damaged."

Toppett murmured agreement. "The boys can have that done by tomorrow for certain, Mr. Stefanski."

Mikolai nodded with approval.

"Number four is blue-smokin'," the foreman commented.

Mikolai glanced once more in the direction of the huge beehive kilns, like big brick igloos at the far side of the yard. He watched the bluish-colored steam from the oxidation phase of the firing process rising out of the last kiln in the line.

"Raise the temperature to vitrification overnight and we will seal it in the morning," he said.

"I'll be stoking that fire, Mr. Stefanski," Toppett promised.

Toppett continued to regard his employer curiously, but Mikolai made no further comment. He had no reason to explain himself. He was simply anxious to return home. As owner of the Stefanski Brickyards, he didn't need to say *why*.

Of course he knew *why*. He also understood the reason that he had been unable to concentrate on the paperwork he'd left waiting upon his desk, the reason he'd been able to think of virtually nothing else but the events that occurred at the victory dance.

He wanted to see Gertrude Barkley. He wanted to stand close to her again. He wanted to look down into her so-familiar face. He wanted to talk to her about her life.

Despite the surprising finale of the evening, his son declaring his intentions for Claire Barkley, Mikolai had not been quite able to block out the memory of holding Miss Gertrude in his arms and hearing her tears of distress.

"I am just an aging spinster who has suddenly discovered that she is disappointed," she had said to him.

His own reaction was also troublesome. Gertrude Barkley was a friend, a good friend, and such an exceptional woman. Seeing her shed tears of regret was unbearable. The memory of it had been haunting him for the last several days. So much so that this morning he had decided to speak with her. And when Mikolai Stefanski decided to do something, he rarely allowed anything to get in his way.

He left the running of his brickyards in the competent hands of his foreman and in the middle of a workday afternoon took the Interurban up the full length of Main Street.

She was not hard to locate. She was, where Mikolai often saw her, at the hazel tree that marked the border of their property. Dressed in a simple plaid work dress that was covered by a bleached muslin pinafore trimmed along the ruffles with green rickrack, she might have been any of the hardworking housewives of Venice, Missouri. But appearances, as always, were deceiving.

He didn't exactly sneak up on her. But he was there, watching her for several minutes before she knew of his presence. She spoiled and coddled the shaded roots of the hazel tree, trying to make it give fruit. He didn't think that it ever would, but he admired her so much for not giving up on it.

"Good afternoon, Miss Gertrude," he called out.

She turned to him, clearly surprised at his unexpected presence. "Oh, Mr. Stefanski. I was just thinking of you," she said. Then, as if realizing the connotation of her words, she blushed rather prettily.

Mikolai nodded. He had been thinking of her almost ceaselessly and somehow he was grateful that he was not the only one still affected by the encounter at the dance.

"What are you doing?" he asked as he slipped off his silk-trimmed fedora deferentially.

"Just putting down an ash ring," she said, indicating the gray powdery contents of her bucket. "A circle of ashes around the base will keep the bugs off."

He nodded thoughtfully. "Better put down in spring than fall," he suggested.

Gertrude nodded, pleased at his rudimentary knowledge of gardening. "I had the ashes today," she admitted, laughing.

Mikolai laughed, too, lightly. It was not something that he did often. And it seemed Miss Gertrude was most often the catalyst for its occurrence.

He came forward and ran his hand assessingly along the rough bark of the tree; he smoothed the downy underside of the sharp-toothed leaves with his fingers. He shook his head.

"This tree seemed so sturdy and strong, but I don't believe anymore that it will ever bear us hazelnuts, Miss Gertrude."

"I haven't given up," she said. "If I continue to take care of it, surely it will reward me eventually."

Mikolai didn't look hopeful. "You have spoiled it, I think. This tree is too lazy to do anything useful."

She laughed. "Trees don't get lazy. At least, I don't think that they do. How would we ever know? You would have me ignore it in the hope that it will learn to take care of itself."

"It seems like a reasonable course of action," he said.

Gertrude eyed him assessingly. "Is that what you are doing with the young people? Just hoping that they will learn to take care of themselves."

"Ah . . ." he said. "Teodor and Claire. What do you mean?"

"I haven't heard any opposition from you for their marriage," she said.

He shrugged. "I have no opposition. I am surprised, but I think Claire to be a wonderful girl. Someday she will make a loving wife and partner."

Gertrude's mouth thinned to a narrow line and she shook her head. "Someday perhaps, but not now. Her whole life is ahead of her. I don't want her to marry too soon and miss her chance at growing up."

Mikolai looked down at her. She was so stern, so sure. His expression was sober but warm. "Claire will get her chance to grow up, though it may not be exactly as we had hoped it would be. She will find her own way. She is a lot like you."

Gertrude nodded and then feigned humor. "That's exactly what I am afraid of."

She set down the empty ash bucket and dusted the residue from her hands. "How do you do it, Mr. Stefanski?" she asked.

"Do what?"

"Just sit back and be so calm. I know that you were upset the other night, but now you seem undaunted by this unexpected wedding talk."

He shook his head. "I'm not unconcerned," he said evenly. "I was angry when I thought Teodor to be so foolish as to get caught stealing into the darkness with a young woman. I was stunned when he mentioned marriage, grateful when he said that it would not be soon, and wise enough not to try to get in the way of it."

"Still, how can you just accept it?" she asked.

Mikolai shrugged. "I trust my son," he said. "That helps. And I know that to keep a thing, you must sometimes give it away."

Gertrude looked skeptical. "Is that an old Polish proverb?" she asked.

"Not a proverb exactly," he said. "But it does go back a long way."

She eyed him questioningly.

"When the first king of Poland converted to Christianity he gave his country to the Holy See."

"He gave his country away?" Gertrude asked, incredulous.

"Yes," Mikolai answered. "He gave it away."

"But that is terrible."

"Perhaps it was not," he said. "Through all the years of invaders and conquerors, inept rulers and unjust occupiers, we have remained always Poland."

Gertrude nodded slowly, thoughtfully.

"Even now," Mikolai continued, "with the land divided between Prussia, Russia, and Austria, Poland remains an entity, intact. And why is that?"

"Because the first king gave it away," she said.

Mikolai nodded. "The Vatican has an interest in it. By giving Poland to the Holy See, the king was able to guarantee its existence for all time, forever."

"And that's what you are doing with your son."

The gleam in Mikolai's eyes could only be interpreted as humor. "Well, I'm not giving him to the church," he said.

He let his teasing words sink into her thoughts until she smiled.

"But I do believe that allowing him to be his own man, to let him go his own way, makes it easier for him to stay close to me."

Gertrude nodded thoughtfully.

"Teodor is a good and dutiful son," Mikolai said. "And if I would ask him to stay here in Venice and go into the business with me, I know that he would. But then I would lose his heart, I think. And that is more valuable to me than his hands."

"Maybe that was Papa's trouble with George," Gertrude said. "He wouldn't set him free, never allowed him to be himself. So one day he just broke loose."

Mikolai didn't comment. He was content for the moment just to gaze at the bright, flashing eyes of the woman beside him and to marvel, not for the first time, at her intelligence and thoughtfulness.

"Of course, Papa wasn't completely wrong," she continued. "People can make some very foolish decisions when they are young."

He nodded. "And that's what you think that these two have done?" he asked. "They have been foolish in throwing away their youth as you think you have been."

"Oh dear," Gertrude said somewhat nervously. "We are to that, are we?"

With a casual grace that was unexpected for such a big man, he sat down on the grass, leaning his back against the trunk of the stubbornly unproductive tree. "Young people often make choices that later in life they come to regret. Isn't that what you were speaking of the other evening?"

Gertrude's face glowed with shame, but she smiled brightly as if to make light of the circumstances. "I was hoping you would be gentleman enough to forget my behavior the other evening."

He raised a bushy eyebrow. "I suppose I could do that if you truly wish it," he answered. "But perhaps I am a better friend than I am a gentleman. As a friend I might be able to dissuade you from such foolish thinking."

He lifted his hand to her, offering a place in the shady grass beside him. She did sit down, but kept an extravagantly prim distance.

"I certainly need not tell you how greatly I admire you," he said.

Gertrude's chin popped up in surprise. "Me?"

"Why, of course," he said. "Undoubtedly you have been aware of the high regard in which you are held by myself and many people in the community for your talent and your spirit."

She laughed humorlessly. "I'm not sure my talent and spirit are much more than tolerated by the city of Venice, Missouri."

He nodded. "You have your detractors," he admitted. "But all those who strive, in big ways or small, are held up to ridicule by those who never had the courage to try," he said. "You have had that courage, and what is more, you have succeeded. I find it very strange that you would have cause to regret your choices."

"You are right, of course, Mr. Stefanski. It would be silly for me to even look back," she admitted with forced gaiety.

"But you do look back," he said.

Her silence was the answer.

He sighed heavily. "In all truth, Miss Gertrude," he said. "I have spent a good deal of my time lately looking back myself. I have regrets also."

"You?" Gertrude's expression was mystified. "What on earth could you have to regret?"

"The same things as you, I would suppose," he answered.

"Now that *is* foolish," she said. "Your life has been so important, so worthwhile, I can't imagine what you might have to look back on."

"Important? What of great importance do you see in my life?" he asked.

"Why the whole town," she said. "Were it not for you, this town would have reverted to cattle pasture years ago. And if not that, surely we'd still be slogging to church through the muddy streets five months a year. And without all those fireproof brick buildings, Main Street would have undoubtedly burned to the ground years ago, with businesses ruined and lives lost. The children wouldn't have that wonderful high school. And think of all the jobs the brickyards have brought to town. The mining men would have moved on long ago without those jobs."

He shrugged. "If I hadn't done those things, another man would have."

"You can't be sure of that, Mr. Stefanski. And besides, no other man would have done things in quite the way that you have."

He was silent for a long moment. "In truth, I am proud of my accomplishments. It was not those things I lament."

"Then what is it?"

He picked a blade of grass and ran its soft, smooth surface against his lower lip. "Lately, I think that I have let my dreams and ambitions get the better of my personal life."

Gertrude's brow furrowed. "But you have had a life, Mr. Stefanski. You had a wife and now a wonderful son."

"I love my son and am very proud of him," Mikolai said. "But had I been a less ambitious man, less driven, perhaps I could have had a half dozen sons and daughters by now."

Her cheeks were flushed at the personal nature of his words, but Gertrude's curiosity overrode her embarrassment.

"I always thought that you grieved too much for your late wife ever to remarry," she said.

Mikolai's eyes widened, clearly startled by her words. "I grieve, of course. I feel grief and guilt almost equally. I vowed never to marry again, and I won't. But that has been as much a convenience for me as an honor to her."

"I don't understand."

"I was fearful that a woman, any woman, would slow me down," Mikolai admitted. "A wife would expect more of me than I had to give her. She would expect more than my name and my money. She'd expect to have *me*, a thing I have never been prepared to offer. So I purposely decided not to remarry. Now that I see my son going off to live his own life, I suppose I am fearful of being left alone."

Gertrude nodded. "I understand what you are saying. Some people feel sorry for me that I never married. But, in truth, it was my choice. I think I always knew that a husband would probably never have allowed me to pursue my writing. My own father was strongly against it. And even if I had found a gentle and tolerant man to marry, children tugging at my apron would not have been conducive to creating fiction."

"But you still feel the regret," Mikolai said. "I feel it, too."

"Even knowing that I chose the right direction, I'm as guilty as Lot's wife of looking back," Gertrude said. "Given the same choices today, I would chart the same course. Still, there is a kind of sadness to my life that lately I cannot seem to dispel."

"You regret not marrying, not having children?"

"Well, I . . . no, I don't suppose I do," she admitted. "It might have been nice to live life instead of writing stories about it. But I am my own woman. I wouldn't want to simply belong to some man."

Mikolai shook his head in approval. "And the world would miss your stories if you had not written them."

Gertrude shrugged his words away. "My work is rather ordinary. Everyone in publishing agrees that if the public enjoys a writer, his writing must not be of much value."

"Is that how they judge? What is good is what no one wants to read?" he said.

She laughed. "I'm afraid that is the way it has always been," Gertrude told him. "So, like the streets and buildings of town, if I hadn't written these novels, someone else undoubtedly would have."

"And like my streets and buildings," he said, "another person would not have written these the way that you have."

She smiled at him, very pleased.

"The gift of putting words upon paper in such a way that people clamor for them is not a skill that should be disreputed."

Gertrude nodded thoughtfully for a moment before agreeing with his words. "I do love writing. But my work has taken so much of my time that sometimes I think . . . I think that perhaps I have missed my life."

"What do you mean? What life have you missed?"

"I suppose I've missed what Claire and Teddy have. I've missed being in love."

"Ah, love." Mikolai nodded thoughtfully. He stared silently out at the manicured perfection of the Barkley garden. "Marriage is not a guarantee of that, you know," he said. "Indeed, I have missed out on love myself, if such a thing truly exists."

"You think it might not exist?"

"Honestly, I don't know. All I have seen of love are some of its substitutes."

"Well, at least you've seen that. I'm not even acquainted with its distant relatives."

As soon as the words were out, Gertrude appeared to regret them, covering her flaming cheeks modestly.

"Surely that's not true, Miss Gertrude," he said. "Didn't you carry a torch for any of the young men who called upon you?"

Gertrude didn't answer at first. It was as if she were deciding if she should speak the truth or merely voice an acceptable lie.

He saw her swallow determinedly before she raised her head high, refusing to be cowed.

"I have been in love, Mr. Stefanski, once. But the gentleman never returned my affections."

Mikolai made no comment, but merely waited for her to offer an explanation. And she did.

"I didn't have all that many beaus. I was not interested in the young men for a very long time. Truly I never considered any man's attentions as serious ones."

"But did not your father insist that you should receive callers?" he asked.

Gertrude nodded. "My father was a very rigid and uncompromising man," she said. "He kept me very sheltered from the world for a long time."

She smiled bravely and offered her next words with a lightness that belied their meaning. "I believe the young gentlemen in town were quite daunted by him."

"I can imagine," Mikolai answered.

"By the time he realized that his behavior was likely to turn me into an old maid," she said, "it was simply too late."

"Surely you are exaggerating," he said.

"No, I am not. By the time I was twenty, I was considered quite on the shelf. It was something he hadn't intended. Shortly before he died he said that I should marry the next man who came through the door."

"But you didn't."

"No, by then, having fixed my heart with such certainty upon a man who did not return my affection, I knew that I could never marry. I'd seen enough of other people's marriages to know that if not for love, there was truly no reason to wed. And the man I loved never came through that door. He never knew how I felt about him."

Anger, frustration, and pity flashed through Mikolai's thoughts. "He never knew?"

"Of course, I could never tell him," she said. "And he never guessed."

"Well, the gentleman was an unfortunate idiot, Miss Gertrude. I can assure you that had this fool known that you would look kindly toward him as a suitor, your father would have had to hire thugs to keep him from your front porch."

Gertrude laughed delightedly at his gallant words. "You are very kind, Mr. Stefanski."

"And I am truthful, also," he said. "A woman such as yourself is rare indeed."

"Why, thank you very much, sir," she said. "Truthfully, I am vain enough to find it gratifying that my single state is due to the gentleman not knowing that I was looking for a husband rather than from simply being undesirable to him."

"You could never be undesirable, Miss Gertrude."

He spoke his words softly, but something in them caused her to raise her head quickly and look closely into his eyes. The moment was a strange one, an uncomfortable one. Mikolai felt uneasy, as if he had opened up a secret room that should have remained closed forever. Hurriedly he tried to shut that room once more.

"It is very sad that the man you loved never knew of it. If only this were Poland," he said.

"Poland?"

"In Poland your father would only have had to dapple your house and the gentlemen would have known his intentions."

"Dapple the house?"

"It's called *tarantowate*. Paint dots on the house. That's what the fathers do in Poland to tell the men in the village, as well as passersby, that there is a marriageable young woman in the house and that the father and daughter would welcome a suitor."

"Are you serious? They paint spots on the house?" Gertrude asked.

"Oh yes," Mikolai assured her. "And it works very well. It gets everyone's attention."

"It most certainly would," Gertrude agreed.

"If a man has been thinking about one of the daughters of the house, he hurries in to make his offer, before the father accepts a quicker fellow."

Gertrude laughed with delight. "Then that's exactly what my father should have done, painted Barkley House in bright polka dots."

"It's not too late," Mikolai said.

Gertrude's eyes widened. "Oh, it is very much too late," she said.

Mikolai looked skeptical. "Well, your brother George is not much of a painter, but I'm sure he could hire it done."

"I could never marry now," Gertrude said adamantly. "I am happy with my spinsterhood and my little apartment. It is not even a thing that I would consider were I alone and starving. I am far too set in my ways to take on the peculiar quirks of a grouchy old man."

"So we've come full circle," Mikolai said. "You have regrets about the life you chose, but still you would not change the one you have."

"No, I don't suppose I would change it. But I still think of what I missed."

"Love," he said.

She blushed. "Yes, love."

Mikolai studied his blade of grass even more carefully than before. Protected beneath the shelter of the hazelnut tree, it was among the last sprigs still green in the autumn. It was still smooth, but slightly dry from the chill of the season. It still lived, but not forever.

"Would you like to take a lover, Miss Gertrude?"

"What!"

Gertrude's relaxed pose disappeared completely as Mikolai watched. It was as if a rigid iron pole had suddenly replaced her backbone.

"You are insulting, Mr. Stefanski!" she said, attempting to rise.

Mikolai laid his hand on her arm. "Wait," he said.

She was silent and still as stone beside him.

"I did not wish to be offensive," he said quietly.

"Well, you certainly are!" she said. "You are no better than the rest of them. Just because I cut my hair and wear fashionable clothes you think that I am little better than scandal and would go off with some strange man in an—"

"Not some strange man, Miss Gertrude. Me."

Gertrude was struck dumb by his words. She stared at him.

"I mean no disrespect, but as we have just discussed, neither of us wish to marry, but both of us would like . . . would like another chance at youth. I thought that perhaps this would be a way."

In wide-eyed disbelief she stared at him.

"We cannot change the lives that we have lived and neither of us can go back to our youth," he said. "We have chosen what was best for us. But perhaps we can take a time out of our life. A time that none other need know about to experience things that perhaps we have not known. To have at least an interesting substitute for some things that we have cause to want."

"A time out of our lives?" Gertrude whispered the phrase over to herself.

"Yes, a special time that none should ever know about but us," he said.

"Mr. Stefanski, I—"

"When I held you in my arms the other night," he whispered, his words almost tangible in their softness, "I felt something. Something I have not felt for a long time."

He glanced up at her. His heart was in his throat and his pulse was pounding. His confidence had deserted him. He felt imprudent and very vulnerable. Beside him, Gertrude sat stiffly, her prim clothing and her pale expression the antithesis of the wanton proposal that he was making. Her silence was accusing.

"Forgive me, Miss Gertrude," he said, finally. "I thought perhaps that you felt it also. If I have offended you, I am sorry. And I will never speak of this again."

Gertrude only stared at him as if dumbstruck. He accepted her silence as horrified rejection.

Mikolai quickly rose to leave, too ashamed to meet her gaze. He felt foolish, loutish, uncouth. He didn't know where the words had come from. He hadn't intended to make such an ungallant proposition. He had probably permanently destroyed any hope of friendship with the one woman he most admired. If he were his best friend, he would have cheerfully kicked his teeth in. He was despicable, loathsome—

"Wait!"

Her word halted him in midstride. He hesitated a long instant before turning around. She was still seated in the shady vestiges of the last of the hazel tree's summer leaves. Her head was held high and her cheeks were prettily pink. He took in the sight of her, deliberately, as if to imprint it upon his memory so that he would always recall her so.

"Perhaps I have answered too quickly," she said, seeming not to realize that she had answered not at all.

She took a deep breath as if she were contemplating a dive into a dangerous pool. Her voice was low and controlled, as if she were measuring every word that she spoke.

"I think, Mr. Stefanski, that I never want to look back on this moment and regret my cowardice."

Chapter Twelve

"IT'S GOING TO be so much fun," Claire assured her aunt as she hurried Gertrude along behind her. "Candlelight croquet is simply a different game altogether. It's terrific!"

Gertrude's very definite lack of enthusiasm went completely unnoticed, as Claire's own attention was focused more adroitly upon a very different game.

She had so much on her mind. It was, Gertrude surmised, as if her thoughts were a gallon and her mind was only a quart-size pitcher. She had hoped to spend the evening hiding away in her room, pretending that she was writing. She would have to pretend. Her real life was suddenly so much more exciting than what she had planned for her characters, she could hardly give a thought to Weston, Alexandria, and Carlisle Place. But even if she couldn't hole up another evening, alone with the thrill of her own thoughts, the last thing she wanted to do was to play a friendly game of croquet. Especially not with the Stefanskis.

After their talk under the hazel tree, Gertrude honestly didn't know how she would even look the man in the face again. She had agreed to engage in some kind of scandalous "time out of life" with him. She wasn't sure exactly what sort of immorality was to be involved, but she knew that it was something shady.

"I really am quite tired this evening," she had insisted to her niece. "I think you should simply go alone."

"Unchaperoned?" Claire asked with feigned horror. "I couldn't."

"Don't be silly, Claire," her aunt replied tartly. "You and Teddy have spent time alone together since you were children."

"Yes, but we weren't getting married then," Claire said.

The young woman gave Gertrude a long hard look that her aunt couldn't interpret and was too churned up to even worry about.

"You do remember that we are getting married?"

Gertrude's expression sobered and she deliberately showed what she hoped was loving concern. "There is really no hurry."

"Oh, but I can hardly wait."

"But you must wait, dear," Gertrude insisted. "Time changes things for people. What you think you want when you are young is often not what you can live with as you grow older."

Claire's expression was unfathomable. "I don't intend to change my mind," she told her aunt emphatically. "When I set my mind on a thing, you know how I am about following through. It would take a reason of enormous proportion to get this idea out of my head."

Gertrude's face was lined with worry. But only a minuscule part of that concern was for her niece's happiness. Her own heart was pounding like a tom-tom. Dwarfing any fears for the exuberant young woman at her side was Gertrude's anxiety at seeing Mikolai Stefanski again.

She had thought three days ago under the fading cover of the bountyless hazel tree that she was ready to reach out to life. She was ready to take chances. That she, Gertrude Barkley, was ready to engage in a grand passion. One that she had dreamed about for seventeen years.

Since that moment, however, sheer terror had overtaken craven curiosity. She didn't know if she could go through with it. How could she ever be that close, that intimate, and keep the secret that she loved him?

"Look at the yard!" Claire exclaimed beside her.

Gertrude did. And it nearly took her breath away. The backyard of the Stefanski house was lit with the glow of candles.

Candlelight croquet was one of the latest crazes of middle-class leisure. Croquet itself was a delightful game preferred by both ladies and gentlemen because of its innate equality. Tennis and golf favored those of muscled physique and athletic ability. But like its less savory cousin, billiards, croquet was a game of challenge and skill. The most tiny and delicate of the ladies could as likely play with as great a mastery as a brawny schoolboy. And furthermore, croquet did not, as many sports, induce a lady to commit the atrocity of perspiring. Candlelight croquet was especially redeeming in this respect.

"Isn't it terrific?" Claire whispered. Gertrude couldn't help but agree.

"It's beautiful," she said.

The wide expanse of the Stefanski house's backyard, unrelieved by either bedded plants or flowered borders, had always appeared stark and desolate. Tonight Gertrude could approve wholeheartedly for the first time of the rather new fashionable notion of *lawn* over *garden*.

The pattern of croquet wickets, two at either end guarding the stakes, one near each corner of the field and at the center, was brightly outlined by the glow of the slender candles that sat firmly in sockets on the side of the curved wire.

"It's like a fairyland," Claire gushed dreamily.

"Isn't it amazing," Gertrude said, "that something so familiar can be so lovely?"

"Yes, it is truly amazing."

The answering voice was low and masculine and behind her. Gertrude turned, startled, to find herself face-to-face with Mikolai Stefanski.

"G-g-good evening," she sputtered.

"Good evening to you, Miss Gertrude," he answered.

The two stared at each other in silence.

Stefanski looked as if he had just come in from work. His snowy white linen shirt was covered by a four-button pin-striped gray vest that matched his trousers. At his throat was a carefully chosen and conservatively tied silk Windsor.

"I asked Aunt Gertrude to help you to chaperone us, Mr. Stefanski," Claire chimed in. "I hope you don't mind."

Gertrude glanced back at her niece, stunned. Mikolai had not known that she was coming? She had arrived in his backyard uninvited! Gertrude was momentarily horrified. How unconscionably eager she must appear! What if he had changed his mind?

She had no time for further conjecture as he stepped forward to graciously take her hand. "I wouldn't have let Teodor talk me into playing this summer game on such a cool fall evening if he hadn't suggested that we would be honored with your pleasant company, Miss Gertrude."

His words and actions were exceedingly gallant, but his face was a somber mask. He was friendly and polite, he even appeared pleased to have her there, but as Gertrude looked deeply into his eyes, she saw more. She saw so much more that it scared her. Hope, anxiety, excitement, wariness, all warred in his glance and she knew his desires and doubts mirrored her own.

This was no small dalliance that they contemplated. It was to be no fevered night of spontaneous impropriety. It was a calculated decision to engage in an illicit act. An act that Gertrude feared would change her life and her expectations forever.

"We're so glad that you've come to join us, Miss Gertrude," Teddy called out across the lawn as he hammered the far stake into the ground.

Gertrude forced her gaze from the man behind her and

pasted a smile upon her face as she answered his son. "Thank you very much."

"You and Father will make great partners," he called back. "But he doesn't have much experience."

"Oh, I'm sure your father . . . I mean . . . oh—" Gertrude's cheeks were blazing.

"Claire tells me that you are a fine player," Teddy continued.

"Oh, that, yes, I mean—" She felt very foolish and attempted a modest shrug. "I have won a game or two, I suppose."

"Then Miss Gertrude is definitely the other half of my team," Mikolai announced. "I have never actually played this game," he confided more quietly. "I have been assured by many who know, that it is quite easy. But I believe I can use your help."

"I'll do what I can," Gertrude answered him.

"Terrific!" Claire declared with delight. "Teddy and I against you two. It's like playing couples, isn't it, Teddy?"

The young man nodded as he came toward them. "Claire and I are both crack players, but we haven't been partnered together in a good long while. I suppose that will even up the competition a bit."

"Even it up?" Gertrude asked.

"Yes, you two being older and wiser are not as apt to make the mistakes that we are," Teddy said, joking.

"Age is no guarantee of wisdom," his father answered. "And I believe that the widely held truth about mistakes is that anyone can make them."

"Well," Claire said with a youthful giggle. "We'll just have to hope that you two make plenty of them tonight."

Gertrude swallowed nervously.

Mikolai cleared his throat.

"Let's get started," Teddy said with excitement. "Since you

are dressed in blue, Miss Gertrude, you and Father can have the blue and black."

Claire sighed. "I guess that leaves us with red and yellow." She rolled her eyes. "You have to be the cardinal, Teddy. I want to be the canary."

The young man laughed. "Shouldn't it be the other way?" he said. "Red for anger and yellow for cowardice. That's more like us; when I miss a shot Claire gets angry at me, so I'm coward enough to shoot carefully."

The young people's light humor was not so easily matched by their elders. As Gertrude set up her ball half the distance between the starting stake and the first wicket, she felt a gnawing excitement that made her hand tremble. But it in no way brought a smile to her face. Her palms were sweaty as she clutched the mallet firmly. She glanced up only for a moment, but it was long enough to catch sight of Mikolai. He was watching her, but looked almost as disquieted as she felt. Her light blue tub-silk shirtwaist had been chosen for comfort and ease of movement. At that moment she felt as if her chest were swathed in a half ton of chain mail. And her mannish-cut navy skirt seemed heavy enough to be made of lead instead of poplin.

She took a deep breath and tried to regain her self-control. She was here. The words had been said between them. There was nothing for her to do except play out the game and pray that Mr. Stefanski would be as loath to actually speak about the other day as she was.

Gertrude drew back her mallet and gave her blue-striped ball a mighty whack. This action drew light applause from her opponents.

With her first stroke Gertrude took the first two wickets easily. However, she blundered both her point shots and had to step aside as Teddy took his turn.

The young man took quick advantage of his position, making four wickets before his efforts too fell short.

"Teddy's halfway to the turning stake!" Claire announced unnecessarily. "You'd better do very well with your shots, Mr. Stefanski, black goes next."

"How exactly do I do this?" he asked.

Teddy showed him where to start and he gave it a very good first try, but he hit the ball rather sideways and it went catty-corner through the first wicket, missing the second.

"That's a rough one to get back," Teddy told him. He looked over at Gertrude. "He's your partner, maybe you had better advise him."

"Please, Miss Gertrude," Mikolai said politely. "Do advise me."

She found it hard to look at him. She had known him so very long. Yet tonight, his words, his look, seemed to take her breath away. They certainly took the words from her mouth.

"Well, I suppose—"

When she glanced up into his face, she forgot what she was going to say.

"I thought I would just hit it back toward the middle," Mikolai said. "Would that be a good course?"

"But you only have one shot, Mr. Stefanski," she answered.

"Can't I just wait here until everyone else shoots again? Then I will get another chance."

She shook her head. "A second chance at this isn't likely," she said. "Claire is up next and if you're in position to take the wicket, she'll probably get you and the wicket, too."

"Oh," he answered, looking more carefully at the glowing candles on the wickets and his own black-striped ball.

"You must always be aware of the players that come after you," she said. "They have almost as much control of your outcome as you do."

On Gertrude's advice, Mikolai took a small shot that only

altered the angle for the wicket. Leaving the way clear for Claire to pass him by, which she did easily, taking two more wickets before she rolled out of bounds.

Through the next couple of rounds it quickly became clear that, age notwithstanding, the young people were roundly trouncing Gertrude and Mikolai. Shot after shot Gertrude fumbled. And although Mikolai's attempts were valiant, it was obvious he was still very new to the swing of the mallet.

Father and son found themselves simultaneously going for the center wicket. Mikolai, however, was heading toward it while Teddy was already coming back.

It was almost sheer luck when Gertrude's bad shot hit the corner of a wicket and accidentally rolled to a stop against Teddy's lead ball.

"Roquet! Aunt Gertrude's made a roquet!"

It was the first truly lucky happenstance that the blue-and-black team had been given. Claire and Teddy were as excited for Gertrude as if she were playing on their team and not against them.

"Knock him off the field!" Claire called with delight.

"Hey!" Teddy feigned an angry snarl. "You're supposed to be on my team."

Gertrude smiled with as much good-natured enthusiasm as she could manage. She just wanted the game over. And the sooner Claire and Teddy won it, the sooner she could go home.

The proper stroke to a roquet was to place the foot upon one's own ball to hold it still, then strike it as hard as possible. The force from the strike would propel the opponent's ball away from a shot and, with luck, out of play completely. Gertrude fumbled around trying to get her foot positioned right. Unfortunately her new spoon-heel high-button boots were not cooperating.

"What's wrong?"

"I can't get a good grip on the ball," Gertrude said with

exasperation. "The soles are too slick and the space between the flat and the heel is too narrow."

"Let me hold it for you," Mikolai said.

Gertrude raised her eyes in surprise.

"That's allowed, isn't it?" he asked Teddy.

"Sure, it's allowed."

"And after all, she is my partner," Mikolai pointed out unnecessarily.

Slipping his own mallet under his arm, he walked away from the others, across the lawn to where she stood, and knelt down at Gertrude's feet. Grasping the ball, he held it firmly, waiting for her stroke.

"I'm afraid I'll hit your hand," she said.

"No," he answered. "You'll hit the ball. You are a woman that I could trust with more than hammered fingers."

She looked at him then. Once more he was not speaking of the things he was trying to say. On one bended knee on the ground before her, he was looking up into her eyes. Asking. Telling. Listening. The mallet was still in her grasp as she waited a long instant, knowing he was going to speak.

His words were low and quiet and spoken so gently they could have been a poem or a love song. "I have secured an apartment above the cigar store on south Second Street," he said. "There is a back entrance off the alley. I can be there tomorrow at three, if that is good for you."

"That's . . . that's fine," she answered.

As the fire of thrill and fear surged through her veins, she raised her mallet and pounded the dead ball with a mighty blow. She did miss his hand, and the force of her stroke passed to Teddy's yellow-striped winner and sent it careening out of bounds.

"What a stroke!"

"Aunt Gertrude, that was great."

"It's the best shot she's made all day."

≈≈≈   ≈≈≈   ≈≈≈

"It's working, Teddy," Claire whispered to her croquet partner. "It's really working."

Glancing up, he observed closely the members of the opposing team standing across the lawn. "It had better work," he complained quietly. "If I have to hear one more well-meant lecture about the responsibilities of marriage, I'll simply lose my mind."

"Did you see him whispering to her when she took the roquet?"

Teddy nodded.

"I bet she was asking him right then about how and when they are going to tell us."

"I don't know," Teddy said.

"It's your turn, Claire," Gertrude called.

Without ceremony the young woman easily knocked her ball through the double wickets at the top of the field and hit the turning stake.

"Two point shots," she announced. "And here is two more."

As good as her word, she shot back through the way she had come. It looked as if she might make up for Teddy being hurled out of play, but she fouled on the third shot and had to relinquish her turn to Mr. Stefanski.

"Father hasn't said one word against you," Teddy told her as they watched the older man managing the wickets with little style, but a good deal of determination. "He talks as if he thinks you'd make a good wife."

"I would make a good wife!" Claire exclaimed. Her raised voice momentarily drew attention to her and she grinned foolishly at the other couple for a moment before they turned their attention back to play. "He's my father, too," she whispered to Teddy. "Of course he would say that."

"Well, it seems that he wouldn't say that to me," Teddy told her. "He wouldn't say it to me if you were *really* my sister."

"Oh, of course I'm your sister," Claire ground out in frustration. "Do we have to go over this again?"

"I just think if it was true, they would have told us."

"We just have to give them a little more time. They are trying to figure out a way to break the news," she insisted.

"I hope so."

"What else could it be? Don't you see how strangely they act toward each other?"

Teddy glanced over at the two and nodded gravely.

"It does seem as if they are hiding something."

"We just need to push a little bit more," she said.

"Push a little bit more! Good heavens, Claire. What on earth are you planning now?"

"I'm not planning anything, really," she assured him quickly. "I just wish that you hadn't made it so clear that we want to wait. Go ahead, Teddy, it's your turn."

He managed to make it back onto the field, but nothing more. He stepped back to Claire's side and watched as Gertrude hit the turning stake.

"That's probably why they didn't tell us that night, you know," Claire commented. "If they thought we were going to get married soon, they would have told us right away."

"Sooner, later, I don't see what difference it would make," Teddy said.

"It makes all the difference in the world," Claire said. "They think that they have time. We're not to marry soon and we'll surely fall out of love with each other as time goes on."

"I can certainly see how that would happen."

"What do you mean by that?"

Teddy shook his head in exasperation. "I mean that there wasn't anything else that I could do. Good gravy, Claire, I had to tell him that we weren't getting married right away."

"I don't know why you couldn't have tried waiting a while before caving in to him."

"Caving in? He started talking about Polish weddings and speaking with your father." Teddy wiped his brow as if the mere thought of such a thing had broken him out in a sweat. "You put too much of this on me, Claire. I'm not used to lying to my father."

"It isn't lying, not exactly," Claire told him. "And it's not going any further than those two."

"It could have gone further," Teddy told her. "He wanted me to speak to your father. I couldn't do that."

Claire nodded thoughtfully. "Yes, I do think that is a complication we should avoid."

"A complication we should avoid?"

"Yes," Claire agreed, nodding. "We'll leave George and Prudence out of this if we possibly can."

"What do you mean *if* we possibly can?" Teddy's tone was extremely wary. "Asking George Barkley if I can marry you is not a *complication*, it would be a complete disaster."

"It wouldn't go over too well, I suppose," she said with a slight chuckle.

"Claire," Teddy said solemnly as he gazed at her smile, "I think this business is going to get us into trouble, really bad trouble. I just have a feeling that things are not exactly what they seem."

"Oh, Teddy, stop worrying," Claire admonished. "I promise we're already in it as deep as we are going to get."

"Up to our necks," he lamented.

"We do have to push just a little," she said. "Just a little, but it won't mean much."

"With you, everything is much," he said.

She slapped him lightly on the arm. "Come on," she cajoled. "George and Prudence are definitely the last resort. Only if these two can't be made to talk will we take it to the Barkley house to be settled."

"George Barkley will likely settle it by punching me in the nose," Teddy declared.

"Oh, stop worrying. It won't come to that."

"Miss Claire," Stefanski called out. "It is your shot."

She turned to grin at the two adults standing across the lawn. Aunt Gertrude and Mr. Stefanski. Her parents. Her real parents. They were still a rather handsome couple standing there next to each other, she thought. They were avoiding each other's eyes. Her smile broadened. Their actions made her believe. And somehow it made her proud.

"Look at them, Teddy," she said. "There is a secret between them, that's as clear as Christmas morning. It's just a matter of time until the truth comes out."

Chapter Thirteen

GERTRUDE WAS SO nervous, she thought she might be developing a twitch in her left eye. Her stomach was also quite queasy. She could only be grateful that she hadn't been able to ingest a bite of food all day. She climbed the ironwork stairs at the back of the Second Street cigar store with indelicate haste.

She feared being seen. More than that, she feared losing her nerve and hurrying home. She raised her hand to knock, but it wasn't necessary. Mikolai Stefanski, looking large and masculine and strangely unfamiliar, opened the door.

"I was watching for you," he said.

She stared at him.

"Come in,"

She did.

Her feet seemed suddenly to have turned to lead, but she forced them across the threshold, past the gentleman she had come to see, and into the cold sterility of the rented room.

She was here. She was actually here. All night as she'd lain awake, she'd assured herself that she would not come. But she had.

Gertrude glanced around her, noting her surroundings as dispassionately as if she were visiting a train station. The walls of the little room were unlightened by either whitewash or paper, and unadorned except for a small shaving mirror nailed above the water pitcher. The afternoon sunlight streamed in through the one dingy window that faced Second Street, revealing the contents of the room. A small, scarred table with two mismatched chairs sat on one side and a rusty iron bed with a rolled-up tick resting on the bedsprings was on the other.

Her heart was pounding and her knees were knocking. She admonished herself for being such a coward. If she was going to leave, it would have to be now.

With slow, deliberate movements, Gertrude removed the pin from her hat. It was a long, thin, dangerous pin with a large jet obelisk at its head. She looked at it for a full minute before removing her hat and weaving it into the black silk braid.

"Where should I hang my hat?" she asked.

Mikolai was still holding his. He looked around for a hook or rack.

"There is no place," he told her.

Gertrude nodded. "I suppose not."

Her chin high, her courage feigned, she walked over to the small table and set her hat upon it. She looked at the chairs and thought to sit down, but she wasn't sure. For the first time since walking through the door, she looked at Mikolai. He looked as uncomfortable as she felt.

"I suppose I should make up the bed," he said.

Gertrude nodded. "Yes, yes, of course, I'll help you. We should make up the bed."

She hurried, with as much grace and dignity as she could muster, to the far side. They faced each other across the width of it. Allowing themselves only one intense questing look before they began, they industriously rolled out the cotton bed tick. It was old and much mended, but had been recently beaten and was as full and fluffy as if it were new. The sheets were mere hemmed cotton and were unstarched. They had, in a manner, been pressed, and once stretched and tucked appeared sufficient enough for their purpose.

"There," Gertrude said with finality as she smoothed out the last wrinkle. She glanced over at Stefanski, who also appeared rather pleased with their joint handiwork.

As the moment lingered, their smiles faded. With great concentration Gertrude clamped down on an overwhelming need to fidget.

"This is all very disconcerting," she admitted quietly.

"Miss Gertrude, if you have changed your mind, I—"

"I haven't changed my mind," she assured him hastily. "Unless you have."

"Me? No, no, Miss Gertrude, I haven't changed my mind."

"That's good then," she said.

"Yes," he agreed. "It's very good."

Silence enveloped them once more. Gertrude glanced down at the round jet buttons that adorned her shirtwaist. She had chosen her costume with the knowledge that she would be removing it. The idea of standing in front of Mr. Stefanski in her camisole and petticoat was suddenly quite real and infinitely daunting. She steeled the trembling in her jelly legs and spoke sharply.

"Perhaps I should undress now," she said.

Mikolai stared at her mutely for an instant and then spoke up hastily.

"Perhaps we should talk first."

"Oh." Gertrude was not at all sure about the appropriate preliminaries, but agreed gratefully.

Quickly he came around the bed and offered her his arm. It was not more than two steps from the bed to the table, but they took them with the formality of entering a cotillion, her gloved hand resting upon his sleeve.

"Please be seated, Miss Gertrude," he said.

She did as she was bid, centering herself somewhat precariously upon the wobbly panel-back chair. He seated himself opposite her and a very respectful distance away.

Her hands had begun to tremble so she clasped them together tightly.

"Mr. Stefanski, I really don't know——" she began.

He held up a hand to quiet her. "Of course you don't, Miss Gertrude," he said. "It is my duty, both as the gentleman and as the partner of wider experience to . . . to make this go well."

His words relaxed her considerably. He was going to take charge. She needn't do anything but follow his direction.

He cleared his throat. "I fear, however," he continued, "that it may not."

Gertrude's eyes widened with concern.

"Have I done something wrong?"

"Oh no, no, Miss Gertrude," he assured her quickly, leaning forward in his chair to grasp her hand. "Please do not think that. It is nothing that you . . . oh no, it is me. I——" He released her hand, straightened once more in his chair, and began pulling at his left eyebrow. "I do not believe that I have ever been so nervous with a woman in my life," he admitted.

"I am nervous, too," she said.

"Well, you certainly should be," he told her, his brow furrowed with concern. "This is, after all, your first . . . your first . . . ah, participation in such an . . . an act. But I have . . . I mean, on numerous occasions, and I . . . well, I just feel differently about you."

She sat silently in her chair.

"My experience has been with . . . with women who were more . . . more experienced themselves. I have never . . . not with a . . . well . . . a virgin . . . not since . . . since my wife."

"Oh yes, of course." Gertrude nodded slowly, reminding herself to continue to breathe.

"I'm not sure that you really . . . that you really should do this," he told her.

Gertrude's chin came up defensively. "You are not attracted to me," she said evenly.

Her words seemed to catch him off guard. He hastened to correct her impression. "That's not it at all! I am very attracted to you, Miss Gertrude."

She didn't believe him. "I do understand, Mr. Stefanski," she said quickly. Rising to her feet, she grabbed her hat. Her cheeks were flaming with humiliation. "I am so sorry to have inconvenienced you."

"Miss Gertrude, you misunderstand," he insisted.

"No, I understand completely," she said. "Please let us speak no more of it. I know that I am neither young nor especially fair."

"That is not—" Mikolai was becoming increasingly agitated. "What I . . . Damn it! I forget my English when I am upset. Miss Gertrude, I—"

"Please let us just forget it all, Mr. Stefanski. It is certainly not your fault that you do not find me attractive."

She was walking now. Her head high, her heart breaking. The poet said *"better to have loved and lost."* Gertrude was thinking that it was better to have always wondered than to have found out the truth. She had offered herself to a man, freely, with no question of vows or ties, and she had been refused. She wanted to cry. She wanted to screech. She wanted the ground to open up and swallow her. She wanted to get out of the room.

She reached the door and grabbed the handle. She had only managed inches of a peek outside before it slammed shut loudly. Mikolai Stefanski was leaning against it.

"Please, you must not think what you are thinking," he said.

"It is no fault of yours, Mr. Stefanski," she said bravely.

"You misunderstand," he said. "That is my fault."

"I am quite all right. And you must not reproach yourself,"

she said. "You can in no way be blamed for not . . . for not wanting me."

"I do want you."

"There is no need to spare my feelings, sir."

"I am speaking the truth."

"Please just let me go."

"I cannot while you believe this . . . this lie."

"Mr. Stefanski, please, I—"

Her words were halted abruptly when he grabbed her black gloved hand and pressed it against the front of his trousers.

"Oh!" she cried.

"My body does not lie, Miss Gertrude," he said evenly. His voice was very quiet in the still, silent room. "Can you doubt my desire for you when you feel with your own hand the evidence of it?"

Gertrude did feel it. The hard, formidable length was pulsing against her hand through the layers of fabric that separated his flesh from her palm. This was a man. A man, the way a man was built. It was bigger, harder, warmer, more real than she had expected. Now she knew at least. She knew what it was to touch a man.

With sudden realization she saw that he was no longer forcing her to that intimate touch. His clasp upon her wrist was gentle, easily broken. Yet, her hand had not moved away, but rather she had conformed her palm to the shape of him and was tentatively though deliberately exploring him.

Horrified, she jerked back her hand and turned her back to him. Her thoughts were flying too wildly to grasp. She trembled with anxiety, or was it excitement?

"See, it has already happened," he said quietly behind her. "I have disgusted you."

"You?" She turned to look at him askance. "Not you. It was me. I touched you."

"I put your hand against me."

"But I kept it there."

"Did you?"

"Well, yes, I—" She turned her back to him once more and fell silent. "You have not disgusted me, Mr. Stefanski," she said quietly.

"I still fear that I might," he told her. "I have so little experience with ladies . . . ladies such as yourself."

"How is it with . . . with the other type of . . . of women?" she asked.

"Well," he said thoughtfully. "It's a game of sorts, I suppose. We tease each other a bit and then we just pull up her skirts and get at it."

The image his words conjured up brought Gertrude to blush. Disconcerted, she returned to the table and placed her hat upon it once more. She was not leaving. Not now. She was not leaving now.

"What about your wife?" she asked. "Surely the first time with her must have been more . . . more solemn."

He did not answer immediately. She glanced up to see his expression lost in thought, his face pained.

"Forgive me, Mr. Stefanski," she said quickly. "Of course this . . . this is nothing at all like your wedding night with your late wife. I cannot think how crass I am to suggest that this assignation be in any way similar to the uniting in wedlock of a man and his wife."

Stefanski's expression returned from the past and he fixed his eyes upon her thoughtfully.

"I was very drunk on my wedding night," he said quietly. "I was very drunk and very young. I don't remember too much of it. But I vividly recall that my bride cried for an hour at least after the deed was done. And she called me a . . . I'm not sure how to say it in English. She said I was a 'big, sweating hog.' I would not wish, Miss Gertrude, to give you justification for saying the same."

Gertrude swallowed the strange emotion that caught in her throat. "I am sure you will not," she assured him softly.

His eyes were deep and fathomless as he looked at her. "You understand that I must touch you, caress you in places that are very private," he said.

She nodded bravely, but her blood was pounding through her veins and her stomach was suddenly filled to the brim with the fluttering of butterfly wings.

He stepped toward her. With great formality he raised her hand to his lips. "I will try to be gentle," he promised.

She nodded.

Slowly he turned her hand in his own. He looked at her once more, as if giving her another chance to flee before he bent to kiss her wrist. It was a gentleman's kiss, light and respectful. The thrill of it pulsed through her and brought a ripple of sensation to the flesh beneath her clothes.

His strong, callused hands smoothed up her arm to the delicate buttons on her gloves. Unslipping them easily with two large masculine fingers, slowly he began to pull down the glove, unveiling the pale, smooth skin beneath it.

"You have very pretty hands, Miss Gertrude," he said. "I think of your hands often."

"You think of my hands?"

He nodded. "I think of them writing stories and digging in the garden."

She smiled lightly, pleased.

He leaned forward and whispered close to her ear. "But now, forever, I will think of them caressing the front of my trousers as you did a few minutes ago."

"Oh my," Gertrude said. She found it suddenly difficult to catch her breath. Tingles of startling gooseflesh crept down her throat all the way to her bosom, the tips of which tightened perceptively as if his hands had touched them instead of his words.

He relieved her of her other glove in the same manner he had taken the first and left it to lie with its mate on the scarred little table, next to her silk braid hat.

"Please tell me if you become frightened," he said as he reached for the button at her throat. "I do know how new this all must be for you."

Gertrude's arms were stiff at her side as she felt him unfastening her shirtwaist. "It is all new," she said. "But it is not as if I have not thought about it, this, many times."

"You've dreamed of having a lover?" he asked, his pale eyes observing her keenly.

She had dreamed of him. "Yes, I have. Not always for myself. I . . . I rarely allowed myself really to imagine . . . to imagine that," she answered shyly. "But I have often dreamed for my heroines, for them there have always been men to love."

Her buttons undone on her shirtwaist, Mikolai began to pull it out from the confines of the skirt. He tried to smile. "I don't think the hands of the gentlemen who made love to your heroines ever shook as mine do now," he said.

Gertrude looked up into his eyes and felt compassion for his fears. She pushed his hands away and, keeping her eyes straight upon his own, slipped her bodice off easily and draped it thoughtlessly across the back of the chair. She stood before him now, her shoulders bare save for the two wide ribbons of white satin that held up her camisole.

He hurried out of his own coat and vest and allowed them to lie where they fell. He gazed at the half-dressed woman before him like a starving man might view a twelve-course banquet.

"Oh, Gertrude," he said as he stepped toward her. "You must be able to hear my heartbeat. It seems to be clamoring like a blacksmith's hammer."

"And mine also," she said.

Gently he caressed the naked, exposed flesh of her shoulders. "You are so smooth," he said.

"Thank you."

"I haven't kissed you yet."

"No, you haven't."

"I think I will."

"Please do."

He took her chin in his hand and bent his head slightly at an angle and leaned toward her. Eagerly she pursed her lips and raised her mouth to his. He hesitated. With the pad of his thumb he softly rubbed against her lower lip.

"Open your mouth, Gertrude," he said. "I want to kiss you as a lover, not as my maiden aunt."

She relaxed her puckered pose and he moved in closer. "Open your mouth," he said. "Just a little bit. Yes, that's right."

He placed his lips upon hers so gently. Yet the firm pressure as he sucked her mouth against his own set off tingling fires from her scalp to her toes.

He relinquished the kiss but pulled back only a hairbreadth to question her. "Do you like my kiss?" he asked.

"Oh yes." Her voice was breathy with excitement and her chest was tight.

"May I embrace you when I kiss you this time?"

"If you like."

"I would very much like."

He slipped his arms around the thin shield of eyelet and cambric that covered her and pulled her tightly against him. Once more he brought his mouth down to hers, tasting and teaching as she trembled against him.

Reluctantly, but without haste, he broke off the kiss again. His eyes were dreamy, lusty, as he gazed at her.

"I can feel your bosom against my chest," he told her.

"I suppose so," she said.

"It's a very soft bosom, Gertrude," he said.

"I suspect that it is supposed to be that way."

"Yes, it is wonderfully soft. But not all soft. I can feel the hardness of your nipples through my shirt."

"Is that supposed to be that way?"

"Oh yes," he answered. "It is supposed to be just that way."

He kissed her again, more thoroughly, more confidently. He allowed his hand to roam more freely along her back and down, down, past the waistband of her skirt to the curve of her buttocks. He clasped her there and pulled her commandingly against him.

His lips left hers and traveled a scorching path to the tender flesh of her neck. "What do you feel of me?" he whispered against her throat.

Gertrude gasped for air, not certain that she could speak. "I can feel . . . I can feel your body," she answered.

"You can feel it," he said. "And is it soft or is it hard?"

"It's hard," she whimpered. "It's very hard."

"Do you like feeling it against you?"

"Yes, I think that I do like it."

"Do you think you would like it inside?"

"Oh, please, Mr. Stefanski, don't tease me anymore. I think I do want it inside me."

He pulled away from her then, but his movements were sure and swift as he found and released the fastener of her skirt. It dropped to her ankles, but she didn't have time to step out of it, he grasped her behind her knees and lifted her up into his arms. She wrapped her hands around his neck as he carried her to the rusty iron bed.

He hesitated a moment as he held her above it, as if savoring a special treat. Then, gently he placed her in the lover's bower they had prepared. He followed her down upon the soft cotton tick and wedged his knee between her thighs.

"Oh, Mr. Stefanski," she whispered.

"Yes, Miss Gertrude" was his answer.

He kissed her then. Passionately. Thoroughly. Feverishly. It was not a kiss as the others had been, a tasting of one mouth upon another. This kiss involved his whole body and incited her. His hands were everywhere, coaxing, pressing, caressing.

His breathing was at a pace so quickened, it was only surpassed by the haste with which he was pulling at her camisole. When the ribbon strap on that garment ripped, it sounded as loudly within the room as if a cannon had been fired.

He stopped immediately. Mikolai stared into her eyes. What he saw there she didn't know, but he released her and sat up on the side of the bed. He stared off into space and seemed quite determined to get control of his accelerated breathing.

He turned back to her finally, much subdued and very apologetic. He smoothed her cheek gently. "I'm sorry to tear your clothing," he said.

"It's not important. I can easily mend it," she told him.

"Would you allow me to buy you a new one?" he asked.

She didn't answer, but her cheeks pinked brightly with embarrassment. A single man buying a woman's underwear was as scandalous an action as a decent woman could imagine.

She almost giggled at her own thoughts. Certainly lying half dressed in a rented bed with a lover sitting beside you was much farther beyond the pale. Somehow, it didn't seem very shameful at all.

Her laughter relaxed him. He looked at her somewhat sheepishly.

"You may buy me anything you like, Mr. Stefanski," she said. "I would be honored to accept a gift from you."

He smiled. Clearly he was once more in control of his passions. "I would consider it a gift from yourself if you would call me by my given name."

"Mikolai," she said quietly.

He reached up to gently touch her face, taking one short brown curl of her hair and twisting it around his finger.

"Let us take this a bit more slowly," he said. "I don't want to frighten you."

"I wasn't frightened," she assured him.

"Perhaps I was," he answered.

A long moment passed between them as he looked at her, warmly, lovingly. His haste and his passion thrilled her, but the regard in this long, friendly look pleased her also.

He glanced down at the bed and suddenly grinned. "Miss Gertrude, I am shocked!" he said, feigning social horror. "Boots on the bed! What would the ladies of the Algonquin Society think?"

"I cannot imagine."

"Well, I certainly can. Mrs. Wentworth would say it was further proof that you have no good sense at all. Naomi Pruitt would agree that it is exactly the kind of thing that a woman like yourself would do. And poor Claudy Mitts would 'oh dear, oh dear' herself into a near frenzy."

Gertrude laughed out loud. She gazed in wonder at the man beside her. Mikolai Stefanski, the rather dour Polish business-man that she had known all her life, was transformed before her eyes into a smiling gentleman with a sense of light good humor.

"However did you get to know the ladies of the Algonquin Society so well?" she asked.

He shrugged. "Just because a man does not speak much doesn't mean that he is not listening. One thing about attempt-ing to converse in a foreign language is that it gives you more time to think about your words before you utter them. Given time to think, I've discovered that much of my own speech is better left unsaid."

She smiled back at him, trying to take in this new image. The eyes of the man she knew so well were now crinkling with smile lines.

"Now let me help you with these boots before the ladies become unhinged."

He was still acting with jovial nonchalance as he pushed the hem of her petticoat up to her knees. Certainly higher than necessary for the unlacing of her black dress boots. His big hands were adept and unhurried. He looked up at her, once more his eyes were lazy as if his thoughts again were lascivious.

"Perhaps next time you put on these boots, you will think of me," he whispered huskily.

The timbre of his voice made Gertrude tremble. "Because you have unlaced them for me?"

"Yes, that," he agreed. "And because of the action required." He pulled out half a length of the shoelace from the eyelets. "It must go in," he said. "And out. In . . . and out . . . in . . . and out."

Gertrude's brow furrowed in puzzlement.

"You don't know what I'm talking about?" It was a question.

"No, I don't."

He threw the boots off the end of the bed. "You will," he said in a tone that sounded like a promise.

He scooted up on the bed upon his knees and pulled her feet into his lap. He began to massage her instep and she sat up in bed.

"Too much?" he asked.

"I'm ticklish."

He nodded and released her feet, only to explore a length of leg covered by black silk stocking.

"Would you like to see my chest?" he asked. "I would like to remove my shirt, but only if you are not offended."

The idea of a shirtless Stefanski upon the bed with her was really quite thrilling. "Please, remove your shirt," she said.

He discarded his tie, slipped his suspenders off his shoulders, and made quick work of the half-dozen mother-of-pearl buttons that had kept it fastened. He jerked its tail out of the waistband of his trousers and threw it from him. The shirt hardly had time to hit the floor before he also discarded his silk fleeced undershirt.

It had all happened so quickly that Gertrude found herself somewhat taken aback by the sudden appearance of his naked flesh before her. She had always thought him to be a stocky, almost portly man. But there was not one ounce of fat on his broad, heavily muscled torso. What there was, Gertrude discovered, was an unbelievably abundant amount of thick brown hair.

"Oh my!" she said.

"Would you like to touch me?" he asked.

She hesitated.

"You can touch me this way," he said, taking her stocking-covered foot and laying it in the center of his naked chest.

Gertrude waited, unsure for a moment before she began to tentatively investigate the hills and valleys he had placed beneath her foot.

"The silk feels wonderful touching me," he told her. He ran a questing hand up the back of her calf and beneath her petticoat. She felt rather than heard the snap of her garter being opened. An instant later the cool air of the room was against her skin as he rolled the thin tube of black silk down to her ankle, baring her limb. "But I'd rather feel the texture of your own flesh," he said.

She allowed him to remove the stocking. He tossed it carelessly over the footboard. "Touch me, Gertrude, please touch me."

She used her foot to explore the thick pelt of chest hair and to discover the hard points of his nipples as he relieved her of her other stocking.

"Such strong, beautiful legs, Gertrude." He caressed them as he spoke. "I am a great admirer of ladies' legs," he admitted. "I've often wondered about yours." He lowered the tenor of his voice measurably. "Lately I have dreamed of them wrapped around my waist, holding me so tightly."

Gertrude found his words almost as startling and provocative as the touch of his hands.

He took her foot from his chest and raised it to his lips where he pressed his mouth passionately to her instep. Gertrude's breath caught in her throat, but was released in a startled cry as his tongue darted out to taste that delicate flesh.

"I know, darling," he comforted. "You are ticklish."

Gertrude felt more than ticklish as he spread her legs on either side of his thighs and came forward to lie full length upon her.

Up on one elbow, her held himself just above her as he gazed down into her face.

"Kiss me, Gertrude," he whispered. "Kiss me."

She did. First just with her lips, openmouthed and tugging gently as he had taught her. Then, she lay her hands upon his shoulders, his broad, strong shoulders, and suddenly she couldn't bear not to touch him, to caress him, to explore the feel of his body, so different from her own.

As one of the same mind, Gertrude and Mikolai sought knowledge of each other. She rejoicing in the hard, unyielding muscles of his back. And he sculpting and shaping the soft yielding mounds of her bosom. The pace of their exploration increased as their need to touch outstripped their patience and caution.

When Mikolai finally unleashed her right breast from the confines of her lacy cambric camisole, he could barely allow himself an instant to gaze and a moment to touch before he had to taste.

Gertrude cried out at the heat of his mouth upon her and bowed her back rigidly to offer him more. Her position allowed him to fix his thigh more firmly between hers and she was stunned by the sudden inexplicable need to press her most tender parts firmly against that thick, unyielding bolster.

He was twirling his tongue around the hard, aching flesh of her nipple. She wiggled and squirmed beneath him, needy, searching.

He pulled back and raised himself to his knees, struggling to regain his control. His eyes were bright with passion, his breathing labored and quick. Her own eyes seemed to be glazed with some warm, glittery syrup that both delighted and incited her.

She felt the cool air upon her wet bosom but it made not half the sensation as the lightning touch of his eyes upon the same spot.

"Mikolai!" His name was a whimpered plea on her lips, but he seemed well able to understand it.

"We've got to get these drawers off you," he said with a firmness of conviction that was indisputably the cause of his tradition of commercial success.

He tossed the hem of her petticoat up over her head and delved near her waist for the fastening. Gertrude pushed the lace-covered satin out of her face and attempted to help him.

The hook released at last, he raised her hips off the bed as if she weighed little more than the sheets and removed the pretty confection of muslin and eyelet that had suddenly become so superfluous.

Mikolai threw the drawers over his shoulder, but didn't look back. His vision was focused solely and most intently upon the naked feminine secrets spread out before him.

"You are so beautiful," he whispered with near reverence in his voice.

His words were somehow more intimate, more frightening than anything that had gone on before. Feeling momentarily vulnerable and exposed, Gertrude attempted to draw her limbs together, but he grasped her knees and held them wide.

"Let me love you, Gertrude," he pleaded. "Let me."

She relaxed. He spread her before him wider still and then released her. Gertrude did not move to hide herself as his hands went to the placard at the front of his trousers. She watched, eager, spellbound, as one by one he freed the buttons that kept him hidden from her. Once the buttons were undone he eased both his trousers and his underwear down over his slim hips, nakedly displaying himself to her.

Gertrude swallowed, her blood still pounding in her ears.

"Am I supposed to say that you are beautiful, too?" she asked.

"Only if that is what you think," he answered.

Gertrude nodded slowly. Her courage seemed to be deserting her. "Not beautiful exactly," she told him. "But . . . but formidable."

He bent forward to plant a gentle kiss on the inside of her knee. "Not too formidable, I hope," he said.

She couldn't quite hide the fear in her eyes. He lay full upon her once more, her legs wrapping naturally about his hips. He kissed her.

"I'll try not to hurt you, Gertrude. That is the very last thing that I want to do. But they say the first time . . . well, they say the first time is not good."

She ran a caressing hand along his cheekbone. "Then I will get through the first time, Mikolai, dreaming about the second."

Chapter Fourteen

MIKOLAI COULDN'T REMEMBER a time when he had felt more daunted by the most pleasant task before him. The afternoon sun shed bars of bright yellow light and shade across the rusty iron bed. The rusty iron bed in which he held Gertrude Barkley in his arms.

She was generous and eager and willing to suffer whatever ignoble pain might be associated with her deflowerment. But Mikolai was not. He wanted her to enjoy it. He wanted to please her. He wanted it very badly. He could never recall anything having mattered so much before.

He brought his mouth down to hers, joining their lips with tenderness and passion. She had puckered up like a schoolgirl no more than an hour ago. Now she met his kiss with practiced eagerness. He gently allowed his tongue to slip inside her mouth, mimicking the movements of the act that he wished to teach her.

She seemed startled at the invasion, so he quickly withdrew. He would not scare her, not force upon her anything that she didn't like. He was hard, aching, but more than his own release, he wanted hers.

He could have called out thanks to heaven when she cried out with pleasure at his mouth on her breast. He wanted that from her, pleasure. He wanted to give it to her. He wanted to feel her having it. But she was a virgin, and this would all be so new to her.

He would take no pride in hurting Gertrude that way. He wanted to fulfill her desires, not relieve her of a useless badge of innocence.

He pushed the sweet bouncy curls out of her face so that he might kiss her brows and her temples. He thought of her tears on the night of the dance at Monument Park. She'd lived her dreams in books and cried that life had passed her by. She had loved a man who had not loved her back. For this, she had missed much of the sweetness of life. And certainly the raw pleasure of sex.

He wanted to give her that. Not just sex, but pleasure in sex. He wanted her memories of their time together to be as fine and as shining as anything her wonderful imagination could have conjured up. He was a man, not a hero in a book, but he wanted to be as loving and caring of her as any man she might create in her stories.

He let his kiss drift down along her throat once more and to the softness of her exposed breast. Her camisole still shielded most of her nakedness and he wished the pretty feminine thing in Hades. If he could get her to sit up, he could pull it off over her head. He tenderly urged the crown of her dark pink nipple into his mouth. He'd get the camisole off in a minute, just a minute or two.

Slow down, he cautioned himself. Give her time. She is a virgin. The truth of that unnerved him.

He knew that there were tricks. Tricks that a man could use to ease his way into a woman. But tricks with Miss Gertrude might not be the thing. She had become embarrassed when he had looked at her most private parts. He couldn't imagine that she would let him put his mouth and tongue upon them. And as for taking her *stallion style*, a position said to aid ease of entry on the unbroken maidenhead, it seemed patently utilitarian and downright unfriendly.

He increased the pressure of his tongue on her nipple, and

she cried out her approval beneath him. He smiled against her breast. With her legs wrapped round his waist, his thigh was no longer there to ease her. But he would make it better. His Gertrude ached with need and he would make it better.

Pushing aside the satin of her petticoat, he slid his hand down to that soft pelt of curls he had viewed so thoroughly earlier. He clasped her and she pressed against him. She was so wonderfully wet.

"So sweet," he whispered. "So very sweet."

To prove his excitement, he clutched her tightly to him, allowing her to feel his erection. Her heard her gasp in shocked surprise. He loved the sound.

She was kneading the muscles of his back, strongly, passionately, lovingly.

His hand had begun to delve into the damp, heated hollow of her female body. With the pad of his thumb he found what had once upon a time been described to him as "the mistress button."

"You press that button," his cousin Jozef had told him and his brothers one bright, blue-skied summer afternoon back in Poland. "You press that button on a woman and the dutiful wife becomes a naughty mistress."

Mikolai pressed it now. The expected result came quickly and with great intensity. Her cry was sweeter than the most beautiful of music and the scoring of her nails upon his back was more welcome than a caress.

He began to ease his fingers inside her. She was smooth and damp and wonderfully warm. The passage was tight; marvelously, thrillingly tight. He didn't want to wait. He didn't want to do things for her the right way. The blood was pounding in his ears. He just wanted to do it. He wanted to do it now.

Forcefully pulling the reins on his own need, he pushed his lusty selfishness back inside the cage of his control and thought again of her. Not of woman and man and mating, but of her, his Gertrude. Dear, sweet Gertrude.

He would control himself. He would glean his pleasure from providing hers. Again he teased and toyed with the mistress button, now stiff and pulsing beneath his thumb.

"What are you doing to me?" Her question was heated and throaty with passion. It sizzled through him, enhancing the play of his questing fingers, buried deep inside her.

"I'm doing to you what you want me to do," he answered her. "Let me touch you more, Gertrude. Let me touch you more."

Whether from his words or her own needs, he felt her relaxing, opening to him.

Gently, lovingly, stroking her tenderly and stoking her fire, he pressed farther inside her. He sought to locate and weaken that tiny wall of inexperience that separated them, but he found no barrier.

He raised his head from her breast to meet her lips once more. As his kiss comforted, he delved yet deeper. What he didn't find there turned his lips from cajoling to joyous.

"Sweet, sweet Gertrude," he whispered.

Mikolai lay his head lovingly upon her breast and sighed into the soft, warm skin. There was no barrier. Thank heaven and fate, there was no painful boundary to be breached. At some time in the course of Miss Gertrude's thirty-odd years a stumble on the staircase, a carriage accident, maybe even a pony ride, had removed any impediment to their full enjoyment of this afternoon.

"Gertrude," he whispered. "I am going to give you all the pleasure that I know how to give."

Her answer was more a breathy sigh than an actual word.

"Yes, oh, please yes," she answered, her words nearly a plea.

He was hard and hot and throbbing with need as he pressed himself to her narrow entrance. Her whole body stiffened with fear at the invasion. He didn't allow her to dwell on that fear.

He took her gentle hands that lay trembling upon the sheets and put them to good use. One he wrapped around his neck that she might hold him. The other he carried between their bodies to the place where they were barely joined.

"Help me, Gertrude," he said. "You have invited me in, now guide me."

In truth he required no help. His need to push farther inside her had him trembling. He held himself back only with rigid control. Yet, he wanted her help. This joining should not be, he was certain, something that *he* did to *her*. It must be a thing that they did together.

"Help me, Gertrude," he begged against her throat once more.

He felt her swallow her fear as she reached out to touch him, oh, so tentatively.

He had to grit his teeth against the power of that hesitant caress.

"Oh yes, yes, my darling," he whispered as he awarded her bravery with kisses. "Yes, I love the touch of your hand upon me."

Those kisses turned to licks and nuzzles as slowly, painfully slowly, she eased him, by centimeters, into her hot, silky depths.

When her hand became more an obstruction than an aid, he pulled it from between their bodies and kissed her fingers with loving gratitude. He pressed her to him that final inch, causing a startled gasp to escape from her throat. He was buried inside her. Mikolai's teeth were clenched in a desperate attempt to maintain control. The sweat upon his brow was not from the sweet labor of his entry, but from the restraint on his nature.

He rocked very gently, assuring himself that he was not hurting her, that he was lovingly, completely, gloriously, inside her. He moaned her name in a delight that was very near physical pain.

She trembled beneath him and he opened his eyes to look down into hers. They were bright and sparkling with a little uncertainty, but there was much desire there, too.

"I always wondered what it would be like, and now I know, Mikolai," she breathed. "Oh, how nice."

Mikolai grinned at her. He might have laughed if the desperate control he was maintaining hadn't been such torture.

"This isn't it, Gertrude," he said. "We've hardly started."

Her eyes widened in surprise at his words, and he began to rock against her once more, this time with more effect.

"Do you like that?" he asked.

Her eyes had become dreamy. "Yes, yes, I like that."

He withdrew slightly.

"Don't . . . !" she admonished him boldly.

He did laugh then, for all that it was difficult. "Oh, my Gertrude. No need to worry." He drew ever closer than before.

She sighed.

She had begun to squirm again beneath him. "It feels . . . it feels . . . I don't know how it feels," she whispered. "But I do like it."

"I like it, too," he told her, trembling as he smoothed her hair from her face, wanting to watch her expression, wanting to see the need in her eyes become fulfillment.

"Then don't stop," she begged.

He didn't.

Slowly, steadily, with determination, he slid into a mutual rhythm that both assuaged the sharp edge of his need and further spurred his desires.

Gertrude was no fainting flower in his arms. She quickly grasped the steps of the dance and moved with him in eager, passionate cadence. Less and less carefully, more and more lustily, he thrust inside her.

She was moaning, startled, awestruck, beneath him. He could feel that change inside her as she clenched and pulled him to her. Still, he was not prepared for the power of her zenith when she reached it. He held her fast, welding himself to her.

Her creature cry was untamed, frenzied. He was hers. No longer aware of where his body ended and hers began, she was wild motion beneath him. She was the beating of his own heart. Her eyes were wide, wide with disbelief. Disbelief, yes, and pleasure.

Her name was ripped from his throat as the molten fire inside was released, his very being joining with hers. Taking with it all thought, all control, all restraint.

"I love you," he cried.

And he did.

In the warm afterglow of their loving, they held each other and giggled and sighed. The slanting light of afternoon revealing their bodies in unshadowed reality, they examined each other like scientists on a geographic exploration.

Gertrude pulled gray hairs from his chest, until he complained that she would make him hairless as a boy. He finally managed to get her camisole off and assured her that her still-firm bosom would be the envy of women half her age.

"Women half my age have no bosom yet," she told him with feigned petulance.

He grinned, that grin that had suddenly become so familiar and so dear. "That just proves my point," he answered.

Cuddling, caressing, kissing, they were loath to leave the secret hideaway that they had discovered and made their own. But eventually they rose and dressed and he kissed her hand and told her good-bye.

They decided to meet every Thursday. Prudence always

went to the Algonquin Society meeting on Thursday and Gertrude wouldn't be missed.

It was a good plan, a very good plan. But by Monday, Mikolai was too anxious to see her to wait four more days and he slipped out to the Barkley garden to ask her to meet him on Tuesday.

She had been more than eager to do so. And after that afternoon of exploring, loving, teasing, they decided that they should meet on Tuesdays *and* Thursdays.

But on Thursday they hadn't been able to get enough of each other, so they met again on Friday.

By Saturday, Gertrude Barkley was walking around in a daze of sensual desire. She hardly ate, never worked, and couldn't put together a coherent thought. Still, life for the rest of the world went on at its regular pace.

"Do hurry, Aunt Gertrude," her niece called out from the doorway of her apartment. "We don't want to be late for the kickoff."

Venice was playing Rolla that afternoon, and after some coaxing from Claire, Gertrude had agreed to attend the game. She was fully dressed and ready to go, except for her shoes. As she bent over to fumble with the laces her hand trembled. In and out. In and out.

"I'm wearing my button-tops," she declared suddenly.

When Claire looked at her curiously, Gertrude flushed.

"Go on downstairs, I can't get ready with you staring at me."

She knew her words were cross, but she couldn't quite help herself. It was extremely difficult to do or say anything coherent in Barkley House when all her thoughts and visions resided across town in a small room above the cigar store on Second Street.

Yesterday they had played sweet games together within their safe little haven. He taught her what he had called "tricks." The memory of them had her head spinning. She'd had no idea that people, lovers, could do such things. And she'd certainly never thought such excess of sensual joy existed. She found his body to be rather fascinating. And she found his ability to make hers respond intensely pleasurable. She sighed out loud with the memory of his lips upon her. And trembled with the resulting desire it evoked. How did married women manage? However did they get anything done? They were free to be with their gentlemen all night, every night. They never had to race the afternoon sun, or jump up and dress so they wouldn't be missed.

They had dallied overlong with such frequency that Mikolai had become quite adept at helping her with all her hooks and buttons. And she had found that with the appropriate incentive she could don her clothing in a quarter of her usual dressing time. Still, they often became distracted by the sight of a soft feminine shoulder or the lean muscles of well-curved masculine buttock.

"We must be very careful," he told her. "Too many people know us. And they know we have no reason to be in this part of town."

Gertrude smiled, trying to lighten the mood. "Maybe they would believe that I've taking up smoking if I am noticed frequenting a cigar store."

Mikolai was not amused. "We must not allow anything to cheapen what we have here together. I would not wish any disgrace attached to your name."

"For myself, I wouldn't care," she told him honestly. "But I wouldn't want to bring shame down upon my family. And I'd never want to embarrass you."

"I would not be embarrassed," he answered. "If it were not a scandal, I would shout it from the housetops that Gertrude Barkley allows me to hold her in my arms and love her with my body. I can hardly believe my good fortune."

She looked up into his eyes and read the truth written there.

She felt the elation of pure good fortune, also. But she put her feeling into a kiss instead of words.

"The man who owns the cigar store owes me a favor," he said later as he checked the alleyway to ensure that no one was around. "He will never mention that I rent this little place. Still, I don't want him to ever see you."

"I will be careful," she promised as she slipped past him through the doorway and hurried down the stairs. She stopped at the bottom, somehow compelled to look back.

He was still standing in the doorway. He was watching her. His expression was solemn. He seemed lost suddenly and so alone. Her heart ached and she wanted to return to him. She wanted to run back up the stairs and into his arms. She wanted never to leave.

The light was fading. She must walk the five blocks to the library and catch the Interurban when it went by. No one must ever know that she had not spent her afternoon perusing dusty books and dreaming about life instead of living it.

"Tuesday?" she had asked in a quiet whisper.

"Monday," he had replied. And he had blown her a kiss.

How could she wait?

Gertrude walked across the confines of her lonely, narrow apartment and sat down at the window. She stared at the bright brick house next door. It was so close. She could throw a stone and hit his window. Yet, it was as far away as it had ever been.

She loved Mikolai Stefanski. And she knew that in his own way he must love her, too. He certainly wanted her. She smiled at her memories of that evidence. And she wanted him. All of him. His days. His nights. His triumphs. His fears. She even wanted his children. She turned away from the window, scolding herself for her own thoughts. She had no chance for such things. Some things were just not meant to be.

For seventeen years she had craved a place in his life. She had that place now. Their secret hideaway, their illicit afternoons, that was what she had with him. What had he called it? A time out of life. He desired her body. He chuckled at her jokes. He even liked her conversation. She should be grateful for what she had.

She had the pleasure of his hot, passionate afternoons. Why did she covet his cool evenings and lazy mornings and his darkest, bleakest nights? She had his love. Why did she still long for his name?

Once more she stared out the window through the branches of the hazel tree to the big brick house next door. Mikolai Stefanski had given her more joy and pleasure and happiness than she had ever found in her life. But she knew, with certainty, that the burden of her long-held unrequited love for him could spoil everything. He had told her once that he'd never remarried because a wife would expect more than he was prepared to give. She must continue to pretend, as she had all these years, that she had no expectations. The strain of that deception might well break her heart.

Chapter Fifteen

❧ ❧

THE FOOTBALL TEAM trounced Rolla handily. Now the talk was flying that if they could beat the powerhouse at Springfield, Venice High School could win the state championship. Claire Barkley found this to be a terrific prospect, but not nearly so terrific as the certain-to-be-forthcoming confession that she was the daughter of an illicit relationship between her Aunt Gertrude and Teddy's father.

As the days passed she had become increasingly impatient to hear the truth. To have it said, once and for all, that she was not simply George and Pru's oldest child, a human being of little concern and less consequence. That she was the unsanctioned issue of a passionate union betwixt two star-crossed lovers made her existence seem so much more purposeful, so much more important.

Claire sighed with appreciable drama at the thought. She could hardly wait for the revelations to begin.

This evening, however, she didn't anticipate any of those revelations to occur. George Barkley, the man who called himself her father, was giving a victory party for the parents of the boys on the football team. This was, Claire concluded, not at all because of his love of football or his team spirit. George Barkley wanted to be Sublime Kalifa of the Crusading Knights of the Mystic Circle. By opening his house to the "less fortunate"—meaning the working-class men and women whose children made up the majority of the football team—he hoped to garner votes for his ultimate election to that noble post.

It was quite easy for George Barkley to throw a fancy party, Claire thought unkindly. It was a wonder that he didn't do it more often. All he had to do was announce that it would be given. Everything else would be taken care of by his wife. After all, it was Prudence's duty to plan parties and do most of the work, too. It was unfair. But Prudence never seemed to mind it. Claire did.

She was stuck in the kitchen helping her mother make the precision cuts of the delicate ladyfingers when she decided to speak her mind.

"You shouldn't let him treat you like this, Prudence," Claire said in a tone that was patently condescending. "George takes you for granted. You are like a slave in this house."

"What a terrible thing to say! Taking care of a man's house and his children is a wife's joy," she said.

Her words sounded to Claire like something her mother had read in *Home Journal*.

"And it is very disrespectful to call your father by his given name," she added.

Claire made a very impolite face before she commented shrewdly, "It's disrespectful to call *him* George, but not to call *you* Prudence. I see how it is. You can't be disrespected? Is that how this works?"

"Oh, Claire, why do you have to twist my words?" Her mother sighed in exasperation. "It is just as disrespectful to me. But I know that it's just your way of being grown-up. Mothers understand that," she said with a smile that was far too pert and cheerful. "Your father simply wouldn't know to interpret it that way."

"He doesn't understand anything except what he wants to understand," Claire answered. "He's so eternally grumpy. All the time he complains about Lester the Pester, but he leaves that brat totally to you."

"Your little brother is not a brat, Claire, and I don't want to hear you say that," Pru admonished.

Claire grinned. "Remember, *brat* means brother in Polish."

Her mother was adamant. "But we do not speak Polish," she said.

Claire couldn't really argue with that and didn't try.

"I don't know why you even put up with him," she said.

"Little Lester?" Prudence sounded truly shocked. "Why, he is my darling boy! Being a scamp is just his little-boy ways, underneath he is a sweet angel."

Claire rolled her eyes in disgust. "I wasn't talking about Lester. I was talking about George. I don't know why you put up with him. He's so selfish."

"Your father is not selfish," Prudence defended. "He just . . . he just has a lot of things on his mind."

"Yes, and everything that's on his mind is about him. What's best for him. What he wants. Where he should be. You should face the truth, Prudence. In the universe of George Barkley, it is not the earth that revolves around the sun. It is the earth that revolves around George Barkley."

"What a horrible thing to say!" her mother scolded. "Claire Barkley, I have a mind to wash your mouth out with soap."

"It wouldn't change the facts, Prudence."

"You don't even know what the facts are," she answered sharply. She began the very delicate process of transferring the ladyfingers to a silver tray. She was so stirred up by her daughter's talk, she was positively heedless of the fragile nature of her creations.

"Your father is a fine, decent, honorable man," she declared sternly. "He has been through things and done things that you can never know about. You think you know all there is to know about him. But you are far too young to understand."

Claire hated her mother's you'll-know-better-when-you-grow-up tone. She answered quickly and with little thought to the consequences of her words. "I think you'd be surprised to find out that I know and understand a great deal more than you think I do," she said.

"What on earth do you mean?" Pru asked.

"I mean that I already know all about the scandal," she snapped.

"What scandal?"

"Prudence, you know what scandal," she said, lowering her voice to a more prudent whisper and glaring at her mother accusingly. "I'm talking about the scandal when I was born."

Prudence's eyes widened with shock and her complexion turned as pale as the crust on the delicate ladyfingers that she dropped unnoticed from her hand onto the gleaming maple flooring at her feet.

"Who told you?" she asked, horrified.

"I figured it out on my own," Claire answered proudly.

"I . . . I . . . oh . . ."

Prudence stood as still as a stone for a long moment gazing at her daughter. Claire kept her expression reproachful. She was not about to allow her mother to brush off what had happened.

To Claire's dismay, Prudence's eyes welled up in tears. She staggered across to the kitchen table and collapsed into a chair as if her legs would no longer hold her.

"I had hoped," she whispered so very quietly, "that you would never find out." Prudence straightened her apron, unwilling to raise her head. "I know what you must think of me."

"What I must think of you?" Claire's question was punctuated by a puzzled humorless laugh. Her mother's obvious great upset surprised her. For all that Prudence was a watering pot and a dishrag, she had been just like a mother to Claire all her life.

"I think you are kind and courageous and did what you thought was best," she said with real sincerity.

Prudence glanced up at her. Her expression was guilt-ridden. Her words contrite. "You don't blame me?" she asked.

Momentarily startled by the question, Claire stared at her in disbelief for an instant before she huffed with annoyance. "Oh, for heaven's sake, Prudence. You aren't to blame for anything," Claire said.

"I'm not?"

"Of course not! I know that George tries to lay everything that happens in this house at your feet," she said. "But surely you can't possibly think of any way that *this* could be your fault."

Pru's eyes widened at her daughter's words.

"If I blame anyone," Claire said. "It's George Barkley! And Grandfather, too. He was just as much in the wrong himself."

"You blame your grandfather?"

"Don't you?"

Prudence appeared confused. "Well, your grandfather was certainly difficult," she conceded. "But he, and George too, they both made sure that we did the right thing."

Claire rolled her eyes. "I'm not at all sure that it was the right thing," she said.

"B-b-b-but, darling," Pru stuttered. "What else could we do?"

"You could have simply left things alone," Claire answered. "I'm sure everyone concerned would have been much happier."

Prudence was dumbfounded. "You think you would have been happier not growing up here? Not living in this house, not having Barkley as your name?"

"Is that what you thought? That calling this house my home

and being named Barkley would be worth what I have suffered?"

"You've suffered?"

"Of course I've suffered," Claire declared dramatically. "Haven't we all suffered? You've suffered. Aunt Gertrude has suffered."

"Gertrude has suffered?"

"Certainly she has. Living in this house, watching you and George, pretending, it's been horrible for all of us."

Prudence covered her face with her hands and began to sob. Taken aback, Claire stood frozen in place for a moment before she dragged up a chair beside her and pulled the crying woman into her arms.

"Mama, don't cry, don't cry," Claire whispered softly. She had seen Prudence weep many times, but this time was somehow different. It was as if her heart were breaking. "Please don't cry, Mama."

"I had hoped," she managed to blubber out. "All these years . . . I had hoped that maybe George wasn't just pretending."

Claire didn't completely understand the meaning of her words, but held her tightly and comforted her just the same. She had never meant to hurt Prudence. It hadn't occurred to her that she might be hurt. That Prudence might actually want Claire as her daughter, that she might be sad that she was not, had never entered the young girl's mind. Lester was Pru's favorite. She was simply Claire. She'd never thought that her mother cared that much. But apparently she did.

"I do love you, Mama," Claire assured her, wiping the hair from Pru's damp cheeks. "I do love you. And I know that you've tried."

"I have tried," Pru admitted through her tears. "I hoped, I prayed, and I really thought that maybe . . . maybe after all these years, but—"

She didn't get to finish her thought. The door burst open and George Barkley, dressed smartly and looking distinguished, stood in the threshold.

"The guests are arriving. I think—" He stopped abruptly and stared at the tableau before him. "Oh, for the love of God, Prudence, what are you sniveling about now?"

His words brought on a torrent of sobs. Claire glared at him.

"This is all your fault," she said accusingly.

"No, it's not," Pru said, patting her daughter. "It's not *all* his fault."

Prudence pulled away from her daughter's embrace and rose to her feet. Determinedly she wiped her teary eyes upon her handkerchief.

"Go on out with the young people, Claire," she said. "Teddy's setting up croquet in the backyard."

"But, Mama."

"Go on," she insisted. "I need to talk to your father."

Pru's unusually firm tone brooked no argument and Claire didn't try to make one. With one last accusing glare toward the man in the doorway, she made her way out of the kitchen.

Leaving the back door open just a crack, she hurried noisily down the steps. On tiptoes she sneaked back to listen.

"She knows," Prudence said.

"She knows what?"

"Claire knows the circumstances of her birth."

The room was in total silence for a long moment. Claire crouched down upon her knees on the porch and eased the door open slightly so that she could peek in.

Her parents stood still, just as she had left them. Her father, hands on hips, was beside the door. Her mother, leaning heavily upon a ladder-back chair, stood next to the table.

"Who told her?" George asked quietly.

Prudence shook her head. "She figured it out on her own."

George nodded solemnly. "Well, I guess we should have

expected that a bright girl like our Claire would learn how to count," he said.

"Don't make light of this, George Barkley!"

"Pru, it's ancient history," he said.

"It's not," she snapped. "We live with it every day."

"You might," he scoffed. "But I certainly do not. It's forgotten."

"Oh no? Then why has this foolish election to this silly post become so important to you? Sublime Kalifa. It sounds ridiculous."

"That has nothing to do with this!" he answered too quickly.

"It most certainly does. You are still trying to get back what respect you think you lost. I'm sorry about that, George. I've said I'm sorry for years now, with everything I've been and done. Well, you are not the only one who lost in this, George. I lost more than you."

"Pru . . ." His word was plaintive.

"I lost something more than my reputation, George Barkley. I lost the chance for a marriage based upon love."

"Oh, don't be silly," he said with an uncomfortable huff. "You know how I feel about you."

"Indeed I do," she said.

Her chin still high and her gait determined, Prudence walked down the hallway to the stairs.

"Where are you going?" George demanded.

"To my room!" she answered, her voice risen in uncharacteristic anger.

In the background the front door knocker sounded loudly. Both of them turned and gazed toward it, but neither moved to answer it.

"I believe I shall lie down and take a nap," she told her husband with purposeful calm.

"A nap!" George was stunned. "Pru? What about the guests?"

She stared at him, not one glimmer of uncertainty in her expression. Her face was red and blotchy and the tears were dry upon her cheeks. She held her head high, regally determined.

"They are your guests, George Barkley," she said with quiet steel in her voice. "And it is your house, isn't it? I don't see that it concerns *me* at all!

"Pru?"

She turned from him and stomped angrily up the stairs. George stared after her, mouth open and, for once, completely speechless.

Gertrude smiled much more broadly than she felt as she passed the tea tray to Mrs. Pugh who had volunteered to pour. Having paid little attention to what was going on, Gertrude hadn't even known there was going to be a party until she'd arrived home after the football game. And now Prudence had retired to her room with a "sick headache" and George was as grumpy as a bear.

She was conscripted into acting as hostess for Barkley House. An arduous task at any time. More so now when she could hardly keep her mind on where she was. With difficulty she maintained a calm decorum, inside she was still shaking.

At the game Claire had once again attempted to press through to the front of the crowd. Today Gertrude had been adamant about keeping out of sight. Mikolai was somewhere near the sidelines and under no circumstances did Gertrude want to stand next to him. Her heart pounded as loud as any drum whenever she saw him. And she genuinely feared that were they to come face-to-face, she might simply lose what meager shreds of self-control she still possessed and throw herself into his arms.

Never in her life had she really tried to control her impulses, but this was one time that she really must.

With that in mind, she had kept Claire with her, in the midst of the crowd, watching the game over the shoulders of the folks in front of them. It hadn't been very satisfactory, but it had kept her away from Mikolai.

At least it had for a little while. At the end of the game, Claire had quite literally dragged her over to Stefanski's Packard.

"I have to tell Teddy what a great game he played," Claire insisted.

She didn't mind at all offering her congratulations, though in truth the game passed her by in a whirl. What she did mind was standing next to Mikolai Stefanski in the sunshine of a crisp, cold afternoon and pretending that they were merely casual acquaintances.

He didn't speak.

She didn't speak.

They tried not to look at each other.

It was a useless attempt.

He was close, very close. His eyes were scanning the crowd around them, but he leaned slightly and whispered to her.

"I have to see you tomorrow."

"Impossible."

"Make it possible," he said.

"I could never get away on a Sunday," she protested.

"I could take you for a drive. A Sunday drive." His eyes were alight with hope. "It is done, you know."

She shook her head almost imperceptibly. "If we were to take a drive together, the people of this town would think that we were courting. They would start watching us. We could never be alone in the rented room again."

He allowed a long moment for those words to sink in before he nodded. "I couldn't live with that."

His words were simple. They were honest. They were sincere. And they had made Gertrude tremble.

That trembling beset her once more as she stood among the uncomfortable crowd of people trying desperately to appear as if they were having a good time.

To the working people of Venice, George Barkley was a different breed. He was a banker. He held their money, if they ever managed to save any. But more likely he loaned them money, if he thought they deserved it, when times were rough. Drinking tea and eating dainty pastries with him was as foreign to these sons of miners and farmers as keeping their shoes under glass.

George, who was never really at his best dealing with people, was even more clumsy this evening than usual. The working-class folks, dressed in their Sunday best, seemed as uncomfortable with one another as they were with Barkley. And without Pru's calm, steady influence, Gertrude feared that the entire occasion might well come to a bad end. For her brother's sake, she tried to maintain a little social dignity. But she was floundering.

Mrs. Acres, who seemed near tears, explained that her husband had forgotten to tell her about the party until that very morning. And she had unknowingly washed her good dress for tomorrow.

"I brought it in and put the iron to it for a good half an hour, but it was still too wet to put on," she said disconsolately.

The faded calico that she wore was certainly still quite serviceable, and Gertrude told her so. But the woman was frustrated and furious.

"I could just kill that man of mine," she complained. "I'm finally invited into the Barkley house and I'm forced to wear rags."

Gertrude had no clue how to answer that. She mumbled something lamely to the effect that Mrs. Acres should return anytime she liked and felt dressed for the occasion. The words didn't appear to offer the woman much comfort.

Her nephew Lester, without his mother and chief guard in sight, was crawling under the furniture and grabbing handfuls of the delicate sweets from the table and stuffing them into his mouth. From across the room Gertrude saw him wipe his sticky hands on her grandmother's hand-crocheted tablecloth. She longed to race over and box the youngster's ears, but it was not something that she supposed a hostess was allowed to do.

Primrose Bounty, Tate Bounty's second and considerably younger wife, was critical. Apparently her two years of working as an upstairs maid in the Campbell house in St. Louis qualified her as an expert on fine household accoutrements.

"Is this the best china you have here at Barkley House, Miss Gertrude? I've seen finer in Mr. Wentworth's store."

"My grandmother brought this with her from Virginia," Gertrude assured her.

The woman sniffed. "It's just plain white. Seems to me that lofty folks like yourselves could afford some plates with a few flowers on 'em."

Aggie Wilson had her own brand of disapproval. "So Mrs. Barkley took to bed with a sick headache."

"Yes, she did."

"Mighty inconvenient time, if you ask me," Mrs. Wilson said. "'Course, I guess some women can just indulge an affliction, while some of us can't."

On an intellectual level Gertrude was impressed that economic class seemed to be no deterrent to cattiness and gossip. The wives of the brick workers could have fit in easily at the middle-class hen party known as the Algonquin Society. Practically, however, Gertrude knew that as the substitute hostess it was her duty to see that the guests enjoyed themselves and left with a good feeling about Barkley House and the Barkleys. How she was going to manage that she simply did not know.

Help arrived rather unexpectedly and in the unlikely person of Mikolai Stefanski.

Gertrude hadn't even heard his knock. She noticed his arrival when his name was called by some of the men. Her head jerked up as if pulled by a string. He was here. She hadn't expected him. He was not one who was given to attending social occasions. And this particular one was given more for the men in his employ than for himself.

She watched him walking through the parlor, politely greeting her guests. He knew them. All of them. Most of them worked for him and the few who didn't had all asked for work at one time or another.

The crowd seem to relax in his presence. They were used to seeing *him* dressed in a suit. He was familiar and unthreatening.

"Evenin', boss."

"Mr. Stefanski."

"Hello, Stefanski, what a game, huh?"

Gertrude watched Mikolai nod politely, respond evenly and slowly. His movement among the people seemed to have no set direction, but with certainty he made his way across the room to her.

He was there then, right in front of her.

"Would you like some tea?" she offered, before she remembered that she had turned that job over to Mrs. Pugh, who was on the other side of the room.

Mikolai smiled. "No, I have no need for tea," he said.

He stood beside her. She knew why he was there. Why he was standing politely at her side. He simply wanted to be close. She wanted that, too. Here in this crowd he could be close without conjuring up undue suspicion. He turned his gaze to the crowd. The folks were stealing glances in his direction and then whispering to themselves.

"What seems to be going on?" he asked.

Gertrude's expression was half desperate. "Pru has gone to bed with a sick headache and I've been drafted into duty as hostess."

"A task at which I'm sure you are very competent," he said.

She shook her head. "Not these days," she answered.

He raised a bushy brow in question.

"I . . . I can't seem to keep my mind on anything . . . anything except my afternoons," she said.

His pale hazel eyes widened and then grew hazy. He nodded as if making a perfunctory flattery and replied so quietly only she could hear. "I would like to get your back against a mattress at this very minute."

Gertrude swallowed nervously and then cleared her throat. He did likewise.

"So how is the evening?" he asked more loudly, attempting to douse the fire that he'd unabashedly stoked.

"I'm afraid things are not going so well," she replied.

"And why is that?" he asked.

Gertrude shook her head. "I'm not sure. The people who are not familiar with this house appear very uncomfortable."

Mikolai turned to survey the crowd. Each and every person that he glanced at smiled at him. Gertrude was nonplussed.

"Believe me," she said, surprised. "Just a few minutes ago everyone was terribly uneasy. But now . . ." She glanced around, puzzled. "They seem to have something to talk about. I can't figure out—" She turned to glance toward him.

The abrupt halt of her words caused him to look at her.

"I know what it is that they are staring at," she said.

"What?"

"You are smiling, Mr. Stefanski."

He raised his brushy brow in surprise and then to the complete surprise of the entire company he laughed out loud.

"You are right, Miss Gertrude. I do seem to be grinning like a fool."

Gertrude felt the warmth in her cheeks. "It's an expression I've grown quite fond of, but it's a new one for the people of Venice."

"Perhaps I should let them get more familiar with it," he said. Then he added more quietly, "And perhaps I can help out a woman for whom I have developed a great affection."

He gave her a slight bow of courtesy and moved on into the crowd. To everyone's surprise, including Gertrude's, he seemed to exude welcome and good humor. The stiff, solemn Polishman proved tonight to be warm and generous.

"Avery," he called out to Mr. Parks. "That boy of yours is passing so well I ought to send a telegram to Jesse Harper at Notre Dame."

"The Parkses ain't Catholic," Tom Acres pointed out unnecessarily before Pete Wilson jabbed him in the ribs.

Mikolai laughed as if the man had made a great joke. "I don't believe the Pope will mind as long as he wins football games," he said.

Good-natured laughter broke out all over the room.

Mrs. Pugh poured Stefanski a cup of tea and half the company decided that they needed a refill.

"I was so proud of my Teodor," he told the crowd. "When he runs through that line, I am breathing so hard, you would think I am running myself."

There was much laughter and understanding at his words. Avery Parks even slapped Mikolai on the back as if they were long companions.

"I know what you mean, Mr. Stefanski," he said. "Every time Paul drifts back for a pass, I think I've got to hold my mouth just right or he'll never get that pigskin down to the fellow in the right colored shirt."

The parents began reliving the afternoon's game, telling it as if they personally had taken the field. Even Dr. Ponder, whose son Delfane was the yell-leader, not a player, talked as if he had personally won the game.

Gertrude watched, pleased and awed. This Mikolai was new, very new, to Venice, Missouri. And *she* had brought him here. She stared at the scene before her, wrapped in an unexpected glow. If only she could capture this moment, this one moment where the world was happy and laughing and her Mikolai was in the middle of it.

"Psst!" she heard behind her.

She turned back, but at first she didn't see anything. Then it was only a familiar hand at the kitchen door that beckoned her.

Puzzled, she unobtrusively stepped away from her post and into the kitchen. Claire and Teddy both stood there. Both looked pale and upset.

"What's wrong?" Gertrude asked.

"Papa didn't tell you?" Claire asked.

"Tell me what?"

She looked over at Teddy as if to ask for advice. The young man shrugged uncertainly.

"Prudence and George had an argument," Claire said. The young girl seemed to be waiting for Gertrude to comment.

Gertrude nodded. It explained George's bad mood and Pru's untimely headache. "These things happen, dear," she told Claire. "It's nothing to be upset about."

Claire hesitated, glancing over at Teddy once more. "Nobody said a word to you?" she asked again.

"No, they didn't," Gertrude said evenly. "And I'm sure that your parents' disagreements are not my concern. Nor should they be yours."

Claire looked at Teddy once more and then stiffened her lip and raised her chin. "They were fighting about me."

Gertrude's mouth formed an O of understanding. She reached over and patted her niece comfortingly upon the shoulder. "I'm sure it's nothing, Claire. Please don't hold yourself responsible."

"They don't think Teddy and I should marry," she said.

Gertrude's eyes widened. "I thought that you had decided to wait to mention it until after college."

"I changed my mind," she said, then with a glance over at Teddy, she rephrased her words. "We've changed our minds. We don't want to wait."

"But, darlings, of course you should wait." She directed her words to both of them. "Marriage is a very important step and one shouldn't take it without proper consideration."

"We've considered it and we are getting married. We are getting married very soon. That is, Aunt Gertrude, unless you can give us any really good reason why we shouldn't."

The two young people stood there staring at her expectantly. Gertrude couldn't think of a thing to say.

Chapter Sixteen

❦❧

It was raining. A slow, steady rain that had started at morning and had continued with unrelenting persistence all day. Inside the little upstairs apartment on Second Street, however, the weather was of little concern. It certainly should have raised some eyebrows when Gertrude left for an "outing to the library" in such inclement weather. But the situation at the Barkley house was so strained, no one even noticed.

For Mikolai and Gertrude, encased in a warm sunny glow of their own making, the gray gloom of the afternoon went unnoticed. They lay together wrapped in each other's arms in the narrow rusty bed, which actually no longer appeared rusty.

As a surprise for Gertrude, Mikolai had bought a fluffy down pillow and fresh sheets of twilled bleached muslin to grace their secret shelter. He'd scoured the rust from the head and footboards and festooned them with garlands of rosemary and bright lengths of satin ribbon.

"It's beautiful," she had said when she saw his handiwork.

Mikolai had smiled with pleasure. But he hadn't told her he had decorated their bed of assignations like a Polish wedding bower.

Gertrude had added her own touches to the room. A lace cloth now graced the scarred table and she'd hung sheer draperies to cover the windows.

"It looks very nice," he told her.

She had gratefully accepted the compliment, but hadn't

admitted that such wifely tasks were things that she wanted to do for him.

They lay together in the languor of satisfaction. After a weekend of unplanned closeness without privacy, they had come together with a wanton hunger for the touch of the other. Their garments had been dispatched with undue haste. And they had fallen upon each other eagerly and without self-consciousness.

"I love those little sounds you make. They are part sigh, part squeal from way back inside you," he whispered as he entered her.

She moaned with pleasure and squirmed beneath him. "I'm not making those sounds, you are," she answered.

He chuckled, pleased at her words. "I confess to being noisy myself," he said. "But I don't see how I can make sounds come out of your throat."

Her eyes were dreamy, teasing. "When you press all the way inside," she explained, "you are so deep, you actually bounce against my voice box."

Grinning, he bounced against it a couple of times, as if to test her theory. It seemed a valid one.

"I love being inside you," he said. "I think about us being like this awake and sleeping. You cannot know how much I crave our union when I am away from it."

Her expression was soft, dreamy. "I do know," she answered. "I crave it. And I treasure it when it is here."

It was there, at that moment, a true union of bodies and of hearts and spirits. Their solemnity softened to sweetness as the pace of their coupling quickened.

She wrapped her legs around his waist and twisted. He laughed as he allowed her to roll him beneath her.

When she was on top, he reached up to clasp her dangling breasts in his hands.

"This is my favorite of the 'tricks,'" she told him. "I can

pretend I am the first woman jockey at a horse race." Her grin widened. "Or perhaps I appear more like Lady Godiva?"

"I don't care who is in the saddle," he told her, his eyes dreamy and his smile broad. "As long as we ride long and hard this afternoon."

And they did.

Mikolai was no longer uncertain about offending this woman of his heart, whose desires seemed so to complement his own. She was no shy, faint flower fearful of his manly needs. She was his lover and his partner and wanted from him part and parcel of what he had to give. He gave her everything. The "tricks" he knew, and even the ones he'd only heard about, had become savory platters in their feast of love. And when they had enjoyed until their strength ran out, they lay sated and content in the lassitude of their lasciviousness.

Later, at his insistence, she wore his shirt. It was meant to keep the chill of the room from her shoulders. Its effectiveness for that purpose was lessened somewhat because she hadn't bothered to button it. And Mikolai was content to allow it to gap open, giving him a pleasant view of her bosom, which he continued to tease and explore.

He himself was wearing nothing at all. And the chill made little impact upon him. Gertrude's hands, leisurely stroking his back, his buttocks, his thighs, kept him quite warm and unbelievably content.

They sighed together as one. It was wonderful being together, totally together. And with the world so far away. They held the privacy of the moment for as long as they could. But ultimately the world outside came sneaking in like a wily thief to steal what they had of value.

"Are Claire and Teddy still talking of marrying soon?" she asked him as she twirled the hair of his chest between her fingers.

Mikolai nodded. "Yes, they still are saying they want to wed right away." He shook his head. "I don't understand it," he admitted. "They say it as if they want me to put a stop to it."

"Will you?"

"No, I don't think so." He was thoughtful as he smoothed a stray curl from Gertrude's cheek. "How can I tell him no? I was younger than Teddy when I wed his mother," he said. "But I do wish they would wait."

"That's what I wish for them, too," Gertrude admitted with a loud, frustrated sigh. "But every time I try to talk to them about it, Claire gets very . . . I'm not sure what it is. It sometimes sounds almost as if she is challenging me to tell her not to. And yet she doesn't listen to my advice."

"I know what you mean," Mikolai said. "It is a puzzle, isn't it? They act as if they cannot wait to wed, but I have yet to see Teddy try to steal a kiss." He leaned down to Gertrude and placed a small sweet one upon her lips. "My son is a better gentleman than me," he said.

Gertrude smiled up at him. "They cannot feel as we do, Mikolai," she said. "I don't think anyone else in the world feels this."

Her words went straight to his heart and warmed him inside and out. He kissed her again. This time with more passion. She purred with pleasure from her throat. When he released her lips, she turned in his arms, pressing her soft, naked derriere tightly against the warmth of his genitals, and relaxed against him.

He rested his head in the crook of her neck and stroked her torso with strong, sure hands.

"George and Prudence are still not saying anything?" he asked.

Gertrude shook her head. "They are not saying *anything*. In fact they hardly ever talk at all, certainly never to each other, and I haven't heard them even mention Teddy's name."

"It's very odd."

"Yes, it is. And it's strange how Claire doesn't want to talk to them about it," Gertrude said. "She wants to talk to me."

"Apparently she already knows what they think," Mikolai observed. "And it doesn't sound as if they are much in favor of it."

"I'm sure they want Claire to be happy."

"And they don't think she would be happy with Teddy?" he asked.

"I think that they just don't know," she answered. "This whole thing has brought back a lot of bad memories for them, I think."

"Bad memories?"

Gertrude nodded and sighed. "I guess you didn't know George and Pru much when they first married."

"No, I didn't," he admitted. Adding thoughtfully, "In fact the first time I ever heard of Prudence was when I heard that she had married George."

"Pru's father was a farmer near Mansfield," Gertrude said.

"Really?" Mikolai was clearly surprised. "Mrs. Barkley certainly doesn't appear to be a farmer's daughter," he said.

"She's tried very hard not to be," Gertrude told him.

She wiggled against him as if trying to be even closer than human flesh would allow. It was not a motion meant as an enticement. She needed to be close to him, to feel safe in his arms as she told him a truth that she had never breathed to another living soul.

"I don't know exactly how it came about or what happened," she began softly as she stared out into the gloomy grayness of the rented room. "But George began seeing Pru when they were only seventeen. He began seeing her on the sly."

"Oh?"

"I didn't know a thing about it. Papa didn't either. He would never have approved. He wanted so much for George. I'm sure he planned on a brilliant marriage for his son."

"Sometimes things don't work out the way fathers plan them," Mikolai said, speaking from experience.

Gertrude sighed and voiced quiet agreement.

"When George rushed into a hasty wedding with a girl we hardly knew, I was puzzled," she admitted. "And when Pru spent the first months of their marriage hiding out in the house and crying, I thought it the most foolish thing that I had ever seen."

Gertrude chuckled lightly in self-derision. Mikolai pressed his lips lovingly against her hair.

"I didn't understand what was happening," she said. "I was older than both of them, but I had lived such a sheltered life, I didn't even really understand how the world worked."

"You are a thinker and a dreamer, Gertrude," Mikolai told her. "Why should you concern yourself with the mundane?"

"Perhaps because the world I live in is quite a mundane one," she answered. "I commented one morning upon how fat Pru had become since their wedding. She burst into tears, of course, but in those days she cried all the time. I just thought she was a crybaby. I probably wouldn't have understood even then had George not barked at me. He told me that she was carrying a child. Honestly, at that moment a faint summer breeze could have knocked me over."

"Ahhhh," Mikolai commented.

"You didn't know?" she asked.

"Truly, I never gave it a thought," he said. "I had so much happening in my own life, I hardly had time to be concerned about anyone else."

Gertrude nodded. "Well, I suppose you were the only one in Venice who didn't notice. For months and months I could think of nothing else. That's when I really began writing for the first time. I thought I was attempting escape through my stories. And yet I found myself constantly trying to put myself in her place. I wrote it all down. As if it were me instead of her. I tried to see how it might be, how it might feel, so that I could understand. I wanted to understand."

"And, of course, you did," Mikolai said with surety.

"Yes, ultimately I think I did understand. But the rest of the world was not so magnanimous."

"I'm sure they were not."

"The gossips had a field day with the Barkleys' seven-month baby," she said.

Mikolai nodded solemnly. "Your father must have been furious. He was so concerned with appearances," he said.

"Yes, I suppose he was upset, but in all honesty he never said a word. He actually seemed to like Pru. That was part of what was so difficult for me. I was very jealous of her at the time of their wedding. Papa seemed to think that Pru was the perfect woman in every way."

"That was good. It would have been so sad for everyone if he had blamed her."

"But he didn't. I don't think he really blamed either of them," Gertrude said. "I think we blamed him for most everything and he rarely turned the tables around."

Her words became soft and sorrowful once more as she spoke. "I had to remind George of that at Papa's funeral. He was really shaken. He was so frightened, so guilty. He felt that his shame had somehow sent Papa to an early grave."

"Poor George."

"Yes, poor George. That's why he's tried so hard, you know," Gertrude said. "He's done everything possible to follow in Papa's footsteps. He's been more rigid and uncompromising than Papa ever was. I suppose he's still trying to make up for that one mistake."

"And no matter what he does, in his own heart he is never quite able to atone," he said.

"You sound as if you know exactly how he feels," Gertrude said.

"I do, I do know exactly."

"You are talking about your wife."

"Yes," he answered. "How did you know?"

Gertrude turned in his arms so that she could look up into his eyes. She did look, for a long time, as the silence in the room was only broken by the sound of the rain against the window-sill.

"I didn't. But it seemed to me what I used to see in your expression. It was like a shadow on your happiness," she said, running her fingers tenderly along his cheekbone. "I have seen it many times in the past, but it is not there now."

"No, no it's not." Mikolai was surprised at his words. "It is gone," he said.

"How did you make it go away?"

He shook his head. "I just kept living," he said. "I just kept living year after year and it faded."

"And it finally just faded away?" she asked.

"No, it didn't fade away completely," he said thoughtfully. "I fell in love at last, for real. The guilt couldn't stand up against it."

She wrapped her arms around his neck. Their kiss was sweet, serene. "I love you, too," she whispered.

They were quiet together for long moments as they looked into each other's eyes. Here, within the safe haven of their little room, all things could be said, all words could be spoken. Love and truth were the same within these near-sacred confines.

Their solemn expressions lightened to joy and they actually laughed. He held her tightly, protectively, against him as if she were a precious jewel to be guarded and cherished. He kissed her again with passion, but with fun also. They rolled playfully on the bed like rollicking puppies before once again they took up the more serious discussion.

"So why do you think that the children's marriage has conjured up such bad memories for them?" Mikolai asked her.

Gertrude shrugged, uncertain. "I suppose because they were obviously once very much in love, the way that Teddy and Claire must be. But their marriage hasn't been a truly happy one."

"I am sorry for that."

"I am, too," she said, sighing. "It is as if they could never get past the guilt surrounding the circumstances enough to appreciate the good fortune they actually have in being married to each other."

"Do you envy them?" he asked in a breathy whisper against her ear.

"Envy them?"

"Being married," he said. "Do you envy them that good fortune?"

Gertrude sat up slightly and pulled the sides of the unbuttoned shirt together, the intimacy between them abruptly broken.

"No, of course I don't envy them, Mikolai," she said. "I told you that I never wanted to marry. Marriage isn't for everyone and I haven't changed my mind. Please don't think that I feel guilty about . . . about what we do here in the afternoons. I don't. I don't feel guilty at all. I guess I have a genuine streak of immorality in my nature, because I simply enjoy just exactly what we have together here. I love you. I've admitted that, but don't think that I, in any way, am trying to trap you or tie you to me. I don't have even the least desire to turn our little 'time out of real life' romantic affair into anything else."

She spoke the words hastily and without meeting his eyes.

He didn't hear the deception in them, however, because he was listening through his own bitter disappointment.

The labor was uneventful, as if giving birth to this child were event enough for the inhabitants of Barkley House. Papa paced the floor. All thoughts of disappointment and blame pushed from his heart by his anxiety.

In an upstairs bedroom, sweating and straining and suffering brought to life a new generation, a human being, a baby.

I had never seen a child born. I had no idea of how difficult and indelicate a thing it was to be. It is a wonder to me that women have managed through centuries to do such a thing. Around campfires and inside great medieval fortresses, near battlefields, and aboard sailing ships, women have taken this journey. This journey that brings life and death so close together, it is almost as if you can see the other side. You can taste the dust of eternity and feel the burst of flower's bloom.

I have seen this journey, now. I have seen it with my eyes and my heart, and I have felt it, though I fear it shall never be mine. It *was* then, almost. Because I wished it so, because I dreamed it so. Because I had written that it would be.

In a cry of agony and a plea of joy, a child burst forth from her mother's womb. A girl child. A beautiful girl child that was half her father and half her mother and in a way all mine.

"She is perfect, Prudence," I said.

She nodded through her tears. "Perfect," she agreed. "Perfect."

These are the last words that I shall write of this. This . . . this dream come true that was my lie and is my truth. Reality calls me from my written words and bids me to live, to live. If prose is to be that life, then let it be prose.

But the mix of life and lie is not prose, it is deceit of the highest nature.

As I hold this child to my breast and look down into her beautiful face, I promise that I shall strive never to covet and I vow to end this liaison of words that is beneath my dignity.

I shall release Mikolai Stefanski, whom I love and always shall, to the joys of his reality and I shall struggle to be a friend to the man that he is, not the man that I have wished him to be.

I shall take up my own destiny in my hands and shall mold it and shape it to the best of my abilities. And I will love what I have made because I have made it myself. How sad that I have waited for persons younger than I to teach me such lessons as these I have learned.

Claire's face screwed up in confusion. She went back over the contents of the diary's last page.

"'Reality calls me from my written words and bids me to live, to live. If prose is to be that life, then let it be prose. But the mix of life and lie is not prose, it is deceit of the highest nature,'" she read aloud. "Gee whiz, Aunt Gertrude. What on earth do you mean by that?" She reread it again and shook her head. "I hate it when you get so poetic."

Claire closed the journal and hid it once more under her bed. She put out the lamp and lay down in the darkness of her room. She had just read her own mother's description of the night that she was born. She wanted to luxuriate in those words to hold them to herself as warm comfort. But they were somehow unsubstantial. These words of the journal, these final words, were like no others in it. It was almost as if they were written by another person.

"She'd just had a baby, Claire," she admonished herself. "She probably wasn't really up to writing."

But though her head accepted that excuse, somehow her heart would not. In her heart there was something, something strange and dark and fearful. In her heart there was doubt.

She pushed those uncertainties from her thoughts. After all, she'd heard her own parents . . . that is, she'd heard Prudence and George admit it.

Her mother had cried. She had cried as if her heart were broken. It was hard to understand. Claire had never meant to hurt her. She had just wanted her real mother. Did Prudence think of herself as Claire's real mother? It was obvious that she did. When she'd skinned a knee or torn a dress, it had been Prudence whom she had run to. And it was Prudence who had always made everything right. When she'd had to have her tonsils out, it was Prudence who went to Dooley's barbershop with her. And it was Prudence who fed her crushed ice until the swelling went down. On the day when she had started her courses and thought she was dying of a bloody flux, it was Prudence who she had run to. And it was Prudence who had wiped her tears and congratulated her on becoming a grown-up woman.

"Mama," she whispered sadly into the darkness.

She loved Prudence. All right, she would admit that. And she loved George, too, grouchy bear that he was. She just wanted the truth. She wanted Aunt Gertrude to admit the truth and then everything could simply go back to the way it was. That's what she wanted, Claire decided. She wanted the truth to come out, once and for all, so they could all return to living the lives they had always led.

"She has to tell me," Claire whispered. "If she doesn't, I can never go on with my life."

The certain knowledge that the airing of the truth would irrevocably change her life she pushed away.

"I have to hear her claim me as her own," she said. "And

then I will go back to being just Claire. I'll be George and Pru's daughter again. I swear it. But I have to hear the truth first. I have to hear it. And I will," she declared. "I will hear those words, if it takes every scheme and plan in the book to do it!"

Claire Barkley had just made a vow of her own.

Chapter Seventeen

TEDDY STEFANSKI WAS having the best afternoon of his eighteen years of life. It was as if he'd been touched by a lucky star. He was playing the best football he had ever played.

It was cold and drizzly. Unrelenting rains earlier in the week had left the grassy field soggy. The damp afternoon had soaked through his navy jersey and streaks of mud were splattered across his face. But the chilly, wet misery didn't touch Teddy. He was happy. He was playing great football and he was confident that his team was going to win. And if they did, nothing could stop them. They were a shoo-in for the state championship.

As Teddy took his stance, he grinned at his opponent. His straight white teeth were like a beacon. When the quarterback called hike, Teddy moved in to block. He took a tough hit, but he held off the tacklers. He did his job and he did it well. The halfback made good yards, not enough for the first down, but enough to keep them in the game.

It was the middle of the final quarter. The score was tied at one touchdown apiece. The sideline crowd was a continuing roar of advice and approval. Venice High School was holding their own, but just barely.

Springfield was bigger and tougher. They outweighed the Venice team at every position. They had cunning and experience. They had a list of plays as long as a parson's coattail, and an ease of communication that would make you think they were all blood kin. All in all, they were an intimidating team.

But today, Teddy Stefanski couldn't be intimidated. He was not making eye-catching plays or scoring points. But he was playing the game and he was playing it well. He was doing the kind of tough, hard work that never gets noticed by the excited folks at the sidelines. The kind of work that makes all those exciting, glorious plays possible.

It was the fourth down. There was less than a yard to go and the team was loath to give up the ball. They were twenty yards into Springfield's territory. On the sidelines the coach looked nervous, but he let Parks, the quarterback, call the play.

Teddy leaned into the huddle, his hands upon his hips. Beside him, Rufus Bounty was puffing heavily. Rufe was the biggest man on the team. He outweighed Roy Bert by fifty pounds. He was a darn good guard, everyone agreed, but he had a passion for bread and potatoes that slowed him down late in the game. He couldn't be counted on to protect the passer. And passing was dangerous business at any stage of the game. In a fourth-down situation, it was foolish. Punting was the safest option. Give up the ball, deep, and work to hold the opponent on downs. It was what a cautious quarterback might call. But cautious quarterbacks didn't win championships. It was short yardage. A running play could work. If they could get the first down they would have a chance to score. If they scored again, Springfield would have very little time to do more than tie.

The situation called for a running play. Which one would he choose? A crisscross reverse might work on a less sophisticated opponent, or a quarterback sneak on a team less powerful. Teddy watched the nervous expression on the face of Paul Parks. It was *his* call and the team would back him up, even if he was wrong.

"Bent 'W' with a closed cousin," Paul hollered out decisively.

Teddy almost sighed with relief. It was a very good call. The kind of call he hoped he would have made himself had the choice been his. They were going to go for it. And they were going for it the hard way.

"Team!" they shouted in unison as they broke up the huddle and hurried to their positions.

The play was a modified wedge formation with a fullback option. It had worked for Pop Warner at Carlisle and for Charlie Daly at Army. Teddy prayed that it would work for Paul Parks at Venice High School.

The team lined up in a close-knit wing formation—the center and guards, point men at the ball. They would all surge forward as a unit. The wedge would ostensibly protect the quarterback inside it who would carry the ball, flanked by the two biggest men on the team.

If the wedge began to break up, Parks would have the option to hand off the ball to Teddy. As fullback, he would be in the tail and, with luck, could find room on the outside.

Teddy went down into his three-point stance, a squat that brought the balls of both feet and the fingers of one hand in contact with the ground. He looked up and found the eyes of an opponent. He grinned broadly through the mud on his face. He always thought a smile put the adversary at a mental disadvantage. Sure enough, the player that he was looking at appeared nonplussed by Teddy's unexpectedly friendly demeanor and hesitated, missing the instant of the snap, starting a second late. In football, a second could be enough.

Teddy did not hesitate. He moved in a precision of harmony with his teammates. The hike from center was perfect and the arrowhead-shaped formation moved forward together as one, according to plan. The play appeared guaranteed for success when suddenly a huge Springfield tackle, big as a house and twice as fast, appeared like magic in the middle of the Venice players. Teddy knew that Paul was going down, and surged forward.

Parks must have sensed he was coming. He turned at exactly the right time, in exactly the right place. He slipped Teddy the ball as easily as passing the potatoes at the dinner table.

Teddy tucked the pigskin carefully against his chest and looked ahead of him. Roy Bert Pugh, the center, was taking the hits repeatedly and fending off the incoming onslaught. Teddy's eyes widened. Just to Roy Bert's right was a hole in the defenders' line nearly as big as the state of Texas.

Teddy didn't wait long enough to ask himself if it was a mirage. He ran for it. He'd made five yards before the defenders even realized that he had the ball. He had the first down. He had done his job. But he could see the goalpost in the distance and somehow the fire of gridiron ambition burned inside of him. He made a run for it. He could hear the crowds howling for joy. He felt the breath of the man behind him against his neck.

Ten yards, he'd made ten yards. He felt as if he had run ten miles. The defender was on his back. He was going down. He saw the ground heading toward him, but he was smiling.

Somehow, though Teddy was never to recall it exactly, his shoe caught in the turf. The momentum of the man on his back pulled his body farther than his foot was able to go. He felt a strange pop from inside his knee. It was almost audible. His mind had barely registered what it might be when the pain arrived in a wave of black nausea. He didn't see anything else.

Teddy came to, in a hazy recognition of where he was, as the tacklers were getting to their feet. He had only remembered the one, but a half dozen seemed piled on top of him. His first thought was for the football. It was still tucked tightly under him. He sighed with relief. That movement caused the pain to shoot through him once more. He almost passed out again.

His left leg was throbbing so violently, it was as if it had suddenly sprouted lungs, inhaling and exhaling in excruciating torture.

"Are you okay?" he heard someone ask. The voice seemed far away and faint. Not nearly as loud as the ringing in his ears.

"My knee," he answered. His voice sounded to him like a soprano, like he was a little kid. He repeated himself, careful this time to speak in his normal tone. "I've hurt my knee."

It seemed like an hour that he lay there in the middle of the field, hurting. People were running around, talking, looking down at him. The referee had made a big production of standing over him and blowing the whistle.

"Get back! Get back! Give him some air!" he heard the coach yelling at the players as he made his way to Teddy's side.

"I've hurt my knee, Coach," he said. His voice sounded like a soprano again and it embarrassed him. He added an angry, "Damn it!" to his announcement, just so he wouldn't sound so much like a baby.

"No need for cursing, Teddy," Coach said. "The doc is here. He's going to take a look at you. He'll say whether you can finish out the game."

The doctor knelt down beside him and picked up Teddy's leg. The pain shot up his body like a rifle. He threw his head back and gritted his teeth against the scream that was trying to escape him. Teddy could have told the coach he wasn't going to finish the game. But he was expending all his energy trying not to sob like a baby.

A very familiar face entered his line of version. He saw his father then, bending over him, his face lined with worry. Teddy immediately felt stronger, safer.

"What are you doing here? Fathers can't be on the field," he muttered vaguely.

His father answered him. He knelt down beside him and held his head, wiping the sweat from Teddy's brow with his handkerchief. He was talking, calmly, evenly. But Teddy didn't have a clue to what he might be saying. His words were Polish and the only ones Teddy recognized were "*Ja*" and "Teodor."

Through his pain, the young man almost smiled. His father never deliberately spoke Polish. But at times he drifted into it when he was angry or worried. Teddy knew that his father must be very frightened to be speaking it to him now.

"I'm okay, Father," he said. "I'm okay, *Tatus*."

Teddy's use of the Polish word for daddy, a word Teddy hadn't used since he was a child, seemed to reassure his father. He smiled lovingly down at his son and then turned to gruffly question the physician.

"What is wrong with my son, Doctor?" he asked.

"Well, the boy is in a lot of pain." Doc Ponder stated the obvious with professional pompousness.

"We can see that, Doc," Coach said impatiently. "Do you think his knee is broken?"

"Could be," the doctor admitted.

"Let's get him to the sidelines," the coach said. "That way we can at least get on with the game. Teddy, do you think you can walk off the field?"

Teddy wasn't sure if he could even sit up without fainting again, but he wasn't given a chance to answer.

"I will carry him," his father said. "I will carry him to make sure that he doesn't hurt himself more."

Gently Mikolai Stefanski, immigrant, businessman, and loving father, swept his son up into his arms as if he were a small boy, not the fullback for the high school.

Teddy relaxed against him, safe in his father's arms. The pain was biting, clawing. He had trouble remaining conscious. But he fought the blackness and the nausea. He fought it because that's what his father would have done.

As he was carried across the field he heard his father speaking to the doctor. "I will take my Teodor home and put him into bed. You come with me and see to him."

"Sure, Stefanski, I'll be over to your house," Doc answered. "I'll come just as soon as the game is over."

"You will come now."

Mikolai's words were spoken softly and without the slightest hint of threat. But they were stated with such authority that the doctor's eyes nearly bugged out of his head. Teddy almost smiled. He knew that tone. He'd heard it more than a time or two himself.

"Sure, Mr. Stefanski, sure. I'll come with you right now."

"You will be fine, Teodor," his father whispered to him.

Mikolai Stefanski hurried to the Packard. Doc Ponder glanced back longingly at the game that had resumed, then followed in his wake.

"Claire, will you calm down," Gertrude ordered, not for the first time. "We are all worried, but you just can't get yourself in such a state."

The young woman had been so impatient with the speed of the Interurban, Gertrude had feared she would jump off and start pushing any second. Now, at last arriving home, she had run across the yard and took the steps up the porch two at a time.

Her niece was understandably worried. Gertrude was also. Her heart had gone straight to her throat when she had seen that Teddy—strong, handsome, young Teddy—was not getting up. On the sidelines, powerless, Gertrude had wrung her hands and watched. When she had seen Mikolai sweep his son into his arms, love and anxiety had welded themselves together into a fierce longing. It was only with great control that she managed not to race toward the man she loved, to throw her arms around him, to publicly declare her feelings for him and beg to share his burdens.

But she hadn't run to him. He had his son upon his mind and certainly didn't need the affections of his *mistress* at such an

inopportune time. Mistress. She said the word over again inside
her head. The term was lowering. The image it conjured in her
mind was even more so. A mistress could have a man's
attention. She could have a man's body. She could even have
a man's love. But she could not share his burdens. A man
wouldn't ask help of his mistress. For help, he had the doctor.
That was who Mikolai Stefanski needed today, not his mistress.

She had watched him lay Teddy in the backseat of the
Packard. The game had already resumed, but Gertrude couldn't
turn her attention to it until the shiny yellow-and-brown car had
disappeared from view.

Determinedly she willed her gaze back to the game. But she
could no longer see it. Plays were run. Whistles blew. Cheers
were cried. All she could see was the man who she loved, the
man who loved her, facing a crisis alone.

"Aunt Gertrude, I know what I am doing," Claire said
adamantly as she charged through the front door of the Barkley
house. "I am not 'in a state,' I simply have obligations to fulfill.
Teddy is . . . Teddy is very important in my life and I'm
going to change my clothes and go over there this very minute.
And no one, no one, Aunt Gertrude, is going to stop me!"

Her tone had gotten progressively higher throughout her
speech and by the end of it she was near yelling as she stepped
into the foyer.

"Keep your voice down!"

The shout startled them both. Gertrude and Claire came to an
abrupt halt. Gertrude lay a hand against her heart and stared
accusingly at George Barkley, who was standing like a
vengeful guard in the doorway of the front parlor.

"George, what is wrong? You scared the life out of me,"
Gertrude complained.

"Chicken pox."

"What?" The question came from both women in unison.

"Chicken pox." George shook his head as if he couldn't believe his own words. "Lester has come down with chicken pox. Pru's got him upstairs trying to take care of him. You'd think it was the plague with the fuss that boy puts up. He has been a whining bundle of misery all afternoon."

George ruffled his hair. It was a tired, anxious gesture of exhaustion that was familiar, but one that Gertrude hadn't seen in many years. The staid Barkley banker looked this afternoon much more like the devilish younger brother Gertrude remembered from her own youth.

"Is Lester going to be all right?" she asked.

George nodded. "Prudence has finally got him quieted," he said. "But I don't want you two to wake him."

"When did this happen?" Gertrude asked. "Lester seemed very much his usual self this morning."

George shrugged. "Prudence noticed him scratching at luncheon. She feared that he might have lice. She tried to catch him for a bath, but he was more wily than usual."

"I know how he can be," Gertrude admitted.

"She finally had to ask me for help," he said. "I chased that rascal all over this end of town. That's why I didn't make it to the football game. When I finally got ahold of him and I got his shirt off, his back and stomach were covered with the itchy things."

"Poor Lester," Gertrude said.

George nodded in agreement. "He's pretty miserable. We salved the little scamp in calamine, but you remember that it doesn't really help."

"No, I don't remember," Gertrude replied as she removed her hat and coat and hung them on the hall tree. "I never had the chicken pox, George, you did."

"Oh Lord, that's right, Gerty," her brother said, his forehead wrinkling thoughtfully. "You were at Aunt Hilly's in Virginia that summer. I hope you don't catch it now."

"Now? Surely I wouldn't catch it now?" Gertrude's tone indicated the absurdity of the idea. "It's a *children's* disease."

"Adults get chicken pox, too," her brother said.

"Well, I won't," she answered with certainty that she hoped would put the matter to rest.

"I haven't had chicken pox either," Claire announced in horror.

George shook his head. "Then Gertrude should keep you away from here."

"Keep her away from here?"

"We don't want her to become ill, too. You may think that you are immune, but how can you be sure that she is?" he said emphatically. "I don't think Pru could handle two patients at once."

Claire firmed her jaw furiously and glared up the stairway with malice. "If that Lester Barkley gives me the chicken pox, I swear I will pull out every hair on his head and stuff them all down his throat."

"Claire!" Gertrude admonished her. "Your brother is ill. I'm sure he wouldn't wish his troubles upon you."

"Oh, yes, he would," she insisted. "Lester the Pester is the bane of my existence."

"Little brothers are just like that," Gertrude assured her as she cast a eye at her own little brother leaning heavily against the door frame. In his exhaustion he looked so much like her George of long ago.

As if he could read her thoughts, he grinned at her. "This is no time to settle old debts, Gerty," he said. "I'll do what I can to help Pru and you two must stay away from the contagion, if possible."

"That's no problem for me," Claire assured him.

"I really don't think there is that much danger," Gertrude assured him.

George nodded. "Still, I'd hate for you two to come down

with it. You two stay somewhere else for a day or two. Just until the little scamp is over the worst of it."

"I hardly think that is necessary," Gertrude assured him. "We'll simply keep out of Lester's room and all will be fine."

"No, I think it better for you to stay away," George said firmly. "Just gather up some clothing and go. I'm sure you can stay with the Wentworths."

Gertrude was horrified. "I do not wish to stay with the Wentworths," she stated emphatically.

He shrugged. "Well, you can stay at the Boston Hotel if you like, but you should not stay here."

"I don't think I'd want to do that either," Gertrude answered.

"Well," Claire blurted in. "You two can argue this without me. Right now I've got to go see about Teddy."

"Teddy?"

"He was injured at the football game."

George's expression reflected concern. "Badly?"

"We don't know. Mikol—ah, Mr. Stefanski had to carry him off the field," she said. Just saying the words aloud caused her lip to tremble. Determinedly she stiffened it. This was no time for emotional displays.

"That doesn't sound good at all," George said.

"The other boys on the team were saying that he'd hurt his knee," she told him. "The doctor went with him, so nobody really knows a thing."

"Did we win the game?" George asked.

Gertrude stared at him mutely for a moment. Her mind was a blank. She couldn't remember how the game turned out.

"Oh, yes," Claire piped in excitedly. "And it was just terrific. Teddy's run set up the touchdown."

"Yes, that's right," Gertrude agreed, sighing with relief that her memory hadn't deserted her completely. "I was so proud."

Claire became impatient once more. "I can't stay here

worrying about Lester Barkley," she said with acidic haughtiness. "Teddy is hurt. I have to go to him."

Her words were crisp and stated with high drama. She took the first three steps of the stairway. Stopping, she turned at the landing. She looked back down at the adults still standing in the foyer. Her expression was somehow accusing. "Of course, you both understand that, don't you," she said. "You realize why I must go."

Her near-angry expression was full of meaning that escaped both of the persons for which it was intended. She stared at them long and hard as if she expected some sort of reply, some sort of explanation.

Gertrude and George could only answer her with two puzzled glances. Her face screwed up in frustration and her tone was accusing as she headed up the stairs.

"Come help me change, Aunt Gertrude," she said. "I want to see Teddy."

Gertrude realized that she wanted to see him, too. Just to assure herself that he was all right, she insisted to herself. But even more than that, she wanted to see Mikolai. She wanted to assure herself that Mikolai was all right, too.

"I'll need to go with you, of course," she said, surprising both her brother and Claire. "You can't go to a gentleman's house without a chaperone."

Chapter Eighteen

CLAIRE'S KNOCK UPON the front door of the bright red brick Stefanski house was forthright and persistent. Gertrude held back, somewhat uncertain. She loved Mikolai Stefanski. She wanted to be there. But she was not altogether sure of her welcome. Her concern heightened when Doc Ponder, not Mikolai, opened the door.

"Afternoon, Claire, afternoon, Gertrude," he said.

He was carrying his leather satchel, as if he were about to leave. But he stood proprietarily in the doorway looking down his long, thin nose at the women upon the porch. "Not the best time to come calling, ladies. Who won the game?"

"We did," Claire answered. "It was terrific. How is Teddy?"

The doctor shrugged. "Knee's shattered, that's not too good," he said. "Doubt the boy will get to play again this season."

"But he will walk," Gertrude said, deliberately keeping her tone even.

"Walk? My yes, he'll walk again. Probably run, too. I told Stefanski that I'd call a specialist I know in St. Louis. See if the man can take the train up here to have a look at him. He's a strong young man. That European peasant stock usually is. Breed them strong, they do, to work in the fields, you know. The patrician families, the people of importance, have a more delicate constitution. Do you read Darwin, Gertrude? No, of course you don't. The man has a point, he certainly has a point.

Not all of it, of course. He's limited in his vision." The doctor shook his head. "My own dear boys," he said sadly. "Why, I've had to use every bit of my skills just to keep them alive."

Gertrude was impatient with the doctor's theories this afternoon and interrupted him curtly. "But you think Teddy will recover soon. There will be no lasting effects from this, will there?"

"Certainly not," Doc assured her. "He'll be fine, of course. But I don't know about playing football."

"He won't be able to play football?" Claire seemed shocked at the pronouncement.

"He certainly won't play anymore this year," the doctor said. "It's a blow, a real blow. The team really needs him. Especially if we are going to play for the state championship. I wish my Delfane could play. I do wish it very much. Not in the boy's nature, of course. As I explained, the Ponders came from the ruling classes. All our breeding went to leadership and intelligence. Not a brawny, gladiator type among us."

"Can I go up and see him?" Claire directed her question to her aunt, but it was the doctor who replied.

"What? Oh . . . I don't think so. That's not at all the thing, for a girl to visit a young man in his sick bed," the doctor told her. "You just go home and tend to your own business and when Teddy is well enough to come downstairs you can visit him in his parlor."

Claire's expression hardened and Gertrude could see from her stance that she was ready to do battle.

"Now, Dr. Ponder," Gertrude began carefully. "I think you don't quite understand, Claire and Teddy are very close and it is just—"

The doctor tutted disapprovingly. "It's not done, Gertrude," he said. "I don't have to ask my wife to know that. I realize that you, Gertrude, have always just proceeded however you saw fit. But you are a Barkley and folks have forgiven you your impetuousness because of that nature."

"Claire is a Barkley, too, Doctor," Gertrude said evenly.

"Oh yes, but she's a Margrove, also, and with mixing among the lower classes, why, we've already seen what kind of lack of personal restraint that can result."

Gertrude's right hand balled into a fist and she was quite ready to plant that fist firmly in the middle of the doctor's long patrician nose. Only the arrival of Mikolai at the door kept her from doing so.

"Miss Gertrude! Claire! I'm so glad you're here!"

Mikolai stepped out onto the porch, effectively pushing the doctor out of the way. "Teddy is looking much better."

"Oh, we are so glad," Gertrude whispered.

"The Barkley ladies tell me that we won the game," the doctor announced. The man seemed totally unaware of the level of tension he had created on the porch. "I'll bet Teddy will be glad to hear that."

"Yes," Mikolai agreed. "I'm sure that he will. Claire, why don't you run upstairs and tell him."

"But—" the doctor began, but wasn't given time to finish.

"Yes, I want to tell him," she said as she hurried past the adults into the house.

"His room is the first one to the left at the top of the stairs," Mikolai called after her.

The doctor's brow furrowed and he looked at Mikolai in reproach. "That's not quite the thing, Stefanski. Letting young people be alone that way."

Mikolai's reply was a long, hard look. "My son just had his knee twisted and torn, Doc," he said quietly. "I don't think he'll be attempting to take liberties with Miss Claire."

"Well, no, of course not," the doctor agreed. "But I did hear about that little peccadillo at the victory dance. Considering the history of that young lady and the way things look . . ."

Stefanski's heavy brow drew together in an expression that Gertrude thought might be kindred to the wrath of God. Although the doctor was a good two inches taller, Mikolai seemed suddenly to tower over him as an uncomfortable silence reigned upon the porch for a long moment.

"In my family and in my house, Doctor," he stated with terse, stern politeness, "I have always been more concerned with the way things *are* rather than the way that they *look*."

The doctor's eyes were wide. Mikolai's stance was threatening. Instinctively Gertrude stepped between the two men.

"I'm here as Claire's chaperone, of course," she announced with a light reassuring smile.

Just moments earlier she had wanted to bloody the good doctor's nose. But she did not want Mikolai to do it. She hoped that her manner would dissolve the tension that swirled around them.

"So I suppose I had better get at my job. So good to see you, Doc," she said, effectively dismissing the man. "You will call Mr. Stefanski as soon as you hear from the specialist in St. Louis, won't you?"

Gertrude half led, half dragged Mikolai back into his own house and shut the door in the doctor's face. Still stiff and shaking, Mikolai stared through the round glass of the door and watched as Doc Ponder made his way down the steps and out to the trolley stop. His jaw was set hard and he continued to look as if he was ready to do some bodily damage upon someone.

"That sorry excuse for a doctor is the worst gossip in this town," he said, seething.

"Let it go, darling," Gertrude whispered to him. "The foolish man is not worth the effort."

Mikolai turned away from the door to look into Gertrude's eyes. His icy hard expression melted in the warmth of her eyes and he wrapped his arms around her and pulled her to his chest.

"Oh, Gertrude, I'm so glad you're here," he whispered.

She needed to hear those words from him. She pressed her body tightly against him. She felt his need for her. Not just the physical need that would be expected. She could feel his heart calling out to her. His emotional need for her at that moment far exceeded any fleshly desire. As he held her close, he garnered strength from their embrace. And as quickly and certainly as he gleaned it from her, he gave it back.

"I wanted to come to you on the field," she confessed. "I was anxious for you."

He removed her hat from her head and tossed it to the floor. Lovingly he stroked the short, dark curls that lay tousled around her face.

"I was scared," he said quietly. "I was so scared. I needed just to hold you, Gertrude. I needed to hold you so very much."

She needed it, too. She needed to be with him, to help him, to love him. She had thought she might not be welcome. She scoffed at her own foolishness now. His arms were her sanctuary. She felt the rightness of it. His arms were exactly where she should be.

Sighing heavily, he leaned back against the wall. He was weary in mind and body and it was as if he could no longer stand up on his own. He would not release his hold upon her, and brought her enfolded in his arms to rest against him and the solid security of the sturdy wall of brick that he had constructed. She felt the warm strength of his embrace and the cool, slick softness of his silk vest beneath her cheek.

He reached down to take her chin between his fingers and raised her face to his lips. "Gertrude, my sweet Gertrude," he murmured before they were both lost in a kiss that was more possessive than passionate.

Her heart beat with wild excitement at the dominance of his mouth upon her own. Their kisses in the secret little room had been poetry and preludes. This melding of lips was different. It was as if he were trying to mark her with his touch, brand her with his own stern, unyielding will. She sighed against him, compliant—even complicit—in his bid of ownership. She reveled in it.

His hands caressed her, coaxed her, but not in a way that was meant to entice. He explored her like a sentimental traveler who had been across these plains and valleys many times. He knew the geography very well, and called the land his own.

It was easy, so easy to give herself over, totally, to make herself a part of him, to make him a part of her. It was so easy. Fear crept in.

"Mikolai, the children," she said as she pulled away. "If Claire were to come down those stairs, think how this would look to her."

There were still stars in his eyes, but she could not see them. He gave his answer like a rough caress against her throat. "Have I not already said today that in my house we care about what *is*, not about how it looks."

His statement soothed her, but her fear kept her wary, deliberately wary.

"I *am* your mistress, Mikolai, but I would just as well that Claire did not know it," she told him.

Her words were like cold water upon him and he pulled away from her. Looking down into her eyes, his expression was troubled, almost hurt.

"My 'mistress'? I hate that word," he said. "It is a coarse word. That word . . . that word is not what you are to me, Gertrude."

She couldn't like it either. Its connotation of cold sin and unfeeling illicitness robbed her of her dignity and degraded her most tender feelings.

"There is no other word," she said evenly. "It is the truth, Mikolai. I will not deny it."

He stroked her temple as if to soften the lines of determination that he found there.

"I went into this with my eyes open," she continued. "I will not be squeamish about the language now."

He folded her into his arms once more, protectively. "There must be a better word for what you are to me," Mikolai insisted. "There has to be a better word."

She shook her head. "No, in English there is not," she said.

He held her tightly, protectively. The hard shell of her brave stance felt to be crumbling within the tenderness of his embrace. "Maybe in Polish they have a gentler term."

He looked down at her for a long moment. Slowly, with warmth of genuine feeling, a smile spread across his face. "Yes," he said. "In Polish there is a word, a better word." He ran one long, loving finger down the side of her face and across the soft tenderness of her lower lip. "It speaks my feelings better than this crude English."

"What is it?" she asked him.

"*Zona.*"

"*Zona,*" Gertrude tried the word upon her tongue. It did rest gently upon the ear without any of the coldness of the English term. "I like the sound of it. It means mistress?"

He hesitated. "It means . . . it means what you are to me."

His eyes glowed with feeling and she trembled in his arms. "Then call me that," she said, burying her face in the smooth silk of his vest once more.

"Yes, I will call you my *zona,*" he said.

"Have you ever called other women that?" she asked him, not able to meet his eyes.

His brows furrowed slightly. "Yes, once, only once, and very long ago, I called a woman my *zona.*" He took her hand and brought it to his lips. "But," he said, "I never felt for her the things that I feel for you. I never really knew this word until I knew you."

❦   ❦   ❦

"Teddy?" Claire's voice was anxious as she slipped into the darkly masculine room at the top of the stairs.

"Claire?" His voice sounded tired, but nothing more sinister.

"Teddy, are you all right?" she asked. The high-rising sleigh-style mahogany bed was almost waist-high to her. He lay sprawled across it, only the top of his nightshirt visible above the crisp muslin sheets.

"Yes, I think so," he answered, rubbing his eyes sleepily. "Doc gave me some powders for the pain."

She nodded gravely. "Do they make you feel better?"

"No, not really better." His tone was groggy and more than a little bit irritable. "I'm just almost too sleepy to care about how it hurts."

"It hurts pretty bad, I guess," she said softly.

"Pretty bad," he agreed.

"Worse than when I hit you in the shin with the croquet mallet?"

He gave a light chuckle.

A smile had been all that she had hoped for.

"I don't know if it was worse," he said. "I didn't get any pain powders that time."

She rolled her eyes dramatically. But she was glad that he was well enough to feel like teasing back. "Do you need to sleep?" she asked. "Do you want me to go?"

"No, no, Claire," he said. "I don't think I can sleep with this knee throbbing like it is. You're my best friend, I guess. I'm glad that you came."

"I had to come. And I'm more than your best friend, you're my brother, remember," she said.

"You aren't likely to let me forget," he said. "Open those drapes, will you? Old Doc Ponder seems to think I'll rest better if this room is as dark as the grave."

"It *is* pretty gloomy in here," she admitted.

"Too gloomy for me," he said. "It's gray enough outside without hiding the light of day completely."

Claire hurried to the window and threw back the heavy damask draperies. The late-afternoon sun was puny, but at least the drizzle had stopped.

"Here comes the Interurban," she said. The window faced the front yard and had an unobstructed view of Main Street.

"Must be twenty after," Teddy told her. "I've never needed a clock in my room, I wake up every morning to the buzz and rattle of the tracks."

Claire shot him a quick grin as she secured the draperies in place with their gold braid sash. From the corner of her eye she could see the doctor making his way through the front gate.

"Doc is leaving," she said. She giggled lightly. "He's running to make the trolley. He looks like a fool."

"He *is* a fool," Teddy said with conviction. "He jerked my leg around like it wasn't even attached to me. And he told me not to worry about healing up. He said the bones of 'agrarian peons' always knit well." Teddy snorted in disgust. "I'd like to pee on him!"

Claire giggled.

"You're laughing," he accused. "You're laughing, and I thought that idiot was likely to kill me."

His statement made Claire turn around abruptly. Her expression belligerent, she glared at the young man in the bed. "He'd better not, and you'd better not let him. I've invested a lot of time in you, Teddy Stefanski. First as a friend and now as a brother. I'm not about to let you just up and leave me here with everything still to be sorted out."

"Oh, I see," he said. "You don't care about me, you just want to make sure that your latest scheme works."

She stomped across the room to stand over his bed, hands on hips. Glaring down at him in an expression of feigned fury, she snarled, "You'd better hush your mouth, or I'm going to make what that Springfield tackler you ran into seem like nothing of any importance."

Teddy grinned. "I can count on you, Claire. You never cajole when you can threaten."

"Oh, you!" she snapped and then grinned back at him. Her tone softened. "You scared me, you idiot," she said. "What were you trying to do? Get yourself killed over a stupid football game?"

"Not killed, never that," he answered with good humor. "Just crippled enough to garner sympathy from all the pretty girls."

She raised a questioning eyebrow. "What about the sympathy of the ugly girls?" she asked.

He shrugged. "I'll take that, too."

"So you have *my* sympathy, for what it's worth," she said.

"Well, it's worth a lot to me."

She pulled a chair up to his bedside and seated herself beside him.

"So we won, huh," he said.

"We did. And if you weren't so full of yourself already, I'd tell you that it was your run that set up the score."

"But I'm so full of myself that you're not going to tell me that."

"No, I'm not saying a word about it."

"Looks like we'll win state then."

"Yes, we'll win state," she said. "But it won't be the same if you don't play."

Teddy shrugged and screwed up his face thoughtfully. "It won't be the same for me, either."

Claire's expression became grim. "Doc says you won't play football again."

Teddy raised an eyebrow. "I think my father is supposed to give me that kind of bad news," he said.

"He's probably waiting to hear from the specialist," she said. "But I thought you'd kind of want to know what's coming."

Shrugging agreement, Teddy nodded thoughtfully at her words.

"Are you very sad?" she asked.

He didn't answer for a long minute. "Yes, I'm sad," he said. "But I'm a little bit excited, too."

"Excited?"

"Well, you know I had things sort of planned out. I'd go to Notre Dame and I'd play football for Coach Harper and I'd see the world."

"Yes, that was always the plan," she agreed.

"But now the plan will have to change."

"And that's exciting?" She was looking at him quizzically.

"It can be. I thought up one whole life for myself. Now I get to think up another."

"Do you want another?"

He nodded. "Yes, maybe I do. I haven't ever really wanted to head back East. I've never really wanted to see the world that much."

"But of course you have, Teddy," she said. "We've always talked about it."

"I know we have," he admitted. "But the truth is that I'm really interested in my father's business and Venice is my home. I never really want to live anywhere else."

Claire's eyes widened, her tone was shocked. "You don't want to leave Venice? I can hardly wait to get out of this town."

"I know *you* can't, Claire," he said. "And I'm thrilled for you. I know that you'll have a terrific time in some big city somewhere."

"I sure will," she said confidently. "There is a whole world out there and I want to see and be a part of every bit of it."

He grinned at her. "I know you do," he said. "You've always been more interested in that sort of thing than I have. After all, it was you who really came up with the Notre Dame plan anyway."

"I did?"

"Of course you did," Teddy said, scoffing at her surprise. "You've come up with every idea I've ever taken up in my life."

She nodded thoughtfully. "Yes, I guess that's true. So now I get to come up with another one."

"No," he said firmly. "This time I want the plan to be mine."

She wrinkled her nose at him disapprovingly and then laughed. "Okay," she said. "So what's the plan?"

"I think I'm going to go to the state university in Columbia and study architecture," he said. "I can get a good education there and won't be so far from home. I can come back and work at the brickyards whenever I'm needed. As soon as I graduate, we can expand the business. Brick is a building material whose time is passing quickly. The future is all concrete and steel and I want to be there."

Claire looked at Teddy as if she'd never really seen him before. "This is really what you want, isn't it? You really just want to be a part of your father's business. It's what you've always wanted."

"Yes, I think it is."

"So you're glad this terrible thing has happened to you."

"No," he said. "I'm not really glad. I love playing football. I'll miss it. But I have to see things as they are. I have to look at fate in terms of its opportunities. This is an opportunity for me to do something different."

Claire was silent, thoughtful as she stared at him. Finally she nodded. "You know, I think I understand what you're saying. I've kind of been there, too, you know."

"Have you?"

"When I found out you were my brother, well, it really changed all the plans I'd ever had for myself. If you think I had *your* life lined up like a row of dominoes, I truly had mine in order. And when I discovered Aunt Gertrude's journal, well, it just turned everything topsy-turvy." She sighed heavily and shook her head. "But, like you, I'm looking for those opportunities."

"Good girl," Teddy congratulated her. He paused for a moment reflecting on what she had said.

"What kind of plans did the journal change?" he asked.

"Well," she hesitated, laughing a little. "Honestly, Teddy, I planned to marry you."

"Marry me!" He sat bolt upright in bed and then groaned out loud at the pain his sudden movement caused.

"Don't upset yourself," she said. "Of course, I don't plan that anymore."

"For heaven's sake, Claire," he said. "You didn't really ever think that we'd be married."

"Well, of course I did. And we would have. I decided that I was going to marry you before we were even in grammar school."

"You decided you were going to marry me before we even went to grammar school!"

"I just said that, didn't I?"

Teddy was shaking his head in disbelief. "We never would have gotten married," he insisted firmly.

"Of course, we would have," she said. "We get along so well together, we were perfect for each other. Just two peas in a pod from the time we were babes, everybody said so. As soon as you'd finished college and were ready to see the world, I was going to be there to see it with you."

"I wasn't going to get any say in this? You were just going to pick the pod and I was going to have to live in it?"

"Oh, Teddy, don't get snarly."

"Why shouldn't I get snarly? You planned my whole life without ever thinking about what I might want."

"Teddy, don't be silly," she scoffed. "You know that you always want what I want."

"Claire, you really think you know everything about everybody, don't you?" he said.

"Not everybody, just most everybody," she corrected. "I don't know why you're in such a snit. You're my brother now, so we can't marry."

"What a narrow escape," he said snidely.

"Don't be rude, Teddy. You're my brother and I love you. I only want what's best for you and now you can go to college here in Missouri and marry Olive Widmeyer. Everything has worked out perfectly."

"Olive Widmeyer! I'd never marry Olive Widmeyer. She makes me nervous," he said. "I shouldn't have even gone to the dance with her. And I wouldn't have if you hadn't put me up to it. I could never marry her. We'd never be comfortable together."

"Sure you will," she said, patting him reassuringly. "After you're married it will all work out fine."

"Claire—"

"We don't have to talk about that now. We've got more important things to consider."

"Like what?"

"Like getting the truth between us and our parents settled once and for all," she said. "I have a plan."

"I don't think I'm going to like this."

"I know. But you'll go along with it anyway."

Chapter Nineteen

❧❧

"I'm not leaving here," Claire stated obstinately. "I won't leave Teddy in his hour of need."

Gertrude and Mikolai looked at each other in stunned disbelief. They stood in the center of Teddy's bedroom, brightly lit by the electric bracket lamps on each wall. Young Miss Barkley was seated in a chair at his bedside, looking extremely composed and sounding extremely confident. The young people had been allowed almost a full hour of time alone. Gertrude and Mikolai should never have permitted such a lengthy piece of privacy, but caught up in their own private drama, the minutes had slipped by.

"Claire, darling," Gertrude began gently. "We all understand how upset you must be. You've had a nasty scare today, but you simply cannot stay here with Teddy."

"He needs me, Aunt Gertrude," she said. "And I'm staying."

"You needn't worry about my son," Mikolai told her, smiling kindly at her dutiful possessiveness. "He is not in any danger and I am here to watch over him. It's a job I've been glad to do for many years."

"I have to be here myself," she said emphatically. "Teddy's had a terrible blow today. I don't mean just breaking his kneecap. I've told him that he'll never play football again."

Mikolai's expression grew weary. "I was going to tell you myself, son," he said quietly.

"I know you were," Teddy answered. "But Claire has

already told me, and truthfully, I think I understood that before I ever left the field today."

"I am so very sorry," Mikolai said.

"Please, Father," he said. "I'm okay. I don't mind, really, I—" Teddy glanced over at Claire and stuttered. "I . . . I . . . I just need to have Claire with me."

"But Teddy—"

"Not in *here*," he said. "I don't mean she must be in this room. But I want her close by. Can't she just stay in the guest room?"

"Of course I can, Teddy," Claire answered for Mikolai. "And that is exactly what I intend."

"Claire, this just isn't done," Gertrude said.

Her niece smiled up at her in that strange and curious way she had of late. "I must take after you, Aunt Gertrude," she said. "I do what I think I should do. I don't hold myself to the dictates of society."

"That's all well and good, Claire," Gertrude replied. "And I think that you, that everyone, should stand up to convention when you think it is necessary. But at this moment, for this reason, Claire darling, it is *not* necessary."

"But I *want* to stay," she said. "And Teddy wants me to, don't you?"

"Yes, I definitely think that she should stay," he said, raising up slightly in bed. His color was much improved from earlier in the evening and the pain in his leg was either ebbing considerably or masked by the powders the doctor had given him.

"Claire must stay with me," Teddy said decisively. "But we needn't throw good sense completely out the window."

"What do you mean?"

"You should stay, too, Miss Gertrude," he said. "You are Claire's chaperone, after all."

"I couldn't stay here." She was clearly horrified. "Two single women do not stay in a house with two single men."

"Well, suit yourself, Aunt Gertrude," Claire said. "I can understand that you might want to safeguard your own reputation, so please don't worry about mine."

"Claire, I—"

"Please, Aunt Gertrude, Mr. Stefanski, I think we should let Teddy rest now. This has all been too much for him."

She leaned forward to pat the young man consolingly upon the arm. Teddy smiled up at her as if she were his private guardian angel.

"Why don't you two continue your conversation in the hallway," Claire suggested. "That way you can say everything that you wish, without disturbing our patient."

"Yes, Claire's right," Teddy told them. "Claire's always right. I think we should all do as she suggests."

Stunned into speechlessness, the two adults followed the young lady's dictates and moved into the hallway where they stood staring at each other.

"This is unbelievable," Gertrude said finally, breaking the silence.

Gertrude glanced around her uncomfortably. She had never been upstairs in the Stefanski house. It was dark, masculine, tasteful in a sparse and orderly sort of way. The ivory-and-claret Brussels carpet runner was eye-catching against the dark pine floors and made up for the lack of wallpaper adorning the walls. A large brass hall fixture that was obviously chosen for its utility rather than its attractiveness shed abundant light in the long, narrow hallway. She liked it, she decided. She liked the upstairs of the Stefanski house.

At the instant she discerned her own thoughts she became wary. She didn't belong upstairs. This part of the house was for the family. She was not part of the family.

A clawing ache seemed to settle in her chest. She closed her eyes tightly and repeated the thought to herself once more. She was not a part of the family. This was not the time away from the world that they had created at the little Second Street apartment. This was Mikolai's real life, his real world. And she was not now, nor ever would be, a part of it. Determinedly she repeated that litany to herself. She was not a part of his real life. In his real world, she was no one.

Mikolai's brow was furrowed thoughtfully as he stared first at his son's door and then at Gertrude.

"You did say that George didn't want the two of you in Barkley House now that Lester is ill."

"What? Oh no, he doesn't," Gertrude said somewhat off-handedly. Then, realizing what Mikolai was saying, she immediately set out to dissuade him. "But I'm sure George would never suggest that we stay here."

"No, I don't suppose that he would suggest it," Mikolai agreed. "But it's really not so terrible an idea."

"It certainly *is* a terrible idea."

Gertrude glanced up and down the hall at all the doorways now closed. She needed to keep them closed. She was no part of Mikolai's real life. She shouldn't know what was behind those doors.

"I think perhaps that you both should stay," Mikolai said.

Gertrude stared at him in near horror.

"Oh, no, I . . . I couldn't."

Her passionate refusal raised his eyebrow and Gertrude felt obliged to explain. Except she wasn't really certain what explanation she had.

She leaned closer to him, her voice lowering to a whisper. "People will hear of it, Mikolai, and what if someone begins to suspect . . . to suspect us."

"Why would anyone suspect us? It must look much more suspicious for both of us to be sneaking away from our lives every afternoon. Here, in front of the whole town, here with the children, we wouldn't do anything here with the children. No one would think it."

"Well, no, I don't suppose they would."

"Not even the more scurrilous gossip would be low enough to suggest that."

"No, certainly not."

"And if you're worried, I . . . I hope you know that I would never try to take advantage—"

"Oh, no, Mikolai, I never thought that."

"So why don't you just stay. You can watch over Claire and . . . and I can watch over you," he said.

He made it sound so simple. As if it were merely a decision about a room to occupy for a night. She knew that it was more than that. It was much more.

Gertrude managed to smile at him, but just barely. Her heart was heavy. She didn't want to be here, here in his house. It wasn't her place.

A flood of feelings, strange sentimental feelings, filled her heart until she feared that she might drown in them. She didn't want to examine how she felt, but she could hardly avoid it. Being here, being within Mikolai's real life, it made her want it to be her real life, too.

No, she could not stay here with Mikolai, not even for one night. It was far too dangerous. She could not stay. But she couldn't simply leave Claire either. That would be unthinkable. George and Prudence would never forgive her. And the girl seemed determined to stay.

"I don't know what to do," she told him.

She felt his hand against her cheek and she looked up into his eyes. His gaze was so penetrating, so knowing, she wanted to glance away. But she did not.

"It's not merely the impropriety that bothers you," he said.

"No, it's not just that," she admitted.

"I know that you are not afraid of me. I know you're not

simply worried about the children." He continued to gaze at her assessingly. "I cannot guess," he said. "So you must tell me."

"I shouldn't stay here," she stated flatly.

He nodded. "And are you going to tell me why?"

"Yes," she whispered. "I suppose that I am."

Mikolai took her hand and pressed it against his cheek. He waited.

"A long time ago," she began, "a very long time ago, when I first began to write, I made up a story."

She swallowed, not quite able to meet his gaze.

"I made up a story in which I was the heroine," she said. "All the things that I dreamed of doing, I did in this story. I walked around turning people into what I wanted them to be. In my little scratchings, I allowed myself to live a kind of life I was too frightened to attempt in reality."

She sighed with weariness, as if the burden she carried weighted her down, and faced him squarely.

"One day, I'm not even sure quite when it happened, the world I created crossed the line into the world where I lived. There were things there. Things that belonged to other people's lives that I took over. Ultimately I trivialized them."

She shook her head with guilt as her heart pleaded for him to understand.

"That is the worst thing a human can do to another human, you know. To trivialize their reality."

"And this is what you fear, that you will *trivialize* my reality?"

"Our . . . our time together is time out of real life. That's what we both said that we want."

Mikolai glanced down the hallway. She saw him looking at the walls, the ceiling, the carpet. Then his gaze returned to her.

"To have you here with me is a chance I am willing to take," he said.

"But what if—" she began.

"What if Teddy never plays football again?" he said. "What if he and Claire never marry? What if George does not become Sublime Kalifa? We can deal with those things when we find them. We do not have to solve our problems before we make them." He gripped her hands tightly as if he could hold Gertrude to him by physical means alone.

"Please stay this night with me," he pleaded.

How could she deny him? She loved him.

Bravely, she gave her Mikolai a smile. "Of course, I will stay," she said.

He smiled back. A broad, warm, welcoming smile that went straight to her heart and welled her eyes with tears.

"It will be good to have my *zona* in my home," he said.

She knew then, like a lightning flash of understanding, she knew. She knew that more than any other reason, and there were many, she knew why she should not stay. It was because she wanted to too much.

Mikolai was nervous. Pacing to and fro across the front parlor was not helping at all. Upstairs, Teddy had awakened from his nap and he and Claire were playing cards. Gertrude had gone over to Barkley House to pack a satchel of clothing for herself and her niece. His heart beating with anxious excitement, Mikolai told himself to remain calm. The silent, stalwart Polish demeanor that had always worked so well for him was nowhere to be found. Gertrude Barkley was to spend the night in his house and he was unrealistically thrilled.

Shaking his head with disbelief, Mikolai walked the short distance to his library. He plopped himself down in one of the tufted leather armchairs and stared thoughtfully at nothingness. He realized with some surprise that he was smiling. Smiling. Alone in his very serious gentleman's study of his richly appointed eclectic manse, he, Mikolai Stefanski, was grinning like a fool. With some hesitation he searched his thoughts to find out why.

Certainly having Gertrude with him in the house tonight was a pleasing thought. But it would not be as if she were *really* here. He would have to guard his speech and actions toward her for the sake of the children. He would not be allowed to sleep with her, although the mere idea of holding her close in his big mahogany four-poster had the same effect one might have imagined if she had run her hand along the front of his trousers. And they would both be aware that her venture into the life of the Stefanski household would be a temporary one.

It was a start, he insisted to himself. Rome was not built in a day and Gertrude Barkley would not be won in a night. But it had to begin somewhere. Mikolai was ready to begin. He need not rush her or frighten her. He had the rest of his life to make her his own.

He paused in his ruminating to look around him. Something had changed. Something inside him had changed. Only a few weeks ago, he was a man whose memories and regrets outnumbered his plans for the future. He had danced a simple sad waltz with a woman he'd known for years and he had changed.

He thought about the question she had asked him the other afternoon about his guilt. He hadn't lied. It seemed that love, his love for Gertrude, had truly made it fade away.

Purposely he allowed his mind to drift back to thoughts of Poland. He picked up those memories with great care and examined them as if they were made of spun glass. The golden fields of autumn were almost as close to his heart as if he were there again, there in Poland. Not the Poland that he knew it to be in 1915, a Poland of warring armies and mixed loyalties, but the Poland of his childhood. The one that existed only in memory.

With the eye that dwelled in his heart, he saw *Tatus* in the field of grain. It must have been a good year. The wheat was nearly as high as the man's waist and was ripe and glistening in the afternoon sunshine. His father swung the big scythe back and forth, moving in that earthly cadence so intrinsic to yeoman farmers. His step never faltering, his stroke never halting; the strong, dependable father of five cut his field with the optimism of a man who would live forever and with the knowledge that he certainly would not.

Mikolai let his thoughts drift to his mother. The images came flooding in. She was making bread in the kitchen, the baby, Rhysio, her favorite son, forever frail and pale and pretty, tugging at her apron. She was hanging laundry upon the fence with such pride in its cleanliness it was almost sin. She was kneeling upon the hard dirt floor in the little church clutching her well-worn beads and praying. Praying, Mikolai knew, for her children.

Matka was silent and often sullen as he was sometimes himself. But *Tatus* would make her laugh. He teased her about her cooking. Pretended to forget her name, claiming he'd had so many wives, it was hard to keep track of them. And he would look down the long table at his family and exclaim in horror that she must be taking in orphan children, he knew he had never fathered so many of his own.

They would all laugh and *Matka* would slap him on the hand with the wooden spoon, as if he were another of her errant youngsters.

In the night sometimes Mikolai would hear them in their bower. They would be whispering, telling tales, sharing secrets. *Tatus* would say something low and suggestive. *Matka* would giggle like a young girl. And then there would be silence. Sweet, soft silence, or very near it, as they sneaked through their private, intimate moments with deliberate effort not to awaken the children.

The children. His brothers. His sister. Himself. He let his

mind follow those paths. In his thoughts once more they were all alive and all together. He and Bartos and Dawid out in the snow searching for the most perfect Christmas bough. Their breath coming out in great clouds of warm air. They broke off twigs and fashioned them into would-be pipes and pretended that they were men out for a smoke.

He remembered his sister, Edda, during one spring masquerade when it was tradition for boys to pester girls. He had come up behind her and shorn off the end of her braid with the wool cutters. Even though he'd covered his face with soot and wore a self-fashioned wig of broom straw, she'd recognized him and instead of bribing him with colored eggs to leave her be, she'd whacked him across the nose with the soap ladle. He'd bled all over his dingus costume and his nose was never shaped exactly the same way again.

He remembered her also with a bride's wreath upon her head. She was brave and beautiful, her chin held high as she sat for a wedding supper with a man twice her age.

How was she now? he wondered. She must have had children of her own. She had wanted children. Certainly she would have been a good mother. She had been a good mother to his little brother, the best he could have had save his very own. Yes, she must definitely have children of her own. She might even have grandchildren. Or perhaps she did not. She was the same age as his Lida. Perhaps she had been dead for just as long.

"Lida."

He said the name aloud and waited for the pain, the guilt to envelop him. It didn't come. His brow furrowed.

He tried harder. He forced himself to picture her as he had seen her so often. She was glaring at him, accusingly. They were in the stinking, crowded bowels of the Swedish ship. The seas were too heavy to be out on deck. And the air in steerage was close and foul with sickness and humanity.

"It will be better in Amerika, I promise," he had told her. It was something he had told her many times over that next, that last, year of her life.

It had been the truth, but not all that he should have told her. He should have told her before they wed that he was taking her away from everything that she knew. He should have told her that her body intrigued him more than her soul. He should have told her that he hadn't loved her, that he only needed her beside him so he wouldn't have to face the new country alone.

Cringing in his heart, Mikolai waited for the guilt to fill him. He waited for the self-hatred that was well deserved to steal upon him like the blackness of night.

It did not happen. His thoughts were of those last moments. Those last moments of her short, unhappy life when the doctor had shaken his head and had gathered his things back into his bag.

She had lain so pale and wan upon the narrow cot. Her hair, her beautiful cornsilk blond hair, was mussed and lifeless, plastered to her brow from the sweat of her labors.

"The baby is crying," she whispered.

He had looked down into her pale blue eyes, disconsolate. "Don't worry about him, *Zona*," he had answered. "Our little one is a strong boy."

"Yes, I hear him," she said. "Will you call him Teodor? Teodor, for my father."

"If that is what you wish," he answered.

"Yes," she said. "I do wish it. It is all that I will ever have to give him."

"You have given him life," he told her.

She smiled. Just a tiny smile, so small Mikolai had almost not seen it through the tears that filled his eyes.

"Yes, I have given him that, I suppose. And you will give him Amerika."

"Yes, I will give him Amerika."

She had reached for him then. The grasp of her hand was weak as she held his. "I have loved you," she said. "I have followed you here because I loved you. And my saddest regret in dying is that I leave you alone."

"I have our Teodor," he said.

"He cries for me," she said, glancing over toward the cradle on the far side of the room. "And you cry also." She was looking up at him, deeply, intently, as if she knew it was the final sight that she would see. "My last wish," she whispered. "My last wish is that your tears may dry and that you love as I have loved."

"I do love you, Lida," he lied.

"No, not—"

Her words were never finished. Mikolai saw the light, the soul, disappear from her eyes. In the tiny upstairs room of a crowded Chicago building, a child lay crying and a father, mired in guilt, sat weeping for his dead wife.

Mikolai took a deep, cleansing breath in the solitude of his study. A tear trickled out of his eyes and he wiped it hastily upon his sleeve. Now the feeling would come, the familiar, almost welcome feeling of guilt and self-loathing. His wife had wanted him to love her. He never had. He never would.

He waited. He waited for the blackness to sweep him. But it did not.

"My last wish is that your tears may dry and that you love as I have loved."

He heard the words again as clearly as he had that day so many years before.

"I do love you, Lida," he had lied.

"No, not—"

Mikolai continued to stare into the nothingness. Suddenly his eyes widened and he came to his feet.

"No, not—"

He had misunderstood and she had tried to correct him. Like

a bolt from the blue, understanding shot through him. She had not wished him to love *her*. She had wished him to love as she had loved him.

"Lida!" he said aloud.

He smiled. She had known love. Even when it had not brought her the dreams that she had wanted, she had known it. She wanted that for him.

And he had found it. After all these years of grief and guilt he had found it. His life was not behind him in deeds undone, people lost, and regrets of the past. His life was all ahead of him. He was in love. Truly in love for the very first time. It was what his first sweet, sad wife had wished for him. And now it was true. His life was just beginning. Now all he had to do was convince the woman he loved to live it with him.

Chapter Twenty

"I COULDN'T SLEEP." Gertrude's quiet words were loud in the empty room. She'd left Claire curled up in the bed that they shared and had come downstairs to find Mikolai. She knew he would be here. She wanted to see him. Yet she hesitated, uncertain, in the doorway.

He looked strong and certain and substantial sitting in the heavily stuffed and upholstered sofa chair. He was dressed casually in gray striped trousers and a white shirt. He wore no vest or necktie, and his cross-back suspenders emphasized the width of his shoulders and the strength of his back. He was a formidable man. And, to Gertrude's adoring eyes, a very attractive one also.

It was late, very late. The big German clock in the front hall had sounded only moments earlier that it was two in the morning. The house was silent and dark except for the small lamp in the front parlor where they stood.

"I couldn't sleep either," Mikolai said quietly as he rose to his feet. "It's silly, isn't it? So many times we've fallen asleep in each other's arms. Cursed our exhaustion because we knew it was time wasted between us. But now because we are in the same house, and because the oblivion of slumber is what we need most, we cannot sleep at all."

Gertrude stepped forward into the room and accepted his outstretched hand. "I just can't seem to stop thinking. It's as if my mind simply will not take a rest. Just when I feel certain that I'm not thinking of anything, I realize that I'm thinking about not thinking about anything."

He smiled at her. "I know. I lay awake for more than an hour and finally decided that I would be happier getting up and dressed."

"I felt the same way," she admitted.

They stood facing each other. She wanted to kiss him, to have him hold her once more in his arms. But this was neither the time nor the place, she reminded herself. If they began to caress each other they would find it hard to stop. And they simply could not let anything happen, not here in his home, under the same roof with the children.

"I suppose Claire finally got to sleep," he said.

"Thank heaven," Gertrude said with a sigh and a shake of her head. "I was afraid she would insist on staying in Teddy's room. I don't know what we would have done if she had."

Mikolai shrugged. "I suppose we would all have spent the night there. Though I doubt that would have been the best thing for a young man with a broken knee."

"How is Teddy?" she asked. "Is he sleeping?"

"Fitfully," Mikolai answered. "His leg is throbbing pretty badly. The doctor left a bit of morphine for him to chew, but he says he'd rather do without it."

Gertrude nodded. "I can't blame him for that. In my estimation, what morphine does best is give the patient bad dreams."

Mikolai agreed. "It's almost better just to be awake. As there are already enough of us who can't sleep."

She smiled at his light humor, but made no comment.

"Come sit with me on the divan," he said, taking her arm. "That's surely safe enough, don't you think?"

She agreed readily, but in her heart she wasn't certain. The evening had been a long one. Just being near Mikolai made her want him. And she was very much convinced that he felt the same.

They had eaten dinner alone together. Teddy, not ready to attempt the stairs, was taken a tray. And since Claire refused to leave his side, Gertrude had taken up a tray for her, too.

Together in the dining room, Gertrude had attempted light inconsequential conversation. The type of unsubstantial talk that would have served for the most distant of acquaintances. Mikolai, unfortunately, would have none of it.

"You should have seen Oleander Wentworth at the game," she had said to him with chatty exuberance. "She jumped and screamed and cheered for the team as if she were sixteen rather than sixty. Then after everything was over and the game fairly won, her face got red as a beet and she had to lie down, right there on the grass."

Gertrude's expansive gaiety was observably forced. "The ladies of the Algonquin Society came running with her smelling salts. And all the time Claudy Mitts kept saying, 'Oh dear, oh dear.'"

Mikolai nodded. He appreciated the humor, but looked beyond it. "Well, you can understand the ladies running to help her," he said. "Mrs. Wentworth and the Algonquin Society are very much tied together."

"Well, yes, I suppose so," Gertrude agreed.

"So they came running when she needed them. Just as you wanted to come running when I needed you."

Gertrude gazed down at the creamed corn on her plate and didn't reply.

"You and I are tied also," Mikolai continued.

Clearing her throat, Gertrude adroitly changed the subject, commenting positively on the fine dinner.

"I don't believe I've ever tasted better," she said.

"Mrs. Thomas does a fine job," he admitted. "She's a very dedicated employee. I could hardly find one better."

Gertrude smiled, thinking that she had discovered a safe conversation path.

Then Mikolai added, "Only a meal cooked with love could taste any better."

He was looking at her closely, assessingly. Hurriedly Gertrude moved on. "It's funny that you should mention that," she tried once more. "One of the characters in my book, Weston Carlisle, finds that the first thing he really appreciates about Alexandria—that's his stepmother—is her fine cooking."

"And doesn't he fall in love with her? Isn't that what you told me?"

Gertrude's eyes widened. "Why yes, yes, he does. I'd forgotten that I'd mentioned the book to you."

"I remember that he fell in love with her," Mikolai said.

"Of course that has nothing to do with her cooking, I mean ultimately," Gertrude explained. "He simply falls in love with her."

"He falls in love with his stepmother," Mikolai considered thoughtfully. "It must be a very desperate match."

"Oh, well, it is," she said. "I mean, she is a widow now and he was never particularly close to his father, being illegitimate and all. And Alexandria married his father when she was very young and is actually more the son's age than the father's. But still, it creates a difficult situation when people are in love who aren't expected to ever be together." Gertrude could hear herself, and she sounded as if she were babbling.

"But you'll find a way to work it out for them, won't you?" he asked.

"Certainly I will," she assured him. "Fiction is like that. There are tremendous stumbling blocks that have to be overcome, but ultimately the characters will, in some way, triumph over their situation."

He nodded slowly. "Triumph over their situation," he

repeated. "It sounds like something that we should all strive for."

"Well, I suppose that in our own way, we do," she admitted. "Still, life is not fiction where both the stumbling blocks and the triumphs are easily tailored to fit."

"That is true. But it seems to me that if Weston and Alexandria can find happiness together, then other people, real people, with not nearly their problems, should be able to work things out fairly easily."

She had just stared at him, having no response to that statement at all.

Again and again Gertrude had changed the subject, yet Mikolai continued somehow to bring it around to words that made her uncomfortable. She was trying so hard not to want him, his house, his life. But Mikolai appeared to be actively working against her. It was as if he were begging to hear how truly desperate she really was for him. And she was very afraid that any moment she might give him what he wanted and blurt out the awful truth.

Now, sitting next to him on the divan, she feared that once again any attempt at small talk would be hopeless.

"Do you remember the night of the victory dance?" he asked her.

"Of course I remember it," she said. It was the first time he had held her in his arms. The first time she had felt the warmth of his body against her own. "How could I forget?"

"I felt so old that night," he said quietly. "I felt like my life was over." He shook his head and then turned to gaze at her. "I thought that all I had left were memories and regrets."

"Well, I needn't remind you how I felt," she said, her tone rife with self-derision. "I was weeping like a baby over some unkind words being told about me."

"But you felt it, too, didn't you?" he said. "You felt as if everything good was behind you and the road ahead was just one endless procession of meaningless sunrises."

She did remember. She still could feel the sting of regret in her heart. "Yes, you know I felt that way," she admitted.

"But you don't feel like that anymore, do you?"

She looked up at him. For a moment she just stared. Willingly she tried to conjure up that emotion, that quaking uneasiness, that sense of loss. Then slowly, slowly, she began to smile. "No, I don't feel that way anymore," she said.

His gaze was warm and welcoming and centered upon her face. "It's as if we have new lives," he said. "We thought that our lives were over, but they are not at all. It's as if we have started out new, or almost new, once again."

She shook her head, almost disbelieving. "It's true," she said. "I . . . I don't feel sad anymore. How silly I was! And you, too." She actually laughed then. It was the best feeling that she had had all day.

Mikolai laughed, too, with joy. "My life is my future," he told her. "A few weeks ago I didn't even understand that my future still existed."

Gertrude continued to chuckle in disbelief. "How strange that we should suffer the same passing fancy."

"Not so strange," he answered. "Especially since we effected the cure together."

"Oh, you mean . . ." She felt the heat in her cheeks as she thought of the intimacies they had shared.

He ran a long finger along the pretty blush of her cheek and raised one busy brow. "Not that," he said, his voice teasing in its scold. "I have heard of things that *that* can cure, but a middle-of-life melancholia is not one of them."

He let his finger follow the line of her jaw and then raised her chin to look at him.

"I meant," he said, "that falling in love with each other has given us both a new start in life."

Gertrude's mouth formed a surprised little O and she had no words with which to answer. She could only look into his eyes.

"Dance with me, Gertrude," Mikolai said. "I want you to dance with me."

Gertrude was startled by his request. "I don't know if we should."

Her protest went ignored as he stepped across the room to the fancy concert Victrola. After only a moment of leafing through the disk collection, he placed the record on the turnplate and set the needle.

The sounds of a tinny orchestra filled the room as Mikolai returned to the divan and offered his hand.

"It is the only polite and circumspect way that I can hold you in my arms. And I'm afraid that if I wait one more moment to hold you. I won't be able to remain polite and circumspect."

Gertrude didn't question his statement. In many ways she felt much the same. She needed his touch. She needed it like air or water. But she feared that once she had taken it, she would have a difficult time doing without it.

She rose to her feet and was swept into his arms. The warmth, the closeness of him, was familiar, pleasurable . . . tempting. With no hesitation they danced, as they had danced that night, as if they were one. So close, so effortless, they had only to glide across the floor. Neither of them had the reputation of a fine dancer, but together their movements were as graceful and synchronous as if they were interlocking parts of the same soft mechanism.

Gertrude felt herself being drawn into his touch, drawn into his eyes. She turned her gaze from him. But she couldn't shut out the sounds of the Emerson Sisters, singing with such perfectly blended harmony, the sweet song from the days of her youth.

"After the ball is over,
After the break of morn

> *After the dancers' leaving;*
> *After the stars are gone;*
> *Many a heart is aching,*
> *If you could read them all;*
> *Many the hopes are vanished*
> *After the ball."*

Sentimental tears slipped from the corners of her eyes and she tried to wipe them surreptitiously with the back of her hand.

"You're crying?" he said.

"I'm being silly again. It's just for the song," she assured him. "It's such a sad, sad song."

He nodded. "Anytime pride and mistrust and simple foolish misunderstanding get in the way of love, it is enough to make one cry."

She didn't comment on his words and he offered no more. It was enough just to spin with light grace around the narrow confines of the front parlor in his arms.

When the recording finished, the disk continued to spin and the needle bounced back and forth in the last unending groove. Mikolai hardly hesitated in the dance. He led her past the Victrola and within the midst of one graceful swirl, he plucked the needle from its scratchy conclusion and set it back at the beginning. Once more the orchestra began to play. Once more they danced.

"I love holding you like this," Mikolai told her.

She smiled up at him. "I thought you said this was a substitute for a more risqué embrace."

"I thought it was," he admitted. "I thought that I was forgoing pleasure. But I find that holding you this way, holding you, close and loving and respectful, without hot passion or wild thrill clouding my appreciation, has a pleasure of its own."

"You merely love to dance, Mr. Stefanski," she teased.

His reply was serious. "I had never danced, never really danced, before I danced with you," he said.

"Teddy? Teddy, are you awake?"

The question came from the doorway and the young man in the bed sighed loudly. He wiggled ineffectually, trying to sit up without moving his injured leg.

"And how would I not be? The *concert* has been going on for hours."

Claire nodded and entered the room, assuming that his being awake constituted an invitation to enter. She was draped in her wrapper in casual disregard of proprieties. She went to the window and opened the shade. The music had been playing downstairs for hours. Dawn was just on the horizon and there had been no letup in the endless repetition of the lovely old-fashioned waltz.

"At least it's not as loud here as it is in the hallway," she told him.

"I don't care about how loud it is," Teddy complained. "I'm just ready for it to stop altogether."

"It doesn't sound like it will," she told him as she crossed the room and plopped down in the chair next to his bedside. "But at least it didn't keep me awake all night. I sleep the sleep of the guiltless," she said.

Teddy snorted. "More like the sleep of the conscienceless," he said. "What are you trying to do to those two, get them back together and break their hearts?"

"If that's what it takes," she answered. She smiled. It was a serene, rather self-satisfied smile. It raised the hairs on the back of Teddy's neck.

"You've got something in mind," he said accusingly.

"Nothing that you don't already know about," she assured

him. "I want Aunt Gertrude and your . . . our father to confess all."

"That is not exactly news," he said.

She didn't respond.

"But now you think you've found a way to make them do that?"

"They are dancing," she said. It wasn't really an answer to his question. "I peeked from the landing and they are just waltzing around in a little circle in the middle of the front parlor."

Teddy shook his head. "Waltzing in the front parlor all night long. Who would ever believe such a thing of a couple that age?"

He shook his head again in disbelief.

"And my father apparently cannot locate another record. 'After the ball. After the ball. After the ball.' How in the world can anyone listen to that sugary sentimentality for hours on end?"

Claire waved away his bad humor. "Old folks love bad music," she explained. "They simply have no sense about what is terrific at all. Now I've been thinking, and I have a plan."

Teddy moaned with despair. "I am crippled, exhausted, and in pain. And you have a plan."

"It doesn't involve much for you," she assured him. "Although I do think that it would go over better if you went downstairs."

"If I went downstairs?"

"That's what I said. I can help you. It really won't be so bad with that splint on your leg. You can hold on to the railing on one side and I can be on the other."

"Why do we have to go downstairs? Couldn't we just do whatever it is you want to do up here?"

"Well," she said with a thoughtful sigh, "we can, if we have to. But I'd rather not."

"I'd rather not try to get down those stairs."

"I think that we have to confront them," Claire said. "It's time that we confront them. Force them to tell us the truth. And I don't think there will ever be any better opportunity than now."

Teddy groaned. "Now?"

"Don't you see? They've been up all night, too. And they've been dancing for most of that time. Not lying around in bed like you've been."

"They don't have any broken knees," Teddy pointed out.

"No," she agreed. "But they are still tired and they'll be very vulnerable."

"You sound like you're planning a frontal attack," he said.

"I am," she answered. "Even more than that. We go in there this morning, when they are tired and sleepy and deal them the final blow. They'll be begging us to let them tell us the truth."

Teddy looked at her thoughtfully. "You mean if we catch them now with their guard down, and hit them hard, we can go all the way," he said.

"Yes, that's it exactly."

"Claire, you really should play football. I think that it's your sport."

She grinned and chucked him playfully on the arm. "Yeah, if I was on the squad, we'd be a cinch for the state championship," she said.

"I still don't know why I have to go downstairs," he said.

"Because part of the strategy of a good football team is to get the best position on a good playing field."

"And the 'best position on a good playing field,'" he said, "is downstairs."

"Right. That means you have to get down the stairs."

Teddy sighed. "Claire, I hate it when you are right," he said.

"Teddy, trust me. I'm *always* right."

He set his chin with feigned bravery. "I imagine it will be easier getting down than it will be getting back up," he said.

"That's the spirit. Now where's your pants?" she asked him.

Chapter Twenty-one

"WE NEED TO talk to you, both of you." Claire's voice broke the sweet spell in the front parlor.

Guiltily Gertrude jumped away from Mikolai's arms. They both stood staring with disbelief at the two young people in the doorway.

"Teddy? How did you get down the stairs?" Mikolai asked of the pale-looking young man who was dressed and leaning heavily on Claire.

"She helped me," he answered simply.

"We didn't hear you," Mikolai admitted.

"How could you with the music playing?" was the young man's reply.

Immediately Mikolai hurried to the Victrola and set the needle to the side and turned it off.

"Sit, sit, Teddy, before you fall down," his father ordered. "You look quite faint."

"This is probably something I should stand up for," he said firmly. But he eased himself into the nearest chair just the same. He looked up at Claire. He nodded slightly, giving her free rein to do whatever she thought best.

"Perhaps we should all sit down," she said. Her tone was downright haughty, but Gertrude and Mikolai, both suddenly aware of exactly how tired they were, followed her directive.

When everyone was sitting, Claire firmly took the initiative.

"While you two have been dancing the night away, Teddy and I have been talking."

Gertrude's eyes widened. She looked horrified. "We kept you awake?"

She glanced over at Mikolai guiltily. He, too, looked surprised and disconcerted. Neither had given a thought to the young people upstairs.

"We don't mind missing a little sleep," Claire assured her. "And it's given us some time to sort out things between us."

"That's good," Gertrude said. "That's very good."

Claire ignored her. "Now we think that it is high time that we four sort out the things that are between us."

Mikolai and Gertrude gave each other puzzled glances as Claire nodded to Teddy, giving him the floor.

"Claire and I have said many times that we want to be . . . to be married," he said, choking only slightly on the last word. "Although you haven't forbidden us, we can both tell that you don't like the idea. Now we want to know why."

The two young people were stone-faced and staring intently at the adults who were momentarily disconcerted.

"Well, I . . ." Gertrude began but couldn't quite get her feelings into words. She looked over helplessly at Mikolai.

"We are not against your marriage," Mikolai said evenly. "We just worry."

"What do you worry about?" Claire asked pointedly.

"Why, the things parents worry about," he answered. "Will you be happy? Are you truly a good match for each other? Whether you are really in love. You are both so young."

"That's it?" Claire asked skeptically.

Gertrude tried to explain further. "Mr. Stefanski and I have seen . . . well, we've seen a lot in our lives and we know that mistakes can be made. Everyone makes mistakes, but when you are young it's easier to make them. And a mistake in who one marries can be the very biggest mistake of all."

"So all you are worried about is our youth and whether we will make a mistake?" Claire said.

"Yes," Gertrude answered. She looked over at Mikolai and he nodded in agreement.

Their answer didn't seem to suit Claire a bit and she turned to Teddy in an expression of hopelessness.

"So you really have no objections to our being married," Teddy clarified. "No real, certain, absolute objections."

Mikolai shrugged. "No, no, I don't guess that we do."

"So you are going to let us get married?" Teddy asked.

His father was slow to answer, but finally nodded. "If this is what the both of you want. Then I think it will be a fine thing. If you are asking my permission," he said, "then you have it. You have my blessing, too."

"Yes, and mine," Gertrude added with a warm smile to the two young people she loved so much. Claire and Teddy turned to look at each other in disbelief before the same word exploded from their mouths.

"What!"

The exclamation was shouted in unison and with such fury, both Gertrude and Mikolai were taken aback.

"You are going to let us get married?" Claire asked, horrified. "You are actually going to let us go through with it?"

"If that's what you want," Gertrude answered. "We just want what you want."

"My God!" Claire rubbed her arms as if a cold chill had spread across her skin. "Have neither of you any morals at all?"

"Morals?"

"What are you talking about?"

"We know all about you," Claire announced furiously. "We know all about your little scandal and you should be ashamed."

Mikolai and Gertrude just stared at the two young people as the words penetrated their understanding.

"Oh!" Gertrude cried out in horror and covered her mouth as she realized at last what was being said.

"We know everything, everything," Claire continued. "Everything. And we've given you chance after chance to confess the truth. But this . . . this permission . . . it's beyond understanding."

"How did you find out?" Mikolai's voice was curt and he directed his question to Teddy.

"We just did," he answered. He was not feeling nearly as confident as Claire and was very unhappy with the look of pure anger upon his father's face.

"You haven't told anyone?" he asked.

"Of course not," Claire answered. "Do you think that *I* would tell?"

"We didn't breathe a word to anyone," Teddy assured him. "We didn't even hint."

"So no one knows," Mikolai said. "And no one knows that you know."

"Well," Claire said evenly, "Prudence and George know."

"What!"

"Well, it wasn't like they didn't know already," Claire defended. "I just let them know that I knew."

"Oh, my heavens." Gertrude felt the tears of shame begin to stream down her cheeks. She had never meant to hurt anyone. She had never meant to scandalize anyone. Now her whole family was aware of what she had done. They were probably all as angry as Claire. She pictured George, helpless and horrified as he determinedly put a brave face on the latest Barkley scandal. And Prudence, her sad eyes welling with tears, as she assumed that somehow this was her fault. They loved her and would stand by her through the latest, most serious of her indiscretions. All the while writhing in shame. Suddenly Gertrude couldn't bear it.

"I'm sorry I—"

Tearfully clutching her handkerchief, she ran out of the house. She didn't have any inkling as to where she intended to go. The morning sun glimmered on the shiny red brick as she reached the porch, realizing that there was nowhere to run. She had played a very serious game with her life and with her reputation. And she had lost. Now, not only would she pay dearly for it, but her family would, too. She hadn't anticipated that. She hadn't anticipated being found out. She had thought only of her love for a man whom she could never truly have. A man whom she had wanted for so very, very long.

"*Zona*," the soft word came from behind her. Mikolai wrapped his arms around her and pulled her backward, holding her tightly against his chest.

She closed her eyes and allowed him just to hold her for long, wonderful moments before she tried to speak. She should shy away from him, begin at that moment to end their illicit affair. But she could not. It felt too wonderful to be in his arms. And even *caught* she was loath to give it up.

"I am so ashamed," she choked out through her tears.

He pressed a tiny kiss against her hair. "Are you ashamed because you love me?" he asked her.

She stroked the strong arms that sheltered her as she shook her head. "You know it's not that," she answered. "I'm ashamed because I've dishonored my family. Because I've hurt them with my own selfishness."

"*We* have hurt them. With *our* selfishness," he corrected her quietly.

She didn't bother to argue. "Poor George has struggled so hard to overcome the stain on his reputation," she said. "And I've never helped. Never. I've always done just what I wanted. Selfishly. Inconsiderately. I always just allowed myself to please myself. And now, see how it has all come to a bad end."

"You could never be selfish or inconsiderate, my *zona*," he told her quietly. "You have only looked for some happiness in your life. That is not a bad thing. It is what you deserve."

He hugged her tightly. She could feel the pounding of his heart against her. It was as if it were in harmony with her own. As if, like the dance, they moved in the same natural cadence.

"And this love of ours, Gertrude. It doesn't have to be a bad end," he whispered.

"What?" she asked. "How can it not?"

Mikolai turned her in his arms. With one knuckle he raised her chin slightly so that he could look directly into her eyes. His expression was warm and familiar and dear.

"It doesn't have to be a bad end," he repeated. "Because we can marry."

Gertrude's eyes widened. She stared at him in stunned disbelief. "You would marry me?" she asked in an incredulous whisper.

"We can take the Packard across the border to Arkansas and be wed this very morning," he said. "If only the family knows, they won't say a word. We will be together and we will make it up to them."

She continued to stare at him mutely as he pushed a stray curl away from her face.

"But you vowed never to remarry," she told him. "You said a wife would expect more than you are prepared to offer."

"That was because I was never able to offer my heart," he admitted. "But you have stolen my heart already."

"Not stolen, surely."

"I know that you had not wanted to marry. I know that your work is more important to you than belonging to some man. But I belong to you, Gertrude. I cannot go on without you."

"Mikolai, my love."

He dropped to his knee then in front of her. He clasped her hands tightly in his own and gazed up at her.

"I am no longer a young man, Gertrude. But you make me feel young again. I feel young enough to take a wife."

"Of course you are young enough to take a wife," she said. "But, Mikolai, please get up. I . . . I am your *mistress*." She breathed volumes of meaning into the word. "Men do not marry their mistresses."

He let his lips caress the sweet familiar flesh of her fingers. "They do if they love them, *Zona*," he answered.

The touch was nearly as unsettling as his words. She stuttered for an appropriate reply.

"B-b-b-but I never . . . I wouldn't have . . . I had no intention of trapping you into anything," she said.

"Trapping me?" He chuckled lightly, as if she had made a very good joke. "A hare taking shelter in his burrow does not think himself trapped," he told her. "Though the space in the burrow be the same as in a cage, he is home and safe and content, and so will I be."

"But, Mikolai, it seems so unfair," she said. "You wanted only a little pleasure."

"And I found more than a *little* with you," he said. "So much, in fact, that I am loath to give it up. Truly I know you had not planned to wed, but the idea appeals to me more as each minute passes by. Tell me you are not repulsed at the thought?"

"No, no, I—"

"I would not hinder your work, my *zona*, not ever. You have penned two novels," he said. "And I hope that for you there will be many more. I would never stop you from that. I want you to continue your writing. I would never try to keep you from it."

It was a reassurance that she knew was true, yet she needed to hear it. Still, she hesitated. He deserved so much more.

"Mikolai, I know so little about being a housewife," she

confessed. "I've let Pru do all the dinner preparation. I am barely competent to boil my own water for tea."

Mikolai actually grinned at her obvious distress. "Had I wanted a woman chained to a cookstove, I could have married a dozen times over," he answered. "I do not want merely a wife. I want Gertrude Barkley."

She laid a hand upon her heart as if to still the wild pounding inside her.

"I didn't even dare to dream of this," she admitted. "I was afraid to dream of it."

"We are a good couple, Gertrude, a good match," Mikolai insisted. "We are two people who love each other and we are a bit too old for making foolish mistakes."

"If we're too old for foolish mistakes," she asked him, "how is it that we find ourselves in this situation?" She made a gesture toward the doorway where they both knew the young people waited inside.

Mikolai shrugged. "I didn't say it wasn't a mistake," he told her, his tone was light and teasing as he gazed once more into her tear-stained eyes, now suddenly bright with anxious animation. "I just said that it wasn't a foolish one."

She smiled at him and shook her head.

"Marry me, Gertrude, my *zona*?" he asked. "Will you marry me today?"

"Yes," she answered quietly, though her thoughts were screaming out the words. "I will marry you, Mikolai Stefanski."

He rose to his feet then and kissed her. A sweet, brief kiss. It was not a touch to incite the fires of passion, but a gesture of affection. The kind of kiss a husband bestows on a wife.

"I love you, Gertrude," he said, smiling down into her eyes. "And I will kiss you better later. When we are man and wife."

The thrill of hearing his words had her trembling and she

started crying again. With a crisp clean handkerchief, he wiped her eyes.

"I've heard that brides often cry on their wedding nights," he said, teasing. "But I never knew of one to cry at her marriage proposal."

His teasing had her smiling up at him through her tears. He bent forward slightly to plant a tiny kiss on the end of her nose.

"Come along, my sweet *zona*," he said. "I think we need to make some assurances to some very moral and upright young people."

Teddy and Claire were whispering nervously together when they returned to the front parlor. Claire's chin was still obstinate and angry. Teddy looked rather unsure.

"Please, let us sit back down again," Mikolai said.

He seated Gertrude upon the divan and sat down beside her. He did not for a moment relinquish her hand and held it possessively upon his knee as if making a statement to the young people before him.

"We are very sorry if you two have been in any way hurt by what Gertrude and I have done," he said. "We certainly did not set out to hurt anyone and we are very distressed that we obviously have hurt you two."

The young people continued to stare at him stonily and he glanced over at Gertrude for courage.

"We want you to know that we do not take lightly the bonds of holy matrimony. And we would never wish for you to do so either. We admit that what we have done is wrong, but we now have decided to make it right."

"To make it right?" Claire asked. "How do you intend to make it right?"

"Gertrude has consented to be my wife," he said. "We will drive to Eureka Springs this morning and be wed."

There was silence within the front parlor. The morning light at that very moment reached the correct angle and streamed in through the east windows, illuminating the tableau of two couples, one young, one not so young, facing each other in moral dilemma.

"How will that solve anything?" Claire asked finally.

Mikolai glanced at Gertrude, puzzled; she shrugged and then looked back at Claire.

"Why, it should solve everything," she said to her.

Claire's jaw hardened and her voice came out angry. "What about your child? Do you never give a thought to your child?"

"Child?" The word was spoken in unison and in astonishment.

Mikolai looked at Gertrude in shocked expectation. She shook her head with absolute certainty.

"There is no child," she answered him. She repeated it for Claire and Teddy. "There is no child."

"What about me?" Claire cried plaintively.

"You?" Mikolai gazed at her in wonder.

Claire looked at her aunt accusingly. "You didn't tell him about me, Aunt Gertrude."

"Tell him what about you?"

"That I'm his daughter!"

"Daughter!"

Mikolai raised his hands in innocence; his tone was of a man completely mystified. "By God, I swear, I hardly know Prudence Barkley!"

"What is the meaning of this?" Gertrude asked.

"You shouldn't have lied to us, Father," Teddy said.

"I'm owed an explanation," Claire insisted.

Everyone began talking at once.

The tower of Babylon could not have been noisier than the front parlor of the Stefanski manse that morning. Louder and louder the commotion grew as each speaker tried to be heard over every other. Finally Mikolai came to his feet.

"Hush!" he ordered, in a voice of authority well known to his employees, business associates, and competitors.

Silence descended.

He nodded gratefully at each now-quieted person within the room.

"Now, Claire," he said as he took his seat again. "Please tell us, slowly, carefully, why you think that you are my daughter."

The young woman raised her chin high. She was still very unhappy and it was clear she blamed it on the two adults.

"I found Aunt Gertrude's diary," she said sharply. "I found her diary and it's all written there."

Mikolai turned to Gertrude and his eyebrow raised in surprise. "You wrote in your diary that I was the father of Pru's child?"

"Not Pru's child!" Claire interrupted angrily. "Aunt Gertrude's child."

Mikolai, his mouth open, looked first at Claire and then back at Gertrude.

"I never had a child," Gertrude said, shocked at the suggestion and honestly nonplussed at her niece's accusation. "And I've never had a diary."

"What?" Claire stared at her in stunned disbelief.

"Uh-oh," Teddy said quietly.

Gertrude and Claire entered the Barkley house quietly. Gertrude's brow was furrowed and her expression worried. Claire was uncharacteristically quiet.

"I just don't know what I will say to them," she whispered to her aunt.

"I don't know how you could be so brave just a few hours ago and have no courage at all now," Gertrude answered.

Claire sighed. "That was before I figured out what an idiot I can be."

She glanced up the stairs and then looked toward her aunt, her expression woeful. "Do I really have to do this?"

"I think that you should," Gertrude said. "Your parents need to hear you say that you love them. And you, Claire, you may need to hear it yourself."

She nodded. "All right, Aunt Gertrude," she said. "But this is really *terrific*, and I mean that in the true and old-fashioned sense of the word." She sighed. "You get them in here and I'll talk."

Gertrude agreed.

As she watched her aunt walk away, confusion still fluttered through her young heart. Claire had thought the journal to be a fact. She had rearranged her whole way of thinking based on it. Her mother had always said that she was too quick to jump to conclusions. This time her mother's opinion had proved to be very true.

She had listened with growing mortification and surprise to her aunt's explanation of the journal.

"It was my very first attempt at writing fiction," Gertrude had told them. "I used the names and characters of people that I knew, because I hadn't figured out yet how to create my own characters."

"Then you and Mr. Stefanski . . . you never . . ."

Aunt Gertrude's face had been vivid red with embarrassment. "Mr. Stefanski and I hardly knew each other at the time," she admitted. "I . . ." Her aunt hesitated. "I found him to be very attractive and occasionally dreamed up stories about him. It was rather simple, really, to go from dreaming about him to writing about him."

Claire watched Mr. Stefanski's face as he looked at Aunt Gertrude. How totally humiliating to have to admit to having had a crush on a man!

Of course, she wasn't alone in her humiliation. Now that Teddy wasn't her brother, he knew that she had planned to marry him. Surely he wouldn't continue to believe that she was still interested in him.

Her brow wrinkled thoughtfully. That really was, however, the consolation prize of not being his sister. It would be perfectly natural for them to marry one day.

She had no time for further rumination as her father stepped into the room. He was big and frowning and looking as grouchy as an old bear.

"Gertrude said you wanted to talk to me," he snarled.

"Sit down, Daddy," she said.

"This better be important," he snapped. "I'm a busy man and I don't have time to waste."

"Talking to your daughter should never be thought of as a waste of time."

The words, spoken by Prudence Barkley from the doorway, were sharp and to the point. They seemed to make an impression upon her husband. He took them to heart enough to seat himself rather quickly.

"You sit, too, Mama," Claire said. "I need to talk to both of you."

When Pru was properly perched upon the edge of her chair, her back as straight as a washboard, Claire, too, sat down.

"I want to talk to you about the scandal," she said.

Prudence Barkley drew a sharp intake of breath as if she had been wounded by a knife. George rose to his feet, his expression a thundercloud.

"I won't sit still for this foolishness and certainly not from you, young lady!"

Claire took a deep breath and willed herself courage.

"Mama, don't cry," she ordered. "And, Daddy, please don't get mad. We need to talk about this."

"It's ancient history," her father declared.

"Not for me," she answered. "I just found out. And I just wanted to tell you . . ."

She hesitated, groping for the right words. "I just wanted to tell you that I love you both and I'm glad that I'm your daughter."

Her words seemed to deflate George. He sat down wearily and stared into nothingness.

Prudence hid her face in her hands.

"I know," Claire said, "that you never intended for me to find out. But I misunderstood some things and I had to be told."

The silence in the room lingered. Claire wasn't sure what else to say. She glanced hopefully toward the doorway, but Aunt Gertrude was not there. And she knew that she wouldn't be. This was something between her parents and herself. Aunt Gertrude, sweet, wonderful Aunt Gertrude had no part in it.

"I don't need to know the details," Claire continued. "I don't think that it is any of my business. And I promise that after today I will never again speak about this with you or anyone else," she said.

Pru was very quiet, but Claire could tell by the trembling in her shoulders that she was weeping.

Her hands trembling as she smoothed the material of her skirt, Claire bravely attempted to look her parents in the eye. It was not an easy task.

It was bad enough to know that your parents even did *that*. To imagine that they did *that* on purpose, and when they weren't even married, was almost more than her adolescent mind could contemplate. She certainly didn't want to talk about it. She didn't want to even think about it.

"I just want you to know that I love you and that I understand how such a thing might have happened," she said.

"You don't understand anything!" George Barkley growled fiercely.

Claire was momentarily taken aback by her father's vehemence.

"George, don't yell at the child," Pru scolded.

"I'm not yelling!" he hollered.

Then, receiving a scathing look from his wife, George moderated his tone.

"You youngsters today," he said, "you think you know everything. But there are things you don't know. Things you can't know, no one can know, until you've faced them."

Claire nodded vaguely.

"You think I married your mother because she had a baby on the way and it was the honorable thing to do. That's what you think, isn't it?"

Claire's expression grew worried. After what she'd been through today a new revelation wouldn't have surprised her.

"That is what happened, isn't it?" she asked uncertainly.

"No, that's not what happened at all," he said.

Claire glanced over at her mother, who had raised her head from the confines of her handkerchief. Her eyes were red with tears, but she was not crying, she was looking at her husband.

"George, we are not lying to the child anymore," Pru stated emphatically.

"I don't intend to lie to her. I'm going to tell her the truth. The whole truth, once and for all," he said, rising to his feet. He walked over to the parlor window and stared out into the mid-morning sunshine. His voice was quiet, constrained, as he spoke. "Claire, I loved your mother the first minute I saw her," he said.

The silence in the room was heavy, yielding.

"I knew I wanted her with me forever. I knew that very first day." He made a low sound that could only be interpreted as a sad, sweet sigh. He stared out at the street beyond the Barkley house's front window and continued what he had started.

"I went out to her daddy's farm on a hayride with a bunch of other boys. We were up to no good. Laughing, telling jokes, spending our daddies' money like there was no tomorrow."

He hesitated a long moment as if lost in the remembrance.

Then he turned back to face Claire. He did not even glance in the direction of his wife.

"She was working in the field," he said. "We were just driving by and we saw her working in the field. She was chopping cotton, Claire," he said. "There is no work in the world harder than chopping cotton." He sighed heavily and shook his head. "It was hot that afternoon, real hot. I guess your mother was feeling the heat in that cotton field. She took off her bonnet and rubbed her hand across her brow." He shook his head and smiled. "That's all she did, Claire. She just took off her bonnet. And that hair of hers spilled out and down her back. It was just glimmering there in the afternoon sun and I thought to myself, my God in heaven, that is the most beautiful hair I've ever seen in my life."

Claire shot a quick glance toward her mother, who was staring at her husband with an expression as bewildered as her own.

"I had to meet her," George continued. "I had to call on her. I found out who she was and where she lived and I went to see her."

George tucked his hands behind his back and began to pace the floor as he talked.

"Her father didn't think much of me. I was a lazy good-for-nothing as far as he could see. Eighteen years old and hadn't worked a day in my life. But he knew that my family had money. And he knew that Pru fancied me, so he let us be together. He let us be together whenever we wanted."

He laughed then. Her father, George Barkley, actually laughed. It wasn't a loud, boisterous laugh, but more a thoughtful chuckle.

"We strolled the lanes together. We gathered wildflowers. I helped her pick berries and held her thread for her as she crocheted. But mostly, Claire, I just talked to her. She liked to talk to me in those days; she thought I knew everything in the world and that I loved her."

He stopped his pacing long enough to offer a great sigh. "Only one of those things was true," he said.

"I promised to marry her. I promised it a lot," he said. "I talked about what it would be like in this house and how much I wanted her here with me."

He turned to look at Pru then, just for an instant.

"None of that was a lie," he said. "I did love her. I did want to marry her. I did want to bring her to this house. But there was a problem. The problem, Claire, was that your daddy was a coward."

George stopped and gritted his teeth together as if speaking the word had wounded him.

"I am a coward, Claire," he said. "Though not your usual kind. I've faced my share of danger and disaster and frightening situations of all kinds. But when it came to facing my father and telling him that I wanted to marry a nobody—a farmer's daughter for the simple reason that I loved her. Well, I was simply too much a coward to do it."

George seated himself in the chair and leaned forward with hands upon his knees as he looked at his daughter.

"My father, Grover Barkley, ran my life from the day I was born until the day he died. I never did, said, wanted, or thought anything that he didn't suggest. That is until that day in that cotton field when I saw your mother's hair. Please try to understand, Claire. I loved your mother and I wanted her to be with me. But I couldn't face my father. I was too afraid to tell him what I wanted, what we wanted. I was too much of a coward."

Claire saw her father's eyes welling with tears. Then her own vision seemed to be distorted with unwelcome moisture.

"I was not sad or scared or even surprised when your mother

told me that she was carrying you. It was what I had wanted. I knew then that my father would have to let us marry. It was the only decent thing for a man to do. And I knew that for all your grandfather's faults, he was a decent man."

George shook his head in self-derision. "The really pathetic thing about it is that I didn't even understand my father. Like me, he loved Pru on sight. I think he would have let me marry her anyway."

Her father fumbled for his handkerchief and covered his loss of emotional control with a feigned cough.

"Your mother loved me and gave me everything that she had. I have given her nothing but shame and embarrassment."

"You've given me two beautiful children," Pru spoke up. There was no sadness in her voice.

Claire glanced at her to see her face glowing with joy.

"You gave me two beautiful children and a good and happy life," she said. "All I ever felt that I lacked was your love."

"My love!" George looked at his wife, stunned at her words. "My God, Pru, you've always known that I love you."

"No," she said. "I never knew. I thought you married me because you had to and that you'd regretted it all your life."

George reached for her hand. She placed it in his.

"I have only regretted that I brought you to this house under a cloud. I was sure you had never forgiven me for taking from you the only thing that you had to offer, your honor."

Pru's eyes were clear. She gazed at him lovingly. "My honor has always been mine and still is. My heart, however, has always belonged to you."

"Prudence Barkley, I love you," he stated firmly. "I always have and I always will. That is all in this town, in this whole world, that has ever really mattered to me."

Claire watched as her parents embraced. Tears were streaming down her face as they held each other close.

Her father pulled back and opened his arms to include her in their embrace. "It's our Claire, Pru," he said. "Our darling, clever Claire. Our little daughter who brought us together."

"Both times," her mother answered.

Chapter Twenty-two
⇜⇝

MIKOLAI WAS STANDING at the window of his study staring at the Barkley house, a stance he had taken quite often in the last few days. When he saw his son, Teddy, hobble down the steps of the front porch and head toward him, he left his post and hurried to meet the young man at the front door.

"You're doing too much on that leg," he scolded. "The specialist said that you should take it easy."

"He also said not to let the muscles get too lazy," Teddy pointed out. "Besides, I can't just sit here in the house all day."

"No, I suppose not," his father agreed. "What's going on at the neighbors'?"

Mikolai's uncharacteristic nosiness went with no apology for his curiosity.

Teddy looked up and shrugged. "Claire's parents seem to be getting along a lot better now. And Mrs. Barkley has apparently finally had enough of Lester the Pester. She's not letting that scabby little scamp get away with anything these days."

Teddy walked past his father and into the house. Mikolai thought the young man might actually not say anything more.

"What about Miss Gertrude?" he asked.

"I didn't see her," Teddy said.

He wandered on back toward the kitchen, unconcerned. Mikolai followed.

"What do you mean you didn't see her?"

"I didn't see her," he said.

"Has she gone somewhere?" Mikolai shook his head. "She couldn't have. I would have noticed."

Teddy sorted through a bowl of apples sitting upon the counter. He looked up at his father and raised his eyebrow in a manner that was quite similar to the way in which his father often raised his brow at him.

"You would have noticed? Surely you haven't been watching the Barkley house every day for the last week."

Mikolai's mouth was set in a stern and unhappy line.

Teddy selected the apple that he wanted and took a healthy chomp out of it.

"You know, there is one thing about this whole ~~scandal~~ misunderstanding that I never could quite figure out," he said.

"What do you mean?"

"I mean when Miss Gertrude burst into tears and you two came back from the porch saying that you'd decided to 'make things right and get married.'"

The son looked at the father assessingly. The father could think of no reasonable reply.

"There are some things, Teddy Stefanski, that are my business and none of your own," Mikolai told him sternly.

Teddy nodded. "That's what I told Claire, but she wanted me to ask you about it anyway."

"Claire?"

"Yeah, you know how she is. Now she's got it into her head that you and Miss Gertrude are in love. She's trying to come up with a scheme to get you two together."

"Oh my."

"'Oh my' is right, *Tatus*," Teddy said. "When Claire decides to do something . . . well sometimes it's just easier to give in and let her have it. She's ultimately going to have it her way anyhow."

Mikolai looked thoughtful and concerned.

His son gave him a companionable pat on the back. "Don't

worry too much about it today. Claire won't be coming up with any plans for at least a week," he said.

"A week?"

"Yeah, they say that Miss Gertrude will still be contagious that long. I'm sure Claire won't want you catching the chicken pox, too."

"Chicken pox."

"Yes. That's why I didn't see Miss Gertrude. I'm afraid she's up in her room suffering with the chicken pox."

Mikolai turned from his son and walked back to his study. At the window he stopped once more to stare at the big, old house next door. It was pure white, glossy white. A giant expanse of white. The exact same color as the day that he had moved into town. He continued to stare at it for long moments. Then the words slipped from his lips.

"Chicken pox."

He smiled.

"I have to see her. I simply have to see her."

Gertrude heard Mikolai's voice outside her door and almost screamed. She wanted to dive for cover. She had been hiding, literally hiding, up in her room for days. From the top of her head to the souls of her feet, she was covered in itchy, scabby sores. And on top of those itchy, scabby sores was a thick layer of flaky white calamine. She was not a pretty sight.

"You can't, you really can't." She heard Prudence attempting to guard her doorway.

"I simply must" was his answer, and an instant later the door burst open.

Gertrude had nothing to cover up with except the pages of her manuscript. She managed to pull one in front of her face and tightly close her eyes. As if, when she couldn't see him, he couldn't see her.

"Gertrude?" He at least hesitated in the doorway.

"Please, Mikolai," she said, "I really look awful."

She hoped that her words would send him away, but they were immediately dashed as she heard him step into the room and close the door behind him.

"I simply must speak to her privately," he told Pru by way of explanation.

The silence of the room with just the two of them was momentarily uncomfortable.

"Teddy told me you were sick," he said.

"Not sick, really," she assured her. "Just itchy and miserable and . . . and I look terrible."

When he didn't say anything further, she felt as if she should continue to make herself clear. "Chicken pox is not dangerous. So you needn't worry about me. I just have . . . well, I have spots all over me."

"Yes, I know," he said. "That's why I came."

His statement was so surprising that Gertrude dropped the paper she held in front of her and stared at him in disbelief.

Getting his first real good look at her, Mikolai's eyes widened.

"Oh my. Chicken pox certainly doesn't look very good, does it?" he said.

She jerked another paper in front of her face, humiliated.

To her surprise, Mikolai stepped forward and pulled it away. He bent down in front of her upon one knee and took her hand in his own. Nervously he cleared his throat.

"After all that confusion with Claire, well, it left things rather unsettled for us. If I remember correctly, I had asked you to marry me and you said that you would."

Gertrude blushed, but fortunately it was not visible beneath the calamine. "You thought . . . I mean we thought that the children had found out. But now . . . well, now it's really not necessary."

"Oh, it may be necessary," Mikolai assured her. "Teddy is

already asking questions about what we meant. And he told me today that Claire has it in her head to, how did he put it, to get the two of us together."

"Oh dear," Gertrude said. "I do hope it doesn't come to that."

Mikolai shook his head. "It might, Gertrude. Indeed it might. And with all the scrutiny of the children, it will be very hard for us to meet in secret anymore."

Her expression was one of distress, but she nodded acceptance. "I'm sure you're right. It . . . it was a bad idea from the beginning."

"Do you regret it?"

"No, I don't regret it exactly. I . . . You know the truth, Mikolai. You know I enjoyed it."

He nodded. "Because you love me," he said.

"Yes."

"And because I love you."

"Yes."

"It seems a quite good reason to get married," he said. "Especially since the children may stir up a scandal if we do not."

"Mikolai, I hate for you to have to marry me," she said.

"And why do you hate that? I want to marry you. I asked you nearly a week ago of my own free will. And today I'm asking you again. I know that you've said you wanted to be a spinster. You said it was a decision that you made. You loved a man who didn't love you back. But now you love me. So any decision that you made when you were very young, well, as you mentioned to the children, the young can make mistakes."

"Are you sure that you want to marry me?" she asked.

"Of that I am very sure. I only want to be certain that you want to marry me."

"I do," she said. The words were most appropriate.

They were quiet together for a moment.

Gertrude raised her eyes to look at her future husband. She

forgot how terrible she looked and gazed at the man before her. He seemed to have forgotten how she looked also, as he gazed right back.

"I do, too," he answered.

They smiled together. He leaned forward to kiss her.

"Be careful, there is a very sore one on my upper lip," she said.

He barely touched her mouth to his own.

"Well, at least we needn't run to Arkansas," he said. "We can have a fancy wedding with all the trimmings."

"Do you want a fancy wedding? All of that bother?"

"In America weddings are no bother. In Poland a wedding can go on for weeks."

"Weeks!"

He nodded. "And impoverish whole families in the process."

She laughed. "Well, I don't suppose there is much chance of impoverishing you and George both."

"But of course you and the ladies may try," he said.

She laughed. "You are getting to have a very American sense of humor," she said.

"It's because my new *zona* teaches me to laugh," he said.

"*Zona,*" she said the word lightly. "I'll miss being called that."

"It is still what I will call you," he said.

"You're going to call me your *zona* even after we are married?" she asked.

He nodded. "Yes, I think that I will."

"What if we come upon someone who understands Polish? What will he think?"

"He will think that you are my wife."

She looked at him for a puzzled moment and then she smiled. "*Zona* means wife."

He didn't bother to make any further comment.

"Do you recall when you were explaining about the diary?"

he asked. "You said that you were very attracted to me when I
first came to town."

She was taken aback by the abrupt change of subject and
blushed, embarrassed.

"I was," she admitted. "I was very attracted to you. I thought
you were the most handsome, heroic man I had ever seen."

"Surely not?"

"Yes, oh, yes. All my characters, the male ones, they all are
you in some way or another."

"Really?"

"Really."

He shook his head in disbelief and then noticed the pink
glowing beneath her face-paint. "You are embarrassed," he
said.

"Yes, I never meant for you to know that. I never meant . . .
You know when I told you that I spent my whole life loving a
man who didn't love me back? You are that man, Mikolai."

"You loved me all this time?" His tone was incredulous.

"Yes," she answered quietly. "I've loved you, Mikolai, for
seventeen years."

He shook his head in disbelief and then laughed out loud.

"You think that is funny?" she was almost indignant.

He threw his arms around her and gave her a loving, playful
kiss.

"Well, yes, Miss Gertrude, I do."

She feigned indignation. "I don't. I pour my heart out to you
and you chuckle about it."

His grin was wide and sappy. "Perhaps you will chuckle
also, when I tell you that I was very attracted to you when I
first came to town."

"What?" She shook her head, disbelieving. "Mikolai, you
don't have to say that."

"But it's true. I found you very interesting. You were so
different from any woman that I had ever known. I wanted to

get to know you better. I even thought very seriously about calling upon you."

"You thought about calling on me?"

"Yes. I even rather casually mentioned it to your father."

"You asked my father?"

"I had no one to speak for me," he explained. "I had to speak for myself. Although I admit I was not very direct."

"What did you do?" she asked.

"I went into the bank one day and laid out my financial affairs as if I were there to borrow money. Of course, I didn't need or want to borrow any money. He knew that, I was sure. I tried to make conversation, to show him that I was a friendly neighbor. Finally, when I thought that perhaps he was getting to like me, I made a suggestion of marriage."

"You suggested to my father that you wanted to marry me?" Gertrude was stunned.

"Not directly, of course," he answered. "That is not the Polish way at all. I asked your father if his house was not too crowded. I told him that I had plenty of room in mine."

Mikolai shook his head.

"Your father was quite insulted and said something about his house being the finest in Missouri. I'm afraid your father didn't understand a Polish proposal at all."

Gertrude giggled. "You were trying to see if he was interested in getting his daughter married."

Mikolai shrugged helplessly. "I didn't understand American ways. I had no way of knowing. And from the way he acted, I thought he wasn't receptive to having me as a son-in-law at all."

Gertrude shook her head, still laughing.

Mikolai was smiling at her. "Of course, now things are different. Now I know."

"Now you know what?"

"Now I know that your father is interested in my becoming your husband."

"What are you saying?"

"Your father is in heaven now, is he not?"

"Well, yes."

"A man in heaven cannot paint his house."

"Cannot paint his house?"

"*Tarantowate*," he said. "Dappling the house so that the suitor knows there is a marriageable female inside. From heaven your father could not dapple the house. So he has dappled you, with chicken pox."

MY FAMILY HISTORY

an essay by
Roberta G. Edwards

Mrs. Pederson
Sophomore English Composition
Venice High School
March 12, 1965

Family history is important because who we are is a lot of times dependent on who the people in our families were. I am very proud of my family. They are not rich or famous, but they are important to me and in some ways they have been important to this town.

I am the youngest of three children born to Robert Donald Edwards and Lila Claire Stefanski Edwards. My father is originally from Indiana. His parents died when he was a little boy and during the Depression his family scattered all over and he doesn't know where they are. He came to Missouri during the Second World War when he was stationed at Fort Leonard Wood. He liked Missouri, so after the war he settled here.

My mother was born in Venice and has lived here her whole life. She worked for the telephone company until she got married and now takes care of my brothers and me. She is very interested in local history and knows a lot about things that happened and people that lived here a long time ago.

My grandparents are Mr. Teodor Stefanski and Claire Barkley Stefanski. My mother is their only child. But my

Grandpa Teddy was married once before. His first wife, called Grandma Olive, died in 1931. They say of her that she was a robust woman until the day she died. She must have been robust because she had nine children, including two sets of twins and a set of triplets. Mama says that it is Grandma Olive's fault that there are more Stefanskis in the Venice telephone book than there are Smiths or Joneses.

Grandpa Teddy and Granny Claire were in the first graduating class of Venice High School. Grandpa Teddy attended the University of Missouri for two years before coming back to Venice to get married and run the family business. Grandpa Teddy was not called up for service in World War I because he injured his leg playing football when he was in high school. That was the only year that Venice High School won the state championship.

Granny Claire went to Simmons College and received a degree in journalism. She worked on several newspapers back East including the *Boston Globe*. In 1931 she was fired from her job (part of the Depression layoffs) and she returned to Venice.

I said to Mama that it must have been fate that Grandpa Teddy's wife had died only six months earlier and destiny made Granny Claire lose her job and return to Venice.

Mama laughed and told me that Granny Claire has never depended much on fate and destiny. But she wouldn't explain to me what she meant.

Granny Claire's parents, my great-grandparents, were George and Prudence Barkley. George Barkley was a banker. He died before I was born, but there is a picture of him that I have seen where he is dressed up in some strange costume, like a sheik or something. Mama says that it was taken when he was Sublime Kalifa of the Crusading Knights of the Mystic Circle. That's a kind of community organization that they had back then. I guess it was sort of like my dad being in the Rotary.

Grandma Prudence lived a very long time. Long enough to see her son, Lester Margrove Barkley, sworn in as governor of the State of Missouri. Uncle Lester is now a judge on the State Supreme Court.

Grandpa Teddy's parents were Mikolai Stefanski, a Polish immigrant, and Gertrude Barkley. Actually, his real mother was from Poland and was named Lida, but he doesn't remember her. Gertrude was also Grandma Claire's aunt, but Mama tells me that in olden times families got mixed up like that a lot with people marrying other people who were related to them by marriage or something.

Gertrude Barkley was a writer and published five novels and a collection of short stories about immigrants that won her an important literary prize.

Mama says I get my talent for writing from Great-grandma Gertrude. I also have her name for my middle one, but I don't like it. I think that if she could manage to write books, get married, and win prizes, she must have done it in spite of that name.

I have one very vague memory of who I think were my Stefanski great-grandparents, Gertrude and Mikolai. I must have been very little, because Mama said that they died before I was old enough for school.

I remember being on this porch. It was very clean and shiny and it was red brick. I'm not sure exactly, but I think it may be the house on East Main Street near downtown where Aunt Arlene and Uncle Pete live.

I can remember her, Grandma Stefanski, laughing and offering me a cookie. She said it was hazelnut and that Grandpa had picked them off the tree, just for "his baby Bobbie." I looked up at the man then. He was sitting in a chair on the porch and he had two canes, one on each side of his chair. He spoke to me. He talked funny, like he had an accent or something, but I could understand what he was saying. He seemed like a big man, but I guess I wasn't afraid of him because I crawled up into his lap and pulled on his big eyebrows. They were the biggest, thickest eyebrows I have ever seen.

She spoke to me then, about the cookie.

"Your grandpa and I planted that tree," she said. "We planted it and we thought we would never have a hazelnut from it. But we did. And we thought we'd never have a little girl, either, but we have you."

The old man laughed and he winked at me. Then he told me a story about an ancient hazel tree and how it protected Mary and the Baby Jesus from King Herod's soldiers. It was a nice story and a familiar one. I liked it very much. When he finished I hugged his neck. He stroked my hair and called me his *dziecka*. He stared off across the porch to the big tree that grew at the side of the house. Grandma looked at the tree. And I looked at the tree, too.

It's all I remember of them. But now, looking back, I think that perhaps they weren't just looking at the tree. Maybe they were seeing things from the past. Things they did. People they knew. Times they remembered. I don't really know. Maybe it was like a symbol, I guess. All I saw was a tree and in those days all a tree was to me was something shady.

National Bestselling Author
PAMELA MORSI

"The Garrison Keillor of romance, Morsi's stories are always filled with lively narration and generous doses of humor."—*Publishers Weekly*

__*SOMETHING SHADY*__   0-515-11628-9/$5.99
Since the day Gertrude Barkley bobbed her hair, her small Missouri town—and her love life—have never been the same.

__*MARRYING STONE*__   0-515-11431-6/$5.50
Harvard-educated J. Monroe Farley has come to the Ozark town of Marrying Stone to research traditional folk songs. But "Roe" is having a tough time keeping his mind on his studies, especially after he meets Meggie Best.

__*RUNABOUT*__   0-515-11305-0/$4.99
Tulsa May Bruder has given up on love. But when a friend helps her to stand tall in front of the town gossips, Tulsa suddenly sees a face she's known forever in a whole new light.

__*WILD OATS*__   0-515-11185-6/$4.99
Instead of getting angry at Jedwin Sparrow's offer to sow some wild oats, Cora Briggs decides to get even. She makes a little proposition of her own...one that's sure to cause a stir in town —and starts an unexpected commotion in her heart as well.

__*GARTERS*__   0-515-10895-2/$5.99
Esme wants to find a sensible man to marry. Amidst the cracker barrels and jam jars in Cleavis Rhy's general store, she makes a move that will turn the town—and her heart—upside down.